BY DESIGN III

BY DESIGN III

A LIFE WELL LIVED

J BOYKIN BAKER

Published by J Boykin Baker Books in Atlanta, GA

www.jboykinbaker.com

Printed in the United States of America

This is a work of fiction. Names, characters, businesses, places, events, locales, and incidents are either the products of the author's imagination or used in a fictitious manner. Any resemblance to actual persons, living or dead, or actual events is purely coincidental.

Paperback ISBN- 9781676839040

Books are available in quantity for promotional or premium use. For information, email info@jboykinbaker.com.

First Edition, 2019

Photo 111320249 © Motortion - Dreamstime.com

Scriptural quotes of Ecclesiastes 3:11 and John 3:16 taken from The Living Bible (TLB)

❀ Created with Vellum

To these dear friends who have enriched my life in more ways than they will ever know:

To my Atlanta Country Club prayer group. We've shared so much over these last decades—private moments of joy, heartbreak, and growth. We know each other so well, as we have been on such a miraculous journey together. You all are loved more than I can say, as you are and always have been my touch stones. Suzanne's dedicated and faithful leadership has inspired and enabled each of us to enjoy a more fruitful life with Christ and His Spirit. Beth, Karen, and Sandy, we love and miss you. Save us a place at the table!

To our travel group. Ben and I have traveled this beautiful world with you three fun-loving couples. What thrills and memories we share! We can't thank you enough for all of your love and friendship over our many years together. We miss and adore you, Henrietta, our vivacious friend, who added laughter and cute stories to every trip.

To the five ladies of my investment group, the "Hi-Rollers." If anyone defects from this group with our many secrets, the rest of us will have to kill you! Over forty years of craziness, laughs, tears, and lots of shenanigans. Ladies, thinking of our trips brings to mind tales that no one would believe. Do these words make you smile: silver, lace, a bad hair night, Saint Peters, art investments, weddings, births, frizzy hair, drapery making, a Bible stand, decorating, and boats? I could go on forever! The love and commitment we continue to share is a true blessing in my life and I love you all dearly. To Karla, our one-of-a-kind, precious sister. We will always have you with us through your jokes, comical tales, our extraordinary memories, and deep abiding love that lasts a lifetime.

To the many women of Widows Mite Experience. We were so blessed to be called to bring clean water and the Word to areas in the United States and to nations worldwide. Each of you worked incredibly hard and gave without measure. Due to your unfailing love and support, I am a better person for having worked alongside you, my sweet friends, and my gratitude has no limits. I will forever love and appreciate you all in ways I continue to discover!

ALL THE RAVES

A confident young woman, a strong family, an emotional story, a forever classic in the making. Mrs. Baker is quite the storyteller! — Liz T., a Southern bookworm from Birmingham

Amazing. I absolutely love your book! — Goodreads review (5 stars)

A page turner, reminds me of *The Notebook.* — Amazon review (5 stars)

Sweet continuation of *By Design I* and *II*. Ms. Baker has a knack for bringing a delightful flare to her novels. Most enjoyable. — Marion N., a Northern Transplant to the South

A romance is not my normal genre. However, the *By Design* Trilogy is an exception. These books will cause you to fall in love all over again. — Alton B., A Huge Fan.

ACKNOWLEDGEMENTS AND APPRECIATION

To Patty Little, my right hand. Your wonderful positive nature and sweet smiles light up long days as you continue to be so very instrumental in bringing words to paper. I count you as a precious blessing in my life.

To Grace Routh and Kelsie Keeton for the perfect cover to By Design III. Your creativity and imagination visually tell an unfolding story.

To Rick Miles, my publicist who has seen me through the writing of this trilogy on so many levels. What would I do without your friendship and professional guidance?

To Amy Miles, the gifted author in her own right, who took time to assure that my words rested nicely on the pages of this book.

To Kristina Circelli for helping this book speak well and correctly. You are such an accomplished writer, editor, and proofreader.

To Kimmie Durham, and North Carolina's own BRB Book Club. You all are so much fun and helped furnish the best Festive Southern Holiday Feast EVER! Let's do dinner!

As always, to my trusted readers. What would I do without your thoughts, corrections, and encouragement?

GRETCHEN'S PLAN

(Gretchen's plan is so instrumental to the By Design trilogy that I have included that plan below for your review.)

Gretchen Boyd had a wonderful life. She was blessed with a successful and loving husband, a sweet and beautiful teenage daughter, supportive family and friends, but most importantly, she had her faith, which she was counting on to serve her well. Gretchen was fun-loving and adventurous in such creative ways. She had always embraced life to its fullest. But now she was sick and her life was changing.

A virulent form of cancer was invading her body and, barring a miracle, it would most likely take her life. It was a devastating diagnosis for herself, but her worst fears were for her only child, Anne. How would her precious fourteen-year-old daughter navigate her future, all of life's decisions, without a mother to guide her? Sadness flooded her thoughts as she visualized each of the special moments in Anne's future that she would probably miss. Choking up, she imagined graduation, her prom, her first boyfriend, her first job . . . her wedding. These thoughts were way too painful; she shifted her attention to her husband.

Edward was a good daddy and he was crazy about Anne, but his work was demanding. There were nights before a court case that he didn't get home until close to midnight. Who would be there for Anne to help her with schoolwork and take her to activities? Who would hold her as she poured her heart out when she'd had a bad day? Who would be there to keep her from being lonely and sad when she'd walk into an empty house?

Gretchen looked at her watch. It was time for her medicine. The pain seemed to be increasing daily, and she needed to get it under control before Anne came rushing in from play practice. She swallowed the capsule with a drink of iced tea. Stepping out of her shoes, she pulled the covers back on her bed and lay down, trying to get comfortable as she winced and waited for the pill to do its job. The thought of her situation was now all too real. Tears flooded her eyes as she began to make a mental list of her family's future needs.

By the end of the next week, Gretchen had hired Ruby Wheeler, a jovial, kind, and experienced housekeeper who could work full time and even stay late when necessary. Ruby had known Anne since she was five from the years she had worked as part nanny, part housekeeper for one of Edward's cousins. She was to start in two weeks so that Anne and Edward could get accustomed to her, and Ruby could get familiar with their lifestyle and schedules.

Next, Gretchen insisted Edward take a day off. She needed to discuss his responsibilities concerning their daughter, things he would not naturally think to do. Through their tears she had gotten a solemn promise that he understood and would always put their daughter's needs above everything.

Then, she interviewed Ruth Kelly, a well-respected grief counselor. After several hours of discussing her medical situation and concerns for Anne and her husband, Gretchen was comfortable with her choice. That night Gretchen gently presented Ruth's card to Edward. She gave him a kiss and told him to put the card where he could easily find it when the time came. Edward looked at the card, back at his wife, and took her in his arms. Not another word was said.

The days passed, and as Gretchen's condition grew worse, all she could think about were the decisions that Anne might face. One afternoon she walked to the back door, turned to a board with old painted hooks, and reached for her tan sweater. She smiled remembering knitting that sweater when she was expecting Anne. It seemed such a short time ago, but Anne was already a budding teenager. Continuing to the porch, she sat down in a rocking chair. It was a startlingly clear autumn day, blue skies overhead, and the leaves were starting to change. The kind of day that makes you want to live forever, but then, no one does. Gretchen held her hands up and turned them slowly; how frail and helpless she felt at just forty years of age. In the last few weeks, she could actually feel herself slipping away. She began to pray.

"Dear God, please give me wisdom and clarity for a plan that will honor you and help my sweet girl in times to come. I know you'll be with her, Lord, and that is such comfort, but please help me leave a legacy that will stand in my stead." While she prayed, her mind began to fill with ideas for guiding Anne on her journey to womanhood.

As she reviewed her thoughts, Gretchen was clear that the design for this plan had to fit any needs or questions that might arise, and it had to equip her daughter to make wise choices concerning subjects as broad as friends, finances, college, and eventually the possibility of marriage. The plan had to be profound, yet simple, so that Anne could recall its steps at a moment's notice. Gretchen searched her memory for past situations the two had tackled. One immediately came to mind.

Years earlier, Gretchen had watched Anne struggle with her allowance, usually coming up short with days to go. She smiled as she remembered the distress her daughter experienced when she had no money left for a movie with her friends. One afternoon when Anne was throwing a tantrum over this very subject and was begging for an advance "just this one last time," mother and daughter sat down on the bed in Anne's room. With some thought, even an argument or two, they developed a system they named the "Three S's," a plan to assist in controlling Anne's spending and temper when things didn't go her way.

Going forward, Anne would divide her allowance into three jars. She could wisely spend the eighty percent in the first jar, save ten percent for emergencies in the second, and still have ten percent remaining in the third to share with children in need or church projects. It took a little time for Anne to get the system down pat, but in the end, a more successful money management process developed. Gretchen nodded as her thoughts began to give birth to a new three-step plan, but this plan would be a guide for Anne's life journey.

She opened the small drawer to her nightstand and picked up a bright floral journal, a treasured Mother's Day gift from Anne. She opened the book to the inscription on the first page: "To the most wonderful mother in the whole wide world, I love you sooo much!!!" Tears filled her eyes. She took a tissue out of her pocket and sat down at Edward's desk. She picked up a pen, turned to a fresh page, dabbed her eyes, and began to write.

A design for the new plan seemed to flow. The first step of the plan would start with Anne identifying her desire or concern regarding a specific issue. With the issue identified, whether it was friends, money, career-direction, or more, the second step would be an evaluation of possible choices or decisions. In the third step, Anne would need to consider how her selected choice would affect the outcome of her intended goal or destiny.

Gretchen knew this three-step plan was not as simple as it sounded. There would likely be struggles and heartbreak along the way, as some choices could be painful. But that pain would be nothing compared to the consequences of Anne being untrue to what she knew was right in her heart. Ignoring her conscience and making compromises could prevent attaining her goal or realizing her greatest destiny.

Feeling tired, Gretchen moved to her bed. Removing her shoes, she tugged at a small woolen throw to lay it over her feet and settled back against the comfort of her pillows. It was time to mentally test her plan. Gretchen smiled as a thought began to materialize. She could use an imaginary scenario concerning friendship. Suppose Anne was introduced to a new friend, but soon found this friend was using cheat sheets on algebra tests. Not only that, her friend would ask to copy Anne's homework. Would Anne value the friendship so much that she would take a chance of her friend's bad habits getting her in trouble? Or would she make the difficult choice to kindly discontinue the friendship and avoid possibly being labeled as dishonest? A label like that could undermine the trust of her teachers, cause suspicion regarding test scores, possibly limit college choices due to lukewarm recommendations, and jeopardize her long-standing desire of becoming an interior designer. Gretchen smiled. *It works!* Her plan was complete. It all basically came down to three questions.

First, what desire or concern came into play?

Second, what choice and commitment were required to stay true to herself?

Third, how could that choice and commitment affect her goal or destiny?

All was ready to begin discussions with her daughter.

About a week later, Ruby had a church meeting, Edward was going to be working late, and the perfect opportunity presented itself. Journal in hand, Gretchen called Anne into her bedroom and patted for her to come snuggle and chat for a little while. It was their normal custom in the late afternoon before dinner and homework. They settled in as Gretchen shared the "new friend scenario." She felt it was a good way to illustrate her train of thought as she introduced her plan.

"Now, let's talk about money. What is your future desire concerning your finances, sweetheart?"

Anne turned over and rested her face in her hands as she

thought and finally said, "Money is not a big deal to me. I would just like to have a lot, and I don't want to give out. And remember, I want to give some to help children."

Gretchen smiled. "So, what kind of choice would it take for you not to give out and to be able to help?"

"Other than asking Daddy if I could have one of his credit cards?" Anne said with a laugh. "I guess a choice to get a job and not spend more than I'm paid." She laid back and put her head in her mother's lap.

"And how would a job and living on a budget affect your destiny?" Gretchen continued as she stroked her daughter's hair.

Anne's eyes lit up. "I would always have enough to do the Three S's. I could help children with the sharing part."

Both smiled as they thought of that earlier lesson. Mother and daughter continued to examine various choices and consequences with school work, activities, colleges, and more.

Yet Gretchen had designed her plan to include an even more serious conversation. She took a breath. "Now, let's talk about boys."

"M-o-t-h-e-r, I really don't have that desire. I hope you're not going to talk about sex stuff . . . that's gross." A flushed rosy glow began at Anne's neck and spread to her cheeks.

Gretchen smiled at her daughter's familiar blush. "But you will have that desire. It may not be important to you now, but take my word, sooner than you know it's going to become important. You will be very attractive to the young men you meet."

"Mother, can we get a glass of tea? I need a snack or something."

Anne wasn't thirsty or hungry, but she was beginning to understand her mother's purpose for the plan and her eyes filled with tears. She wiped her face as tears spilled and angrily turned to her mother. "I don't want to learn all of this stuff. I want you to be here to help me. I don't want to grow up without you!"

Gretchen took Anne's hand. "I know."

She tenderly wrapped her arms around her daughter. Anne settled back against the soft pillows and the two snuggled in silence until there were no more tears.

Gretchen gently restarted the conversation and whispered, "We'll have a glass of tea a little later. Let's think this through."

She knew the discussion was difficult for Anne and took it slowly, but she needed to persist. "Suppose you're out with a young man and he starts making sexual advances that seem rather exciting . . . you'll have a choice to make. Will you want a trial run or will you save that part of yourself for the man you marry? The choice to wait will require a serious commitment and, trust me, it will not be easy. Making love is a beautiful part of a committed relationship, but can have painful consequences outside of marriage. Painful breakups, health issues, unplanned pregnancies, and sadly, even the pressure of an abortion. The choice not to wait could seriously affect your destiny."

"M-o-m-m-a, all of this seems a million years away."

Still, as they talked, Anne could tell how important their conversation was to her mother and reluctantly decided to listen as she rubbed the back of her mother's hand on her cheek.

"It does right now, sweetheart, but you'll need to be committed to your choice before you face a crisis in the heat of the moment. I pray that you will carefully think through how your decision could affect your life. Always remember, sweetheart, make your decisions knowing that your worth is invaluable."

Gretchen fluffed her pillows and sat up a little straighter. "Let me tell you a couple of stories to help you better understand. One of my friends had a strong desire to care for children. She and her husband had two biological children and adopted three others. Several years later, she learned of three young sisters who desperately needed a home. She was faced with two choices. Would she raise her existing family just as it was, or would she adopt the young girls, and nurture them as well? Not an easy decision. How would the addition of three more children affect her home and family life? After much thought and prayer, she made the choice to follow her heart and adopted the sisters. Today, because of that heartfelt choice, her destiny has mushroomed into a ministry for orphans. That one unselfish choice has improved the lives of thousands of children.

"Now, let me tell you about another friend who because of insecurities had a basic desire to ensure the happiness of others, even at the expense of her own. Because she wanted to please, she chose to give in to a young man's fleeting satisfaction, and with that choice, her life evolved into an unwanted pregnancy and a desperate abortion. Deserted by both the father and her parents, and filled with guilt, that unfortunate choice directed her life down a sad and negative path. Thankfully, with prayer, she was able to forgive herself, and even wrote a book, *Heavenly Appointments*. A sweet story aimed at helping other young women come to terms with guilt and embrace forgiveness.

Even though it took time, better choices have her back on track for a more positive destiny with a wonderful husband and three beautiful children."

Gretchen looked intently into her daughter's eyes. "Anne, as hard as you try to make the very best choices, there may be times when you will make a mistake. Just remember, you can go back to the plan by making better choices. You have the power to choose again, follow your heart, and move your destiny in a better direction."

Gretchen paused. "But, my sweet girl, even with God's grace, because of His love for us, there are consequences when we're disobedient and don't follow our hearts. Those consequences can cause a delay or disruption in His best plan for us. My prayer for you, my sweet girl, is that your goals and desires will be so meaningful that you will seek strength and wisdom to make the best choices. And that those choices will allow God to give you the desires of your heart as He reveals His perfect destiny for your precious life."

Thirteen years later . . .

Anne smiled through tears as she reflected on her mother's careful design for her future, and for the most part the plan had worked beautifully. Sure, she had made the typical mistakes, but nothing serious. It only took once to realize that bouncing a check, confiding in a gossip, or drinking more than two beers were bad ideas. So . . . nothing major.

In fact, the plan had been working for all the important choices in her life until Anne gazed into the dark brown eyes of Bradford Young.

INTRODUCTION

Life—with its decisions, its pitfalls, and its joys continues to define Anne and Brad's journey. But at what price? Can even their love survive unexpected events that are beyond their control?

A thought from the author...

I truly feel you will enjoy *By Design III: A Life Well Lived* so much more if you have gotten to know Anne and Brad with the first two novels of the trilogy. In the first book, *By Design: A Love Story with a Twist,* you will witness the couple's tragic youth, their opposite and sometimes difficult personalities, and their many struggles as they fight the commitment involved in a passionate new love. In the second book, *By Design II: Matters of the Heart,* you will see the couple learning compromise as they establish life together in their new home. Despite frightening complications as they start their family, interest peaks in helping other women and children facing similar circumstances. May you enjoy all three books as much as I enjoyed writing them for your reading pleasure.

Love to all,

J Boykin Baker

CHAPTER ONE

WHAT? WHAT'S WRONG?

ANNE OPENED HER EYES TO BRIGHT RAYS OF SUNLIGHT POURING through the bedroom windows. Noticing they seemed a little too bright for six-thirty, she looked at the clock. It had stopped at three. She grabbed her watch from the bedside table; it was seven-thirty. Brad was due in surgery at eight, the same time that the children's carpool would arrive. She reached over and shook her husband. "Brad, get up! Get up!"

He sat straight up in the bed, trying to open his eyes as he looked around for the emergency. "What? What's wrong?"

"It's seven-thirty. You said you had an eight o'clock surgery scheduled. You're going to be late!"

"No way! I didn't hear the alarm!"

"We must have had a power outage. The clock stopped at three o'clock."

Brad glared at his wife. "We haven't had a power outage. Dammit! It's that clock. I asked you two days ago to get a new one. It's been acting up for weeks, and you know I don't like to

1

rely on my cell phone!" Still fussing, he rushed toward the shower.

"Well, don't 'dammit' me! You'd still be asleep if I hadn't woken up!" she fussed back as she ran to wake the children.

Going into the twins' room, Anne hurriedly said, "Get up and get dressed quickly! We overslept." She ran to the closet, grabbed two outfits, and threw them on their bed. Neither girl had moved a muscle. She shook their bottoms. "Get up right now!" Then she ran into Little Brad's room.

He was sitting on the side of the bed, rubbing his eyes, as he asked, "What's all the commotion?"

His mother gave him a quick kiss and explained, "We've all overslept. Get ready for school right now."

Anne ran down the stairs to start coffee. She heard Patsy crying, turned around, and ran back up into the girls' room. "What is going on?"

Patsy screamed, "Gretchen put my shoes on!"

"I can't find mine!" Gretchen cried.

"Give your sister those shoes right this minute. If you can't find yours, put on any other pair. Just hurry up!" Anne ordered.

Brad yelled from their bedroom, "Where are some of my blue scrubs?"

"They're all still in the dirty clothes. Just wear green ones!" Anne yelled back.

She started for the stairs again as Little Brad called out, "Mom, where is my backpack?"

Anne continued down the steps while answering, "You'll have to find it yourself."

She started the coffee, put Pop-Tarts in the toaster, poured three glasses of juice, and waited for the cup of coffee to finish brewing. She quickly poured the hot liquid, half and half, and a spoon full of sugar into a cup and stirred just as Brad rushed into the kitchen. He found Anne standing by the door holding out the steaming cup. He took the coffee with a scowl and walked out to his car without a word.

Anne yelled, "You're welcome!" as she slammed the door behind him.

She took the two Pop-Tarts out of the toaster, added two more, grabbed three plates, and put them on the table as she added the grape Pop-Tarts and a few green grapes to two dishes. Going back to the bottom of the stairs, she hollered, "You three have got five minutes to get down here for breakfast!" She rushed back to the kitchen and filled the third plate with another toasted pastry and grapes.

Little Brad came down first, still looking for his backpack.

Anne remembered that he had done his homework in Brad's study last night. She ran over to the room, grabbed the heavy, navy backpack, and brought it back to her son.

Little Brad looked inside. Frowning, he huffed, "My language book isn't in here."

She stared into his eyes as her own widened. "Then go get it! It's in your daddy's study."

With a mouth full of Pop-Tart, he mumbled, "Why are you so mad?"

Anne watched as he walked into the study and felt a tinge of guilt. When her son came back in with his book, she gave him a hug. "I'm sorry, sweetheart. I'm not mad. I'm just trying to get y'all ready for school . . . we're running so late."

Rushing back to the bottom of the stairwell, she yelled again, "You girls have two minutes to get down here!"

Gretchen came down barefooted. "I can't find my shoes anywhere so I just won't wear any. They're the only ones that match my outfit," she whined.

Patsy rushed past her sister and scurried into the kitchen to eat her breakfast.

Anne looked in Gretchen's direction as she washed six strawberries. "Did you check the great room? You take them off in there lots of times."

Gretchen ran into the other room and over to the sofa. "I found 'em!"

"Great! Now get in here and eat."

Within five minutes a horn blared in the driveway. Anne realized they didn't have time to brush their teeth, but decided with a shrug, that was the least of her morning's problems. She waved to Cynthia, this week's driver, then gave each one a hurried peck as they walked out the door gobbling the last bites of their pastries, and carrying several grapes and a strawberry in their napkins. Anne called out as cheerfully as possible, "Have a wonderful day!"

Breathing a deep sigh, she walked over to pour herself a cup of coffee. Mug in hand, she collapsed in Brad's large, leather chair in the great room. Anne was still fuming over Brad's "get a new clock" comment. Getting her husband to the hospital, eight-year-old twin daughters, and a ten-year-old son out the door was bad enough on a good day. But this morning had been the pits.

Looking around at her house, Anne frowned. Her home was showing the untidy effects of her housekeeper, Margie, being absent way too long. Margie had been home with the flu for over a week and with Anne's crazy schedule, the dirty laundry was piled sky-high in the utility room.

Finishing her coffee, she set the dryer to fluff the load of clothes that had dried the day before. After ten minutes, she felt they were bound to have less wrinkles. She folded the clothes, put them in the laundry basket, changed a load from the washer to the dryer, started a third load to wash, then ran upstairs to put on her warmups from yesterday. Dashing to her car, she set out for the McDonald's drive-thru. Ordering two sausage and egg biscuits and a cup of coffee, she drove to Margie's. Walking inside her friend's, as well as her housekeeper's, home, Anne opened the refrigerator and poured a glass of orange juice. After placing the juice, the McDonald's bag, and the cup of coffee on the dining room table, Anne called, "Your breakfast is on the table! I love you. Gotta go!" As she rushed out, she added, "Lordy, I do hope you are feeling better."

Driving back to her neighborhood, Anne laughed to herself. *It has to be at least noon by now.* Looking at her watch, it was just nine-thirty. Hurrying in the back door, she ran to the dryer to grab the load of clothes that were drying before the dryer stopped, hoping to minimize the wrinkles. In her hurry, she had totally forgotten her cell phone which she had left in the drink holder in her car. Placing the still-warm load of clothes on hangers, she looked down; there were still three baskets of laundry begging for attention. Clothes in hand, she walked upstairs to hang the wrinkle-free load of blue scrubs in Brad's closet. Feeling overwhelmed, she looked at all of the cleaning that needed to be done in the children's messy rooms. Plus, apparently, it was up to her to go out and buy a new clock. Amazon was a possibility, but it would be more fun to involve the children. Tears formed in her eyes; she hated the way she and Brad had left each other that morning. He had never left without some sort of goodbye kiss, even if it was just a quick peck.

Brad rushed through the doors of Doctor's Hospital. Not waiting for the elevator, he ran up the steps to his assigned surgery suite. The anesthesiologist took one look at him and commented, "Take it you've had a rough morning."

"It's a long story," Brad said. "Are we ready?"

One of the nurses sighed. "We've been ready for thirty minutes, Dr. Young."

Brad rolled his eyes as he reviewed the patient's file and scrubbed impatiently. Then he took a deep breath and walked into surgery.

As the children entered their different classrooms, all seemed to be on track for a typical day. The girls' primary class was with their favorite teacher, Mrs. Hayes, whose first assignment for the morning was for each student to discuss what his or her parent(s) did on their jobs or in their daily activities to help their community. After several children had taken their turns, it was soon Gretchen's opportunity to speak.

She stood and proudly announced, "My daddy is a doctor. He helps women have babies."

Then Gretchen turned to Patsy and whispered, "You can tell them about Mama and how she helps ladies at the Center."

Patsy disagreed a little too loudly, "I'm going to tell them about Daddy too!"

Gretchen stared at her twin. "Just do what you want to." She huffed as she shrugged.

Mrs. Hayes intervened, "Both of you can talk about your mother and your daddy."

Apparently satisfied with the compromise, Gretchen resumed her story, "Sometimes he does operations when ladies don't feel good."

Richard, the young boy sitting beside Gretchen, started laughing. With a snicker, he looked around at his classmates and announced, "My daddy says the twins' daddy is a lucky doctor 'cause he gets to look at naked women all day!"

Gretchen immediately turned toward the boy as she blurted out, "That's a big lie!" She proceeded to draw her fist back and followed through with a direct punch to Richard's nose, hitting her classmate as hard as she could manage.

Mrs. Hayes, now in shock, came rushing over to the two children. She looked at Gretchen in disbelief. "Young lady, sit down in your seat right this minute!"

By this time Richard was whimpering and wiping a little blood from his nose. Mrs. Hayes instructed the class to read quietly while she took him to the school nurse.

Patsy leaned over to Gretchen's ear. "You're in big trouble, Sissy."

Gretchen began to cry; all the other children sat quietly, as they were stunned. There had never been a fistfight in their classroom before today.

When Mrs. Hayes returned to her class, she asked Gretchen to come with her. Patsy got up to join her sister, but the teacher told her to sit back down. Patsy started crying, but reluctantly did as she was told. She put her head on the desk and hid her face as her sobs grew louder.

Mrs. Hayes took Gretchen's hand and quickly walked her down to the administrative office. She explained what had happened and asked Mr. Elder, a kind and compassionate headmaster who also happened to be a golfing buddy of Brad's, if he would call one of her parents to come to the school and discuss the situation.

Gretchen began to cry hysterically. "Please don't call my mama! Only call my daddy. I don't want my mama to know what Richard said. It might hurt her feelings really bad." She couldn't imagine what her mother would think of her daddy looking at naked women.

Mr. Elder then called Brad's office and was told that Dr. Young was just coming out of surgery. Miss Davis advised him to call Gretchen's mother if something was needed. He explained that calling Anne was not an option; Gretchen was sobbing uncontrollably and only wanted her daddy. Miss Davis assured that she would pass along the message and that Brad would get to the school as soon as possible.

By now, Brad's morning patients were lining the waiting room. Miss Davis looked around and shook her head, knowing that this was not going to be a good morning. She called the OR and asked that Brad call her back as soon as possible. She then called Dr. Young Sr., who was now retired, and suggested he come in to see Brad's morning patients as his son was needed at the children's school. Brad Sr. assured that he would be there within thirty minutes.

Just then Brad returned Miss Davis' call.

He asked, "What's up?"

"Gretchen is in Mr. Elder's office and he wants you to come to the school as soon as you can."

Brad put his hand on this forehead. "What a morning! What in blue blazes has she done now?" Brad asked, raising his brow, as Gretchen always seemed to find a way to get into trouble. "Can you please call her mother and ask her to get to the school? I've got patients waiting."

"I guess it's not that simple. She only wants her daddy. I've called your dad and he's coming in to take your morning patients." Miss Davis continued, "You need to go check on Gretchen. Something must really be wrong."

Having just walked out of surgery, Brad took a record-setting shower, then hurriedly put on clean scrubs before leaving for the school. Sliding into his car, he called Anne. Getting no answer, he slammed his phone onto the console. "Great! Where is she?" he said aloud in a thoroughly pissed tone. Then he thought back to his wife's rushing around trying to get everyone out of bed and ready for their day, even handing him that cup of coffee as he left. He felt bad and knew he owed her an apology. He sighed as he thought back to a normal morning. He missed having held her and those early morning kisses. No matter what his day brought, those sweet kisses made every day better. If he had ever needed her kisses, it was today.

As he continued down Peachtree to the children's school, every vivid Gretchen scenario passed through his mind. Had she forgotten her homework, said a cuss word, or possibly broken something? Pulling up in front of the large brick building that was the private school Brad had attended over thirty-five years earlier, though a much larger campus now, he double-parked and rushed up the steps to the solid wooden doors. Brad had no idea what to expect. He took a long breath and hurried inside.

CHAPTER TWO

WHAT NOW?

PASSING THROUGH TWO SETS OF DOUBLE DOORS, BRAD RUSHED down the long hallway of shiny, wooden flooring. He couldn't believe, with everything concerning his daughter sweeping through his thoughts, that there was still room in his addled brain to notice the never-changing cleanliness of the school, but he was thankful for any small diversion. Reaching the administrative office, he could see through the windows on either side of the large check-in desk. The twins were quietly sitting in chairs just outside of the headmaster's frosted glass door. Because both girls had been so upset, the teacher had decided it would be less disruptive to send Patsy to join her sister. Brad stepped inside. As his daughters looked up, both girls ran over to their daddy and put their arms around his waist.

"Daddy, Gretchie's in a lot of trouble," Patsy began as the sobs started. "She . . . she punched Richard Powell in the nose!"

The three sat down and Gretchen laid her head on her

father's shoulder. "He said something awful, Daddy! He said you look at naked women all day and I told him that's a lie . . . that's when I hit him."

Patsy cupped Brad's face in between her hands. "You don't look at naked women all day . . . do you, Daddy?"

Brad had to think. He did not look at naked women ALL day, so his response was truthful. "No, I do not."

"Then I had a right to hit him, Daddy!" Gretchen exclaimed. "Because he was a big fat liar!"

The door opened and Mr. Elder walked out to call the girls in, as he greeted their father. "Dr. Young, if you and your daughters will come into my office, we can sort this out."

Brad looked back and forth between the girls and the headmaster. "I have a pretty good idea of Gretchen's involvement in this situation. But what did Patsy do?"

"She's here as moral support for her sister. They were both crying uncontrollably to be together," Mr. Elder explained.

"I'm not surprised. They've been that way since the day they were born. From what I have gathered, Richard Powell said something inappropriate and Gretchen let him have it." Brad shook his head and looked back at Mr. Elder.

"That about sums it up. I've already had a discussion with Richard's daddy. He made him apologize to Gretchen." Mr. Elder then looked directly at Gretchen. "She would not say that she was sorry, but as Dr. Powell left, he said he would be in touch with you tonight. Dr. Young, your daughter has got to understand that she cannot take matters into her own hands . . . literally. We are set up to handle problems like this without her help." He smiled faintly and patted Gretchen on the head.

She looked at her daddy's face and cried out, "Patsy and I

want to go home."

Patsy, still sobbing, chimed in, "Right now, Daddy!"

Mr. Elder assured Brad that they had their assignments for the next day and it was okay if they wanted to go home. Both girls took one of their daddy's hands as they stood to leave.

Patsy peeked over at Mr. Elder and said, "We'll see you tomorrow and we'll act nicer." Brad left the school with his hands grasping two, now happier, little girls.

Pulling in the driveway, the girls asked their daddy if they could go straight to their room. They had decided their father could tell their mother what had happened as Anne had been very clear with her children about settling an argument in a physical manner. They knew she was not going to be the least bit happy with Gretchen.

The minute Brad and the girls walked through the back door, he called Anne's name. She came downstairs, passing the girls as they raced up. Brad was standing at the bottom of the stairs running his fingers through his hair. He took her hand and pulled her toward his study.

"I've been trying to call you!"

"My phone must be in the car," Anne thought aloud. She looked up the stairs and asked, "What is going on?"

"I have just been made to feel like the biggest pervert in the city of Atlanta!" Brad fussed.

"What are you talking about? And why are the girls with you?"

He explained about the naked women, Gretchen's response to Richard Powell, and how she only wanted her daddy to come to the school because the naked women comment might hurt her mother's feelings.

"How hard did she hit him?" Anne grimaced.

"Well, I understand there was a small amount of blood involved," he answered.

"Oh, Brad. I know the girls were so embarrassed. They're not old enough to understand."

"Well, I'm going back to the office. And you can explain everything!" Brad turned toward the door.

"Why can't you stay and we'll explain this together? It's your job that has caused the problem."

"I beg your pardon?" Brad turned back to look at his wife.

"Explaining where babies come from is your job. And I'll tell you another thing. If I were Richard Powell's daddy, and my specialty was proctology, I wouldn't be talking to my son about what other doctors look at all day."

Anne couldn't help but laugh, which finally brought a smile to Brad's face.

"Anne, I'm sorry about this morning. I acted like a jerk."

"Yes, you did. But I know you so well, my love. I know how important it is for you to never keep a patient waiting." She walked closer to Brad and continued, "After lunch, I'll take the children to the mall to buy their daddy a new clock. And I'll pick up the book, *Where I Came From?* And you and I, Dr. Young, will read the book to them together . . . tonight!"

Brad reached out and pulled Anne into his arms. He gave her a long kiss, then smiled as he said, "Let's see . . . their bedtime is eight-thirty. I'll be home by ten." He grinned. "But feel free to start reading without me."

Anne put her hands on her hips and glared. "I'll see you by eight-o'clock. I mean that, Brad Young."

Brad walked back into the doctor's building after stopping to inhale a few Varsity hotdogs. As luck would have it, he came face to face with his colleague, Richard Powell, Sr. the minute he stepped inside.

Dr. Powell looked embarrassed as he walked up to Brad. He lowered his eyes and apologized. "My son deserved what he got. That was an awful thing for him to say."

"They're just children," Brad said as he started to laugh. "But I've given Gretchen full permission to tell the class what you look at all day."

"I hope you're kidding . . . but, if not, I deserve it. From my literal point of view, your specialty beats the hell out of mine."

The two laughed, shook hands, and went their separate ways. Both men had a new understanding concerning the plight of daily parenting.

After another goodbye kiss, Anne had watched Brad drive away. She was feeling so much better as he left this time. But now to deal with the twins. Walking up the stairs, their mother entered the girl's room.

Patsy stood up first. "Mommy, it was all an accident."

"Pattie Cake, it was not an accident," Anne corrected as she looked at Gretchen, who by now had big tears rolling from her eyes "Gretchie, what Richard said was not nice at all. But you should not have hit him. That was not nice either."

Anne sat down in the big, fluffy chair in their room. Both

girls ran over and scrambled up into her lap. After Anne gave them a stern "talking to" about their mother and daddy's expectations concerning their behavior at school, she gave each twin a kiss. Then she suggested they go downstairs and get some lunch before starting on their homework. She promised that when their brother got home, she would take them to the mall so the three could pick out a new alarm clock for their daddy.

As the girls ate their macaroni and cheese, and some applesauce, Anne went back into the laundry room to deal with more dirty clothes. She loaded the washing machine for the fourth time that day. While sorting clothes, she thought about the incident at school and had to admit to herself. *He actually does look at semi-naked women most of the day.* Then she smiled and thought, *and this naked lady during wonderfully romantic interludes.*

At three-thirty, Little Brad came bursting through the back door. He ran up to Anne and began, "Did you hear what Gretchen did today? She got into a fight at school! With a boy! And, Mama, did you hear what he said? If I'd been there, I'd have helped her knock him into next week!"

Anne put her arms around her boy and gave him a tight hug. "Go put your books up and get a snack. We're going to buy your daddy a new alarm clock. We need to go pretty soon, Daddy's going to try to get home early tonight so we can have some family time." She walked back to the laundry room as she mumbled, "I'd bet my last dollar he'll be late."

CHAPTER THREE

ONE MY WAY...WILL EXPLAIN

GRETCHEN WAS CURIOUS AS SHE LOOKED THROUGH THE DINING room window, waiting to see her daddy drive in the driveway that evening. She remembered how family time could be good or bad. However, even "family time" concerns didn't keep the three Young children from having fun while they selected a new alarm clock. With the clock in hand, when they arrived home, the three ran upstairs to gift-wrap their father's new black and chrome surprise. Anne ordered pizzas, made a chopped salad, stirred a pitcher of sweet tea, and fixed plates for the children while they wrapped. After eating, they all ran upstairs for baths, to get ready for bed, and to prepare for the family discussion.

It was now twenty minutes after eight and Brad wasn't home yet. Looking out of the front window, Gretchen frowned. "He's always late." Anne picked up her cell and dialed his pager. She was determined that her husband was not about to wiggle out of reading this book.

A text response came through in second. "On my way. Will explain."

After office hours, as Brad was hurriedly getting ready to leave for home, Miss Davis, his office manager, asked for a few minutes of his time. He motioned for her to come in and sit down with him on the sofa in his office. She began to explain, "Brad, I've been suffering from one headache after another. I'm worried." Looking at her eyes, he could tell she was right ready to cry. "I seem to be having increasing difficulty performing my duties at the office. I just can't concentrate. That's not fair to you."

The tearful look on her face was really concerning to Brad. He had never seen her this serious or apologetic.

First, Brad asked if she had taken time for an eye exam recently. She explained that she kept that appointment once a year religiously, in dreaded fear of losing her eyesight. He then asked if there was any unusual stress in her life. With that question, the floodgate opened, releasing Miss Davis' tears. Brad walked over to his desk for the box of tissues, returned, and set the box on a coffee table in front of them before taking his seat.

"About two months ago, my sister, who lives in South Carolina, called to tell me that she had been diagnosed with Alzheimer's." She leaned toward the coffee table to take one of the tissues, then wiped her eyes. "She's seeing a doctor at the Mayo Clinic down in Jacksonville. He's got her on some medication and she seems to be feeling better about her situation . . .

but . . . she's two years younger than I am. Our mother and grandmother ended up dying from this horrid disease. With the headaches . . . and not feeling as sharp as before, memory lapses. I can't seem to remember even familiar names. I'm just afraid."

"Miss Davis, I hate to have to tell you this," Brad began, "but what you're describing is probably just age-related. To be truthful, I can't remember names. But to help remove all doubt, let's get you set up for a complete workup. Then we can put any fears behind you. With your permission, I'll make a few calls tomorrow. That way you can relax and put these justifiable, but most likely false concerns to rest."

The two agreed. Brad made a note to make the calls his first priority the next morning. Just as he finished placing a reminder sticker on his keyboard, his pager went off.

After a quick text, he walked into the business office, helped Miss Davis get her things together, then he walked her to her car. Giving her a hug, he promised to lock up and assured her that everything would be just fine.

Looking at his watch, he laughed. *By the time I lock up, if I circle the block four times, they'll be in bed.* Anyway, maybe it would be good if he and Anne read the book first, planned their strategy, and figured out how they were going to handle the "burp" situation. He smiled, remembering the girls asking several years ago how they got out of their mommy's tummy. He laughed recalling the look on Anne's face when he had told them their mother burped and there they were! What had seemed like a good idea at the time was now coming back to haunt him. He hoped they had forgotten the comment, but quickly realized Gretchen never forgot a single thing.

Driving into their neighborhood, Brad glanced at the clock on his dash. Eight forty-five; he had a reprieve.

As Anne sat with the children saying their prayers, she suggested they pray especially hard for their daddy because he was late again. Hearing his car pulling in, she kissed the children goodnight. But they had heard him too.

Little Brad rushed into the twins' room, with the wrapped clock in hand. The girls jumped up and all three ran downstairs.

Their daddy was thrilled with his new clock and raved over the beautiful wrapping. He took them upstairs to help him plug it in. Then he tucked each one of them back in their beds. When he came downstairs, Anne had two dinner plates prepared and on the table.

As the two sat down to eat, Brad explained his idea about a joint-preparation before reading the book. Then he shared Miss Davis' concerns for hers and her sister's health. Brad looked around at the mess in the kitchen and back at Anne, who appeared thoroughly worn out. "How's Margie feeling?"

"She's hoping to be back by Monday." Anne sighed "Four more days." But just as quickly, she smiled and added, "You have a closet full of blue scrubs!"

After the couple cleaned up the kitchen, Brad took her hand. "Anne, even as difficult as everything was with the twins today, and talking to Miss Davis . . . the worst part of my day was how I acted this morning. You work so hard to look after our family and I know it's been tough without Margie. I'll try to be a more helpful husband."

"I felt the same way about my day. I couldn't help but just sit down to cry after you left. I didn't get a goodbye kiss and even worse, we didn't have our time to cuddle before our day started."

He pulled her close and gave her a slow, passionate kiss. "We have plenty of time for kisses now. Let's go take a shower, get ready for bed, and we can cuddle all you want." He had that familiar twinkle in his eyes as he added with a laugh, "If that's what you want to call it."

Anne couldn't help but laugh too. With his arm around her, they walked upstairs and into their room. Brad turned and locked the door.

CHAPTER FOUR

YOU LEAD...I'LL FOLLOW

THE NEXT MORNING, WHILE ANNE LAY IN BRAD'S ARMS, THE TWO agreed that both mother and father should take the children back to school after yesterday's incident. They would drive separate cars so Brad could go straight to his office afterward. At breakfast, Gretchen whispered to her daddy, "Did Mama cry about the naked ladies?"

Brad smiled at the twin and said, "No, ma'am, everything was fine with your mother. Together, she and I are taking you to your classroom today."

Patsy overheard and asked, "Mama can hold Gretchen's hand. Will you hold my hand, Daddy?"

With that, an argument about hand-holding ensued between the twins. Little Brad looked at his mother, somewhat embarrassed. "I'd let you hold my hand, Mama." Then he shyly added, "But boys don't do that."

Anne laughed and looked at the family's brown lab. "I guess I'll have to take Bo Jr. for hand-holding."

Patsy laughed at the idea. "Mama, that's silly. They don't let dogs come to school." She stood and walked over to her mother and gave her a kiss. "I'll hold your hand, Mama."

As Patsy and Anne hugged, Brad decided the girls needed clarity of his expectations for the morning. "Ladies, when we walk into the school, we'll first visit Mr. Elder. Gretchen, you are going to apologize for the punch to Richard's nose and then we'll go to your classroom. We'll ask Miss Hayes to meet us in the hall and you two will apologize to her for all the commotion you caused yesterday."

Both girls looked down at their breakfast, but they were no longer hungry. They whispered as they reviewed their daddy's plan while they slowly walked out the door. After Little Brad took his last bite of pancakes and bacon, he gave Bo Jr. fresh water, put on his jacket, and followed his family to the cars.

A little later, Anne and Brad walked out of the school delighted that everything had gone so smoothly. Gretchen's apology was accepted. Mr. Elder even gave both twins a pat and their teacher could not have been any more understanding as she lovingly ushered the girls back into the classroom.

Reaching the parking lot, Brad leaned against his car. Pulling his wife close, he softly kissed her lips. "I think that went remarkably well, Mrs. Young."

She gave him another quick kiss and replied, "Yes, it did. Now, I have to run." She turned and clicked to unlock her car. "Margie's waiting for her McDonald's breakfast. By the way, let me know how everything goes with Miss Davis. Give her my love."

∾

When Brad arrived, he walked straight to his private office without even stopping for a cup of coffee. He picked up his phone and made several calls, after which he entered the business office. He asked Miss Davis if she was available to talk. The two walked back into his office and returned to their usual seats on the sofa.

"I have some appointments set up for you. One is for extensive lab work later today," Brad began. "I think it's best to begin with the basics on your blood work. Once we get those results, we'll have a clearer picture of what our next step should be."

Miss Davis shook her head and said, "Brad, it's the end of the month. I can't be away from my desk today . . . there's just too much to finish up."

"This was not a suggestion, ma'am. What you've got to take care of in this office is for me and I'm saying that it can wait. Besides, there are two others in that business office to whom you can delegate. This is too important and I care about you."

"Where and what time?" Miss Davis asked as she shook her head.

"Let's start in the lab here and then I'm sending you down to the lab on the first floor for any needed tests we don't run," Brad explained, then added, "I would imagine that you'll be out most of the afternoon. Once we've received all of the test results, then we'll likely schedule you with an internist."

She nodded.

"If you don't have a preference, I know who I'd like for you to see. In my opinion, Jess Wilkins is the best and extremely thorough."

"That's fine with me," Miss Davis replied.

"I've written the orders for our lab and sent the other orders downstairs. Your appointment there is at one-thirty. I'd like our lab work to be finished before you go down for the other test."

She stood and said, "I'll make sure I'm on time, but just so you know, you have certainly fouled up my day."

Brad stood, smiled, and gave her a hug before she walked back to the lab.

After lunch, Brad tried to check in with Anne and, as usual, she didn't answer her cell. He laughed as he thought, *I bet her phone is in a buggy in the grocery store or under her car seat.* He buzzed Virginia out in the business office. "Virginia, will you do me a favor? Will you see if you can get Anne a second cell phone with her same number? I'll feel better if she had a backup."

That afternoon during a brief lull between patients, Brad tried his wife again. This time she answered. "I tried to call you back," she defended. "I saw that I missed your call, but I couldn't find my phone earlier. I was told that you were with a patient."

"It's okay, I've ordered you another phone. That way you can keep one in your car and one in your purse."

"Brad, I have trouble keeping up with one phone! I do not want to keep tabs on two."

"Anne, I have ten minutes and I don't want to spend it arguing about telephones. I called to see how you want to handle the reading of that book on sex with the children. Let's get that out of the way . . . I do not want to keep thinking about it. Should we read it all at one time; read it together?" Brad asked. "Or do you want to read it to them earlier today and then we could all have a question-and-answer period later?"

"Brad, this is not a seminar at one of your medical events.

We'll read the book and then we'll just lovingly and carefully talk with our children."

"Well, you lead and I'll follow," he suggested.

"Dr. Young, what is your problem? You explain this every day!"

"Not to nine-year-old girls and an eleven-year-old boy. Yes, I talk about this every day but I'm not responsible for the repercussions of the choices following those discussions. Or what could happen if I don't cover everything in an understandable manner for children at their ages. This topic is too important to mess up. I'm used to talking to grown-ups; this is uncomfortable and totally different."

Anne started laughing, which she could tell he didn't like as he curtly replied, "I'll be home by seven and we're getting this out of the way tonight."

She stifled another laugh and said, "You don't have to worry, I've read the book. It's thorough, but in a limited and loving way. Therefore, it won't be difficult to explain to our children at their ages. So, my precious Dr. Young, take two aspirin and call me when you are on your way home."

After all of their afternoon activities, Anne could tell the children were ready for baths and dinner. The twins looked especially tired and she wondered about their latest plan for the book discussion. Maybe tonight wasn't the best option, but on the other hand, they did expect to read before bedtime. She was helping them clean their rooms when she heard the back door open. It was only six-thirty, so there was plenty of time for the book and any questions.

Brad yelled upstairs, "What's going on up there?"

"We're just picking up the girls' room a little bit," Anne answered.

He walked upstairs and looked in the twins' bedroom. It was a wreck. "What happened? It looks like a bomb went off!"

The girls ran over to give their daddy a hug as Patsy said, "We've been cleaning out our closet and our drawers. Mama says we've outgrown everything."

Little Brad walked into the room and gave his daddy a high-five. "Mom says we're having last night's family time tonight. What's that all about? I finished my homework."

"Let's go in our bedroom to read tonight," their daddy suggested.

Anne walked into her dressing area and picked up the book, but before she could speak, Brad, with a determined whisper said, "I googled that book, we are not reading that tickling or sneezing part, that can wait. Just skip those pages for now. Are we clear on this?" Anne nodded as she tried not to laugh at this new prudish side of her husband.

Brad and the girls laid down on the bed. Little Brad sat at the foot of the bed with his mother. Anne began the conversation. "Daddy and I have a special book we'd like to read together with you tonight."

The children were quiet and looked at her, obviously waiting to hear more.

With no way to dance around the issue. Anne began to read. The book began with brief descriptions of male and female anatomy. A pin-drop could have been heard in the bedroom. The next section explained how the two anatomies fit together.

Anne looked at Brad, skipped the three controversial pages, and continued.

The girls were wide-eyed and completely still. Little Brad squirmed and drummed his fingers on the footboard as he asked, "Can I go to my room?"

"This is important," Brad said, "and, no, you cannot go to your room quite yet."

As the book progressed, illustrations showed the sperm uniting with the egg and then moved onto pages of the developing embryo. Finally, it pictured a healthy and fully developed baby following delivery.

Anne asked the children, who had been completely silent, if they had any questions.

Gretchen looked at her daddy and asked, "What happened to the burps?"

Brad had to confess, "When you two were little, this was too complicated to explain. So, I made up the part about the burps."

Little Brad interjected, "I don't have any questions. Can I go to my room?" Avoiding their eyes, he added, "But, that stuff is disgusting! I'm not doing that. I don't want any children."

Anne gently discussed the book, especially the beginning, with an emphasis on love. She re-explained the basics from the standpoint of how married couples love each other and want children. She looked at her husband to indicate that it was time for him to contribute.

"What your mother said is right." Brad nodded.

Anne huffed as Little Brad asked to go to his room yet a third time. Before she could answer, Patsy said she had a question.

"Mommy, did you and Daddy do that?"

"Yes. We wanted to have three precious children."

Gretchen patted her mother's hand. "I bet you were glad we were twins, so you only had to do all of that stuff just two times to get your three precious children!"

Brad looked away to hide his smile while Anne bit her lip.

Little Brad crossed his arms and asked with open irritation, "May I please go to my room, right now?"

Brad got up and put his arm around his son's shoulder. "Why don't we go to your room and the two of us can talk a little more."

That gave Anne a chance to ask the girls if they had any more personal questions.

Patsy asked, "Mama, did it hurt when we came out of that place in your bottom?"

Anne patted her little girl and said, "Not too much, the doctors gave me medicine so it wouldn't hurt too badly."

"Anything else?" Anne asked. She looked at Gretchen.

"Well, I'd like to say . . . this whole thing is a nightmare. What you have to do . . . then where the baby comes out . . . as far as I'm concerned, the burps sounded a whole lot easier."

Anne smiled. "I know this is a lot to figure out at one time, but it all comes together beautifully to form a family. As you get older, it will become much more important to you. One day you'll fall in love, get married, and all of this will seem very natural."

The girls looked at each other and rolled their eyes.

"But, girls, there's something else we need to talk about. Mommies and Daddies discuss this with their children at the time they believe is appropriate. Daddy and I felt you were ready, but your friends' parents may have different opinions about their children. Therefore, we don't talk about this with others. If you have any thoughts later, just know that Mommy and Daddy will always answer any questions for you."

Again, Gretchen piped up. "Mommy, this has been a very busy day with school, band practice, and everything tonight. I can't take anymore. Can we say our prayers now? I'm ready to go to sleep."

Patsy, in her sweet way, said, "Mama that was a very interesting book. But I'm sleepy too. Can we go to sleep in your bed?"

"Certainly." Anne pulled the covers back and tucked the twins into her bed. After prayers and kisses, she cut the light out and closed the door.

Brad sat down on his son's bed as Little Brad crawled under the covers. "Son, do you have any questions?"

"Dad, I'd already heard about all this. Some of the older boys that help coach our baseball team told us about it one day when some pretty girls walked by in shorts."

"Well I'm not surprised, but your mother feels that you and I need to have our own discussion about sex."

"No problem, Dad. What do you need to know?" Little Brad asked with a grin.

"You are so funny!" Brad smiled. "Anything we need to clarify?"

"Not tonight. Maybe later . . . much later. And don't call me, Dad. I'll call you."

They both laughed, but Brad felt he needed to add one more

thing. "Son, as you get older, what we've discussed tonight will become very interesting to you." Little Brad sighed. "Just remember young girls may seem mature, but when it comes to sex, they can be fragile. You are to always treat girls with respect and remember, no means no in any situation. Do you understand?"

"I got it, Dad."

"As you get older, we'll talk more, but always know you can come to me with any questions."

"Okay, Dad. I really need to get some sleep."

Brad kissed his forehead and the two said prayers before Brad left to go downstairs to join his wife.

Walking in the kitchen, he sat down at the table as Anne fixed his plate of chicken pastry, string beans, cucumber slices, and cornbread. He laughed as he explained that their family time was old news for Little Brad. Anne was surprised, but as she thought back to her high school days, she was thankful her son had heard about sex in the proper manner tonight. Then she laughed as she shared Gretchen's comment about the process being a nightmare. Brad was pleased and actually hoped both twins continued to feel that way for a long time. Anne handed him his plate and a glass of sweet tea as she joined him at the breakfast room table.

"And just why do you hope she thinks of sex as a nightmare?" Anne asked as Brad picked up his fork.

He smiled. "That way, she won't have any interest in doing 'it!'"

"Suppose she meets someone like you?" Anne smiled. "Who tries desperately to change her mind?"

"That's not funny, Anne."

"Not funny now that you have daughters, huh? Bet my daddy wouldn't have laughed at the pressure you put on me either."

"That's different," Brad lamely tried to explain.

"It wouldn't have been different to my daddy," she assured.

Brad changed the subject. "Anne, you know that three-step plan of your mother's? You need to teach that to the girls . . . make sure they understand it well and that they are as dedicated to waiting as you were."

Anne glared at her husband as he took another bite. "Dr. Young, I think you're a wee bit of a hypocrite." She thought, then suggested, "I'd be happy to loan you my notebook so that you can work on the plan with Little Brad as well . . . Of course, you'll need my approval on just how you explain the plan." She laughed as she took a sip of his tea. "Now, tell me about Miss Davis."

Brad put his fork down. "I'm really concerned about her. It could be nothing or it could be very serious. The test should be back sometime next week."

CHAPTER FIVE

THE ATTACK

MISS DAVIS ARRIVED AT THE OFFICE EARLY THAT THURSDAY morning; she was hoping to peek at her lab tests before others began to file in. If there was anything that could cause an emotional response, she wanted to have the tears under control before anyone else came into the lab. She had always been a private person, even as a child with two sisters, a brother, and overly rigid parents. Maybe that's how her need for solitude evolved. Her parents never showed any emotion and would reprimand the children for crying at what they believed to be inappropriate times, especially any time the family had visitors. Having worked for Brad Sr. since her mid-twenties, she took great pride in the fact that she had stoically led the office for more years than she cared to remember. Now, she didn't want to destroy her image by breaking down in front of anyone, let alone Brad for a second time.

Walking back to the lab, Miss Davis pulled her chart up on the computer. Everything in the beginning seemed fine, but the notes toward the end were a little confusing. There were several words she didn't recognize in their context. She clicked off; there was no more time for investigation as she heard several other employees talking and walking down the back hallway toward the lab. Sharing morning greetings with the other early arrivers, she grabbed a cup of coffee from the lounge and went back to the business office to try desperately to get some of her monthly report completed.

Brad had surgery first thing, so it was nearing eleven before he made it in to the office. She watched the phone and saw his line light up. Shortly after it dimmed, he walked into the business office and asked if he could speak with her privately.

Again, they sat down on his sofa. Sensing her nervousness, he took her hand. "We have the reports on most of your lab work, and there doesn't appear to be anything going on that makes me specifically concerned, but I have made an appointment for you with Dr. Wilkins. He'll see you tomorrow afternoon at four. Miss Davis, I know this is very personal. But have you been having any medical issues that you haven't mentioned?"

She thought for a few minutes and answered, "Not that I can think of, although, I have been really tired lately. As we discussed, I chalked it up to the joys of aging now that I'm sixty-three."

Smiling, Brad said, "We'll wait until tomorrow and if it's okay with you, I'll have a talk with Jess after your appointment." Just then, one of the midwives called his cell in a panic. He was needed in Labor and Delivery ASAP. He excused himself and rushed toward the back stairs.

The midwife met Brad in the hallway and exclaimed, "Dr.

Young, we've got a problem! Fran Ivy's husband seems to have lost his mind. He doesn't want anyone in the delivery room, but Fran is crying out for her mother. Her husband is throwing a fit."

Brad took a deep breath. "Here goes!" he uttered as he walked in the delivery suite. "Mr. Ivy, what seems to be the problem?"

The man pointed to his mother-in-law. "I want her out of here right now!"

Just then a pain hit the patient and she screamed out as she involuntarily pushed and called for her mother, extending her hand toward the frightened woman. Brad assumed his position to deliver the baby. At that moment, the husband rushed around and pushed the older woman away from his wife.

Brad called to one of the nurses, "Get security."

With that, the man walked over and knocked Brad to the floor as he told the doctor to get out of the room. By this time, another contraction hit hard. She screamed again for her mother while Brad got to his feet and grabbed the man sharply, putting his arm behind his back as two security guards entered. They took over and escorted Mr. Ivy out of the hospital, explaining that any further disturbance would end up with him in jail, rather than in the parking lot.

Brad got back into position and after several more propelling contractions his hands caught a sweet little girl with a head full of red hair, just like her mother's. He placed the baby on his patient's stomach while cutting the cord. Then the nurse took the new baby to the side of the room to clean her up. Brad removed his gloves and assured both the mother and grand-mother that the baby was healthy and absolutely beautiful.

The grandmother started to cry as she said, "I'm so sorry about what happened, Dr. Young. Our daughter left Mark a couple of weeks ago . . . She was afraid of his temper. She's been living with her daddy and me. Our son-in-law was a good man. He briefly played football for the Falcons until he damaged his knee during a practice session. At first, they injected cortisone, but that didn't seem to help much, so they prescribed pain medications."

Her daughter looked away and the woman continued. "Within a few short weeks he was addicted . . . There's been trouble ever since." She extended her hand. "By the way, my name is Mary Beth. Fran and the baby will be coming home with me and my husband."

Brad shook her hand. "I know this is hard and I'm sorry. But from what I've just witnessed, you'll need to take measures to keep him away from Fran and the baby. I suggest a restraining order." He looked at the door and added, "Immediately. Let me know if there's anything my office can do for Fran or the baby. I'll be by to check in later."

The nurse placed the newborn in Fran's arms as Brad walked in the doctor's lounge to shower and change. He looked in the mirror at his reddening shoulder. He had hit the floor harder than he realized. Moving his arm in circles, he could already feel it beginning to stiffen. He stayed in the hot shower a little longer, but as he thought of the room full of patients waiting for their appointments, he hurried to dry off, dress, and get back up to his office.

By the time Brad said goodbye to his last patient that afternoon, it was nearing seven. He looked at his desk and saw five messages that he needed to return. The first was to Dr. Jess Wilkins.

"Jess, it's Brad."

"I hear you had some problems in Labor and Delivery today."

Brad laughed. "Never had that happen before."

"I've only had an incident like that once and trust me, once is enough," Jess said. "I had a man start a war with his wife in the exam room. They were screaming so loudly I didn't even bother going in the room. Just called security."

"Unfortunately, I was already beginning the delivery when I realized this man really was crazy," Brad said with a sigh. "But all ended well. How was Miss Davis today?"

"There's something weird going on with her counts. I asked for some further tests. Either she's not telling us the whole story or whatever is happening isn't causing any further symptoms. I should know something by the first of next week. I'm trying a new lab; they're supposed to be faster. I'll let you know the minute I hear back." He paused and added, "Are you playing golf this weekend? I'm trying to get a foursome together, including my son and his roommate, who are coming in to town. The roommate is sharp, and already into his OBGYN residency at Wake Forrest. I thought you two might like to meet. He's hoping to come to Atlanta to practice."

Brad's practice was growing so fast. He didn't want to miss any opportunity to solicit good help. "Count me in if Anne hasn't made plans that I've forgotten about."

By the time he finished the other four calls, it was pitch black outside. He was starved and ready to get home. If he remembered correctly, Anne was fixing her mother's special beef stew tonight. He cut off the lights and walked out the back entrance, locking the door behind him. As he entered the elevator, he reflected on his unusual day. Shaking his head, he sighed as he rubbed his shoulder during the descent to the ground floor. After greeting the cleaning crew in the lobby, he walked out of the doctor's building. As he headed through the parking lot to his car, he thought he heard a noise like footsteps behind him. But when he turned around to check, he didn't see anyone. Walking up to his car, Brad suddenly felt something firm and cold press against his neck.

"You tried to take my wife and baby away from me today, told them to get a restraining order. Who do you think you are, trying to ruin my life?" The voice was shaky and loud. The cold firmness against his neck pressed into his skin harder. "Now, it's my turn. You're a dead man, Doctor . . . whatever your name is, you S.O.B."

At that moment, Brad felt the pressure of a blow causing Mark Ivy to fall sideways to the concrete. He turned to see Sam, the parking supervisor, on top of the downed man. They were struggling to grab the gun that had fallen out of Mark's hand. It was just several inches away from the struggling men, laying on the ground. Brad rushed over and kicked it as hard as he could before stepping on Mark's arm to hold it in place. In minutes, a security detail came running up, as Sam had hit his emergency beeper the moment he observed the man following Brad. Within minutes a police car arrived and Brad's assailant was taken away.

Brad watched the security detail as they helped Sam get into their car. He laughed and said, "Doc, I'm too old for this! My legs aren't working right." Sam was still shaking.

Brad put his hand on Sam's shoulder and disagreed, "They worked just fine tonight, Sam. Thank you for saving my life. That man was just crazy enough to have pulled the trigger."

"Just doing my job, Doc."

"How late do you stay?" Brad asked.

"I usually leave by seven," Sam said as he continued to brush off his pants. "My replacement didn't show tonight. But you know what? You know when you have a feeling . . . something's not quite right? Well, I had that feeling loud and clear tonight. Figured I'd take a walk around and check on things. That's when I saw that man walk up behind you. I knew I had to get him off-balance, somehow. I just didn't plan on him taking me down with him!" He rubbed his legs. "Anyway, all is good. When you tell your pretty wife about tonight, you might mention that she owes me a Varsity hotdog lunch!"

Brad smiled. "Sam, if there's ever anything I can do for you, just let me know. Hotdogs are too easy."

As the doctor walked away to get into his car, he realized he was shaking too. He put his hands on his head, then leaned against the steering wheel. "Thank you, Lord, for Sam. Thanks for taking care of me tonight."

On the way home, Brad called Miss Davis. He explained that Dr. Wilkins added a few more test to her work up, but that Jess hopefully should have all results back by the first of the week. Finishing the conversation, he pulled in his driveway.

When Brad walked in the back door, he could smell Anne's stew. He knew the children were already in bed and wondered if Anne would be as well. But when he heard Barry Manilow's music, he knew his wife was still awake. He held his arms open as he watched her come running down the stairs toward him.

"Dance with me, it's *My Baby Loves Me*," she cooed.

He pulled her in close to his chest, but barely moved his feet. He was just loving the feel of her in his arms. "I love you, Anne Young."

"I love you, too." She pulled back and looked in his eyes. "Are you okay?"

He smiled. "I will be after some beef stew."

"I waited for you to have dinner," she said.

"Good, I've got a lot to tell you, sweetheart."

CHAPTER SIX

A SAFETY ISSUE

Before Brad could begin any details about his day, Anne butted in. She promised he would be excited, then explained that the school reports for children had come in that afternoon. Rushing into his study, she returned with three printouts.

"They'll need a signature," Anne said as she handed the papers to Brad.

The first one he read was Little Brad's. His face lit up. "The boy's doing well!"

Anne handed him a pen. Brad nodded, then signed the report. The next paper was Patsy's and again, Brad smiled. "Couldn't get any better than this," he said. He signed the second report and then reluctantly looked at Gretchen's. Her grades were perfect as he expected, but his shoulders quickly sagged as he read the note from her teacher. Apparently, Gretchen had a habit of interrupting with questions before the teacher could finish explaining the subject material. Brad shook his head as he said, "What are we gonna do with her?"

Anne laughed. "Darling, I know this looks like a negative to you. But I see it as a positive. She has a curious mind and is detail-oriented. That'll come in handy as her curiosity continues to develop. As she gets older, she'll figure out what's appropriate . . . and when it's okay to ask questions. She'll develop a filtering system as time passes. Gretchen and I have already discussed it, but I think it will be good for you to talk to her as well."

Brad signed the report and added a little note about his and Anne's discussion with Gretchen on appropriate timing, then Brad relaxed and finished his supper. Looking at Anne, he could tell she was sleepy; he had seen her stifled yawns several times during their meal. But as she couldn't stifle her next yawn, his sleepy wife asked about Miss Davis. Brad explained that the additional test showed nothing of consequence so far, but they were waiting for a few more results from Jess. He thought back to the parking garage and decided to wait to share his wild tale. He knew that filling Anne in at this late hour would only keep her awake all night. If she heard the slightest sound, she'd keep him awake all night too.

As they cleaned up the kitchen, Anne asked, "Oh yes, what did you have to tell me?"

Brad put the last plate in the dishwasher. "I was just going to tell you about Miss Davis. I knew you'd want to know."

It was nearing ten-thirty when they walked upstairs to get ready for bed. Just as Anne stepped out of the shower, her cell rang. Grabbing a towel, she rushed over and grabbed the phone from the nightstand, hoping the rings hadn't woken the children. It was her friend, Laura, whose husband was one of Brad's associates on the hospital board.

"Oh Anne, I just heard about Brad! Is he okay? Joe said if it hadn't been for Sam, Brad would've more than likely been shot. This is just horrible! Thank the Lord for Sam."

Anne was horrified by Laura's words and of the images crossing her mind. Not having any idea what she was talking about was even more frightening. Brad just stood there; he could tell by the terrified look on Anne's face that someone had spilled the beans. Their eyes met as Anne said, "Laura, he's just fine. Thank you so much for calling. Can I call you back in the morning?" Still looking at her husband, she added, "Brad's just telling me all about it now." She put her phone back on the nightstand.

Brad, looking at Anne, said, "I was going to tell you in the morning. I could see you were so tired and I knew you wouldn't sleep a wink if I told you about the incident tonight." He held his arms out and said, "I'm fine, sweetheart. Come here." He cradled her in his arms as he felt her tears on his chest. "I'm really okay, sweetheart."

That night Anne lay in bed thinking of how close she came to losing Brad. How close she came to not having Brad there for his children. She realized that every day when she sees her children out the door, her husband off to work, she has no idea what the day will bring. Brad was safe and quietly snoring beside her while all she could do was stare at the ceiling. She had never felt this restless or, for that matter, this helpless. Brad was right; sleep wouldn't come.

Eventually she conceded to the non-stop thoughts and got out of bed. She walked to the doors of each of the children's rooms. Peeking in, Anne saw that all were safe and sleeping soundly. Gretchen was out from under her covers, so she walked over and pulled them back in place. The twin stirred a little. Anne put her Pooh Bear back in her arms, and added a light kiss on her forehead. Gretchen looked up at her mother, smiled, closed her eyes, and went right back to sleep.

Anne turned around and walked out to the stairs. Feeling thirsty, she headed to the kitchen and poured herself a glass of ice water. As her mind raced, Anne remembered that there had actually been nights before when she had this same sense of fear. What if one of Brad's patients had died and the family blamed him? What if some person struggling with addiction broke in to look for a prescription pad? The what-ifs, which Brad dismissed, were now all too real. She was convinced, now more than ever, that they needed a first-class security system. She would take care of that first thing in the morning whether Brad thought it was necessary or not. For the first time that she could ever remember, she felt that she and her family were vulnerable. Vulnerable in terrible ways that were now so frightening to her.

Just then, she heard a noise and jumped as she turned toward the sound, her heart racing. Brad was standing there. "You scared me to death!" she said, bursting into tears.

He walked over and put his hands on her shoulders. "This is exactly why I didn't want to tell you earlier. I know that imagination of yours can go wild."

"Brad Young, I need for you to tell me everything that happened last night and you'd better not leave out a single detail!"

He gave her a kiss and said, "I promise I won't."

After listening intently, she said, "We're getting a security system in the morning."

"If it'll make you feel better, put bars on the windows, I don't care. Just come back to bed." He took her hand as they walked back upstairs. It was after two in the morning and both had a lot going on in the day that would be dawning all too soon.

As they climbed back in bed, she snuggled into the safety of his arms and whispered a prayer of gratitude for the safety of her husband and for Sam. As she closed her eyes, Anne had an unsettling feeling. She shuttered as she silently asked, "What will happen to that man? Will they keep him in jail? Could he try again?"

CHAPTER SEVEN

TEARS AT FIVE GUYS

AFTER TWO CUPS OF STRONG COFFEE, ANNE CALLED THREE security companies to give estimates with the condition that she'd have the figures by noon and the system installed by dark. Then she left to drop off some paperwork at the Center. When she and Brad had started this non-profit to help young mothers and their children, they had no idea that it would take such a huge chunk of their time and resources. But witnessing the satisfying results ensured no complaints.

A little later as Anne was trying to find her grocery list when Margie walked in. The Youngs' housekeeper was feeling good enough to come to work. Anne had never needed her more. After being told that people would be coming to give bids for a security system, Margie gave Anne a hug and said she was thrilled as she informed. "Well, I can tell you right now, when we get the bids, I'm gonna want the one with the most bells and whistles! I want every window and door in this house protected. You know the Causbys down the street? They had their house broken into about a month ago. The thieves put all of her jewelry in a pillowcase. Took it right off the pillow on her bed! Put silver in another pillowcase! Neighbors say it was somebody who worked for Mr. Causby at his construction company."

Anne sighed. "I need to tell you something." As Margie paced, she explained what had happened to Brad the night before. After tears and lots of questions, Margie began to calm down. Anne gave her a hug, told her to take it easy, and not over exert today. Then she left for the grocery store. She was running late. As she drove out of the driveway, she felt bad about leaving Margie. After hearing about Brad, Anne knew that woman was going to have a jittery day.

As the Young children walked into school that Friday morning, several of their friends came rushing up to say they had over-heard their parents talking about what had happened to their daddy. Within minutes, Miss Davis got a phone call from Mr. Elder at the school. He asked to speak with Brad. She explained that he was in surgery and would return the call when he was free. Hearing the dismay in the headmaster's voice, she decided to call the children's mother.

When Anne answered, Miss Davis explained that there must be some kind of issue at the school. Immediately Anne regretted Brad's insistence that they not tell the children what had happened to him. He had actually laughed and said he didn't want them as paranoid as their mother. Anne did a U-turn and instead of pulling in to get groceries, she drove to the school.

Walking through the heavy doors and down what seemed to be an endless corridor, Anne saw her children sitting in the main office. The girls were crying and Little Brad was trying to calm them down. Her son looked confused as she heard him tell the girls to "Hush! Nothing is wrong, who told you that?"

Mr. Elder offered his office as a place for Anne to talk to the three. She took their hands as they walked inside, thankful for the privacy. She first explained how the hospital had a security system that takes good care of the doctors and nurses. They took special care of their daddy last night and he is not hurt. She continued, "He is fine."

The placating explanation did not satisfy Gretchen and she immediately said, "Suppose the man comes back? And what if he tries to hurt Daddy again! Mama, Daddy couldn't pick us up this morning because his shoulder hurt. Did that man do that?"

Anne explained that the man was in jail and that he couldn't hurt their daddy or anybody anymore.

Patsy then asked, "Will anyone try to hurt us, Mama?"

"No, darling." Anne rubbed her hand. "You have absolutely nothing to be afraid of."

Little Brad wanted to help his mother out. "That was just a mean man. Daddy doesn't know many bad people." He looked back and forth at his sisters. "Except for you two. Acting bad like you have this morning was real mean as far as I'm concerned!"

An argument commenced between Gretchen and her brother as Patsy just cried. Anne asked Mr. Elder if she could take the children to get lunch. She wanted to a chance to settle them down and promised to bring them back for the afternoon classes.

By now, Brad had gotten the message and called Anne. He met them for lunch at Five Guys and tried to reduce their fears. Leaving the restaurant, Little Brad patted his daddy's shoulder and said, "Dad, you were almost a goner! I think you need to be more careful."

Anne's cell had rung several times at the restaurant as Brad had been talking to the children. She had answered and listened carefully each time, then approved the third security system estimate. By that night, a crew of ten men had the Young house fully secured with two different types of alarms on every door and window, and full exterior motion-detecting lighting had been installed. But Anne couldn't help but obsess, would it be enough?

CHAPTER EIGHT

A SURPRISE FOR ANNE

FOLLOWING A FULL TUTORIAL ON THE NEW SECURITY SYSTEM ON Saturday, Brad shook his head and left for his two o'clock tee time with Jess Wilkins, his son, and his son's roommate. He had almost stopped playing golf because of all the children's activities, but today the weather was great and golf would be nice. Anne and the girls were going to a birthday party and Little Brad was attending a baseball camp that lasted all day. Meeting the fellas in the bar, they ordered a beer as Brad asked questions, trying to get to know the two young men. Tom, Jess's son, was studying medicine with the hopes of going into research. Walton Hood, his roommate, was well on his way in gynecology and obstetrics. Brad asked, "Where are you from, Walt?"

"A small town in North Carolina that you've probably never heard of . . . Smithfield."

Brad smiled. "I am very familiar with Smithfield. That's my wife's hometown. I think I've met everyone there and in the surrounding counties at her aunt's parties. My wife's name is Anne. She was Anne Boyd before we married."

"I know Anne!" Walt said. "I used to work some in the summers for her daddy. I'd help him with their yard. I raked up tons of pine straw. He'd let me fish in the pond when I finished. I was there the day he got a phone call about a new grandson. I think that's the last time I saw him before leaving for college . . . I was sorry to hear about his death. He was a good man." Walt looked away for a minute, then back at Brad. "I only saw Anne a couple of times, but he sure got excited whenever she was coming home." Walt thought back and added, "You've got a mighty nice wife, Dr. Young. And she was always so friendly to me."

Brad smiled.

"You know what else I remember? Mr. Boyd would always have Ruby fix lunch for me when I was working. I did some work for his sister, Miss Francis, too."

Brad started laughing. "That woman is a real Southern belle! After my wife's mother died, her Aunt Francis was mighty important in her life. If you get a chance, you need to come by. Anne would love to see you." Brad ordered another round of beers and said, "I hear you hope to practice in Atlanta."

"Yes, sir. I'd like to live in a big city for a while. Being single with no one special in my life . . . After I've passed my boards, I just want to enjoy myself for a while. Atlanta seems like the perfect place to be."

Brad smiled. "I felt the exact same way and was having a great time. But then one day, Anne walked into my life. Nothing else seemed to matter or has ever been the same."

Just then their tee time was called. The foursome walked out to their carts.

Late that afternoon, Brad called home. Anne had just come home from picking up Little Brad from his camp. "How would you feel if I brought Jess, his son, and a fella named Walt home for supper?"

"Sounds fine. What would you like to serve?"

"Why don't I run by The Varsity on the way home?" Brad asked.

"The children would love hotdogs. I've got pickles, beans that I can bake, chips, and everything we need to go with a picnic supper. I've also got two of Estelle's pecan pies in the freezer . . . and some ice cream."

"I'll be home around six. They'll want to go home and change first. Let's plan on eating around seven-thirty."

"Tell Jess to bring Carol too, if she's not busy," Anne suggested. Carol was Jess's wife, a retired nurse, and a faithful volunteer at the Center. Anne loved her sassy personality.

That night, when the group walked in, Anne immediately recognized Walt.

Brad looked at Walt and back at Anne. "I invited a surprise for you."

Anne walked over to Walt and gave him a hug. "It's been a long time! I understand from Aunt Francis that you're almost through with your residency."

The two reminisced about Smithfield as Walt and Carol

helped Anne carry trays into the breakfast room. Brad walked in to see if he could help with anything as Jess and Tom pitched horseshoes for an audience of three raptly impressed children.

Walt set several bowls of pickles on the table and turned to Brad. "Dr. Young, there's something I need to tell you that I think you may find sort of miraculous. You're one of the reasons I decided to become a doctor."

Brad looked confused as Walt continued, "I would sit down at the pond with Mr. Edward and we'd discuss my future. One day he asked me three questions. The first was . . . what were my goals for my future?"

Brad looked at Anne and grinned.

"I'd never thought much about that, but two things came to mind. Helping people and to make enough money to support a family well. You know, not having to scrimp and stress about saving for the kid's college days . . . like my parents had to for me. I wanted to be able to bank some money and pay off my own college loans as quickly as I could."

"Then he asked me what it would take for me to realize that goal. We went through discussions on lots of different careers, but then he told me about you. About how his son-in-law was taking care of women and bringing children into the world. He said you were able to support his daughter in a nice lifestyle and that you were still financially able to help others." Walt took a deep breath as he remembered. "He gave me lots of examples of things you did. Hard stuff . . . like early morning surgeries and deliveries in the middle of the night. But he said you loved your calling. That you had followed your plan, achieved your goals, and were heading toward a fine destiny. Isn't it weird how we met today?" He looked around the kitchen and out of the window at the children playing and added, "And that I got to meet your family."

Brad walked over and put his arm around Anne. "What this lady has taught me is our lives are all part of a great design, and I'm more convinced now than ever that we need to talk when you're ready to join a practice. Let's see what happens." Brad pulled out his wallet, walked over, and handed Walt his card as he patted him on the back.

Anne thought of her daddy and about her mother's three-step plan. She walked into the powder room to grab a tissue. Looking up, she thought, *Mama, how many lives have you touched?*

Following the restful weekend, Brad received a phone call from Jess Wilkins on Monday morning. All of Miss Davis' test results were complete; her counts were within acceptable limits. There were no signs of dementia or early onset of Alzheimer's. Jess' diagnosis was that she was suffering from anxiety, which he believed was wreaking havoc on her nervous system, and her B12 levels were extremely low. Hopefully, with all the test results in, she could relax with the knowledge that there was no deathly physical basis for the fatigue and memory loss. An anti-anxiety medication and B12 shots would be prescribed for her to get all under control. Regular exercise, fish oil vitamins, and a good light-hearted book were strongly suggested. His office would be calling her this morning. They'd arrange an appointment for her to come in to discuss his findings and his recommendations.

Brad was relieved; Miss Davis had been with the practice long before he was there and he had come to respect and care for her both professionally and personally. He walked out of his office to begin seeing patients. He passed by the Business Office, smiled, and handed Miss Davis several papers as he said, "You're A-OK. Dr. Wilkin's will fill you in this afternoon."

CHAPTER NINE

THE FRIGHTENING ESCAPE

By now, months had passed and Mark Ivy occupied no place in the Youngs' thoughts; however, the Young family occupied Mark's every thought. But as far as the Youngs were concerned, Mr. Ivy had been sent away to dry out and to serve his time; that was that. Though Brad had decided not to press charges against Mark, the hospital wasn't nearly as sympathetic. Their legal department wanted to make an example of the dangers of addiction along with their commitment to protecting their staff. According to the hospital's attorney, Mr. Ivy was going to face a four-year prison sentence for assault with a deadly weapon, which would give him plenty of time to beat his addiction.

What no one knew was that while Mark served time, those empty days and nights only added more hours for him to be consumed with his bitterness. He still blamed Brad Young, and his advice about the restraining order, for the loss of his family. That was much easier than placing the blame where it justly belonged . . . on his shoulders. A few weeks after he began his prison term, Mark was struggling with withdrawal as he had easily acquired drugs in the county jail. Now, effects from the lack of pain meds were taking a toll. But, as the days passed, his confused thinking took a manipulative turn and he pondered the merits of rehab. He was now convinced that if he carefully complied with every rule for a drug-free life, he might possibly get out after a year or two with the leniency of time served and possible community service. For him, that simply meant he could take care of things quicker.

A week later, Mark discussed his change of heart with his lawyer. The gullible man seemed pleased with his client's contrition and willingness to change his life. He was even willing to argue for Mark to serve his time in a secure rehabilitation facility instead of prison. In front of a lenient judge, the lawyer successfully argued that prisons were already way too crowded and that Mark could possibly figure out how to secure drugs in a prison environment.

Two months later, Mark was transported to rehab at a less than secure, antiquated facility in Dublin, Georgia. What had seemed secure to the State was all too easy for this scheming patient who could charm birds from the trees when needed. His observations of the guards' whereabouts were on high alert and by the third week, a new thought had surfaced in Mark's much clearer mind: the possibility of escape.

As he carefully watched the staffs' every movement, Mark noted that several guards passed the nights by playing cards, leaving two of the back hallways watched only by outdated cameras. They assumed all were asleep. They also seemed to ignore anyone who walked the halls late at night suffering from insomnia. Besides, with what the staff assumed were proper cameras, it wasn't like anyone could actually go anywhere. However, during his daily exercise and walks, Mark had watched the cameras carefully and realized that if he timed things perfectly, he could access an exit at the end of the second hallway. But was the door locked? Each time he had seen a guard pass through that door, there was never an attempt to check or ensure that the door was secured. Not one guard had used a key, but was the exit door on some sort of automatic lock? If not, where would the exit take him? Would his escape lead to another locked door? A dead end? Or possibly freedom? In his mind there was now no option. He had to take this chance.

The next week he waited until he heard the guards laughing as they argued over their card game. He had timed the camera's scan of the two hallways several times before tonight and knew exactly how many seconds he had to clear the second passage and get through the door. After much planning, it was time to make his move.

Leaving his room, Mark removed his shoes and tiptoed along the edge of the first hall, listening to snoring patients as he passed each door. He walked toward the opening of the second, longer hallway and waited until the old shaky camera's scan moved beyond his next step. As the gray metal cylinder slowly moved to scan in another direction, he hurried to the possibility of an unlocked door and, hopefully, an outside exit. Reaching for the handle, he held his breath until the metal lever moved in his hand; his breathing returned. Passing through the opening, he held the heavy door to make sure it closed silently. Then he turned and quietly ran down the steps.

His hopes sank. It appeared that he had come to a dead end. Panicking, he rushed to hide behind the stairwell to think as he put on his shoes. But to his surprise, as he looked to the left, he was looking at another door. Walking over, he placed his fingers on the handle and counted silently to three. With every ounce of his strength, he then quickly pulled down on the handle. Mark heard a click; the door opened. Cool fresh air rushed in, flooding his face. It felt good and tasted like freedom. He closed his eyes and breathed in, all the time wondering where he was and if there were any more obstacles, more cameras or silent alarms. With nothing sinister in sight, he stepped out.

Checking the area for barriers, he didn't see a fence or any kind of containment structures. He feared this setting was way too easy. *There has to be a trap of some kind.* He stepped close to the building, almost hugging the concrete as he moved step by step. Coming upon a window, he heard laughing. It was the guards. Dropping to his knees, he breathlessly crawled past. Finally rounding the corner, he stood. Mark trembled even as he tried to be still. In front of him was a dark, secluded parking lot. He counted at least twenty cars before crouching and running to the first row of automobiles; surely one had to be unlocked. He waited, no alarms or lights came on.

Crawling along the row, Mark reached up, carefully trying each door. No luck. He cursed and crept over to the second row. The first car was unlocked. It was a rough-looking older Honda Civic, but it looked great to Mark; that car could be his ticket out. After silently opening the door on the driver's side, he searched for a key. He felt a smooth rounded top of a key, exactly where he had hoped, under the floor mat on the driver's side. He shook his head and thought, *what a fool*. Sliding into the seat, he slowly closed the car door, then looked around to make sure he was alone before starting the car and driving away as naturally as his nerves could manage. With the lazy supervision, it was unlikely that he would be missed until morning's light.

From Dublin, he drove to the small town of Forsyth, Georgia. He had a cousin, Pete, there, whom he hadn't seen in years. He remembered that with the death of his uncle, his cousin now owned the little automotive store on the town square, as well as the gun his uncle kept next to the cash register. It was in an old cigar box, tucked away on a lower shelf. He and Pete use to take the gun out to a friend's farm to shoot cans off of the fence post, so he knew the feel of the piece.

His next thought was to get rid of the white uniform from the rehab center. Figuring there could be extra uniforms in the maintenance area, he drove to the back of the store, and parked in the dark alley. As he walked up to the back entrance, a motion light came on, sending his blood pressure sky high. Mark rushed over to a darkened corner and found a few bricks and stones around a flowerpot. Picking up one of the bricks, he threw it at the light. The brick missed the bulb and hit the metal shade before it fell to the ground with a loud thud. Mark cursed and stepped back into the shadows as he threw again. The edge of a brick on his second toss caught the light perfectly. The safety of the darkness returned as glass fell.

Trying the door, he cursed again; it was locked. He ran back to the car to look through the glove compartment for anything sharp. He finally located a AAA card. Hurrying back, he slid the plastic into the side of the door as he worked to jimmy the lock over and over. Finally, the old rusty lock lifted, the handle moving as he slid the card up. He opened the door and stepped inside the shadow-filled building. Carefully, he walked to the maintenance lockers, feeling around, and grabbed a uniform and slipped it on. He zipped up the heavy material while slowly walking over to the cash register and pulling that old cigar box from the shelf. The silver barrel gleamed upon opening the lid. Mark checked and was relieved to find the cylinder was fully loaded. It was a fairly old pistol, but would probably work well enough to accomplish his needs.

If he couldn't have his family, one way or another, this Dr. Young wouldn't have his either.

A smile came to his face as he thought about the justice of his plan. Grabbing some money out of the cash register, he hurriedly ran out to continue the drive to Atlanta. Turning on the radio, Mark relaxed as he leaned back. He was feeling confident. Thus far, his journey to justice had gone undetected.

As he got closer to the Atlanta skyline, the thousands of sparkling specks grew brighter. He looked around to get his bearings. At the next familiar exit, he turned right to follow a route that he suspected would take him to Peachtree. His hunch was correct. Minutes later he pulled into the emergency room parking lot of Doctor's Hospital.

Unzipping the gray and black maintenance suit, Mark put the gun in his belt. Closing the suit again, he got out of the car and walked inside the automatic glass doors and directly up to the rounded information desk. With charm oozing, he began a conversation with the sleepy-looking young woman behind the counter.

"Hello, there. I know it's late and you're probably as tired as I am, but I've got Dr. Young's car. I was pretty sure he wanted me to deliver it to him here at the hospital, but if he's left for the night, I probably need to drop it off at his home. Can you check and see if he's still here?"

She explained that she would first need to check with her supervisor and walked away from the desk. Within minutes, she returned and said, "He must be at home. He hasn't checked in here tonight for any deliveries."

Mark, thinking fast, said, "Man, am I gonna be in trouble. He was adamant about needing this car first thing in the morning. Do you, by any chance, have his home address? I'll just drop it off there."

She pulled a directory out of the drawer. "Oh, he lives in Brookhaven. That's not far from here." And then, against all rules, she yawned and called out the address.

"Much obliged, Miss," Mark said as he turned around and quickly exited through the glass doors. Walking to the car, he overheard several men talking as two men were getting set up to start repainting yellow lines on the sides of each parking space. Glancing over, the man giving directions looked up at Mark as he immediately got in the car, turned his face away from the man, and slowly drove out of the lot.

Sam continued the conversation with the men about the painting, but couldn't shake the familiarity of the face he had just seen. *Who was that man?* Minutes later it dawned on Sam. It was Mark Ivy. Sam had sat in the courtroom as a witness for the hospital at Mark's trial. He knew that face. Something wasn't right, Mark had gone to jail for years.

Sam rushed into the emergency room and up to the information desk. He asked, "The man who was just in here in some kind of uniform . . . gray and black. Why was he here?"

"He was delivering Dr. Young's car."

"What did you tell him?"

"I told him Dr. Young wasn't here. I gave him the doctor's home address. He said he would be in trouble if he didn't get it to him tonight." She began to cry as she second-guessed what she had done.

"Oh my gosh, you didn't!" Sam scolded as he paged security, then he called the Brookhaven police department. He looked back at the confused receptionist and said, "Give me the Young's address, now!" Hitting his pager again, he texted the address to security and instructed a detail to leave for that location immediately. Then he repeated the same on his cell with a police sergeant in Brookhaven. He added a brief explanation about Mark Ivy and his concern for Dr. Young and his family's safety.

Finally, Sam rushed out as the young girl yelled, "I'm sorry! Did I do something wrong?"

Anne looked at the clock; it was nearly midnight. Brad's flight was to arrive right about now. He had attended a medical conference in Los Angeles for the last three days and she couldn't wait for him to get home. She had stayed awake as long as she could, but was now sleepy. She walked upstairs to start getting ready for bed.

The master bedroom was at the front of the house. As a light flickered through the side window, she noticed a car passing by on her street. Maybe Brad took an earlier flight. She peered out the window and disappointedly saw that it was an older car that had stopped in front of the neighbor's house across the street. In the stillness of the night, she heard a car door close. Another thought crossed her mind, this one uncomfortable. She couldn't remember setting the alarm. An uneasy feeling coursed through her stomach as she rushed down the stairs to check the system. Thankfully, the alarm was on and no lights were flashing, all the doors were locked. Relieved, she turned to walk back upstairs but stopped. Her son had been taking trash to the street from the basement that afternoon. Had he reset the alarm down there? Just then, her yard was flooded by the security lights.

Motion detectors had been activated. Anne heard what sounded like footsteps on the side porch. Bo Jr. began to bark; the steps stopped. She was paralyzed with fear as the only sound now was the low, snarling growl from their dog. Anne stood at the bottom of the stairs and listened as her heart pounded. She had no idea what to do. Then she heard a strange sound like someone messing with the side doorknob. Next, she heard the tall, porcelain planter as it shattered on slate floor of the side porch.

She rushed upstairs to wake her children and try to get them to safety, but where? All of a sudden, she saw red and blue lights flashing through the large foyer window as cars and emergency vehicles pulled into their driveway and parked on her lawn. She could hear voices calling out and footsteps running around outside in several different directions. Then she heard banging on their front door.

"Anne, it's Sam. Are you okay?"

Anne swallowed hard and slowly walked back down the stairs to the front door. She peeked out the glass side panel and saw that it was indeed Sam. She opened the door and fell into his arms.

"Oh, Sam. I was so afraid. What's going on? What is happening?"

By this time, Bo Jr. was barking loudly again. Anne ran over to calm him so that he wouldn't wake the children. Sam followed. "Anne, where is Brad?" he asked.

"His flight should have landed thirty minutes ago. He's been in LA."

Then both Sam and Anne heard what sounded like a gunshot in the distance. Anne's eyes widened. "What on earth is going on?"

Sam ushered Anne over to a chair. He had her sit down as he explained seeing Mark Ivy at the hospital. "I had just gotten to the emergency department to check on a restriping project when he came out of the emergency entrance. It took me a few minutes, but I recognized him. He had been in there looking for your husband. When he was told that Brad wasn't there, he was given your address . . . supposedly, to deliver Brad's car."

Just then the security detail and a policeman knocked on the door. Sam walked over to answer. Anne could hear Sam asking about the gunshot, but she couldn't make out the mumbled words. The police officers stepped inside to make sure Anne was all right. She asked about the noise that sounded like a gun being fired.

"Mrs. Young, he won't be bothering you anymore. We cornered him on the golf course. He took his own life. We had him in our sights and told him to drop the gun . . . His last words were, 'I can't go back.' It was over."

Sam looked at the tears in Anne's eyes. He asked the officer if they could handle any further business in the morning. He could clearly see that their explanations were not what Anne needed right now. The officer agreed that a detective would call on the Youngs tomorrow.

Then the hospital security team turned to Sam and asked, "Are you staying until Dr. Young gets home? We can probably reach him on his cell by now."

"You may want to wait on that call," Sam said, worried that Brad would be frantic. "I'll stay here until he comes home."

Before the emergency vehicles had time to pack up and leave, Brad pulled into the driveway. He had never seen so many flashing lights. All he could think about was his family. He parked and ran through the open front door. Anne and Sam were talking in the great room. He grabbed his wife's shoulders. "Are you okay? Are the children okay?" He took her in his arms.

After assuring Brad that all was well, Sam explained the night's events. Brad walked over and put his arm around Sam's shoulder as he said, "You're the best guardian angel anyone could ever have. Thank you, Sam."

Looking at the couple, Sam smiled. Then he turned and walked to the front of the entrance foyer. Brad followed, thanked him again, and said goodnight as he locked the door. Walking back to his wife, he took her in his arms again. "I'm so sorry, sweetheart. I'm so sorry I wasn't here to keep you safe."

Anne broke down as her anxiety poured out in deep sobs. He held her until she could calm down. Taking her hand, they walked upstairs in silence. Brad leaned over and kissed her wet cheek. "I will never tease you anymore about your vivid imagination. You were right about the security system, sweetheart."

She finally smiled as she looked back at him. "That system was something that I never wanted to be right about, my love."

After finally getting in bed, they couldn't seem to get close enough to each other as she snuggled into the reassuring comfort of his strong, yet gentle arms. He was home. She and her children were safe.

The next morning, while the children ate their breakfast, their parents explained that someone had tried to break into their house, but their new security system had kept him out and had kept them safe. They wanted to fill the children in with a brief explanation before classmates had a chance to frighten them with whatever story they might have heard. After dozens of questions, mainly from the twins, they seemed satisfied with their parents' answers. Now all they could think about was telling their friends about the burglar, and about how brave they had been. The fact that the three had slept soundly through the commotion didn't seem to play a significant role in their courageous tale.

CHAPTER TEN

A SOBERING REVELATION

WINTER HAD BEEN SURPRISINGLY MILD SO FAR THIS YEAR; IT WAS now well into February. With the Christmas season behind her and no snow to cripple the city, it was the perfect time to get outfitted for the Doctor's Hospital Auxiliary Ball, always held exactly on the fourteenth of February. Anne had woken up with Valentine's Day on her mind. Knowing she needed to call Sissy, her Birmingham fashion-designing friend from college, she picked up her phone. She'd get Sissy on the hunt once again for that perfect outfit. The children were spending the afternoon and night with Brad's parents, Patsy and Brad Sr. Estelle, the Youngs' housekeeper, who had always served as Brad's second mother, was taking all three to buy Valentines for school. Afterwards, she and their grandmother had plans to help the children get their cards ready for school parties on the fourteenth. That night their grandparents were taking the three to a fun dinner at Chuck E. Cheese.

Anne smiled as she thought of Valentine's Day activities and surprises, knowing she would get her usual. She could already picture red roses. Lots of them from her husband. She had found Brad a soft, cashmere sweater in his favorite shade of blue. And the first of next week, Margie and the twins had plans to make heart-shaped cookies and pink iced cupcakes with red hots sprinkled on top. They would be perfect for the children to take to their class parties as Valentine treats. Patsy had asked for cookies, while Gretchen requested cupcakes, so double-duty was on tap for the baking. In her normal patient way, Margie had smiled and said both requests would be just the perfect Valentine refreshments. Once Anne had her red dress for the ball, she'd actually be way ahead of schedule. For once! Brad had called earlier that day, saying he had a board dinner to attend at the hospital, which meant Anne didn't have to worry about supper. Margie had a doctor's appointment and had left for the day. Anne had the afternoon all to herself to do some decorating.

Brad walked into the hospital dinner a little early. He was seated next to Charles Billings, a cardiologist. Although not one of his favorite people, Brad had to admit Charles had been exceptionally helpful with Anne's daddy and his heart condition prior to his death. The two men had a little time to talk hospital business before dinner was served. While they talked, it occurred to Brad that Charles was the only bachelor out of the many colleagues attending the dinner.

Brad asked, "Who's your date for the Doctor's Valentine thing?"

Charles raised his brow and said, "My sister. She's in town for a few weeks visiting our parents. I figured it'd be something she'd enjoy."

"I thought for sure you'd be married again by now," Brad said as the two were served a steak dinner. He had quickly calculated that Charles had been divorced for at least twelve to thirteen years and he never had any children with his first wife.

"Nope. Just haven't met anyone." Charles hesitated as he unfolded his napkin. "You know, Brad. You're a very lucky man. Beautiful wife, healthy children . . . I have to admit I envy you." He looked just past Brad's shoulder and stared at nothing in particular. "You know, I did find someone I truly cared for several years ago. She was everything any man could want. Just being around her made a man feel good."

Brad leaned in and asked, "Charles, why didn't you marry her?"

Charles breathed a heavy sigh. "She was taken."

Brad looked quizzically at his colleague. "I'm surprised you gave up so easily."

"Oh, I was ready to fight for her. But he swept her away before I could do anything to stop it."

Before Charles could finish his sentence, a memory raced across Brad's mind. He remembered a comment that Charles had made to Brad Sr. years ago. He and Anne had broken up for a few weeks prior to their engagement. Charles had sent him a message through his dad. The quote was, *All's fair in love and war. Game on.* Then Brad recalled how Charles had flirted with Anne at Barnsley during an AMA retreat. Anne had been Brad's date and he had not liked the attention she was receiving.

Charles could see by the look on Brad's face that he was

putting the pieces together. "Like I said, Brad. You're the luck-iest man I know."

Brad patted his colleague on the shoulder. "Sometimes it doesn't hurt to be reminded. Thanks, Charles."

That night when Brad arrived at home, Anne was covering the house with red, white, and pink Valentines and anything else she could find that was red or pink, including lots of ribbons. The designer in her never let a holiday go by undecorated, nor thoroughly celebrated. He watched his wife rush around placing huge hearts on the mantel. She then put a red-heart collar on Bo Jr. Brad watched his wife, in her soft red warmups, as her dark hair bounced on her shoulders while she moved from area to area with more decorations.

Every now and again, she would turn and ask, "How does this look?"

"Absolutely beautiful." She mistakenly thought he meant the decorations.

Brad continued to gaze at her with eyes of renewed admira-tion. He remembered that first week when they had broken up, and the call letting him know that one of his other colleagues planned to call her, not wanting Brad to think he was going behind his back.

He thought again about Charles' comment on how lucky he was. But through Anne, Brad had learned that luck had nothing to do with anything. He now understood that he was blessed with his incredible wife and the three children their love had produced.

Walking over, he cut the music up. It was Barry Manilow's

Mandy. Then he walked toward Anne and took the box of decorations from her hands. He placed it on the table, then whispered, "Dance with me, sweetheart."

That night, Brad's kisses lasted a little longer; he held her with a renewed yearning.

CHAPTER ELEVEN

HEARTS AND FLOWERS

EARLY THE NEXT WEEK, THERE WAS A KNOCK AT THE FRONT DOOR. Margie called out, "I'll get it." Within minutes, she yelled up to Anne, who was trying to get dressed for the day, "Oh boy! A box from Birmingham just arrived."

Anne came to the top of the staircase. Leaning over the railing with a gleam in her eyes, she called, "Let's see if Sissy has worked her magic." Knowing it had to be her red dress, she rushed down the stairs. The two took the box into the guestroom. Laying the box on the bed, she and Margie pulled the ends open. At first all they saw was white tissue paper that seemed to explode all over the bed. Then a shimmering red fabric came into view. Anne pulled the dress out and held it up.

"Ooh, la, la!" Margie exclaimed, "Mighty pretty and a wee bit sexy . . . don't you think?"

Anne searched the box for more fabric and was delighted to find a matching jacket. Margie insisted she try on the outfit right away. It was a glimmering scarlet silk that draped softly in front and on the extremely low back. With a slit along the left side, it was a straight sheath with scarlet-jewel spaghetti straps. But the modesty of the bolero jacket trimmed with a matching jeweled zipper and large cuff buttons assured the outfit's acceptability for the Valentine Ball. With her dark hair and eyes, all shades of reds were Anne's favorites. And besides, Brad loved her in bright colors.

Margie swept all the paper back into the box, while Anne smiled, twirled around several times, and danced upstairs in her slinky new dress. Her Valentine's to-do list was almost complete.

The next day, the twins were especially excited to leave for school with red velvet bags full of Valentines to pass out to their classmates. They looked so cute in the dresses their grandmother had bought them, red velvet and tiny hearts on a white sweater. Anne asked Little Brad if he was going to wear his new red sweater.

"Mom, I'm not taking Valentines and I'm not wearing a red sweater. Boys don't do that; we just eat what the girls bring!" He smiled as he rolled his eyes.

"What is this bag full of Valentines?" Anne asked as she pointed to a bag with the name *Brad* written on the side.

"I just did them to make Gaga happy. I'm not taking them to school."

Margie handed Anne the boxes of red and white Valentine cookies and pink cupcakes for the girls' classroom. The whole household had worked so hard on baking and decorating. Walking to the car, Margie gave the girls kisses and hugged

Little Brad as she passed him a cookie to eat on the way. "I have extras if you'd like to take some to your class."

The boy shook his head, much like his daddy's habit, but still managed a huge smile. "Thank you but I'll eat all of mine after school."

Depositing the girls, their brother, Valentines galore, and their sweet treats, Anne ran by to see the seamstress about picking up Brad's sweater. She had asked that a small monogram by placed on the sleeve's ribbed cuff to finish off his Valentine gift. She stopped to select two large yard plants for Estelle and Margie, as their favorite pastime was gardening. Next, she picked up tickets to see Tony Bennet in concert at the Fox Theater for Patsy and Brad Sr.

Picking up Bo Jr. at the house, Anne dropped him off for his annual checkup with the vet. She then drove to the Youngs' with gifts and cards in hand. Patsy asked if Brad Sr. could help with Anne's busy schedule by picking up the children around five that afternoon. All three were eating dinner and spending the night with their grandparents while Anne and Brad enjoyed a stress-free Valentine's Ball. She gratefully accepted the offer; her day was filled to the brim.

Patsy handed Anne a card and one for Brad, as well. She smiled and said, "Open these tonight when y'all get home from your party."

Estelle gave Anne a heart-shaped tin filled with red tea cakes. "You tell that spoiled Southern boy he'd better share these with you and those babies!"

After goodbye hugs and kisses, Anne left to get a spray tan. That dress was way too revealing for winter white skin. Before she knew it, there was barely enough time to pick up Bo Jr. and the children for their afternoon surprise. Thankfully, Margie had already been preparing the table for an afternoon Valentine's party.

When the three walked into the breakfast room after school, red and pink balloons were hanging from the chandelier. Large red boxes were placed at each child's typical seat at the table. Little Brad, being the oldest, got to open his first. Inside was a plastic bag with a big red bow that contained a dozen of Margie's cookies, along with a brand-new football and a signed Braves baseball cap and ball. He hugged his mother and Margie before taking his box and going upstairs to his room. In his opinion, he had enjoyed enough celebrating of this "mushy" holiday.

The twins tore into each of their boxes at the same time. Again, there were the plastic bags with big red bows, full of cookies. The boxes also held new red sweaters; tights; red, white and black, plaid skirts; fuzzy pink Valentine pillows; and all kinds of baking supplies, even spring sprinkles to help Margie with the next big holiday bake-off. Asking for glasses of milk, they opened their cookies.

Calling Little Brad to come downstairs, Anne gave him a hug and whispered for him and his sisters to give Margie their homemade cards and the big, green plant for her yard. Their housekeeper wiped her eyes and hugged the children. Margie, now pooped, couldn't figure out why, but her favorite times at the Youngs' were the busy days of holiday chaos.

Just then the doorbell rang and interrupted the celebration. Little Brad ran to the door and called out to his mother, "Mom, it's for you!"

Anne smiled as she hurried to the door. She had a pretty

good idea of what had arrived. *He didn't forget.* Standing at the front door, the delivery man was holding a large bouquet of red roses and white baby's breath.

"Who is that from, Mama?" Little Brad asked.

The twins rushed up to see what had come and scolded their brother immediately. "They're from Daddy, silly! He sends them to Mama every Valentine's Day."

While Anne set the vase in the center of the dining room table, the delivery man returned with two small, red buckets filled with pink sweetheart roses and another pink crystal vase filled with pink roses, Brad's gifts for his girls, including Margie.

The twins were ecstatic and rushed up to their room with the small buckets splashing water everywhere as more tears welled up in Margie's eyes. Anne sat down to read the card that was attached to her roses. Little Brad looked at his mother. "I hope there's no more flowers! I sure don't want any."

"I think your football was from your daddy, smarty," Anne explained.

Pulling her card out of the envelope, she smiled as she read, "I have a special evening planned, sweetheart. You'll never know how much I love you. Happy Valentine's Day." She placed the card back in the envelope and smiled as she murmured, "I do know, my love!"

Brad was to get home shortly after five that Valentine's Day. The couple were to be at the ball by seven. Anne had the children packed and ready to go to the Youngs' for the night. She had just stepped out of the shower, wrapped herself in a towel, and was drying her hair. Brad drove up just as his dad pulled into the driveway. After helping pack his brood into Brad Sr.'s car, he helped Margie to her car with her new plant and roses. He then grabbed a handful of the red tea cakes that were sitting on the counter, some milk, and walked upstairs to their bedroom. Taking one look at his wife, he suggested, "We've got a little time!" He walked over and tried to loosen her towel.

"No, we don't!" She held the towel tightly. "We're supposed to pick Doris and Jeff up at six-thirty." She winked and added, "But I love the idea of the special evening you have planned."

"Later," he said with a grin. He looked at her more carefully and shook his head. "Has your skin changed color?"

"Yes, it has. It has a tan!"

"In February?"

She nodded and suggested he go get ready.

As he showered, Anne fluffed her hair, added makeup, dressed, and walked downstairs. Grabbing her mother's red purse from the top shelf of the coat closet, Anne checked in with Doris to make sure their babysitter had arrived on time.

Anne had already laid out Brad's tux with all of the accessories, but she could hear him calling her name. He was asking where she had hidden his black shoes.

"Bottom shelf of your closet, where they've been ever since we moved in," she answered. Walking to the bottom of the staircase, she could hear him mumbling; he still couldn't find them.

"Bottom shelf!" she reiterated.

After another minute, Brad finally called back, "Found 'em . . . you didn't hide them good enough," he laughed.

When Brad came downstairs, Anne was in the dining room

and had just leaned over to smell her roses. She looked up to find him staring at her. She smiled and said, "They're gorgeous, my love. Thank you so much."

"They're not the only thing that's gorgeous. I've never seen you look any prettier."

"When you get the bill for this dress, you may feel different- ly," she said with a grin.

He laughed. "Don't think so. No, ma'am. Not with you on my arm tonight!"

They kissed softly. She added, "And you look mighty hand- some, Dr. Young."

With a smile, she placed a rose in his lapel. Then they walked out and into the evening.

After arriving at Doris and Jeff's, they got kisses from little Jeffey when his sitter brought him out to say goodnight. Anne handed him a big red bag full of Valentine's surprises that she knew would keep him happy as they left. Twenty minutes later, the four entered the ball and found their table. It was filled with good friends, and golden bottles of pink champagne were flowing.

That evening the conversation was lively as they enjoyed plates of prime rib, baked potato casserole, chopped salad, and yeast rolls. The dessert course offered the best red-velvet cake Anne had ever tasted. Dancing then lasted for hours as the big band sound filled the room. Since most of the golfing doctors and Brad belonged to the same club, the hospital tended to choose that location for this annual gala. Besides, the white and gold décor lent itself nicely to bright Valentine colors.

The night was wonderful as the band played one love song after another while couples filled the dance floor. Brad held Anne tightly as they slowly danced the night away. Later in the evening as Anne and Brad returned to their table, Charles Billings walked over to say hello. After chatting with Doris and Jeff, Anne and Brad, and the others, the band struck up a familiar tune, *My Funny Valentine*.

Charles looked at Brad and asked, "May I have this dance with your wife, Doctor Young?"

A million thoughts ran through Brad's mind as he recalled their conversation several weeks back. "Just this once," he replied in a somewhat serious tone.

Charles took Anne's hand and proceeded to the dance floor. Brad turned back to continue several ongoing conversations, but he couldn't help glancing over his shoulder at his wife every now and then. He watched Charles laughing and talking with Anne as the two danced. Maybe it was his imagination, but after the two men's conversation that had skirted the topic of Anne, as they danced, there seemed to be a new softness on Charles' muscular face. *Hum,* he thought. *Well, you just dance away, my friend, 'cause she'll be going straight home with me.*

Or so he thought.

CHAPTER TWELVE

HURRY...HE'S BURNING UP

DORIS AND JEFF SAID GOODNIGHT AS THEY WALKED UP THE GRAY slate tiles to their porch. Anne snuggled up to her husband as they waited for their friend's porch light to come on. Meeting them at the door, their sitter was frantic. She had tried to call them several times that night with no success. Their five-year-old son, Jeffey, was running a fever. She began to cry. "I called and called! He's so hot!"

But there had been so much noise at the ball, no one had heard the phone. Doris yelled back to Anne, just as their car started to pull away.

Brad opened his car door. Anne frantically asked, "What's the matter?"

By now, Doris had run inside and Jeff called out from the door. "Jeffey is sick!"

Brad looked at Anne. "He's probably fine. He's just a child. They get sick, sweetheart."

Anne turned to open her door, more than a little perturbed. "We need to get out of this car and go check on that precious little boy!"

Brad huffed; this was not his expected ending to their Valentine's evening. He and Anne rushed into the house. Jeff ushered Brad into Jeffey's room. Doris had just sat down on the bed; she placed her hand on her little boy's forehead. She turned back to Brad and said, "Oh my goodness. He's burning up!"

Brad leaned over to check and said, "Get me a thermometer."

As Anne and Doris looked for the thermometer, Jeffey went into a convulsion. His father froze at the foot of the bed.

Brad yelled to Anne, "Bring cold cloths! Hurry!" He picked up the little boy and handed him to Jeff. "Let's go."

The minute they got to the car, Brad pulled a tongue depressor and gauze from a medical bag in the trunk, wrapped the depressor in the gauze, and passed it to Jeff. "Put this in his mouth on his tongue."

Anne and Doris scurried out behind the men bearing several cold, wet towels. With Jeffey wrapped in the cloths, they hurried to the emergency room.

Within thirty minutes of their arrival, the doctors had Jeffey stable, but the fever was still a problem. While icing him down, the little boy began to cry and say, "The sunshine is blinking on and off . . . on and off . . . on and off." The fever was causing hallucinations.

Nearly an hour later, Jeffey finally began to feel clammy. His temperature had come down some, but what had caused the fever, or the pain now reflected in his eyes? That was the unanswered question. There had to be infection somewhere in the child's body. After a thorough exam with no clues, Brad had a thought. He pressed on Jeffey's right side. The boy cried out in pain. His medical team now felt sure that all was stemming from the child's appendix.

Brad and the ER doctor rushed the boy to another room for a scan, which verified the medical staff's suspicion. Jeffey was rushed to a surgical suite for an appendectomy.

Brad came out with paperwork for Doris and Jeff to sign. "Don't think about all this red tape. Just sign here." He pointed and added, "We don't have any time."

Doris started crying. "I don't want him in there by himself."

"They've got everything ready. I'll scrub, Doris. I'll be in there with him," Brad assured. "I'll make sure they take good care of your little boy," he promised.

Brad was putting on his scrubs as the pediatrician walked into the prep area with a blank stare. "It'll be another forty-five minutes before we can get a surgeon freed up." Then he looked at Brad as if a light had come on. "Haven't you taken out an appendix or two?"

"More times than I care to remember," Brad said as he thought back to his surgical fellowship. "Let's go."

In no time, the surgery was completed. They had found and removed a severely inflamed appendix. Brad was amazed that it hadn't already ruptured. If that had happened, infection could have spread throughout the child's body and could have possibly been a fatal complication. Brad lowered his head and whispered a prayer of thanks. Jeffey was such a special child to everyone. All Brad could think about was his birth mother,

Betsy, and the short life she had sacrificed to bring her son into this world.

Walking out to the waiting room, Brad filled Doris, Jeff, and Anne in on how well all had gone. Then he asked the parents to come to the recovery room with him. He explained that they could sit with their son as he woke up. Anne followed close behind. Soon Jeffey began to stir a little. He opened his eyes while his mother kissed his small face. Brad turned to Jeff and smiled. "He'll be in the hospital for a couple of days, but will likely be doing a lot better than you two or Anne."

Brad showered, changed into fresh scrubs, gathered all the pieces of his tux in a bag, and walked back into recovery to get his wife. He was tired and just needed to go home. Anne was torn; she wanted to stay, but she knew Doris would call if they needed anything. Walking over, she kissed little Jeffey's forehead, then took Brad's hand.

When they walked out to their car, Anne looked in her husband's eyes and said, "You do know you're my hero."

"I like thinking that," he admitted.

A thought nagged in the back of Brad's mind on the drive home and he debated on asking Anne a question. He wondered if she had any idea how Charles Billings felt about her. He began slowly. "Did you enjoy the dance tonight, sweetheart?"

"I did! I think it was the best gala the hospital has had so far." She looked back over her shoulder as they left the hospital. "But right now, all I can think about is Jeffey . . . and Betsy. I was so afraid of cancer cells."

Brad took her hand. "Sweetheart, that baby was insulated in his mother's womb. You don't have to worry about that."

She burst into tears. "I know Doris was thinking the exact same thing. I felt so sorry for her . . . and of course Jeff.

Anne's sobs brought back all the emotion she and Brad had experienced the night Betsy asked Doris and Jeff to be Jeffey's parents. Her husband knew how much Anne missed Betsy and how much she loved that little boy. His question was of no consequence. Now surely wasn't the time. It could wait.

CHAPTER THIRTEEN

THOUGHTS OF BETSY

BRAD AND ANNE, JUST PULLING INTO THEIR DRIVEWAY FROM THE hospital, watched the sun beginning to appear above the horizon. He was exhausted from the unexpected surgery on a little boy that meant the world to so many. The couple walked upstairs, hoping for even a little sleep. They undressed in silence, as each thought of Betsy and her fight for Jeffey's little life. That little boy's mother had become such a good friend as she struggled through that last year as both cancer and a new life grew in her fragile body.

Anne remembered their many times sitting together waiting for various medical appointments, and how the two had bonded with a hope that never materialized. Hope for a miracle that would allow Betsy to live and raise her son. Then Anne thought of the night God intervened to bring Doris and Jeff to the realization that Betsy's son could become their son as well.

Brad, on the other hand, was remembering the birth of that little boy and how he had rushed to lay Jeffey in Betsy's arms, minutes before she drew her last breath. He remembered taking her hand and helping her explore his perfect little body, just as he had promised. Brad had prayed with every fiber of his being that she would live long enough to hold her child.

Getting into bed, the two kissed softly. Closing their eyes, they snuggled under the covers. But sleep wouldn't come for Anne. She finally reached over to scratch her husband's back as he drifted off. Smiling, she thought of how instrumental this man of hers had been in the life of that little boy, and how important Jeffey was to their entire family.

Shortly before seven, Brad's pager rang. So much for sleep; he was needed in Labor and Delivery to bring yet another life into this world. Rushing into the bathroom, he took a quick shower before heading out the door. Anne ran downstairs to at least send him out with a hot cup of coffee.

Listening to the sound of his car's engine, she walked to the dining room window as he pulled away. She wasn't sure if it was just her emotions or the lack of sleep, but she sat down and began to cry. Not the tender tears that came so easily for Anne; these were loud, uncontrollable sobs that came due to the emergency of the evening and her love for this selfless man who gave everything he had to his family, friends, and patients. In that moment of intense compassion, she felt such a need to have the children in her arms.

Her time with Betsy had taught her an unprecedented depth of gratitude. Anne took a sip of coffee, walked back upstairs to their bed, and cried herself back to sleep as she called her husband's name.

. . .

Anne felt a kiss on her cheek when Brad joined her after returning from the hospital. She looked at the clock and it was just a little after noon. "That was a pretty quick delivery," she said as she cuddled up against him.

"Yes, it was." Brad smiled and added, "It was Todd James' grandchild and she came quickly for a first baby. Mother and child are fine and you've never seen such a happy family. I got there just as the pretty little girl was ready to make her grand entrance. After congratulating the family and making sure the new mother was doing well, I couldn't wait to get back here." He smiled. "Back to you. I talked to Mom on the way and they're going to keep the children until tomorrow morning. We'll all meet at church, so we can get some sleep." He looked at Anne and realized she was crying. "Are you okay, sweetheart?"

"I'm okay. But I think I'll go pick the children up later this afternoon."

He cocked his head and looked at her quizzically. "Have you lost your mind? Remember, I promised you a very special evening? It'll just be one evening later."

"Can it be an afternoon later?" she asked. "After everything that happened . . . and thinking about Betsy . . . I just want to hold my children in my arms."

But then, Anne suddenly jumped up and rushed over to the dresser to take two cards out of a drawer. She ran back over to the bed and handed one of them to Brad. "These are our Valentines from your parents. I nearly forgot about them! We were to open them last night."

"You open your card first," he said as he laid his card by his side.

In the fatigue of her emotional state, she began to read it

aloud as tears trickled down her cheeks in a steady flow. "To our sweet daughter-in-law—when you came into our lives we had no idea of all the joy you would bring. If we could have selected a wife for our son, it would have been you. And then you presented us with the three loves of our lives and you share them so graciously. Having them with us for this Valentine's weekend is such a precious gift. Always know how loved you are—Mom, Dad, and Estelle."

"Oh, Brad, that was so sweet," Anne said. "Maybe we should let the children stay until church tomorrow."

Brad laughed. "Works for me!"

"Now read your card," she said as she tried to peek inside.

He took the card out of the envelope and began, "Dear Son —thank you for bringing Anne into our lives. She has been so dear to us while fulfilling our dreams with three beautiful grandchildren. You could not have picked a more perfect life-partner. We love you—Mom, Dad, and Estelle."

Brad sat up. "Wait a minute! They didn't say anything about me and I'm their son! All they talked about was you and the children! I helped with those three . . . you couldn't have had them without me!"

She laughed. "Why, Brad Young, you're jealous!"

He pulled her close as thoughts of Charles Billings came to his mind. "Maybe I am a little jealous. But I agree with my parents. I couldn't have chosen anyone better." He gave her a long kiss, leaning her back against the pillows.

Anne put her arms around his neck and looked into his eyes. "I think you promised an exciting evening."

He kissed both of her cheeks, then her forehead as he whispered, "And I never renege on a promise."

CHAPTER FOURTEEN

THE RESCUE

TWO YEARS LATER, WHILE ANNE WAS PLANTING LARGE, RED geraniums in the pots on their front porch, she was thinking of how quickly time had passed. Little Brad was a budding teenager at thirteen and the girls already had signs of puberty at eleven. Her thoughts were interrupted by a call from the senior pastor at their church. He explained that there had been a police raid at an apartment building on Pharr Street. Eight young girls who were being trafficked had been rescued. Either they were going to have to stay in a social services facility or the church needed to find housing. With the emotional and physical needs these girls faced, he immediately thought of the Center and was asking if there was any possible room available. Anne shook her head; she knew they were on overload, both at the resident's building and at the Center itself, yet there was no way she could turn them away. She agreed that if he could give her twenty-four hours, they would make a place for all eight.

Anne could hear his voice crack as he said, "Anne, one of

them is only fourteen years old. We'll work out something at the church tonight and we'll bring them to you tomorrow. It will be late afternoon to give you as much time as possible."

Contacting the board, Anne found all were in agreement. They would work out something for these young girls.

Driving to the Center later that morning, all Anne could think about was the youngest victim. She was not much older than Little Brad and the girls. "How can there be such evil?" she asked herself.

Upon walking in, the first thing she saw was their big conference room. Anne's eyes widened; ideas began to take shape. By one o'clock, all the furniture had been removed and the conference room was being prepped for new beds and chests to be delivered by five. She had ordered four sets of bunkbeds, fours chests of drawers, and some lamps. She had a crew already building closets at each end of the room. Painters were to come first thing in the morning while Anne and two other volunteers would shop for sheets, towels, bedspreads, toiletries, and the works. Outside of the day room, there were bathrooms with showers, which would allow convenient access from the conference room.

By three o'clock the next afternoon, the little dormitory was fun with bright, feminine colors. The room was now a soft shade of pink with fresh flowers on every chest of drawers and a big, fluffy stuffed bear on each bed. Anne's children had made a huge sign that was hung from the mahogany door frame. It read, "Welcome! We All Love You!!!!" with lots of smiley faces. Everything was ready for the eight special new guests.

. . .

Anne watched with gratitude as all the dedicated ladies at the Center walked over to hug and greet the new arrivals. After giving them time to settle in to their new surroundings, two of the volunteers then took the girls back to the clothing closet, which held volumes of clean donated clothes from lots of Atlanta's generous women and their children. The girls seemed excited and enjoyed "shopping" for jeans, skirts, blouses, sweaters, shoes, socks, undies, night gowns, makeup, and a couple of purses.

Anne couldn't help but tear up as she watched each girl fold and place her new wardrobe in a chest of drawers and their closet with such care. Afterwards, she ushered them to the bathrooms so they could take nice warm showers, brush their teeth, and put on clean clothes. That night a spaghetti dinner, and ice cream with cookies, was served on a long folding table in the day room.

Anne stayed late that night as she and others took turns talking to the young girls. Ranging from fourteen to nineteen, she couldn't imagine how they had lived through the torment they had experienced. She gave each of the girls a new, small devotional book as they climbed into their new beds. Explaining how she and her family said prayers together each night, she asked if they would like to do the same. Two other volunteers joined to interpret for two of the young girls who spoke Spanish. All closed their eyes and bowed their heads as Anne prayed. She then kissed each of their foreheads and told them they were safe and she hoped they would get a good night's sleep. Tired but satisfied, Anne left for home.

. . .

Three of the other volunteers took turns spending the nights until the Center was able to hire a kind and gentle house-mother. Her position would handle the overnight shift and any personalized care for the new residents. One of the secretaries worked on getting the girls registered at the closest school or at least a nearby tutorial program. There were so many pieces involved in pulling together a new life for these eight girls, each with such different needs. The medical needs were more exten-sive than Anne had expected, and psychologically, all eight needed special care. Later that week, the board gathered into the lounge to discuss their crowded situation. All knew the Center was stretched to its limits with space issues and finan-cial concerns. They prayed for guidance.

CHAPTER FIFTEEN

COMING OF AGE

ANNE'S EYES HAD BEEN OPENED AT THE CENTER THAT WEEK. Talking with the rescued girls led to the realization that she and Brad needed to have serious discussions with the children about lots of dangers. That morning she listened to the breakfast conversations and began to understand that her children were on the brink of coming to age. The twins were talking about "a hot new boy" at school and Little Brad seemed to have noticed a girl named Molly, though he displayed irritation if the girls mentioned any mutual attraction between the two. Anne sighed and thought, *it's time to bring out the notebook.* Patsy and Gretchen were now twelve and Little Brad was fourteen. It was time for all three to be introduced to her mother's plan. Anne got busy and started making arrangements. Then she called Brad's office and left a message for him to call when he had a free moment.

Not long afterwards, her cell rang. "Hello, sweetheart, you need me for something?" Brad asked.

"I've decided I want to take the girls to New York. They have next Friday off due to a teacher's workday, no ballgames, and it'll be the perfect weekend to go. Spring is such a beautiful time in the Big Apple . . . The weather will be good and I just want some girl-time with them."

Brad listened as he sensed there was more to come.

"I also want you to have some time alone with our son," Anne said. "Maybe y'all could spend the weekend on the boat? Or go to some wonderful golf course?" She drew in a breath and added, "It's time to tell them about Mother's plan."

Brad was quiet for a few minutes, but he agreed with her on the timing. "I think I'll take Brad to Sea Island. He loves that course."

"Sounds perfect to me," Anne said.

"I'll get Miss Davis working on reservations for all of us."

"She can work on yours if you'd like, but I've already made mine," Anne admitted.

"What? Y'all aren't staying at the Plaza?"

"No. This is going to be a fancy girl's weekend. The Ritz has that enchanting little boutique hotel around the corner from the Plaza. Everything about it is soft and feminine . . . and wonderfully English. They have a small suite and it'll be just right for the three of us."

"Are you sure it's safe?" Brad asked in a protective tone.

"Absolutely. They even offer a driver to take us from dinner to the theater and so forth."

"So exactly what are your plans?" Brad still sounded concerned.

"I've made reservations on Delta to fly out on Friday morning. We'll get there in time for lunch at the Tavern on the

Green. Then we'll do some shopping and I got tickets for us to see a fabulous play that evening. We'll have a late dinner at the hotel after the play. Saturday, we'll shop all day! Then I made reservations at the Brooklyn Café for dinner that evening. Sunday morning, I'll just cuddle with my girls and stroke their hair while I read from Mother's notebook. We'll have a late brunch at the Plaza . . . the girls love their Sunday buffet. Then we fly back to Atlanta around four.

"I'm running out to the store today to buy the girls notebooks . . . and one for Little Brad. I'm going to copy everything concerning the plan into the three notebooks. I'd like you to plan a similar weekend with our son."

"Well, he and I have been talking about a father/son trip. This will be just the ticket. My only concern about your whole idea is that I'm not too sure about you ladies being in New York by yourself."

"Brad, we've covered this a long time ago. Remember when I designed the Greens' apartment?"

"Do I ever!" He thought back to his worries when Anne was just fine. "But I mean it, Anne. You use a driver any time after dark. And you'd better call me every day."

"I promise," Anne assured.

"I've got patients waiting. I'll see you tonight," Brad said. "I love you, Anne."

She smiled on the other end. "I love you, too."

When Anne picked up the girls from school that afternoon, she took them to a new little dessert shop she'd found in Buckhead.

After a hard time deciding which desserts to try, Anne settled on getting the sampler platter and three forks. They sipped Cokes and tried each of the sugary delights as Anne asked if they would like to go on a girls' trip.

With her mouth full of a tiny raspberry tart, Gretchen said, "Sure! When do we leave?"

Patsy swallowed and asked, "To where?"

"To New York!" Anne said with a big smile. "We'd leave next Friday and come back on Sunday."

"What are we going to do in New York?" they both asked.

"We'll shop for summer clothes, see a play, and . . . do all sorts of fun things." Both girls began to fire lists of what they "needed" to find on their shopping expeditions. Anne laughed and said, "I think we can handle that."

"Mama, what do we wear to all these places?" Patsy asked.

"Don't worry. I'll help you pack," Anne promised.

Brad looked at his watch. If he left now, he'd get to Little Brad's golf lesson just in time to pick him up. He was proud of his son's progress; he had become quite the young golfer. He was even lifting weights to build up his arm strength. Glancing at his desk, Brad noticed a trip itinerary that Miss Davis had compiled after having cleared his schedule for the following Friday. She had booked Chuck to fly him and his boy to Sea Island that morning. As it just so happened, the golf pro had time to play a round with them Friday afternoon. He'd also arranged a foursome with another father and son for Saturday.

All meal reservations had been made at several of Brad's favorite restaurants at St. Simon's and they were good to go. Brad had time to talk to Little Brad on Sunday morning before church and they'd fly back to Atlanta after lunch.

Putting the itinerary in his pocket, Brad left. Later, when the two fellas walked into the kitchen at home, the girls in a rather "yah-yah" tone exclaimed, "We're going to New York! It's just girls."

Little Brad turned to his dad and smiled. "That's okay. We're going on a trip. Just boys."

His statement peaked the girls' curiosity and Gretchen asked, "Where are you going? I bet it's not New York! And I bet it won't involve shopping."

Little Brad looked over at his mother and shook his head. "Thank goodness!" Then he looked back at his dad. "We're going to Sea Island to play golf. Bet you're not doing that!"

Patsy looked at her daddy, then she repeated her brother's comment, "No! Thank goodness."

The next week was spent preparing for the two very different, and yet very similar, trips. Brad needed a new driver, so of course, Little Brad said he did as well. While they were at the golf shop, they bought new gloves and two dozen balls. The two spent nearly every late afternoon or early evening that week at the driving range making sure their game would be up to par with the golf pro's.

The twins, on the other hand, with Anne's help, planned outfits for each day and night. The guest room bed was full of dresses, jeans, and comfortable shoes. Not to mention all of the accessories. Looking at their little-girl suitcases, Anne decided it was time for new luggage. Gretchen, whose favorite color was red, found the perfect set at Macy's, while Patsy insisted on going to Belk to find just the right purple-colored set. With those purchases, they were finally ready to pack and impatiently wait for Friday to come.

CHAPTER SIXTEEN

SHARING THE LEGACY

THE ATLANTA AIRPORT WAS AS CROWDED THAT FRIDAY MORNING as usual. But by planning well, Anne and the twins got to their gate with time to spare. After a short, uneventful flight, they landed in the Big Apple. Anne had arranged for the hotel car and driver to pick them up and before they knew it, the car was pulling up to the Ritz. It was white-painted brick with black trim and seemed small in comparison to other hotels they had stayed in previously. But when the girls walked inside, they immediately loved the feminine Laura Ashley décor.

Gretchen whispered to her mother, "Daddy and Brad would've hated this place. But I love it!"

Patsy agreed. "This is way too fancy for them."

The beautiful floral-printed wall coverings were breathtaking and the plush velvet sofas were filled with fringe-trimmed throw pillows perfectly placed across the backs. That cozy sight caught their immediate attention as they tried out each sofa's comfort level. Then the girls moved to the silk plaid lounge chairs with ottomans to match. All the seating was so pretty as it sat on rugs that showcased tiny little prints that matched the sofas and chairs. The woodwork was antiqued in muted hues of green, and the top of the reception desk was a soft-white, glistening marble. Even the chandeliers added a feminine touch with several cream-colored prisms and small, colorful pinstripe shades.

After checking in, the three followed the bellman to the elevators. When the doors opened, the panels inside repeated the same floral print that was featured in the lobby. The girls felt as if the whole hotel was one large, floral garden.

Patsy grabbed her mother's hand. "I could live here, Mama. Isn't it gorgeous?"

"Yes, it certainly is," Anne said.

When the elevator opened on the third floor, Gretchen rushed out first. "I bet our room even has these same pretty flowers on the walls."

The bellman opened the double doors and took their bags inside while the twins ran from room to room. "I told you!" Gretchen said. "Look at the shower curtain and the draperies in our area. It's the same flowers!" She definitely had an eye for design and spotted even the smallest details, just like her mother had done at Gretchen's age.

The entire suite was beautifully and intricately decorated with florals, plaids, and stripes in colors of yellow, green, blue, and red. All the primary colors stood out beautifully against the white backgrounds. The rooms really were exquisitely English in their feel and look. Anne was reminded of London's finest homes with all of their shiny chinches, silks, and velvets.

After settling in, the girls were ready to begin shopping.

"Before we go, have a seat," Anne said. "We're going to play a game. It's called 'a color of the day' game and I used to play it with my mother in New York when I was your age."

The twins looked at each other with question marks in their eyes, then back at their mother.

Anne explained, "First we have to decide on one color. Everything we purchase today has to have a touch of that color in or on it . . . even if it's just on the tag or the box. Gretchen, you can pick the color for today and Patsy, you can pick our color for tomorrow."

Gretchen thought as she looked around the suite. "I like all the yellow they've used in the fabrics in this room. My color for the day will be yellow."

Patsy looked at her mother and rolled her eyes. "I was going to pick yellow for tomorrow. That's not fair!"

Anne laughed; it was so typical. She thought of a compromise. "You can both pick yellow for today. Then you both have to agree on a color for tomorrow."

While freshening up, Anne could hear the girls. Gretchen was claiming yellow as her idea, while Patsy was already saying that tomorrow's color would be her idea. Anne just shook her head before heading to the door. "Let's go, ladies."

After shopping at Bergdorf Goodman all afternoon and finding yellow on every purchase, they grabbed pieces of pizza from a sidewalk vendor before calling the hotel driver to come pick them up. He could take them to the theater, then take their bags of treasures back to the hotel to free up full hands for clapping as they were mesmerized by *The Lion King* at the fancy Minskoff Theater on Broadway.

. . .

Saturday involved more shopping in the Garment District, but the agreed-upon color of the day was blue. Poor Gretchen; she had found a white winter coat that she immediately fell in love with, but there was no blue, not even specks anywhere on the coat, label or tags. Patsy ran over to a sales desk and came to her sister's aid. She had picked up a blue pen from the cash register. In blue, she wrote "Sold" on the tag. The girls hugged and Gretchen got her white coat.

After lunch at Brendel's, Anne watched the twins move through the various departments, looking at the perfumes and jewelry. Such grown-up selections. All Anne could think about was their first trip to New York and their Pooh Bears. Wasn't that just yesterday? Now they were teenagers, the same age she was when her mother got sick. Anne pulled a tissue from her purse and wiped her eyes. It was still hard for her to watch her girls doing such grown-up things. Especially because they looked so much like the grandmother they never knew. Anne's mother would have loved every minute of this trip to New York.

After lunch and knowing that the following morning would begin with a serious conversation, Anne wanted today to be filled with fun. She and the twins took a carriage ride to the Metropolitan to visit some of the paintings the girls had studied in last year's art class. That evening, dressed in their finest clothes, they had dinner at the Brooklyn Café where they chatted non-stop about the days' adventures and sights. As they ate dessert, their mother could see that the twins were exhausted; sleep would come easily that night.

. . .

Anne treated the girls to breakfast in her bed on Sunday morning. Taking the tray back to the cart, she returned to fluff her pillows and snuggle with them for some girl talk. Patsy and Gretchen began by hugging their mother and telling her how much they had enjoyed being in New York. Of course, they were still excited about each and every item they had purchased. As both thanked Anne, they laid their heads on each side of her lap so that she could stroke their long, brown hair while they chatted. After a few minutes, Anne reached under her pillow and pulled out her mother's notebook.

Gretchen saw the familiar journal and said, "Mama, you've had that flowered book for as long as I can remember."

"It's very special," Anne replied.

Patsy said, "I remember you told us once that it belonged to Grandmother Boyd."

Anne began to explain, "I was your age . . . just thirteen . . . when my mother got very sick. She was concerned about how I would manage without her. So, she wrote down lots of ideas to help me. Those words are in this notebook. Words she felt I would need to know." Then Anne asked Gretchen to go open the top drawer of the chest against the sidewall.

Gretchen pulled the drawer open, looked in, and took two notebooks out. "Mama, these notebooks look like yours. But they're new."

Anne patted for her to come back to the bed and reached for the two notebooks. "I have copied everything out of my book into these for the two of you." Their mother handed each girl one of the journals.

Patsy and Gretchen opened their books and began to carefully flip through the pages. Somehow, they immediately sensed the importance of the contents.

"Your grandmother devised a plan that has been instrumental in all of my life's biggest decisions. Including marrying your daddy." Anne took her time and moved page by page, step by step, as she explained Gretchen's plan to her girls.

The twins listened intently. It was as if their grandmother was speaking to them through their mother. When Anne closed her tattered notebook, she asked the girls to tell her what they had learned.

Patsy was the first to reply. "I learned a lot about how we need to act with boys. And I learned that I should think about three things before making a decision."

Gretchen raised her hand. "I want to tell what the three things are. First, I have to think about what my goal or desire is. I guess that's what I want to do or be. Like if I wanted to be an interior designer."

Anne smiled.

"Then I have to ask myself what I need to do to make it happen. I'd have to go to college, study hard . . . maybe go see hotels like this one for decorating ideas . . . and get a job with a design firm. Then I have to think about how all of this would affect my destiny."

Patsy nodded in agreement.

"That could mean that I might move to another city and be decorating an office when I meet a smart, handsome man like Daddy! I might get married and have fabulous twin daughters and a grumpy son," Gretchen added with a grin.

Anne laughed. "Well, that's how it happened for me. God may have a different plan for your destiny."

"But, Mama, what if we make a mistake?" Patsy asked.

"Let me read you that part again," Anne said.

After finishing a repeat of that section, Patsy said, "I remember. I start the plan over, but I might have some consequences I don't like from my mistake."

They talked for nearly two more hours before Anne felt the twins had the plan down pat. She asked each a question to make sure there was no hint of confusion. But both girls could repeat, "Find my desire, figure out what it will take to achieve that desire. Finally, how will all of this affect my destiny, which means the future?"

Patsy kissed her mother's cheek as she said, "Grandmother Boyd must have been very smart."

Gretchen laughed and said, "That's why I was named after her! I'm very smart too."

Anne hugged each of her girls. "You're both very smart. I'm sure you'll follow your grandmother's plan when big decisions have to be made."

"Did you always follow the plan?" Gretchen asked.

"I tried very hard to, but sometimes it was difficult," Anne admitted. "Did I make mistakes? Absolutely. But not nearly the number of mistakes I would have made without the plan. Ladies, when you don't have peace in your heart about something, you'll know you're headed for a mistake. Just remember, my sweet girls, I didn't have a mother who I could go to and talk things over with to keep from making mistakes. You do."

Both twins looked at their mother with a mixture of respect and sadness.

"There is nothing that the three of us will not always be able to talk about. It might be boys, money, or friends . . . whatever. I am here to help you answer the three questions your grand-mother left for all of us."

Gretchen wiped some tears from her eyes as she took Anne's hands. "I'm so sorry you didn't have your mother. But reading this notebook today helps me know what a good mama you had. It helps me know her."

Patsy agreed, "I feel like we've gotten to know her really good this morning. And, Mama, we're so glad we have you."

Anne pulled the girls close and kissed the tops of their heads. "Well, I'm glad I have you two as well. At least ninety-nine percent of the time." She grinned as she looked at the clock. "It's twelve-thirty, ladies, and we have reservations for your favorite brunch at The Plaza in one hour. Let's get ready."

Waving goodbye to Chuck, father and son placed their golf clubs and duffle bags into the trunk of the bright-red rental car. They set out immediately for the course at Sea Island. Stopping at the Cloister, they checked in and left their bags at the bell-man's station. Then father and son hurried to grab a quick lunch so they would be on time for their two o'clock tee time with the pro.

After eighteen difficult holes, Brad got the key to their room and the two walked up to the second floor, neither wanting to admit to exhaustion. Brad looked around. He almost felt guilty being here at the Cloister without Anne; it was one of her favorite destinations. She'd always oohed and aahed over the European influence of the design, especially the muted tiles and those prissy colors throughout. After showers and a change of clothes, the two headed back to the car to go get a seafood dinner at St. Simons.

On the drive, Brad asked, "Want to tell me about this young lady, Molly?"

His son looked a little embarrassed. "She's just a friend, Dad."

"Your mother says she's very pretty, that's she's a good athlete and has the reputation of being an honor student."

Little Brad simply said, "Yup." He turned and pointed out the window. "Look, Dad. There's another golf course."

Brad grinned at his boy's feeble attempt to change the subject. He remembered trying the same thing with his own father years before. He continued, "Well, your mother told me that you went out with Molly and her parents not too long ago."

"Yup."

"What does her daddy do?"

"He's in some kind of business."

"Well, what did y'all talk about when you were together?"

"We went to Cherokee for dinner and her daddy and I talked about golf and how expensive the club's dinners had gotten. I just ordered a sandwich."

Brad smiled. "How'd you like her mother?"

"She was nice."

"Anything interesting happen?" Brad kept trying.

"Nope. I ate all of my sandwich." Little Brad turned his face toward his dad and asked, "How much further? I'm hungry."

"Here we are," Brad said as he pulled into the parking lot. The restaurant was a large, brown barn and the lot was full of cars.

"I hope we don't have to wait," Little Brad whined.

"We have reservations and we're right on time."

Brad had never seen anyone eat as much as his son did that night. Fried shrimp, deviled crab, flounder, slaw, a huge baked potato, and a salad. *But, after all,* Brad thought, *he is a growing boy.* As they ate, they talked about the Falcons and their promising season. Little Brad opened up with that topic and turned into a chatterbox. He had already figured out what games the team would win, which ones would be squeakers, and the two they'd likely lose.

Finishing dinner, they ordered desserts. Brad patted his son's shoulder between bites. "I'm glad we have this time together, son. We need to plan a boy's trip once a year."

"I'll say, Dad! It's good to get away from the twins." He wiped his mouth and added, "And Mom's getting kind of nosey. You know, I'm older now and I can make good decisions."

Brad gave his son a doubtful look. "You mean like the decision to come in thirty minutes after your curfew last week?"

"Dad, my watch stopped!" he defended. "I didn't think it was that late."

"Your mother loves you. She just worries. That's the way all mothers are."

"I bet it was hard to grow up without a mother," Little Brad said.

"It would have been horrible without Estelle," Brad admitted.

"I love Estelle, Dad. I really love her cooking."

"Me too," Brad agreed.

"And Dad, Gaga and BB are the best; they're the best grandparents in the world. I can talk to them. We talk about lots of stuff."

Brad smiled and nodded.

After more sports discussions, they headed back to their room for an early night. Both wanted to be ready for golf again the next day.

A full day of golf on Saturday and dinner at a little restaurant by the pier in St. Simon's gave father and son another great, but long, day. The two crashed when they finally returned to the hotel, not even taking time for television and the news. Little Brad had enjoyed his lowest score ever, putting his daddy to shame. His father couldn't have been prouder. He fell asleep mumbling with pride, "He's a good boy."

Brad woke up bright and early on Sunday and reviewed the notebook his wife had prepared for their son. Her notes concerning Gretchen's plan brought back so many memories, one in particular. He thought back to the morning at Barnsley, the resort he and Anne had stayed at for the AMA conference when they were dating. He had never experienced anything quite like the love and desire he had felt for her on that sleepy Sunday morning. He remembered it all so well, but her tears and determination had put a stop to any thought Brad had of consummating their relationship until they were married. As he reflected, he didn't think he'd cover that incident in the upcoming discussion with his son, but he knew he had to be ready if Little Brad asked any personal questions. He shook his head; this could end up being a lot harder than he had imagined.

Looking over at the other bed, he saw that his son had begun to stir. "I'm going to order room service. What would you like?"

"I'm starved, Dad. One of everything on the menu."

After a huge breakfast, Brad pulled out the new notebook and took a deep breath. He handed the journal to his boy and explained, "Son, your mother and the twins are having the same conversation that I'm about to have with you this morning. You know the notebook that your mother has kept all of these years . . . the red one with the flowers on it?"

Little Brad nodded. "I think it was her mother's."

"Yes, it was. And it's very important to your mother and to me." Brad began to read Gretchen's notes to his son. As he got to the last of the writings, it had to do with how Anne was to behave with boys. Even when it was difficult and she was tempted.

Little Brad raised his eyes and said, "How'd you handle that, Dad?"

Brad thought before answering. "I tried to handle it well most of the time because your mother had been clear about how she felt regarding sex before marriage. I repeat, very clear. The way she felt was mighty important to her. She and her mother had discussed the possibilities of painful breakups, diseases, unwanted pregnancies, and pressured abortions when your mother was only fourteen years old. And when I met her, she was still committed to not letting her mother down."

Little Brad looked away, but his dad continued, "Son, I was in love with your mother from the minute I saw her. But I didn't realize how much until months later. When you love someone, sexual desire is a real part of that relationship. It gets complicated, and there are a lot of girls who don't feel like your mother did."

"I know what you're talking about, Dad. There are a lot of girls who are on the pill and the boys talk about what they do. There are several girls my age who don't worry about stuff like Mom did."

"Well, just like the boys who are messing around with those girls . . . you're going to face the same desires. But just like in your grandmother's notebook, your desires for sexual gratification can cause some serious problems for your more important desires, such as college, a meaningful career, or a guilt-free relationship.

"Let's use an example. Suppose you and Molly dated for a number of years and the kissing starts to involve playing around the edges some. You'll want more as time goes by. So, in the heat of the moment . . . as your grandmother said, you decide to go further and Molly gets pregnant. How would that affect your destiny or as we would say, your future?"

Little Brad thought for a minute before he spoke. "That's a good question, Dad. I guess we'd have to get married and I'd need to get a job. The cost of college would be a lot with a wife and child to support. I'd never want her to get an abortion. I wouldn't even think about that."

Brad felt some relief at his son's astute understanding and continued, "It could mess her life up, too. College, the disappointment of her parents, and son, a baby is full time."

Little Brad frowned and nodded.

"So, before you make any decisions, even when you're facing a whole lot of temptations, you have three questions to ask yourself. Not just about Molly, but concerning any big issue.

What's your desire or goal? What will it take on your part to attain that goal? And how will the choices you make affect your destiny or your future? My prayer for you, son, is that you will live a long, happy and healthy life. How well that life is lived depends on choices you make."

"I understand, Dad. And this has been a really good talk."

"I'm glad. But remember, I'm here for you to talk to about anything . . . anytime. We can work through your decisions, whether it's colleges, careers, or women. We can do it together."

"Thanks, Dad. And if you ever have a problem with Mom, I'll help you out."

They both laughed as they dressed to head for the small airstrip, where they would board the flight back to Atlanta.

Anne and the girls had been home for about an hour when the fellas drove up. After stopping by to see BB and Gaga on the way home, both Brads had filled up on Estelle's tea cakes. The girls met them at the door; they couldn't wait to show their daddy all of the new purchases. Little Brad immediately blurted out to his mother that he had beaten his daddy both days on the golf course.

That night, the family dined on chicken pot pies that the two Brads had thought to pick up on the way home. As all got ready for bed, they reminisced over their trips, but soon gave in to exhaustion. It had been a busy weekend and the Monday morning alarm would sound early. Lights were out by ten and Anne and Brad fell into bed. Both felt good about their times with the children and the fact that their Grandmother Boyd's plan had been passed onto the next generation.

Anne asked, "How did the talk about girls go with your son?"

His daddy sighed. "I think it went well. He sure wasn't going to give me much info on Molly at the start of the weekend. But by Sunday, I think reviewing the plan helped him see a bigger picture about taking responsibility for your actions. How about the girls?"

"Same, I think they realized there were some pretty serious consequences that they hadn't considered concerning lots of big decisions. And then I told them that there was nothing more fun than sex!" She giggled and gave Brad a kiss.

He pulled back. "You did not tell them that!"

She laughed. "No, I didn't. But I'm saying it to you."

Brad reached over, pulled her close, and gave her a lengthy kiss. Then he said, "Hold that thought." He jumped up and locked their bedroom door. Getting back into bed, he took her into his arms again as he whispered, "I missed you, every perfect inch of you!"

CHAPTER SEVENTEEN

JEALOUSY COMES CALLING

AFTER NEW YORK, IT WAS TIME TO GET BACK TO DECISIONS concerning the Center. The next Tuesday, board members met to discuss possibly bringing in two additional physicians to hopefully take turns volunteering one afternoon a week. With the eight new girls in need of so much care, their medical team was stretched tight and they could certainly use more professionals. Several names had been suggested, including Jack Baker, a pediatrician Anne had known for years; Charles Billings, a cardiologist and first-class surgeon she had done work for in her "designer" life; a psychiatrist whom Anne had never met, but whom the other board members held in high esteem; and a semi-retired internist who had a sterling reputation in Atlanta. Anne requested time to discuss the options with Brad Sr. and her husband before the board made any final decisions. She was pretty sure they would want to ask Jack Baker, the psychiatrist, or Charles, but felt it best to double-check.

Following the children's nightly bedtime routine, Brad sat

down to watch his recorded episode of *Jeopardy*. Anne walked into the laundry room to get clean sheets for their bed. Carrying them upstairs, she remembered that she needed to ask Brad about the possible physician additions to the clinic. After laying the sheets on the bed, she came back downstairs to the great room.

"I need to ask you some questions about a meeting we had today at the Center," she began.

"Shoot," he said as he looked up from the television screen.

Anne explained their need for more help and shared the names of the recommended doctors.

Brad thought for a minute and said succinctly, "Any of them sound fine . . . except Charles."

Anne's eyes widened. "We were thinking a cardiologist would be a wonderful asset for our women clients, especially the older ones who are raising grandchildren. His time could also free up slots on the schedule for you and your dad's afternoon."

Brad looked back at the television. He had no comment.

She put her hands on her hips and asked, "Bradford Young, why has there always been some mysterious strain in your relationship with Charles?"

He looked up at her and fumed, "I don't know what you're talking about."

"Excuse me! You know exactly what I'm saying," she retorted. "I've sensed the tension for years."

Brad hit the mute button on the remote and looked at Anne. "Well, since you've brought up the topic, I have a question. Are you aware that Charles seems to have some sort of feelings for you?"

She looked away. "Brad, that's ridiculous."

"It's not ridiculous. Has he ever said anything to you? Because he certainly has indicated his feelings for you to me!"

"Before we were even engaged, I decorated his medical office." She walked over to Brad and put her hands on his shoulders. "One night when I had stayed late with the installation crew, Charles stayed late as well. I knew . . . as women do . . . that he was interested. Actually, I had known it for quite a while."

Brad sat up straighter and looked into at his wife's eyes.

"That night we discussed the possibility of dating," Anne admitted. "But I had already met you, my love. Therefore, there was no chance."

"Why haven't you ever told me about this before?" he asked sharply.

"There was nothing to tell! There was never anything between us."

"Well, I just think you could've mentioned it . . . at the time."

"If I had said anything back then, it would have looked like I was trying to make you jealous. As you well know, I am not one to play games."

"Well, what happened after that?" Brad thought back and added, "From what he said to me, something must have happened."

Anne's eyes narrowed. She softly said, "He called and asked me to dinner."

"Well? What was your answer?" Brad asked impatiently.

She walked out of the room, saying only, "With that attitude, you'll never know!"

"Anne Young! Get back in here right this minute!" he ordered.

Ignoring him, she walked upstairs, past the rooms of sleeping children, and tried to quietly slam their bedroom door. She waited just inside, thinking Brad would follow, but the doorknob never turned.

Anne sighed; she couldn't believe how he was acting. But she couldn't help the grin that crossed her face. *After fourteen years of marriage, he can still get a little jealous.* She waited long enough to allow her husband to cool off, then tiptoed back down the stairs and walked into the kitchen. Pouring two glasses of sweet tea, she walked back into the great room and handed him one.

She leaned down and gave him a kiss on the top of his head. "I do love it when you're jealous, Dr. Young. For your information, I declined his invitation. Brad, the only time Charles and I have ever even held hands was when we were dancing at Barnsley and at the Valentine dance."

"I'm sorry, Anne," Brad said. "But I know that he really cared for you . . . and I just don't like it. I think it would be a mistake for him to have anything to do with the Center."

"That's all you had to say, my love. As far as I'm concerned, his name is off the list. But it is nice to know that after all these years, you still want to protect me."

Brad took her hand. "I guess sometimes I put myself in his place. I can't imagine living without you."

She gave him another kiss, but this time on his lips. "That, my love, you never have to worry about. I was yours from the minute we met."

Taking her tea, he set both glasses on the table beside his

chair and pulled her down onto his lap. "Is there anything else I need to know about?"

She rolled her eyes and said, "Let me think."

"What?"

"Just kidding. I'm going back to the laundry room to fold more clothes. If you're interested, I could always use some help putting the sheets on the bed."

Ignoring her subtle request, Brad picked up his latest medical journal to catch up on some reading as she walked out of the room. He was relieved to have that looming question finally answered. He looked down to the first article and saw that it was written by Dr. Charles Billings of Atlanta Georgia. Brad shook his head. *You've got to be kidding me!*

He closed the magazine, stood, and walked upstairs to help his wife make their bed.

CHAPTER EIGHTEEN

SOMETHING WONDERFUL

WITH THE TWO NEW PHYSICIANS ON BOARD, A PEDIATRICIAN AND a psychiatrist, the eight trafficked young girls were making positive strides. They were getting one-on-one attention from the staff and volunteers, who gave their time on a regularly scheduled day. Soon the Center had placed two of the English-speaking girls in part-time jobs and were investigating another ministry in Atlanta that furnished housing, a tutorial program, and transportation for any girls old enough to be employed. That would make room for additional rescues at the Center as space became available.

Less than three months into their new schedules, the younger rescued girls were happy and settled. But Gayle Roberts, the Center's administrator, was worried. On Tuesday she came to Anne with a question. She had a serious concern about the legitimacy of taking the Center from daycare to residential care. Did it compromise their mission statement, and more importantly, did it require a different license from the

State? She was also worried that if the wrong person discovered what they were doing, it could affect the daycare license. Worst-case scenario, far beyond any bad press, their daycare license could be pulled. Anne had to admit that all of the same concerns had crossed her mind. But she had decided they would deal with those issues only if they arose. She laughingly told their administrator that asking forgiveness was more time efficient than asking permission.

Gayle laughed. "Anne, I'm sure that strategy probably works with your husband, but we're talking about Uncle Sam and he's not as understanding! We need to come up with a more permanent solution . . . in a hurry."

Anne knew it was time to begin a search for another residential building. She asked for a financial report to see where the Center stood with any available funds. As she checked, Anne sighed. Most of their reserves had been spent on the conference room redo. She could feel her stress level rising. She knew there was no way to fix their license concern right now. But what Anne didn't know was that an elderly woman in Atlanta who needed a project. She also didn't know that something wonderful was about to happen that involved Charles Billings.

Sarah Bellamy had just celebrated her eighty-fifth birthday. She never had children, but had been blessed with a loving husband and sixty years of marriage. Bruce Bellamy had owned a very successful textile business and upon his death two years ago, Sarah has become a very wealthy widow. But during the past year, her health had begun to decline. There were no family members left whom she felt close enough to call for help, and she knew it was approaching the time to enter an assisted-living accommodation. Following the advice of her cardiologist, the elderly woman began looking around in Buckhead for a quality facility to call home in Atlanta.

As the days passed, Sarah was troubled. She had so much to think about besides her search for a new residence. Another primary concern was to find a credible and deserving beneficiary for her estate. It was important to her to make all financial plans before poor health robbed her of that ability. She knew her church would be included in her final decision, but she wanted more. She wanted to leave a legacy for children, a dream left unfulfilled in her own life's journey. During her last appointment with her cardiologist, Dr. Charles Billings, she had mentioned another meeting she had later that day with her attorney. She explained her wish to do something important with her wealth, something for children.

Charles took her hand and said, "That is an admirable desire. I have a suggestion." He pulled a brochure from the center drawer of his desk and handed it to Sarah. "I know these women personally and I can vouch for the incredible job they're doing in our community. I'd be happy to make arrangements for you to talk with Anne Young to get more information. It may or may not be a good fit."

"Does this Anne Young work for the organization?" Sarah asked.

"Well, sort of, she's a volunteer. She and her husband, Dr. Brad Young, and his parents founded the Center over ten years ago."

"Dr. Brad Young was my gynecologist! I went to him for years."

"I think you must be talking about his father. The younger Dr. Brad joined his dad's practice when he completed his fellowship."

Sarah's eyes seemed distant as she explained how kind and gentle Brad Sr. had been when he had to tell her she would not be able to have children. Her eyes brightened as she said, "If he's involved, I think this might just be the perfect solution. Could you and Mrs. Young meet with me to discuss this together? Would you have time?"

"It would be a privilege," Charles said. "I'll be happy to set up a time to get together."

As Anne continued to review the Center's financial report the next morning, things just seemed to get worse. Further costs associated with the eight new young girls became agonizingly clear. Besides the conference room redo, there was the salary for the new housemother, along with personal and medical expenses for the eight recues that had eaten up quite a chunk of their yearly budget. She handed the report back to Gayle as she said, "I need to go home. I needed some quiet time to think about a possible solution."

Walking to her car, the thought of asking Brad or his parents crossed her mind. But they had given so much. The money from her daddy's estate was another possibility. But the long-range plans for those funds were to open two more centers in different areas of Atlanta. She just needed to clear her mind. There had to be a way.

Opening her car door, Anne paused as her thoughts were interrupted by the buzz of her phone. "Hello?"

"Anne, it's Charles. How are you doing today?"

"Fine. On my way home from the Center," Anne said.

"That's kind of what I wanted to talk with you about . . . if you have a minute."

"If you've got a million dollars you'd like to donate, I've got all the time in the world," Anne said laughingly.

"Are you ladies having a financial crunch?" Charles asked.

"We are and you know, you can only go to the same wells so many times. But we know the Center is more God's will than ours. He'll make a way."

"Well, I have someone I'd like for you to meet. She's interested in talking with you about the Center. Her name is Sarah Bellamy and she's an elderly patient of mine. She's a widow and has some fairly serious health issues. She was at the office today and asked to meet with you and me about getting to know the Center better."

Anne sat down in her car. "You've got to be kidding! This could be an answer to prayer."

"She's pretty headstrong, so you shouldn't count your chickens before they hatch. She's coming in next week for a follow-up and I told her I'd see if you were available to join us. Maybe we can have lunch at the office and talk . . . if that works for you."

"I'll make it work and I'll bring lunch," Anne assured. "Does she have any dietary restrictions?"

"Nope. I've told her to just enjoy herself and to eat whatever she wants to at this point in her life."

"Margie will come up with something wonderful. Give me the date and time, I'll be there."

"Eleven-thirty next Thursday."

"You've got a date, Dr. Billings."

Charles laid his phone down on the desk. He could still picture Anne when he first met her. He looked around his office and remembered her hanging the art late one Friday night. He had tried to take her to dinner, but she had a prior commitment with Brad. It was several weeks later that he heard the two were no longer seeing each other. Immediately, he had called and invited her to dinner. Sadly, she declined and had asked for a raincheck. In desperation, he must have called her six or seven times after that, but she always had an excuse.

Charles had then thought he would be creative. He called Ben Wilson, her boss at the time, to inquire about extra art for his new offices. He asked to set an appointment with Anne to visit some galleries with him to help make selections. While discussing a time, Ben had Martha, his secretary, check Anne's calendar. An appointment was set up for the following Friday at four-thirty, per Charles' specific time request. Charles had hoped that Anne's working late on a Friday might be rewarded with a dinner date.

Understanding the unspoken honor code among his colleagues, he needed to figure out a way to let Brad know of his intentions. The next Monday morning after entering the

OR, he had run into Brad Sr. "Dr. Young, I've got a message I would appreciate you giving your son. If you will, just tell him 'all's fair in love and war; the game's on.' He'll know what it means." Dr. Young looked a little bewildered, but Charles had no doubt that he would deliver the message.

Looking back on it all now, Charles thought it probably hadn't been his best move. Warning Brad of his intentions was shortsighted. The next thing he heard was that Brad had proposed to Anne on a Tuesday and the Friday gallery appointment had been canceled.

Many years had passed since the Youngs' wedding and Charles had dated several other women, but somehow Anne was still on his mind much more than he cared to admit.

When Anne got home that afternoon, she and Margie sat down and planned lunch for her appointment with Charles and Mrs. Bellamy. Anne had wanted something light and fresh, but lots of it so the meal would be filling for Charles. They decided on tomatoes stuffed with chicken salad, a congealed fruit salad, some tea biscuits, and cheese straws. For dessert, Margie suggested individual lemon tarts. Of course, she would pack a container full of sweet tea to round out the lunch. She walked over to write the appointment on the calendar as Anne left to pick up the children.

Margie was beginning dinner as Brad walked in a little early from the office. She jumped and said, "Oh, you frightened me! I wasn't expecting you this early."

Brad laughed, apologized, and asked, "Where's my wife?"

"She's gone to pick up the girls and then they are going to watch the rest of Little Brad's baseball practice."

"What time does he finish?" he asked, wondering if he had time to join them.

"I don't know. It should be on the calendar," Margie said as she continued cutting up a chicken.

Brad walked over and was amazed at how crowded their calendar always looked. Checking, he saw that he'd be too late for today's practice. He looked for the next one so that he could try his best to make that practice. He stopped his search at, *Bringing lunch to Charles Billings? What in the hell is that all about?* "Margie, are you making lunch for Charles Billings?"

"Yup. And a Mrs. Sarah Bellamy. She's his patient, I think . . . an older lady. Apparently, he wants to introduce her to Anne. She's got money . . . might be donating some of it to the Center." She held up crossed fingers.

Brad asked how much longer before supper as he walked into the great room. Sitting down in his chair, he fumed as he thought of this lunch that Charles had conveniently planned. Moments later, he smiled. He had a thought of his own.

CHAPTER NINETEEN

A PROFITABLE LUNCH

Anne's Thursday appointment with Charles, and the potential donor had arrived. She tried to dress for business, but chose an older tailored suit and plain shoes; simple and not "designery" looking at all. She even took off one of her necklaces. Anne wanted to be seen as understated, but in a professional light. After a few more slight changes to her outfit, she walked down to the kitchen. Margie had just finished packing the basket of lunch items she had prepared. She turned to look at Anne.

"What happened to you?" she asked. "I don't think I've ever seen you look so dated and dowdy."

"I'm not trying to look quite so stylish. I thought I might need to tone it down. I only want to be seen as business-like."

Margie huffed. "Well, if I were meeting with you . . . to maybe give you some money, I'd rethink my whole mindset. Heavens, I'd be afraid you'd spend it on yourself! Now you head back upstairs right this minute. Don't come back until you look like the Anne I know and love! Speaking of donations, I'd give that suit to the Center immediately. Where on earth did it come from?"

Anne shook her head and walked upstairs to start over. Reappearing with a spring in her step, she knew she looked nice as Margie nodded her approval. "Hand me the picnic basket, bossy," Anne said with a smile. Both laughed as she walked out the door.

Arriving at the Doctor's Building, Anne walked in and took the elevator up to the tenth floor. She surprised herself as she actually checked to make sure Brad wasn't in the hallway. Somehow, she knew he would not be happy about her meeting with Charles. Moving the heavy picnic basket from one hand to the other, she opened the door to the cardiology suite. The receptionist ushered her back to the lounge.

"I'll let Dr. Billings know you're here," she said as she left the room.

Anne had just enough time to place a tablecloth, linen napkins, floral-rimmed plates, sterling flatware, and the crystal glasses of tea before Charles and Mrs. Bellamy walked through the door. Introductions were made and the three sat down for lunch.

As their conversation began, a familiar voice could be heard in the hallway. "They're right back here, Dr. Young."

Brad walked in the lounge and over to Mrs. Bellamy first as he said, "I heard you were in the building and I wanted to say hello." Then he turned to Anne and Charles and said, "I met this lady fifteen years ago when she was a patient of Dad's. Sarah has always been one of my favorites."

Sarah started laughing. "That's only because I brought a container of my favorite bourbon balls every time I came!" She turned to Anne and added, "Your husband came over to our home one day and he and I spent the whole afternoon trying to make bourbon balls. I decided it was easier to bring them to him than to try to teach him anything about cooking!"

"I understand," Anne said with a knowing smile. She asked Brad if she could fix him a plate, but he declined. Something about a conference call in a few minutes. He gave Sarah and Anne a kiss on the cheek and said goodbye.

Before going out the door, he looked at Anne and said, "I need for you to stop by the office for a few minutes before you leave."

She nodded. Anne could only imagine what he had to say.

The three continued their earlier conversation and Anne explained the new need for housing young girls who had been trafficked. She briefly shared her concerns about breaking every law in the state of Georgia by housing them in the Center, which had only a daycare license.

Sarah asked, "What will it cost to purchase a new building?"

Anne pulled a folder from her briefcase and handed it to Mrs. Bellamy. "This is a prospectus we put together last week. But I have learned through experience that we need at least a ten percent contingency."

"When would you need the funds?" Sarah asked.

"Mrs. Bellamy, to be honest . . . as soon as possible. I know it's a lot of money but I remember my mother telling me on several occasions that 'I had not because I asked not.'"

Sarah smiled. "That's one of my favorite scriptures."

Charles looked at Anne as he made his first comment. "Sarah, if I were going to trust anyone to use my money well . . . it would be Anne Young."

The older woman looked at Anne. "Could I ask a favor? Could I be a part of making this a reality?"

Anne took her hands in her own. Looking at Sarah's raised veins and loose skin, it was almost painful for Anne. She loosened her grip. She listened as this gentle woman continued.

"I've never been able to decorate any rooms for youngsters. You see . . . I never had any children," Sarah explained. "I'm old and not good for much anymore. But I just believe that if I had something exciting in my life . . . well, maybe I'd feel better."

"May I call you Sarah?" Anne asked.

"I would love that," Sarah replied.

"Sarah, there is nothing that would give me more pleasure than to have you involved in helping us choose colors and fabrics . . . in making this a beautiful home for young girls." Then Anne added, as her sincerity was obvious, "We would love to have you as a volunteer, whether you donate or not."

Sarah's eyes widened as she thought of something that might be useful. "Anne, I own a building. It's not very close to the Center. It's more in the Druid Hills area over near Emory. The University used it as a married housing complex for years until they began a larger building campaign. It's just sitting there . . . Would you like to check it out and see if it could work?"

Anne was thrilled. "When could we see it?"

"I'll arrange for someone to meet us there this weekend if you have an hour or two available on Sunday afternoon."

"If you don't mind me bringing my husband and children, we can come any time after church."

Sarah was transforming into a different person right before Anne's eyes. "I'll have lunch at my home on Sunday and we can go after that. Right after we finish our meal together! How many children do you have?"

"A son who is now fourteen and twin daughters who are twelve."

"Well, I'll have a kid-friendly lunch," she said as she turned to look at Charles and added, "and you'll have to join us!"

"I'd love to," Charles said with a smile.

"I'll call Bradford . . . I always called Brad Sr. that, and I'll invite him and Patsy also. We'll just make this a family affair. Charles, you can be my date or feel free to bring one. And, as far as the money you need, we'll sort that out once you've seen the building. But I don't want you worrying about it anymore. You'll have every penny you need." Sarah smiled and added, "Now, I want to eat one of those desserts. Lemon tarts are my favorite."

After finishing their tarts, Charles escorted Sarah to a car waiting out in front of the building; she'd had a chauffeur for years. Anne had hugged her goodbye, then stayed to clean up and pack dishes away. By now, Charles had patients waiting, but he stopped back in the lounge to see if he could help Anne with anything.

"Charles, I don't know how to even begin to thank you," Anne said.

"I think that fine lunch was pretty good payment," he said with a grin. "You know the funny thing about this? The money isn't as important to Sarah as being part of the plan for young ladies. Did you see her countenance change? She's been looking at the possibility of an assisted-care facility and you just handed her back her life. Your gift is much more important to her than anything she'll be giving. She'll have a purpose."

He walked over and gave Anne a hug as tears streamed down her cheeks. She was in awe of God's incredible timing.

"I'd love to stay here and talk with you for the rest of the afternoon, Mrs. Young. But I'd better start seeing my patients. Let me carry the basket down for you first."

"I'm just going over to Brad's office. I'll get him to take it down, but thank you. Charles, you'll never know how much today has meant to me."

"You'll never know how much being able to do something for you means to me, Anne."

But Anne did know.

Leaving Charles' office, Anne walked four doors down to Brad's back entrance. She set the basket down after entering and checked to see if Brad was in the office. Speaking with several employees on the way, she found his office empty. So, she took a seat and decided to wait, but after nearly thirty minutes, she walked over and opened his desk drawer to take out a piece of notepaper. She wrote, "Gotta pick up the girls. I'll see you at home tonight." Then she drew a heart.

Laying the pen down, she frowned. *I've just wasted a half-hour and now I'm going to be late getting the girls.* Walking down the hall, she grabbed the basket and rushed out.

CHAPTER TWENTY

THREE HUNDRED TIMES TWO

ANNE COULD HEAR AN ATTITUDE IN BRAD'S FOOTSTEPS AS EACH stomp met the wooden floors. She was sitting at his desk in the study, having just finished a phone call to Doris to check on Jeffey's latest accomplishments. She heard Brad call her name a little louder than normal. Walking out of the study, she found him in the great room adjusting the TV.

"You're home early," Anne said in a cheerful tone.

"Want to tell me about this afternoon?" he grumbled.

"Brad, Charles was kind enough to set up a meeting with Sarah Bellamy. This could be important," Anne explained.

Gretchen walked into the room and said, "Hey, Dad. Are you mad at Mama or something? 'Cause your voice certainly sounds like it. I'm gonna need three hundred dollars Monday morning."

"And what on earth do you need that kind of money for?" Brad asked, ignoring her first question.

"I need it for a cheerleading uniform. But never mind!" She started to cry and stormed out of the room.

"What in the hell is wrong with her?" Brad asked, now even more irritated.

"She'll be thirteen soon. Hormone issues," Anne said. "Patsy's going to need the same amount. They both made the cheerleading squad for next year and they are so excited. We can talk later. Right now, you need to go congratulate your daughters. It's a big deal . . . like when Brad made the Junior Varsity baseball team his freshman year."

Brad just shrugged and walked upstairs. Both girls were sitting on the floor discussing their daddy's attitude. He knocked on the doorframe and asked, "May I come in?"

Patsy looked at her father and said, "Only if you're going to be nice about the uniform money."

Gretchen added, "Just because you're mad at Mama doesn't mean you can act that way to us."

"I'm not mad at anybody and I'm sorry. I should have asked about the money in a nicer manner." He smiled and added, "I'm so proud of you both. Cheering should be a fun time for y'all. Of course, you can have the money for the uniforms."

Gretchen looked up smugly. "We don't need the money anymore."

"What do you mean?" he asked. By now he was getting a headache.

"I called Gaga and told her how you acted . . . and that you said the word 'hell.' I heard you when I walked upstairs. She said you should be ashamed of yourself and that she and BB would give us the money. And Estelle said she had made a big pot of chicken pastry, but you're not getting any!"

Brad walked over and asked if he could have some hugs. Of course, the twins popped up and settled in his arms as he sat down on the bed. "Girls, could I ask a favor? Will you call Gaga back and tell her thank you, but your daddy will buy the uniforms. And please tell Estelle I'm starved. Hopefully, we can all have some chicken pastry for dinner. Finish your homework and if Estelle doesn't bring it over here, I'll drive us all over there to eat with them."

The girls were now happier as Brad asked. "Where's your brother?"

"The guys are playing touch football over at Stewart's," Patsy explained.

"I need a kiss on each cheek," Brad said. Both girls obliged as he got up to go back downstairs. On the way down the steps, he shook his head. *How did they call Mama that fast?* Walking back into the great room, he couldn't find Anne. Then he saw her car pulling out of the driveway. He sat down in his chair, picked up a magazine, and turned on the news. *Where is she going now?*

Anne walked back in the house about twenty minutes later. "There's more supper in the car if you'll go get it." She sat the pot of chicken pastry on the stove and turned on a burner to warm it up a little.

Brad came back in carrying a plate of cornbread and a pot of string beans. "Man, this smells good. I didn't get lunch today. I took my only break to figure out what you were doing." He set the plate and pot down on the counter and took a plate out of the cabinet. "Anne, I don't mind you being with Charles . . . What I mind is that you didn't tell me."

She walked over and put her arms around his neck. "I'm sorry. I should have told you."

"Well, I hope it won't happen again," Brad said.

She rubbed his shoulders in massaging circles and moved up his neck and down along the top of his back.

"That feels good," he moaned.

"It won't happen again. I promise." She gave him a kiss, a long, seductive kiss. "You okay now?" she asked.

"I'm sure I will be later tonight when the children are asleep," he said with a twinkle.

"Yes, you will, my love." She kissed him again.

The back door flew open and Little Brad ran inside. "Are y'all kissing in the kitchen? I could've had a buddy with me! That would've been embarrassing."

Anne started laughing. "Let's see . . . Gretchen was upset because she thought we were mad at each other. Your son's upset because we're kissing . . . Guess we can't win!" She rolled her eyes. "Teenagers . . . We're in for a rough patch, Dr. Young."

Patsy came running in the kitchen and asked, "Are we ever going to have supper? I'm starved to death!"

"You mean a rough decade, don't you?" Brad asked as he fixed the children's plates while Anne just smiled, and poured tea.

CHAPTER TWENTY-ONE

ANSWERED PRAYERS

BRAD WOKE UP AT FOUR THE NEXT MORNING, DRENCHED IN perspiration. He shook Anne's shoulder and asked why the house was so hot and humid. She gave him a startled look and wondered why he woke her for that. *How on earth did she know?* But she had an answer for him, "It's almost summer in the south, silly." Brad glared, got up, and walked over to check the thermostat. It was seventy-eight degrees. Hitting the switch by the door, he cut the ceiling fan on before getting back in bed. Anne turned over and promised to call an air-conditioning repairman first thing in the morning. She then suggested he move to the downstairs guest room; it was always cooler on the lower level. Besides, that floor had its own air-conditioning system and it was probably working just fine. But Brad was snoring before she finished the last part of her monologue. She, however, laid awake, tossing and turning. Finally giving in, she got up. The clock read six a.m.

Turning off the alarm to allow everyone a few more minutes

to sleep, she walked downstairs for coffee. An hour later, she carried a fresh cup up to Brad and sat it on the nightstand. She leaned down and kissed his cheek. "It's time to get up, my grumpy love. Your coffee is on the nightstand. I'm going to wake the children."

Brad grabbed her arm, yawned, and asked, "Why don't you come back to bed for just a little while?"

"After keeping me up last night and waking me up at four o'clock, now you want to play nice?"

He looked at her with that twinkle and moaned, "Uh-huh."

Shortly after seven, Anne unlocked their bedroom door and left to wake the children. She laughed. She could hear Brad singing happily in the shower.

After getting everyone successfully out the door, Anne sat down in Brad's big leather chair to rest for just a moment. She must have dozed off and when she woke up, she heard Margie banging around in the kitchen.

"Good morning," Anne called as she stretched.

"Well, good morning, sleepyhead. You finally woke up."

Anne jumped up, remembering the air conditioner, and went straight for her phone. After being assured that a technician would come to the house before noon, she and Margie sat down together for a cup of coffee, a bowl of blueberries, and bananas and a fresh blueberry muffin.

After taking another bite of her blueberry-filled breakfast, Anne noticed that Margie was all smiles. She had even giggled a few times, which was unusual at this hour. "You look like the cat who swallowed the canary! What's up with you this morning?" Anne asked.

Margie held her hand out. There was a new ring on her finger. "I'm getting married!"

Anne stood up and rushed around the table to hug the bride to be. "I'm so very happy for you! Have you set a date?"

"Tommy wants to get married as soon as possible, but I want a Christmas wedding like you had, Anne. Will you help me plan? I don't know about all these things, but you sure do. We just want something simple at the church and a reception in the fellowship hall. But honestly, I still don't know where to start."

Anne squeezed her again and said, "Don't you worry about a thing. We'll start planning this week. Your job is to figure out the date. Tommy's a good man. This is just wonderful!"

Anne remembered the day she met Tommy. She smiled. He was the new assistant pastor at Margie's church. Anne had called this budding relationship from day one; she could see that Margie was really attracted to this young man. She had even asked Anne if Tommy could dedicate the residents building at the Center, which was named for Estelle. He had done a beautiful job that day. The young pastor handled the service with such love, and it seemed that the scriptures he selected and the prayer he voiced were divinely inspired. Anne had no idea that their relationship had come this far, but she couldn't have been more pleased for her friend.

Margie interrupted her memories by asking, "Anne, will you be my Matron of Honor? And I want the children in the wedding too."

"I would be honored and the children will be so happy."

"I thought I'd see if Brad would do a reading. That way the whole family will be part of the biggest day in my life," she said with a huge smile.

Anne walked over to one of the drawers and pulled out a spare notebook and began to write. "This will be our wedding planner," she said as she wrote. "First priority: select a date."

After talking over preliminary plans, Anne walked upstairs to shower and dress. She was playing tennis at eleven and then having lunch with some of her friends. Her big project for the afternoon was to make sure everybody had clean clothes for church on Sunday. They had an important lunch with Sarah Bellamy after church.

The Youngs left for church that Sunday morning as Anne reviewed table manners. They were more dressed up than normal and as she instructed on proper responses, no one complained or fussed. Yesterday afternoon, Anne had spent some time talking to Brad and the children about how important this lunch could be for lots of young girls. She didn't want to be embarrassed by bad manners or someone answering questions without "yes, ma'am" or "no, ma'am."

After the service, the family drove up to a large Victorian home in Druid Hills. The house was stark white with soft green shutters and intricate stained glass in panels that radiated glowing colors on rocking chairs that sat on the front porch. The lawn was manicured to perfection and flowers of all kinds framed the house nicely, with pink dogwoods adding a calming color against the white. Anne could understand why Sarah Bellamy was feeling the need for something smaller. She realized just how large the house was as they drove up the long driveway.

Parking, the family followed old brick pavers that led to the wraparound porch, Anne reminded the children of their best behavior one last time, looking at Brad as she spoke. Little Brad walked up to the front door first and rang the bell. A man in a formal black suit opened the door and invited the family inside. "Please come in," he said. "Miss Bellamy is in the dining room." He pointed to the room on the right.

They walked through the large arched opening and saw that Miss Bellamy was placing flowers in a bright-blue vase on a lovely antique sideboard.

She smiled. "I played hooky from church this morning. I wanted to pick flowers. Have you ever seen such beautiful colors?" she asked as she placed the last two blossoms in a vase. She walked over to the family and looked first at the girls. "You two must be the twins, Patsy and Gretchen, I believe. I had a long talk with your grandmother yesterday and she told me all about you two."

She turned to their brother and said, "Let's see . . . you must be Little Brad. Your grandmother says that she can't keep grass in her backyard because of all the divots you and your grand-daddy dig while hitting golf balls."

All three children laughed and Gretchen said, "Miss Bellamy, they make pure holes out there in Gaga's pretty lawn!"

Sarah laughed, then walked over to hug both Anne and Brad and shared how glad she was that they were all able to join her at home. "I'm sorry your mother and daddy couldn't make it, Brad. But I understand they already had plans."

The doorbell rang again. Charles Billings and a young woman walked into the dining room. Sarah asked Charles to introduce his companion and they all sat down together for a turkey with all of the trimmings lunch that included a large bowl of macaroni and cheese for the younger palates. After strawberry parfaits, the guests were to follow Sarah and her chauffeur to the empty building she had earlier described.

Driving up, Anne was flabbergasted. It was a three-story building and looked to be in excellent condition from the outside. She thought it almost looked like a small hotel with lots of windows and a more commercial entrance of large glass doors. She couldn't wait to go inside.

The children were given a large box by Sarah's chauffeur that contained all of the elements for horseshoes. They got everything set up and played outside in the large yard while the adults toured the building. Walking in, Anne was looking into a large area that she imagined as a welcoming seating area. There was a small built-in desk on the left and behind were mailboxes in rows of six. With all the natural light coming from the large windows, the room was so cheerful.

The group walked farther back and Sarah pointed out a room with washing machines and dryers in rows. She then directed them to a bank of two elevators down a hallway. Sarah hit the button and they stepped inside the opened cab.

Charles looked at Brad and said, "I have to admit that I've never even noticed this building before."

Brad agreed; he didn't remember seeing it either.

They exited onto the second floor and stepped out to a hallway lined with doors on each side. Suite after suite included a living room, a kitchenette, two bedrooms, and a bathroom. Anne walked off the measurements of the bedrooms and decided each would easily hold two twin beds. One larger suite would be perfect for a housemother. Anne counted and there was a total of eight suites. They re-entered the elevator and rode up to the third floor. It held the exact same layout, another eight suites.

"What do you think, Anne? Could this building serve your purposes?" Sarah asked.

Anne nodded. She was overwhelmed; the building was almost too perfect. She couldn't imagine the price tag.

"Sarah, it's unbelievably perfect. But I know it must be a very expensive building."

The older woman smiled. "It may not be as expensive as you think."

They entered the elevator and descended back down to the lobby. "Shall we go back to my house and discuss things further?" Sarah asked.

Anne looked at Brad and knew he was missing a televised golf tournament that he was dying to see. *So be it,* she thought. The children could enjoy exploring the grounds around the Bellamy home to pass the time. She wasn't about to pass up this possible opportunity.

Sarah looked at Charles and his date and said, "We'll need you as well, if you have time."

Charles looked at Anne and smiled. "I wouldn't miss this for anything."

Returning to the Bellamy home, Anne noticed that the dining room table was already pristinely cleaned from their lunch. They walked in, sat down at the dining table, and all waited for Sarah to begin the conversation. Another man had joined them and she introduced him as her attorney, George

Mason. Brad and Charles were both familiar with George as he belonged to their club and was a scratch golfer. Sarah asked George to lead the conversation.

"The Bellamy building that you toured today was built in 1946. It was used for corporate employees until 1957 and from there, the property had been 'moth-balled.' The building wasn't used for nearly twenty years and you can imagine how much had fallen into disrepair. Finally, the facility was leased by Emory. The University refurbished it for married student housing, an uncommon but attractive accommodation for a university at that time. All of the repairs were paid for by the Bellamy Corporation as a donation to Emory. It was used for that purpose until three years ago.

"Now, it's empty again. It would be disheartening for Mrs. Bellamy to see it go back into disrepair. Therefore, she would like to donate it to the Center. Knowing that the building itself is expensive to maintain, Mrs. Bellamy would like to start a trust for furnishings, utilities, maintenance, and decorative needs that she would like to help oversee. Her accountant will be responsible for paying all invoices through the trust. That is . . . if the Center is in agreement."

By now, Anne didn't know whether to laugh, cry, or check her ears. Had she heard this correctly or was it a dream?

Brad leaned over and took her hand, which brought her mind back to the table.

"Sarah, I don't know what to say . . . except thank you. You and I will have a lot of work to do to get the interiors beautifully decorated so that we can make this fabulous building into a lovely home for girls who have suffered in so many ways."

Charles' friend, Heather West, spoke up, "I have lots of time. May I volunteer to help with this project?"

Sarah looked at Heather and said, "I'm not as young as I used to be and it would be very helpful to have an assistant to make sure I don't fall down on my end of project responsibilities."

Anne laughed and said, "We'll just call ourselves 'the designing women,' and I can't wait to get started! We'll call it the Bellamy House."

George spoke up again, "If everyone is in agreement, I need Anne and Brad's signatures as founders. Then I'll need two witnesses. Charles, you and Heather will be fine."

He put the paperwork in front of Sarah and, after she signed, the others followed suit.

Just then the children came running in the front door. Hurrying up to Anne, Little Brad whispered in her ear, "The man in the black suit just gave us presents. Are we allowed to take them? We really want to."

Anne looked up and saw Sarah smile before she said, "Please allow them to accept the gifts. They're from me."

Brad said it was fine and thanked their generous hostess.

When the three opened their packages, Little Brad's was a box of a dozen Titleist Pro VI golf balls that he couldn't wait to share with his granddaddy. The girls' boxes contained beautiful little Kate Spade purses. Gretchen looked at her mother and whispered, a little too loudly, "These kinds of purses are very expensive."

Sarah laughed. "I have an 'in' with the designer."

Before they got ready to go home, Anne, Sarah, and Heather

chatted for a few minutes while the men snuck peeks at the golf tournament on their phones while they discussed the leaders.

Brad whispered into Anne's ear on the way to the car, "Believe it or not, today was better than bourbon balls or golf."

In the car, Anne picked up her cell and called Gayle. She couldn't wait another minute to share the good news. They wouldn't be going to jail over licensing restrictions after all.

CHAPTER TWENTY-TWO

WEDDING PLANS

LOOKING AT HER CALENDAR, ANNE CLOSED HER EYES WITH A SIGH. School was back in full swing after their Thanksgiving break and the days were flying by. Margie's wedding would be here sooner than she wanted to admit. She knew it was time for the bride to find a dress; so many times, wedding dresses needed to be altered and who knew how long the shipping would take once the choice was made? Panicking, Anne took the liberty of making an appointment at the bridal boutique in Phipps Plaza. She made another note to remind Margie that it was past time to order invitations. Calling a local stationary shop, Anne set up an appointment with them as well. On a roll, she called her standby florist and set up a third appointment. "We had a start," she mumbled.

That afternoon, Anne received a call from Margie's fiancé, Tommy. He was trying to plan a honeymoon and wanted to ask Anne how to go about making arrangements. This was all new territory, as small-church pastors tended not to take expensive trips. Anne asked where he was hoping to take Margie. He mentioned that she wanted to go someplace warm. Asking if he had considered the Caribbean, Tommy answered, "That sounds nice, but expensive."

Anne mulled over a few ideas and then asked, "What if our travel agent took a look in that area and came back with a few suggestions?"

Tommy agreed. "I just want it to be some place Margie will like."

"Why don't I give you our agent's name and phone number? You can call, tell her what you're thinking, and that we referred you. She'll come up with the perfect location."

That night, Anne shared Tommy's call with Brad while they laid in bed discussing their respective day. Brad laughed and said, "I remember planning a honeymoon. When I got the figures for our two weeks in Paris, I nearly had a heart attack. Poor Tommy, he's in for sticker shock."

Anne gave Brad a slow kiss. "Well, I'd like to think, Dr. Young, that you found Paris worth every penny."

He thought back to the long, late afternoons and their love-filled nights. He looked at his wife with that tenderness she loved and said, "It was worth every penny and more, Mrs. Young."

"You've been promising me for . . . let's see . . . over seventeen years, another trip to Paris," she reminded.

He laughed. "We still have that 'Paris state of mind' you're always talking about. As much as I'd like to . . . after that first trip, I don't think I can do a second trip justice." He wiped his brow. "Nope, I can't do that trip justice anymore."

Now Anne laughed. "And that's perfectly okay, my love. There are lots of museums we didn't get to see."

A week later, Tommy called. "Anne, do you know how much a trip to the Caribbean runs? Even if we only stay five days, it's over three thousand not counting airfare. I was thinking maybe I should change our plans . . . but I mentioned the idea earlier to Margie and now she's excited. I was wondering if you could talk with your agent and just see if she could scale it down a bit."

Anne assured him that she would try her best, knowing all along that she and Brad would work out anything for Margie. But how could she pull off a little conniving without Margie finding out? Her friend was extremely proud and even more private about her finances and always made it hard for Anne and Brad to help her in any way.

Anne decided to call the travel agent and simply ask her to tell Tommy that she had found a special discount and could bring the cost down to twenty-five hundred, including airfare. It would be the truth; she had found a discount with Anne and Brad's help. Tommy was ecstatic and the honeymoon was booked.

By the end of November, Margie had found a lovely dress. It flattered her nice figure and was perfect for her age and modest disposition. This bride, in her mid-thirties, wanted straps, and a high neckline. The dress was white with lots of lace and beading, and when Margie tried it on both she and Anne agreed, this dress was the perfect choice.

After alterations were made, the box was shipped to Anne's.

When the dress arrived, the twins asked Margie to model. Both girls clapped and exclaimed that they couldn't wait to get married and wear a long, pretty, white dress.

Anne shook her head and said, "I certainly hope we have plenty of time before that day!"

By December, the selected invitations had been dropped in the mail. The florist had their instructions and a photographer had been hired. Now, all they needed was a caterer. Margie didn't want a full meal, just punch and hors d' oeuvres. She wasn't too picky about the foods, but she specifically asked for ginger ale and lime ice cream punch. The caterer came back with a menu of shrimp, chicken bites, Swedish meatballs, rolls with pulled pork, fresh fruit and cheeses, and a few vegetable trays with a toasted onion dip. Margie agreed to everything but the shrimp and the altered menu was approved.

When Anne got home after helping Margie finish up wedding details, she pulled out the photo album from her own wedding. As she slowly turned the pages, she came to picture of her father. Thanksgiving had just passed. That holiday was always a hard time of year for Anne. Since their marriage, Brad and Anne had spent Thanksgiving with her daddy, that was, until his death. She could still see Little Brad and his granddaddy in their fishing vests headed out to the pond. Anne missed him so much and the memories of those Thanksgivings brought an overwhelming sadness. Anne closed the album. With all the hustle and bustle of getting ready for a wedding and Christmas, she didn't have the luxury of dwelling on the past. The future festivities would keep her way too busy.

. . .

It was soon the twenty-third with the wedding just hours away. Anne and the twins each wore red dresses. Both Brads were in dark suits with red boutonnieres. Margie looked gorgeous in her lovely gown. Tommy smiled as nerves calmed when he took her hand. The ceremony was beautiful as the senior pastor led the vows. Brad read from the book of I Corinthians and one of Margie's friends sang the Lord's Prayer. Estelle, Patsy, and Brad Sr. sat on the first row and beamed with excitement for the couple. Proudly, they watched their three grandchildren standing there, now looking far too grown up.

After the reception, the twins passed out small white bottles to all the guests as they lined up to send the couple off through a mass of clear bubbles. Husband and wife were on their way to the Caribbean.

Two days later, all of the Youngs celebrated Christmas while the three children found time to complain about missing Margie's turkey dressing and gravy. More than that, her red velvet cake was missing too. Anne thought about Margie and Tommy relaxing in the warm Caribbean sun and smiled. She suggested a toast to the newlyweds over the family's simple, but adequate Christmas dinner.

CHAPTER TWENTY-THREE

THE CHARM BRACELET

ANNE TOOK THE LAST OF THE PRESENTS OUT FROM UNDER THE Christmas tree and placed them on the dining room table. She had called Sarah Bellamy's landline several times earlier in the week hoping to schedule a time for her and the children to deliver her gifts. Each time she was told that Mrs. Bellamy was not available, but Anne was determined to reach her today. She called the Bellamy residence shortly after nine feeling confident Sarah would finally be at home. To her amazement, Anne was again told that Mrs. Bellamy was not in. Confused, she walked back into the kitchen to begin preparing breakfast for her sleepy family, still in bed, enjoying their Christmas vacation. Her cell phone buzzed; it was Gayle at the Center.

"Anne, have you heard what's going on here? It's the sweetest thing you've ever seen. Mrs. Bellamy brought all of the girls from the Bellamy House over here every single day this week, including Christmas Day. They had a Christmas lunch with candy canes and gifts for every woman and child! I talked with Sarah's butler a few minutes ago and she also had a Christmas Eve party with a lovely dinner and gifts at the Bellamy House. Earlier yesterday, she had a Christmas Eve brunch with gifts and surprises for the staff. Her butler said she has done nothing but work on these projects for two weeks and that he's never seen her this excited!"

Anne laughed and said, "God sent us a guardian angel and the nice thing is . . . this has changed her life too."

"Well, she and her nurse are in the daycare reading to the children as we speak. Anne, you should see the way all the children run to Sarah the minute she walks in here. She has a whole new family of little ones."

"Finally, I know where to find her!" After hanging up, Anne ran upstairs, dressed quickly, and ran around the bed to give Brad a kiss. "Wake up! You've got to fix breakfast."

Brad slowly opened his eyes. He saw that his wife looked like she was ready to head out the door. He whined, "Where are you going?"

"To the Center. I should be back in a couple of hours. But your children are going to wake up starved and today, that's not my problem."

Brad sat up, placing his feet on the floor. "Is the coffee made?"

"No, I haven't had time. You can make it," Anne said.

"I don't know how to do that new coffee thing with the pods."

She glared. "Figure it out. You're smart!" With that, she ran downstairs, grabbed the gifts, and left.

. . .

154

Walking into the Center, Anne looked around and smiled. She and the staff had worked for weeks decorating as they ensured every room look festive. She heard Christmas music playing and could smell spiced tea as she walked to the childcare area. Anne stood just outside the door and watched through the large, glass panel.

Sarah was sitting in a big, comfortable chair that she had evidently brought with her and a little girl was sitting in her lap. Nearly twenty toddlers and preschoolers were huddled around the chair intently listening to *Frosty the Snowman*. The look on Sarah's face was sheer delight.

As soon as the story ended, Anne opened the door and walked inside, clapping her hands. Sarah's nurse began passing out cookies to the children, each one having been decorated just like Frosty, with a corncob pipe and a big black hat.

Approaching Sarah, Anne said, "I have been trying to call you for a solid week! But you, evidently, don't stay home anymore. We wanted you to come and have Christmas dinner with us and we wanted to give you these." Anne passed her one gift at a time from the large shopping bag.

Sarah replied, "I'm so sorry we didn't connect. But I had plans and I have been very busy. But I do appreciate the gifts." She peeked at the tags and said, "Oh, I see that some of them are from the children!"

"Yes, they are, but you can't open those quite yet. The children will want to be with you." She pulled out one of the boxes and added, "But this one is from Brad and me, you can open it now."

Sarah smiled as she started to untie the ribbons and remove

the wrapping. It was a gold charm bracelet. She began to tear up. "How did you know of my love for charm bracelets?"

"Brad's daddy remembered that you had called their office many years ago, asking about a lost charm bracelet that may be in the exam room you had occupied. He said they looked everywhere, but to no avail. The next year when you returned for your physical, he asked if you had ever found that special piece of jewelry . . . but he remembered it had never shown up. We decided it was time for you to have a new charm bracelet!"

Sarah pulled the bracelet from the box and ran it through her fingers.

Anne explained, "Each disc has the name of a young girl who has been housed at Bellamy House. Next week, we'll be adding six more names. This bracelet won't take the place of the one you lost, but it will be a forever-reminder of the children whose lives you have changed." Anne leaned down and kissed her cheek. "We love you, Sarah, and we are so very thankful for you."

Sarah held her arm out and asked Anne to fasten the bracelet on her wrist. She then took Anne's hand and said, "I will guard this one with my life. I love it! Thank you so much."

Anne pointed to the box. "Now, if you'll look under the paper in the box, there's something else. Brad, through trial and error last Saturday, made you a small batch of bourbon balls . . . all by himself."

Sarah laughed as she dug through the paper. "Are they edible?"

Anne shook her head. "Probably, if you're on a deserted island and you're starving."

. . .

Later that afternoon, Brad and the children joined Anne at the Center for the some of the yummy Frosty cookies and to help Mrs. Bellamy open the rest of her gifts.

CHAPTER TWENTY-FOUR

AN UNEXPECTED VISITOR

With Margie on her honeymoon and all of the Christmas decorations to take down, Anne was primed for a full week of cleaning. She grinned; at least with Brad at work and the children back in school, she had plenty of time. Walking over to the closet to pull out boxes, she began to remove ornaments from their sheading tree. Having just removed the last of the children's pipe cleaner angels, Anne heard the front door bell ring. She walked into the foyer. Looking out the side panel of the front door, Anne saw a young woman with a toddler wrapped in her arms. There was a brisk wind whistling that morning and her two visitors seemed to shiver from the cold as they stood on the front porch.

Anne opened the door and asked, "May I help you?"

"Mrs. Young, my name is Fran Ivy. May I come in? I'd like to talk with you for a few minutes . . . if it's okay."

Anne stood there processing the name Ivy through her memory. It didn't ring any bells. "Certainly." She smiled. "Come on in, you must be freezing," she said as she moved to allow the young mother to enter. "How can I help you?"

Fran hesitated before asking if they could sit down. Anne sensed her nervousness and motioned for them to follow her into Brad's study. To lighten any tension, she said, "What a beautiful little girl you have and I love her gorgeous red hair." Then Anne walked to a basket and pulled out a children's book. She gently handed it to the little girl with a smile.

"Thank you. Her name is Markie. She's named for her daddy." Fran paused, as she waited for Anne to reply.

Now, everything was beginning to connect. Anne remembered the name, Mark Ivy. Suddenly, she felt uncomfortable and totally vulnerable.

Sensing Anne's uneasiness, Fran said, "I'm here to tell you how sorry I am about what happened to your husband and the frightening situation my husband put you through. I've wanted to make this right for a while now, but I just didn't know how. After a wonderful Christmas Day with my little girl, I knew it was time for us to meet."

Anne looked at Fran and swallowed hard.

"Your husband has a big heart. Dr. Young delivered my daughter and tried to warn me that my husband was sick and could possibly be dangerous. He suggested I take out a restraining order . . . which my parents did immediately. The problem came about when my mother mentioned to Mark that your husband had been the one to recommend the order. I'm sure in his mixed-up mind, he then had someone to blame . . . your husband."

By now, Anne's pulse had slowed down and she could see that Markie was getting restless. She suggested the two follow her into the great room, where there were toys and other books. "Would you like a cup of coffee or something to drink?" she asked.

Fran nodded. "That would be nice." Over coffee, the two women talked and consoled each other over the circumstances that had brought them together. Honest conversation can shed light on so many things. When Fran and Markie left, Anne had a new understanding of what life could be like when situations unexpectedly change. Mark Ivy had been a good husband and was excited over the upcoming birth of their child. He had a solid career as a professional athlete. But one injury had dismantled everything. Anne reflected on her own life, her children, and her husband. She felt overwhelmed by a wave of pure love; it was clear that what had happened to Fran Ivy and her family could have happen to anyone.

When Brad came home later that night, Anne told him about her visitor, the cute little girl, and the new understanding that visit had provided. Fran had brought closure to a terrifying night that had remained too vivid in Anne's thoughts, as well as in an occasional nightmare.

Brad took his wife in his arms. "I'm glad her visit made you feel better, sweetheart. But, Anne, it is not a good idea to open the door to people you don't know. We've been through this before . . . You need to be more cautious."

She lowered her head. "Brad, she had a baby in her arms, it was so cold, and somehow the door just flew open."

He smiled and shook his head before giving this baby-loving wife of his a tender kiss.

CHAPTER TWENTY-FIVE

A DEVASTATING FALL

MARGIE MOVED HER PILLOW OVER AS SHE SNUGGLED UP TO Tommy. He was fast asleep by her side. She still couldn't believe he was her husband as she repeated that word aloud. She held her hand up and turned the wedding ring on her finger. The last seven days together on the tropical island of St. Thomas had been more romantic than she had ever dreamed. She was finally experiencing the love she had only hoped was possible. Passionate love was real and this man was her handsome husband.

She thought back to when she first saw Tommy and how her heart immediately skipped a beat. She remembered his navy-blue suit and could still hear the whispers from others floating down the pews. Apparently, Margie wasn't the only admirer who took notice. That was the day of his first sermon, which he had taken from the gospel of John. Tommy was filled with energy and his voice almost shouted enthusiasm as he quoted scripture after scripture on the love of Jesus. She could still see the look on his face, the light in his eyes and how he couldn't even stand still as he talked with both hands pointing to the truth of every word he spoke. She was sure that day's sermon was the moment when she fell in love.

Sighing, she took in a deep breath; it was now time to return to the world of work and commitments. At least she was returning with a partner. She had missed Anne and the children and their Christmas together, but she would see them soon. The flight home from St. Thomas was at three that Monday afternoon and they'd arrive in Atlanta by five. As much as she hated to leave their beautiful suite in this very pink hotel, she had to admit that it was time to get back to real life.

Anne was packing her car with all the "welcome home" signs. The children had made the posters for greeting Margie and Tommy at the airport. She smiled as she saw a misspelled word. Just then, her cell rang. It was her mother-in-law; her voice was shaking.

"Anne, the ambulance just left."

Anne felt her knees buckle as she grabbed the phone more tightly with one hand. She steadied herself against the car with the other.

By now, Patsy was crying. "I cannot tell you how many times Brad Sr. and I have told Estelle not to go up those stairs! Her knee gave way as she was coming down." Patsy took a breath, but continued, "She fell from the landing all the way down . . . all the way down to the bottom . . . I heard her hit. She just laid there. I got to the phone as quickly as I could. She was in so much pain."

Anne took several deep breaths, opened the car door, and sat down in the front seat.

"Brad Sr. is waiting at the ambulance entrance right now. He just happened to be at the hospital for a board meeting today. I knew you'd want to know. He's calling Brad now."

"Patsy, I'll come get you if you want to go to the hospital too," Anne offered.

"No. I won't be any help. But please go and let me know what's happening."

"I'm on my way right now," Anne said as she pulled out of the driveway.

She couldn't find any open spaces, so she parked in a tow-away zone and ran inside. When she got to the information desk, they were expecting her and took her straight back per Dr. Young, Sr.'s earlier instructions.

By now, the ER doctors had Estelle sedated and were preparing to take her back for x-rays. Anne walked over to her father-in-law and asked, "Dad, do we know how bad it is?"

"My feeling is that she has broken her hip and possibly her knee. She was in excruciating pain when they brought her in."

Anne looked around. "Where's Brad?"

"He's in surgery, but should be through in about thirty minutes," Brad Sr. said. "He's going to be so upset . . . but who's with Patsy?"

"No one. She's in the sunroom and she's promised not to move a muscle," Anne said.

"I don't think she's got any business coming up to the hospital, but we're going to have a hard time keeping her at home," he said.

"Dad, she's stronger than you think. I'm just going to go get her. Maybe by the time I get back, we'll know more about Estelle." She ran back out to the car, hoping security hadn't yet seen her illegal parking option and, fortunately, found the car hadn't been towed.

When Anne walked into the Youngs' home, she saw Patsy wringing her hands and rocking in her chair. "Oh, Anne! I'm so glad you're here. I can't stand not knowing."

"Let's get you in the car. You'll feel better once you get to the hospital."

"What about the children? Who's picking them up?" Patsy's voice rose.

"I'll pick them up after I get you to the hospital. They have afterschool activities and will be busy for a few more hours."

"Well, who's going to pick up Margie and Tommy?" Patsy was clearly worried about everyone.

Anne thought and said, "I'll get Brad to send somebody from the office."

"Oh, Anne, this is just horrible"! Patsy cried.

Anne wrapped her arms around her. "I know. But she's in great hands and we just have to trust that it isn't as bad as it seems."

When the two got back to the emergency room, Brad Sr. was coming down the hall. He gave his wife a kiss and said, "They've assigned a room for Estelle. Room 322 on the orthopedic floor. She's just gone back to x-ray. We probably won't know anything for another hour or so. You'll be more comfortable waiting in her room."

The two took the elevator up to the third floor in complete silence, each lost in a myriad of worried thoughts. Once Anne had Patsy settled in Estelle's room, she called Miss Davis. Brad had just come out of surgery, had been told about the fall, and was already down in x-ray. He would be calling Anne as soon as he knew something. Miss Davis asked about Patsy and if she was needed to help. Anne explained that her mother-in-law was with her, but that she did need someone to pick Margie and Tommy up at the airport. Miss Davis assured Anne that someone would be waiting at the airport and would bring the couple straight to the hospital.

After hanging up, Anne texted Margie's flight itinerary to Miss Davis. She hated for Margie to find out about her Aunt Estelle from anyone else, but there was no other option.

Within minutes, Brad entered the room and walked first to his mother to take her hands. "Dad is with Estelle . . . It's not good. She's fractured her hip in three places and nearly every ligament and muscle in her knee is involved. She's going to need immediate surgery for her hip and we'll worry about the knee later. Dad's also concerned that she's broken several ribs from the pain she's describing. He's going to scrub for the surgery simply to calm Estelle and assure her that he'll be close. But at seventy, we have to really watch her for any further complications."

"Oh, Brad. Do you know how many times we told her not to go up those stairs?"

"Mom, we both know Estelle. She doesn't listen to a word anyone says. It's not your fault. You just need to be here when she comes to the room. She'll want to see your face." He gave her a kiss, then looked at the clock and said, "But that will be hours from now."

Anne sniffed as Brad walked over to give her a kiss. "Where are the children?" he asked.

"They have activities at school and should be done around five."

"What about Margie and Tommy?"

"Miss Davis has that under control."

"I might have time to go with you to get the children. We can tell them Estelle fell, but I don't want to bring them up here," Brad said. "If Margie and Tommy are coming and Mom is here, it's better for you to be with the children. I'll come back to the hospital and keep you posted on everything that's going on. I'll get someone from the office to come here and stay with Mom until Margie gets here."

"I can stay with Patsy another hour before we leave to get the children." Anne began to cry.

Tears began to spill from his eyes. "Those three are going to be devastated."

"I'll keep them busy," Anne promised.

Brad's pager beeped. He looked at Anne. "I'm the only staff surgeon here, sweetheart. It's an emergency C- section."

"Can't someone else handle it?" Anne begged.

"Sweetheart, we've got three doctors out with the flu. We're all on overload, but I'll be home as quickly as possible." He rushed out.

Patsy looked at Anne. "Isn't it always that way, darling? I

guess it's normal that patients have to take priority. Still doesn't make it easy, but there's probably a spouse and maybe even some children that will be waiting on the doctor who will be taking care of our Estelle."

Anne nodded and sat down to wait with Patsy.

When Brad walked in the door later that evening, the children were doing their homework and his supper was still warming on the stove. He sat down on a barstool as Anne turned the burners off and fixed his plate.

In between bites, Brad filled Anne in, "Estelle is still in surgery. From the looks of the x-rays and her doctor's reports, she is going to need extensive physical therapy once she leaves the hospital. They actually won't keep her at the hospital long. We know a great rehab center in Jonesboro. We've already made her reservations." He sighed and continued, "Our other concern is Mother. She can't be by herself and she's very particular. Daddy can be there most of the time, but she will want a female nurse."

Anne stopped her husband. "Why can't we call and see what Chandler's doing?" She was the nurse that Patsy had for so many years before his mother was able to come home. "Those two adore each other; I have her number. I've kept in touch from time to time."

"Great idea. Call and let's see about her situation," Brad said as he sighed and took another bit of the chicken pastry Estelle had brought over yesterday. Tears ran down his cheeks.

"If it doesn't work, I can make it without Margie. I'll get a cleaning service and you'll just have to pretend to like my cooking."

Brad wiped his cheek and smiled. "I'm praying for Chandler."

That night they sat down with the children and explained what had happened to Estelle. The twins started to cry as she was one of their very favorite people and was so instrumental in their lives.

Little Brad crossed his arms across his chest and looked at his daddy. "How many times have we all told Estelle not to go up those stairs? Daddy, she doesn't mind any better than we do!"

Brad smiled. "No, son, she doesn't."

Anne heard her cell ringing in the kitchen. She ran to answer it. Shortly afterwards, she walked back into the room with a big smile on her face. "Chandler will be here by Tuesday, prepared to stay."

CHAPTER TWENTY-SIX

THE SAD GOODBYE

THE ONLY WAY BRAD COULD HAVE DESCRIBED WEDNESDAY WAS that it was one of the worst days of his life. Two physicians were still out with the flu, leaving them shorthanded for the number of expected surgeries and deliveries. But even short of help, his priority remained Estelle. She had just been transferred to the Jonesboro facility and he had hired a private nursing service to make sure her every need would be met. But that didn't relieve him of feeling the need to be with her daily, regardless of his patient volume. To make sure that happened, he had carved out a window of time from four to six each day to get to Jonesboro, have time with Estelle, and get back to the hospital if he was needed. Today, Anne and the children were to meet him in Estelle's rehab room.

He was getting ready to walk out the door to begin his drive when Miss Davis walked in. "It's the rehab center in Jonesboro."

Brad picked up. "Dr. Young, we hate to have to tell you this .

. . but Estelle has been taken to the emergency room at the local hospital. We think she's thrown a clot. She's in terrible pain."

"I'll be there as fast as I can. Thank you for calling," Brad uttered. He was beyond aggravated. *Why didn't they send her here? We could take better care of her here.* But it was too late; she had already been transferred.

After reaching his car, Brad pulled out of the doctor's parking lot and headed straight for Interstate 75 toward Jonesboro. Then he called Anne. She didn't answer. He left a message to meet at the Jonesboro ER rather than the rehab center. "Bring the children and come as soon as you can."

Thirty minutes later, he pulled in front of the ER, left his car running, and ran inside. He showed his ID to the front desk receptionist and asked to see Estelle. The parking attendant rushed in. Having seen the MD on Brad's car tag, he took Brad's key to park his car. A volunteer quickly ushered him back. A physician, having been alerted that Brad had arrived, stepped out of a treatment room and walked up the hallway to meet him.

"I'm so sorry, Dr. Young. There was nothing we could do. We think it was a pulmonary embolism. Her heart just stopped. I'm so sorry."

Stunned, he asked, "Where is she?"

He followed the doctor to the treatment room where Estelle was laying. She looked peaceful and, when he took her hands, he could still feel her warmth. Brad's mind filled with memories —those long-ago Friday nights when he'd come home to spend the night with Estelle, they'd make popcorn and watch cowboy movies, then she'd tuck him into bed, in a room she'd fixed just for him . . . how she'd sit on the front porch and watch him play with neighborhood boys in a park across the street . . . how she'd hold him when she knew he was missing his mother. Then he laughed. How she'd fuss at him when he didn't finish his homework. Estelle had been an incredible mother to him all those years. He leaned down and kissed her cheek, and then he kissed her hand. "What are we going to do without you? Who's going to make my tea cakes? Who's going to love my children like you loved me?"

Brad sat down beside Estelle and stared at her beautiful face. That face was waiting for him every day when he came home from school. He rubbed her hands and thought of the millions of times those hands had put bandages on his knees, held his face, wiped away tears, and had rolled out strip after strip of pastry to make his favorite dish. The only thing that gave him any sense of comfort was that he knew there was no doubt in her mind about how much he loved her.

The doctor came in and asked if Brad would like for Estelle to be transferred to one of the funeral homes in Atlanta. Brad wiped his eyes. "No. Can we stay right here until my wife and children get here? They need to say goodbye."

"Certainly. We understand. If you need anything, just let us know." He turned to leave Brad alone with the woman he would miss more than words could ever explain.

Calling his father, he explained everything that had happened and began to cry.

Brad Sr. breathed deeply and said, "She sure loved you, boy."

"I know, Dad. And the only comfort I have is knowing how much we all loved her."

"Son, I'd be there, but I can't leave your mother. I'll call Estelle's church so they can start making arrangements."

. . .

A little later, Anne and the children walked into the treatment room. Anne had explained what had happened to Estelle on the way to Jonesboro. But all three were still crying when they walked in. They saw Brad's tears and Estelle's stillness. They rushed over to their father.

"Why couldn't you save her, Daddy? You're a doctor," Gretchen cried.

Patsy took Estelle's hand and just began to softly kiss it.

Brad looked at the twins and said, "If I could have saved her, I would have."

Little Brad put his hands on his daddy's shoulders. "We know you would have, Daddy."

Anne gave Brad a kiss and then walked over beside Estelle and bent down to kiss her forehead. She whispered something to her dear friend and then kissed her again.

"What did you say, Mama?" Patsy asked.

"I told her to make sure to save a place for all of us . . . a house right beside her. Then one day we can all be together again."

Gretchen's eyes widened. "Can she do that?"

Anne smiled and said, "If anyone can do that, it would be Estelle. And she's going to make sure lots of angels have special instructions to take good care of you three and your daddy."

As they left the hospital later that night, the five walked out in silence. All were lost in the thoughts of a woman who was irreplaceable. She had been the rock of their family as long as Brad could remember. Now, he had to go face his mother and the grief that would leave her devastated. Estelle had been the only one whom Patsy felt was loving enough to entrust her own son to, knowing she would raise him as her own. He may have lived through some difficult times with his mother's absence and with his practice, but nothing came close to today. His heart was shattered and even Anne's love couldn't soothe his pain tonight.

CHAPTER TWENTY-SEVEN

LOVE WINS

SUMMER HEAT HAD PEAKED AND NIGHTS WERE THANKFULLY getting a little cooler. September was right around the corner. Activities for each of the children had doubled with cheerleading practice, baseball tryouts, swim meets, and Little Brad's golf lessons. Of course, Anne or Brad tried to attend each event. She was also working with Sarah and Heather on the Bellamy building. Some of the wall's paint colors that Sarah had insisted upon were not Anne's favorites, but she managed to bring it all together with rugs, bedding, and accessories. They had already moved another six girls in and another housemother had been hired. Another six young girls were to be moved in next week.

Brad, on the other hand, was watching his practice seem to double and he was trying to hire three new doctors. The first person he contacted was Walt Hood; Brad wanted to feel out his current situation. Walt had just taken his boards and the scores were due back next Thursday. Brad offered a position and Walt accepted, contingent on passing scores.

Needing more space, Brad had leased an adjacent office that had just become available. That gave Anne another design project, as the area needed to be totally remodeled to fit obstetric care needs. It seemed she didn't have enough hours in the day.

One afternoon when Anne sat down with Little Brad for a breather, she asked him about his friend, Stewart. It had dawned on her that she hadn't seen as much of him lately. He lived close by and often played basketball with Little Brad, sometimes staying afterward for dinner.

Anne could tell that Little Brad didn't want to answer her question and she wondered if the two had had a disagreement. She asked again, then said, "I miss him!"

"Mom, he doesn't think you'd want him to come over here anymore," her son finally confessed.

Anne's eyes widened. "What are you talking about? Of course, we want him over here."

"Mom, Stewart says he's gay. He knows we go to church and pray and stuff. He says Christians don't like gays."

Anne was caught off guard, not knowing what to say. She hoped she had never given that impression; she loved Stewart. "Son, what he thinks is simply not true. There are all kinds of things described in the Bible as being good or bad. There is probably no one on earth that has not crossed one of those lines at some point in their life. Do I want people to do things that I feel might not lead them in the best direction? Absolutely not, but I'd never stopped loving them because of it.

"You know, Brad, you're never going to agree with everything that people whom you love do. But you never quit loving them because of those actions. Love is always there no matter what."

She felt the need to continue, "Would I pray for them to make excellent choices? Of course, but it wouldn't change how I felt about them if they didn't. I want people to pray for me to make excellent choices as well, and I hope they never stop loving me, even if I did something that concerned them. You tell that precious Stewart that your mother loves him dearly. He will always be welcome in our home and for supper."

Little Brad kissed his mother's cheek and said, "I'll tell him, Mama."

The next night when Anne got home, it was late and the children had gotten hungry. They had already sat down at the table, waiting. She looked in the breakfast room and saw Stewart sitting with Little Brad and the girls. They were all laughing and talking as they always had. She quickly warmed up supper and smiled as she watched several bites of macaroni and cheese, string beans, and bites of baked chicken disappear between the laughter.

Walking over, she said, "You four better eat good. Margie made a great meal and there's banana pudding in the refrigerator for dessert." Anne remembered that was Stewart's favorite and knew Margie had made that treat especially for him. She kissed each of them on their heads. Stewart turned to kiss Anne's cheek in return. That small gesture brought tears to her eyes. She walked upstairs to have a moment by herself.

CHAPTER TWENTY-EIGHT

DO I WANT TO HEAR THIS?

ANNE OPENED THE REFRIGERATOR. SHE WAS ALL SET TO SNEAK A little bowl of banana pudding for breakfast, but the children had eaten every bit of it. Sighing, she went to the pantry and took out a box of Cinnamon Toast Crunch. The children were still asleep; she had to admit that she loved these few peaceful moments to herself before the onslaught of chaos. Brad had left close to four that morning for the hospital; not his favorite schedule, but babies emerging from the womb didn't notice the time. Due to a half workday for the teachers, the children's schedule wasn't starting today until early afternoon, so she was just letting them sleep. She had about a half-hour before Margie would walk in.

She laughed. "A bowl of cereal and a cup of coffee sound great together this morning." Before she could finish a second spoonful of cereal, her cell rang. She sighed. "So much for breakfast."

"Anne, I hope I didn't wake you," Margie began. "I'm not

going to make it there this morning." She sounded frazzled. "Tommy and I have a meeting with the senior pastor at nine-thirty. I think I'll be there by one if that's okay."

"Of course," Anne assured. "And if you need to take the day off, it's fine."

"Thanks, but I'll be there later. I'm hoping you'll have time to talk."

"I'll make time," Anne said. "I'll see you when you get here."

As Anne put the phone down, her heart sank. Something had been bothering Margie for close to a week. Anne had assumed it was just part of adjusting to the complications of married life. But maybe it was more. Without Margie this morning, Anne headed for the laundry room.

By noon, she had the final load in the dryer and was taking a basket of folded clothes up to her room to put away. Little Brad had been up for over an hour and had taken Bo Jr. for a walk. She peeked in the twins' room and saw that all the girls were still asleep. They had had a sleepover and Anne could still hear them giggling when she and Brad went to bed well after midnight. After getting the clothes positioned in the drawers, she sat the basket with the remaining girl's clothes outside their door.

As she started to walk away, she heard Gretchen say, "Take that off right this minute! That's mine, not yours."

Then Patsy screamed, "You wear my stuff all the time!"

Anne wondered if she should intervene, but decided against it. This argument happened on a regular basis and somehow the girls worked it out. Her only issue was that the twins' company would have to listen to the drama of their loud discussion. She laughed as she thought, *they've got sisters. They'll understand.*

A little later, four girls came bounding down the stairs announcing their weakened state from hunger. Anne put cinnamon rolls in the oven to warm, cut up a cantaloupe, fried some bacon, and set the table. After the girls finished their brunch, the group walked over to the tennis courts at the Club.

Anne had gone back to fold the last load of clothes when she heard Margie coming in the back door. Walking into the laundry room, her housekeeper asked, "Where is everybody?"

Anne just smiled and said, "Isn't the quiet just wonderful? They've all gone in different directions and it's just you and me."

"Could we sit down and talk?" Margie asked. She had the saddest look on the face.

Anne took Margie's shoulders in her hands and quietly asked, "Am I going to want to hear this?"

"Probably not," Margie said as she shrugged her shoulders.

Anne poured two glasses of tea. They sat down in the great room.

Margie began, "You know that our church sponsors an orphanage in Guatemala. And another one in Costa Rica." Anne nodded.

"Things are not going well at either place. We found out two weeks ago that the couple who has been in charge of those sweet babies has been embezzling money. The children aren't getting fed on a regular basis. Our pastor suspected something several months ago and sent Tommy down to see what was happening."

Anne shook her head and continued to listen.

"Some of the stories told by the workers absolutely broke his heart. He fired the couple on the spot and then two of the elders from our church were sent down to see if they could help. Tommy has actually flown down a few times with needed supplies."

"Anne, you know how much I love your children. I can't imagine what my life would have been like without your three. But now . . . Tommy and I have a chance to do something for children who really need us badly. Little children who need love and attention. Our children here . . . your children . . . are getting older. They don't need me as much anymore. I miss being needed. Tommy and I have an opportunity to take over the management of both facilities. We're so excited, but I can't go without your blessing. I love you too much, Anne."

Anne took Margie's hands as tears rolled down her own cheeks. "Of course, you have my blessing. We all want nothing but the best for you and Tommy. But you've got one thing wrong, Margie. There will never be a day in my family's life when we won't need you. I love you too, we all do!"

The two embraced as tears fell. When they finally got control of their emotions, Anne asked, "When do they want y'all to leave?"

"In two weeks. But I've got so much to do to get ready."

"What can we do to help?" Anne asked. "The children have saved some of their allowances to help children and Brad and I would love to help. Why don't you make a list? The children and I will spend the next two weeks making sure everything on it is checked off and ready to go with you."

· · ·

Two weeks later, the Young family stood and waved tearful goodbyes as Margie and Tommy left to start a new chapter in their life together.

On the way home, Gretchen summed up what they all were silently thinking. "Mama, not having Margie is depressing."

A week later, Anne hired a cleaning service and a lady from the Center to help with the laundry. Every morning at nine o'clock, she thought of Margie and how lonely it was without their daily conversations. But then she remembered how loving Margie had always been with the twins and her son. Anne pictured that same tender woman taking care of babies who needed her far more. Those thoughts seemed to wash away at least some of the emptiness.

CHAPTER TWENTY-NINE

A FAMILY TIE

IT WAS POURING DOWN RAIN WHEN ANNE WALKED INTO THE Center. She was soaked to the bone despite her heavy rain jacket and umbrella. It was a driving rain and the umbrella offered little protection. The receptionist, Lori, looked up and said, "Let me get you a towel. After you dry off, there are some people waiting to see you. They got here about ten minutes ago. It's a couple with two children, so I thought they'd be more comfortable in the playroom because the little girl is younger and there are toys there."

"Did they give their name?"

"A Mr. and Mrs. Donald Phelps," Lori said.

The name didn't register, but Anne was curious. After drying off, she walked into the playroom and spotted the couple at a child-sized table playing with a little girl. An older boy was sitting quietly by the bookshelf flipping through the selections. Anne walked over and introduced herself.

The woman stood and said, "You don't know me, but I've

heard some really good things about you and I wanted to meet and thank you. I spent a few days recently with my mother and she was telling me how you helped Betsy when she was so sick. I'm Susan, Betsy's younger sister."

Anne's eyes flooded. She reached to give Susan a long hug. "Oh, Susan. You're alive. You have no idea how many times I've thought of you!" She stepped back and added, "I can certainly tell you're Betsy's sister. You're beautiful too."

Susan smiled.

"You have a handsome little nephew and his name is Jeffey," Anne said.

Susan tilted her head in surprise. "Betsy was pregnant? She had a baby?" She looked at her husband. "Excuse me, this is my husband, Matt. I'm sorry I didn't introduce him earlier." Matt stood, shook Anne's hand, and then put his arm around his wife. He wanted to hear more of what Anne had to say.

Anne suggested they go into the lounge, where they could talk privately. She introduced the daycare worker to Susan's children and asked her to please get them a snack. After which, the three walked out and into the quieter room.

Sitting down, Anne first told Susan how much Betsy loved and missed her. She then explained the complicated situation and Betsy's brave determination to give life to her son. Susan put her face in her hands, as she was having a hard time controlling their emotions. Anne continued Betsy's story and told them all about Doris and Jeff and the divine intervention that allowed Jeffey's adoption before Betsy's death. She shared how Betsy was able to hold little Jeffey before cancer took her life.

Susan had question after question, which Anne patiently

answered. Most of the discussion was about her nephew. Anne had an idea. "Excuse me for a few minutes," Anne asked. "I need to make a phone call and I'll be right back."

Anne stepped into an office and called Doris. When she answered, Anne told her to sit down; they had something important to discuss.

"Doris, you are not going to believe who is sitting in the Center. It's Betsy's sister, Susan, and she knew nothing about Jeffey. She has her husband and two children with her."

Doris spoke up, "Anne, can you bring them by? I'd love for them to meet Jeffey."

"I was hoping you'd say that."

"I just made a big bowl of chicken salad. Why don't y'all come over here and we'll have lunch?"

"That sounds perfect. Give us thirty minutes with this rain."

Doris complained, but couldn't repress a smile. "My house is a mess and I don't want her to see me looking the way I do. Give me an hour."

"No problem," Anne promised as she put her cell back in her pocket. Walking back into the lounge, she told Susan and Matt about her conversation with the adoptive mother.

Susan stood to give Anne another hug. "I've been so worried about this visit and the sadness of losing Betsy before I could be with her. I didn't realize I'd ever get to meet her child . . . I have a nephew and our children have a cousin. It's wonderful."

After they went back to the playroom for the children, they entered the parking lot for their cars. Susan and Matt followed Anne, rain and all, to Doris' house. Anne was glad they had agreed on an hour; the traffic was bumper to bumper on

Peachtree all the way to Peachtree Dunwoody. By the time they reached Doris' driveway, it was nearly an hour and a half. She figured her friend would appreciate the extra time.

Doris had seen them drive up and had already opened the door to greet them. Umbrellas in hand, the five, trying not to drown, rushed up to the open foyer. Jeffey was standing beside his mother, wondering who Anne had brought over to see them.

Anne made introductions and walked over to Jeffey to give him a big hug. It was still hard for her to believe that he was already nine years old and getting so tall. "Are you enjoying the Thanksgiving break from your school?"

"I was until Mama just made me go clean up my room."

Anne started to say something about his aunt, but stopped. It would be better to let Doris handle the explanation.

Doris looked at her son and said, "You know how Daddy and I have told you about your mother?"

Jeffey nodded.

"This is your Aunt Susan, your mother's sister, and her husband, Matt." She looked at the boy and girl and added, "And these are your cousins."

Susan interjected, "John and Brooke."

Jeffey asked, "Do y'all like to play with Legos?"

Both nodded.

"I have a whole Lego room. Wanna go see it?"

They followed Jeffey as Doris started laughing. "This house has been overtaken by Legos." She invited the adults to come into the breakfast room as she talked and prepared lunch at the same time. She fixed bowls of macaroni and cheese for the children and cut-up apples. After setting those plates on the table, she dished up plates of chicken salad, grapes, and crackers, poured four glasses of tea and three of milk. After she called the children back in, they all sat down for lunch. Doris asked Jeffey to say the blessing.

He looked at his mother shyly and asked, "The one I learned last week?" It was a most appropriate blessing, as it indicated gratefulness for unseen blessings.

"That would be perfect."

Over lunch, Anne and Doris got to know Susan and Matt even better and Jeffey was having fun with his cousins. Around two, Anne excused herself. Even with no school during the holidays, practices were mandatory with weekend games and the girls needed to be picked up. She asked Susan and Matt to come back anytime with the children. Hugging Susan, she looked at Doris and told her she'd call her later.

Pulling into the children's school, Anne could still picture Betsy with her feet up on the ottoman, slouched into that comfy chair in the garage apartment. She looked up and whispered, "Betsy, I like Susan and her family. I know you would have enjoyed today as well. They love your son. It's been a really good day."

Within minutes, Anne's car was full. Gretchen started talking as Patsy was asking her to slide over on the seat; she was getting wet. Little Brad jumped in the other side, fussing, "I still don't know why I can't drive my car to school."

Anne just closed her eyes. Yes, it had been a good day until now. She'd be glad to get home and talk to Doris. Susan had made a comment that Doris didn't seem to like. Anne thought about that part of the conversation; she wasn't sure she liked it either.

CHAPTER THIRTY

EVERYBODY DOES IT

THE FOLLOWING MORNING AS ANNE WAS FINISHING HER FIRST cup of coffee, her cell rang. It was Doris.

"I hope I didn't call too early, Anne. Is everybody still sleeping?" Doris asked.

"Not too early at all. I'm having my coffee. Brad has already left for a delivery and the children are taking advantage of this opportunity to sleep."

"I was so excited for Jeffey to meet his aunt and uncle and cousins yesterday. He talked about it for the rest of the day and even asked when they were coming back. But . . . something was mentioned yesterday that really bothered me."

There was no doubt in Anne's mind as to what Doris was referring. "I was concerned as well."

As Anne was leaving Doris' yesterday, Susan mentioned that they were going to be in Atlanta through the weekend after Thanksgiving and that they would love to take Doris, Jeff, and Jeffey out to lunch. More importantly, that Susan would bring her mother for the visit. The minute those words left Susan's mouth Anne had tensed up. The last person she wanted to meet was the woman who had been so selfish and mean to Betsy.

"I don't want Jeffey to meet that woman," Doris began. "I don't want her in his life at all. I remember Betsy telling me how she had said Betsy would have to find someone else to care for her when she was so sick. How am I going to handle this?"

Anne thought for a minute and replied, "How did you leave it with Susan?"

Doris sighed. "I told her it sounded lovely and she said she'd call me on Friday. Should I just say it's not a good time? That we can't make it?"

"I think that sounds reasonable. But you're not closing the door. It could easily come up again."

Doris sighed even more loudly. "Why don't you call her? You're good at this kind of thing. I'm not. I talked to Jeff last night about it and his response was, 'That's not going to happen. I'm not having lunch with that woman … and neither is my son.'"

"Let me think about this and I'll call you back," Anne said.

Susan had given Anne a card with her phone number on it. Anne walked over to pull it out of her purse. She carried it over to the breakfast room table and stared at the number, willing herself to make a wise decision. She certainly didn't want to hurt Susan's feelings, but she agreed with Doris and Jeff. This meeting could not happen. Period. Anne punched the number into her cell. No answer. Politely, she left a message for Susan to give her a call.

Noises from upstairs brought Anne's attention back to the moment; the children would be hungry. She opened the refrigerator, took out the bacon, and began searching for the eggs. They were nowhere to be found. The twins came running into the kitchen, but stopped short and looked at each other. Their mother was looking for the eggs. Turning around, they tried to tiptoe back upstairs. It was too late; Anne had heard them.

"Ladies, where are my eggs?" She could tell by their body language alone that she wasn't going to like the answer.

Patsy turned around and looked at her mother. "We borrowed them."

Gretchen thought that sounded pretty good, so she concurred, "Yes, but we're going to buy you some more today."

"What did you do with my eggs?" Anne persisted.

"Mom, it'd be better if you didn't ask," Patsy tried to explain.

"What have y'all done now?" Anne asked as she glared.

"Everybody did it . . . We got together last night and egged the cars in the parking lot at Westminster. Their team was getting on our nerves saying they were going to whoop us Saturday night." Patsy looked down after this admission.

"Who exactly is the 'everybody' that egged the cars?"

"The junior varsity and the varsity cheerleaders," Patsy answered.

Gretchen laughed a bit nervously and said, "We figured there was safety in numbers."

Anne put her hands on her hips. "Both of you know better than that. We don't egg anything in this household. Your daddy is going to be furious!"

"We won't do it again," Patsy promised.

"But it felt really good," Gretchen added with a grin.

"And, Mama, don't worry. We'll just have bacon and cereal for breakfast," Patsy offered.

"Well, you're both going to tell your daddy tonight."

Gretchen rolled her eyes. "Why should we bother him with this? It's too late to take it back . . . and I can't afford to lose another penny of my allowance."

"Me either," Patsy agreed.

"Will you two promise me that you will never do this again?" Anne was buckling.

"Yes, ma'am. We promise. We promise," they said over and over.

After the girls finished their breakfast, they said they were meeting some of the other girls to go to the mall. Anne could at least put a stop to this privilege. "I don't think so. You're not out of the woods yet." She pointed toward the laundry room. "There are baskets of clothes to be folded and put up. Then your room needs to be dusted and vacuumed. Your bedsheets need to be changed . . . and your bathroom needs to be cleaned."

The twins knew not to argue; it was a better deal than their daddy finding out about the eggs. They ran to the laundry room to start their chores; maybe if they hurried, there would still be time to meet friends.

"Is your brother up?" Anne asked before they got out of the room.

"He's not here, Mama. He went to spend the night with Gaga and BB. I think he was going to take them for a ride in his Jeep this morning," Patsy said. "Sorry, he told us to tell you last night. They really like that Jeep and so does Bo Jr.!" Gretchen said. "Brad took him to Gaga and BB's when he left."

Anne and Brad had been to a party and were late getting

home. They had noticed the Jeep was gone, but assumed he had told his sisters where he was. The girls were already asleep, so they figured they would ask in the morning. Even though she had been concerned about his whereabouts, she was actually delighted that her son was spending time with his grandparents; they had a special bond.

Before heading upstairs with the laundry, Gretchen stopped back in the kitchen. "Mom, Gaga said we can have Granddaddy's car when we get our license. He's thinking about getting a new one."

"I don't think this is your best time to bring that up, ladies," Anne said as Patsy popped back in the room, hoping to hear her mother's reply. Anne couldn't help but stifle a laugh when she heard Patsy whisper to her twin that they'd ask their daddy.

As Anne was cleaning up the kitchen, her cell rang. "Anne, this is Susan. We had such a good time yesterday. Jeffey looks so much like his mother. He even has Betsy's dimples . . . I hope you can join us for lunch on Friday."

Anne swallowed hard. "Susan, there's something we need to talk about. Betsy and I had a lot of conversations when she was sick . . . some of which were about your mother. Did you know that she didn't offer to help your sister? Betsy never heard a word from her the whole time she was sick with cancer." Anne took a deep breath and added, "We would prefer not to get her involved in Jeffey's life and we hope you understand."

Susan responded more quickly than Anne thought she would. "Anne, you don't have to worry about that. Mother said some nasty things last night when I told her about Jeffey. She called that sweet little boy a horrible name . . . We will never, ever bring up a visit with her again. To be honest, I can't wait to leave this house. I should have never come back. Some things never change . . . not even when you pray so long that they will."

"I'm sorry, Susan. I know that must be painful. I'm sorry I won't be able to join all of you for lunch, but I know you'll have a great time. Please let me know the next time you're in town and hopefully we can get together."

Anne clicked off and then called Doris to report her conversation. Then she told Doris about the eggs.

A relieved Doris started laughing and said, "Do you remember our freshman year at VCU? The eggs off the fire escape?"

"Doris, if you ever mention that to my girls, I'll never forgive you!" Anne warned. They were still laughing as they said goodbye.

CHAPTER THIRTY-ONE

PACK YOUR BAGS

BRAD WALKED THROUGH THE BACK DOOR A LITTLE EARLY ON Thursday afternoon. By the look on his face, Anne could tell there was something exciting about to happen. He was all smiles.

"What's going on with you, Brad Young?" Anne asked as she walked over and gave him a kiss. She shook her finger and added, "You better not have bought another car!"

He laughed. "No, it's not that. I just came from a meeting at the hospital. We're joining another group of doctors from New York General. We're forming mission teams. Our first trip has already been planned."

"Oh . . . where?"

"Fifteen of us are headed to Guatemala the first of July. That gives me plenty of time to brush up on my Spanish and help plan the logistics of this first trip."

Anne sat down on one of the kitchen stools. She wasn't smiling. "How long will you be gone? Can spouses go?"

"I think it'd be fabulous if you want to go. In fact, if you want to leave a week early, the two of us could take some time to see the country. But then, it would probably be better for you to come home. I'll be in really tough terrain for ten days of brutal work. We're going to start establishing clinics in mountainous areas and there will be a lot of walking in the summer heat. We need to hike through several areas that have never been cleared and honestly, we don't know the full extent of what we may run into. Many places are so high up in the mountains that the buses can't even make the trip. Like I said . . . a lot of walking."

"Where will you fly in to?" Anne asked.

"Guatemala City. One of the physicians traveling with us was telling me about a coffee plantation in Antigua that has a quaint little hotel with very nice amenities. Even a swimming pool and a five-star restaurant. It's not Paris," he said with a grin, "but I bet it could be." Brad leaned over and nuzzled Anne's neck as he worked his way up to her lips.

Now, she was smiling. "That sounds wonderful, my love. Then I can picture where you are when I'm not with you."

"I'll get Miss Davis working on the reservations."

Anne cocked her head. "One question. Wouldn't that be a wonderful educational trip for the children?"

Brad shook his head. "Well, there goes Paris." But he had to agree. "It would be good for them to see how other areas of the world live."

Anne thought further. "Why don't we tell them tonight at supper and add a challenge? We could ask each one to bring a new fact about Guatemala to the table every night for discus-

sion. I think that will add to their enjoyment of the vacation."
She pursed her lips. "Brad, is any part of this trip dangerous?"

He knew he needed to be careful with his response as he considered her overactive imagination. "Sweetheart, it probably could be. But we'll be with a big group and as we divide up, each smaller group will have a guard and an interpreter. Anne, I've known for years that this was something I was supposed to do. I made a promise when you recovered from the birth of the twins. I need to honor that promise of gratitude for bringing you back to me, sweetheart. I supported you with the Center and now I need your support on establishing these clinics."

Tears slipped down her cheeks as she looked into her husband's eyes. "Don't you worry for a minute, Dr. Young. You have my full support."

After a kiss, Brad suggested, "Let's wait until the arrangements are made and all's a go, before we bring it up with the children?" He walked into the study. Sitting down, he left Miss Davis a message asking that she contact their travel agent to get the ball rolling. He had forgotten to mention one detail to Anne and walked back into the kitchen as she started supper.

"There are some female physicians going on this trip. Just want to make sure I still have your support."

Anne laughed. "I may have to think about that one!"

A week later, Brad and Anne met with their travel agent. She had a list of activities the family could choose from, including zip-lining, a helicopter ride over a volcano, hiking trails, shopping expeditions, and visiting the Mayan ruins, as well as a museum, a zoo, and a tour of a coffee plantation. Since they would be staying at the resort on the coffee plantation, that tour was assumed. Brad suggested they take the list and discuss it at supper with the children.

Reading over their itinerary, Anne decided she and Brad should go to the mall and visit the small travel shop to get Guatemalan maps and books for the children to begin their study of the country. She looked at her husband and laughed. She could tell he was much more excited about this trip than any of the children would be.

Anne called Margie from the car to tell her about their trip. Both women couldn't wait to see each other in Guatemala City.

Running into Phipps Plaza, Anne and Brad grabbed the travel materials, and then he left to pick up Little Brad from baseball and the twins from swim practice.

She left to get dinner from La Paz. She then set the dining room table with a sombrero centerpiece. She poured lemonade into margarita glasses and placed napkins, each a different bright color.

When Brad walked in the door, he said, "Yum, something in here smells really good!"

Anne rushed past him straight into the dining room. After distributing tacos and chips with a queso dip, not exactly traditional Guatemalan food, but close enough and something familiar that the children would eat, she placed a book and a map at each table setting. Gretchen followed her mother and asked, "Are we having a party?"

That comment brought the other two running into the dining room. Brad came to the table. "Well, it's kind of a party. An educational party."

Little Brad picked up one of the books. "Where's

Guatemala?"

"That's what we're going to talk about over tacos. Go wash your hands," Anne ordered.

Picking up one of the books while the children cleaned up, Anne reminded Brad, "Margie and Tommy are at an orphanage in Guatemala City!"

Brad smiled. "Wouldn't the three love some time with them?"

By this time, the children were walking back in with nice clean hands. Everyone sat down as Brad said the blessing. The children were thrilled over tacos and thought lemonade in the special glasses was fun.

Gretchen looked around the table and asked, "Why does this look like a party? And what are the books for?"

"We're going to take a trip to Guatemala!" Anne announced.

"All of us?" Patsy asked.

Anne nodded and the children began asking one question after another. Brad explained the details of the trip and the children became even more excited. He read the list of possible activities and it became very clear that the boys and girls could separate on some of the options, and thus accomplish more. Brad and Little Brad checked zip-lining, hiking, and the helicopter ride. All the girls checked shopping, the Mayan ruins, and the swimming pool. But Gretchen convinced her mother and sister that everyone had to do zip-lining. She wasn't missing out on that adventure. Brad gave them their homework assignment about bringing a new Guatemalan fact to the table each night.

Anne remembered a recent conversation with Margie. She raised her hand and said, "I already know a fact! Did you know there are a lot of places in that country that don't have clean drinking water? A church had to put a well in for the orphanage we help sponsor for Tommy and Margie."

Patsy frowned. "Where do they get something to drink if no one builds a well?"

"From rivers, sometimes from mud puddles after the rain," Anne explained.

"That's so sad," Patsy said with tears building in her eyes. "Who wants to drink muddy water?"

After more water conversation, Anne explained that their daddy would be staying longer to help set up medical clinics in the mountains and that he might see a place that needed water. Their family could then help to donate for a well if they'd like. It could be drilled so that those children could drink clean water.

"Can we help find the place, Daddy? Can we look while we're there?" Patsy asked.

All three chimed in, they were in agreement about finding a place. Anne smiled as she watched their blossoming sense of generosity.

Brad took his wife's hand. "They have your heart, Mrs. Young."

Anne shook her head. "I'm not the one going to Guatemala on a medical mission, my love. They have their daddy's compassion."

Then Anne and Brad told their children that they had another big surprise. Together the girls cried, "What, Daddy? Tell us, Mama."

Brad smiled. "We'll have some time with Margie and Tommy."

CHAPTER THIRTY-TWO

ZIP-LINES, CLEAN WATER, AND PRAYERS

JULY HAD FINALLY ARRIVED; IT WAS TIME FOR THE FAMILY TRIP TO Guatemala. The children had faithfully studied the country's fact sheet. Father and son had their hiking gear packed and Anne and the girls had packed cool cotton clothes and comfortable shoes. Once they landed, Brad had hired a car and driver to take the family to the orphanage, where they would spend the day with Margie and Tommy. Anne had a suitcase full of toys for the children to give to Margie. They couldn't wait to get there.

The reunion was full of hugs, kisses, and tears. Margie introduced her family to everyone at the orphanage and laughed as she watched all of the children playing with each other and the toys Anne had brought. Tommy and Brad spent their time in the ministry's clinic discussing the normal needs and medications that were a must in this mosquito-infested area of the world. Brad was grateful for Tommy's insight as he texted several requests for additional equipment and medications to his mission's procurement coordinator.

Soon it was time to say goodbye to Margie and all of their new friends. Again, there were more hugs and tears, but Margie promised she and Tommy would come to Atlanta for a visit before too long. That helped make their departure a little better as they all waved goodbye.

The Young family found the country to be both beautiful and inviting. The bright colors and fresh fruit in the marketplaces were even more vibrant than any they had ever seen. The hotel was right in the middle of the coffee plantation in the little town of Antigua and the perpetual coffee aroma was pungent. Outdoor cafes spotted the grounds and boasted delicious food and even better desserts. Of course, the shops carried every kind of coffee and bug spray known to man. The family lathered up daily. The girls picked out cool and colorful Guatemalan outfits on their shopping spree and the entire family zip-lined through the lush green rainforest. The view above the foliage was breathtaking and the cool air on the ride brought relief to the hot day.

Little Brad looked over at the mountain on the morning of his helicopter ride and noticed that the volcano was smoking. He pointed out cinders flying in the air. His daddy called the tour guide and learned the ride had been canceled due to signs of activity with the volcano. Little Brad was disappointed, but relieved to hear that it happened regularly and would likely cease in time for another day's adventure.

With the opening in their schedule, it was the perfect time

for Brad to tell the family about a nearby village. It had a school and a small medical office staffed by a young nurse from the United States. It was a few miles up the mountain and it had no clean drinking water. The children listened with excitement, realizing this could be the village for them to help with a well. They had been diligently saving their allowances and doing extra chores to earn even more money.

Brad arranged for a small van and the family headed toward the village. The van had a difficult time making it up the steep, dirt road, filled with holes and rocks. The bumpy ride seemed to be fun for the children, as they were jostled around. Finally, the Youngs made it to their destination.

Upon seeing the meager surroundings, the children became unusually quiet as they exited the van. Patsy took her daddy's hand and asked, "Where are their houses, Daddy?"

Brad pointed to a few small shacks made from tin signs, branches, and rope. The adults of the village were sitting on crates or walking around. The children were playing games the Youngs had never seen before, improvising with rocks and sticks.

The nurse from the village came out to greet them and introduced the family to some of the village leaders. Anne had brought two bags full of balls and Frisbees that she thought might be good ice breakers between the children. She had even put a few dolls in one of the bags, dolls she had purchased at the airport in Guatemala City.

Gretchen looked at her daddy. "I have to tinkle."

Brad explained that they didn't have any bathrooms. But the nurse offered to take Gretchen to a little place in the clinic that offered some privacy. Gretchen and Patsy followed the nurse to an area behind a curtain with a small pot on the floor.

Gretchen looked at the nurse with obvious panic in her eyes. She asked, "How do I use that?"

The nurse explained how to squat over the container. Then Gretchen asked how to flush. The nurse held out a tissue and told her not to worry about that part.

When she and the nurse walked back to her parents, she whined, "That was awful, I tinkled on my shoe! Why don't they have bathrooms?"

"They have so little here," the nurse began. "When I first came to Guatemala, I was as shocked as you. But now I have learned to adjust to life as they know it. In fact, I've learned a great deal from all of the wonderful people here in my new big family."

Patsy looked at the nurse. "This makes me so sad."

Miss Little, the nurse, put her arms around the girls. "Do you know what would make the biggest difference for this village? What could help them grow vegetables and not get sick from drinking dirty river water?"

Patsy and Gretchen's eyes widened. They both exclaimed, "A well!"

"You're absolutely right. They need a well for clean water."

The girls looked up at their daddy. "Can we drill our well here, Daddy?" Gretchen asked. "Can this be the place?" Patsy added.

"I think this could be the perfect place," Brad answered.

Anne and Little Brad agreed. However, Gretchen had more questions. "How long does it take to drill a well?" She looked at her mother and added, "Do we have enough money? How much does a well cost?"

Anne explained that it would probably cost four to five thousand dollars for a well. Their faces dropped and they looked at Brad.

Little Brad, the realist, said, "We don't have that much money."

Anne wanted to plant a seed. "You know, when we started the Center, I didn't have enough money. But I had some money that my mother left me and I used that."

Little Brad looked at his sisters. "We have some money that Granddaddy Boyd left us."

"Do you remember where it is?" Anne asked.

"It's in the bank," Gretchen confirmed.

"Well, you could take enough money out of that account for a well, if you are really sure it is something you want to do."

All three were positive. Little Brad pulled an envelope out of his pocket. "This is the money we saved from our allowance and chores. What do we do with it?"

Brad looked at the nurse and asked, "Miss Little, I bet y'all could use some bandages and medicine."

She nodded. "We certainly could. We have very little to work with as far as medical supplies go."

Little Brad looked at Gretchen and Patsy with raised eyebrows. They nodded yes and he handed the envelope to the nurse. "Maybe this can help buy some medicine."

All three children then took the bags of toys and headed out to meet and play with new friends.

Anne and Brad went to the van and opened the cargo door. They pulled out baskets from the hotel and crates of bottled water that they had stocked before leaving Antigua. The baskets held sandwiches, homemade cookies, and lots of fruit.

After the children had played for a while, the Young children invited their new friends to join them for lunch. Anne and Brad motioned to the parents to come over for the picnic as well. Before eating, Little Brad said a blessing he had learned in Spanish before the trip. He then moved to the side of the table as the large group swarmed toward the food. There was plenty for everyone and the Youngs left a village of full tummies, waves, and smiles when they pulled away. Miss Little rode along with them to purchase more medical supplies in town with the children's gift.

A gentleman from the Antigua drilling company came by the hotel the following morning to thank the children for supplying the funds to drill the well. He assured them that it would be starting their water project within the next thirty days.

Little Brad immediately challenged him with the fact that thirty days was a really long time and that the children in the village needed water now. The man grinned and offered ten days. Little Brad smiled and said, "That's much better."

Brad shook his head as he looked at his son. "I surely hope he's not planning on going into politics!"

Two days later, Anne and the children boarded their flight back to the United States after a tearful farewell with Brad. It was more than a challenge for Anne to leave him in another country, but she understood his need to help on this mission. As she turned to wave one last time, she was reminded of all sorts of danger. She thought, *Lord, please protect him. He's such a good man.*

Anne took her seat and focused on the children. Their exhaustion was evident; it had been a whirlwind of a trip. Anne smiled thinking of the suitcase the three had brought to her when they were waiting for their car in the hotel lobby. It was full of their clothes. They had asked if Miss Little could come get their case. They were leaving it for the village children. She had been delighted at how well they had behaved, as well as thankful that changing the lives of their new friends for the better had become a tangible goal for each of them.

As they waited to take off, a strange feeling washed over Anne. She turned to her children and said, "We need to remember to pray really hard for your daddy. For his safety and for the safety of his entire team. Just remember that when you say your bedtime prayers." Anne looked out the window and muttered, "In this heat and these mountains, our prayers can help him stay safe and sound."

These sudden strange feelings were somehow new and different as Anne laid her head back against the seat. Maybe even a little frightening. Maybe having to do with stormy weather as she looked at dark cloud formations outside of the plane's small oval window. She looked back at the children. "We should pray for sunny skies and nice breezes for Daddy." Little did she know how important those prayers would be.

CHAPTER THIRTY-THREE

THE COMING STORM

BRAD WAS WAITING AT THE AIRPORT IN GUATEMALA CITY WHEN his fourteen colleagues landed. After greeting one another, they sat down in the conference room at the city's hospital. There the group decided on their marching orders. Each team was divided into three groups. Teams of five were assigned three villages in which to provide and instruct medical care over the ten days of their volunteer mission. The clinics were to be established in remote mountainous areas. They would each have a Jeep for traveling the rough, rocky terrain. The volunteers in Brad's group were primarily from Atlanta and had worked together before on community projects. Familiarity with each other's area of expertise was a comfort as they faced a completely new challenge in the mountains of Guatemala.

There was a surgeon, an internist, a dentist, and an ophthalmologist, and Brad was to handle gynecology and obstetrics. His team took the map for their first location and headed to Antigua. The head of the mission's group had established

Antigua as their base for supplies and medical inventory. After dinner and a good night's sleep, each team loaded their Jeep and trailer and were on their way by five o'clock Monday morning. The Jeep's driver also served as the guard and an accompanying interpreter sat in the far back with Brad.

After three hot hours on the road, they pulled into a small village. The team immediately started preparing different areas for their tents to provide various specialties. Even though Brad had been diligent about brushing up on his Spanish, he was extremely grateful for the interpreter. As the first day passed, Brad was surprised at how young most of his patients were. They came in with various concerns and questions, were examined, and then given the appropriate vitamins and medications as needed. Several young girls already had a child and were pregnant with another. It became quite clear to Brad that most of the villages had a strong Catholic tradition and he was not to mention birth control. He questioned the sensibility of that edict as the girls seemed to look even younger over the course of the day.

Things were moving rather smoothly until a girl in obvious labor came in near the end of the day. Well into the night, she was still breathing and pushing, but to no avail. Brad called in the surgical volunteer and both decided that a Cesarean was their only choice. After checking her vitals, the procedure began. In less than an hour, the young mother was holding her healthy baby.

When Brad pulled his blanket up later that night, he couldn't get his mind off the young mother. He thought, *if we hadn't been at this village on this particular day, she and her baby would have more than likely died.* He knew the statistics of death in childbirth were quite high here; now he knew why. So many women were facing their pregnancies completely alone; a few might have the untrained help of an elderly woman serving as a midwife. In reality, teenage mothers trying to deliver healthy babies was a life-and-death gamble; their bodies simply weren't ready.

Later the next day as Brad talked with some of his colleagues, he learned that it was nearly impossible to even get an OBGYN doctor to come on these trips. Most felt it was an exercise in futility. For every child saved, they lost another and, in numerous cases, the mother as well.

After the three stiflingly hot days in the first village, it was time to pack everything up and move to the second location. Brad looked around at all of the women he had seen and tragically realized he was leaving them to an uncertain fate. He wondered which ones would eventually deliver their babies safely and which would not be so fortunate. But he had no choice; it was time to move on.

Arriving at the next village late that same day, the team shared a simple meal and hoped, even with the heat, to sleep in preparation for the three busy days to follow. The first two days seemed familiar, young girls and older women—either too young or too old to be having babies. On the third day, a woman about Anne's age came into the clinic.

Brad could smell the woman's bleeding and, through the interpreter, he learned she had been bleeding for months. When he examined her, Brad knew she needed a D&C; she had evidently miscarried a late-term pregnancy. He scrubbed and completed the procedure, but the infection he found appeared to have already spread to other areas in her body. He gave her a supply of antibiotics and instructed her to take them twice a day until they were all gone.

Lying on his cot, as he tossed, turned, and perspired most of the night, all he could think about was what a real clinic could accomplish in these mountains. The woman with the bleeding issue could have the care she needed. But he had to leave the next morning and would not be returning. He fell asleep wondering if he was helping in the least; his specialty needed more follow-up clinical care. He hoped the woman would recover. He prayed she would take the antibiotics as prescribed.

Rain came overnight and thankfully cooled the air; however, the water added more difficulties for their drive to the third village. A wind had come up as well, which actually felt good after seven days in the harsh heat. Finally, the team made it to their last village safely. It was the place where their interpreter, Mario, had spent his childhood.

Looking at Brad, Mario smiled and said, "Dr. Brad, we have lots of babies in our village! My sister's baby will come any day now."

"What's your sister's name? How old is she?" Brad asked.

"Her name is Rosa and she's fifteen. She got married last summer. She's very pretty," he said with a smile. "But she sure has a big belly!"

Brad smiled back. "What is her husband's name?"

"Jose," Mario answered. "I'll introduce you to my whole family."

After unloading the Jeep and trailer, the men waved goodbye to the driver and he headed back to the city to refuel. Just then a beautiful and very pregnant young woman ran up to Mario and gave him a hug.

"Dr. Brad, this is my sister, Rosa," Mario said as he led her over to Brad and the team.

"Good Morning, Rosa. You must be close to term. Have you been able to see a doctor?" Brad asked.

Mario listened to her response and answered in English, "She said she saw a doctor four months ago and he told her the baby would come in this month. She asked if you would check her while you are here."

"Of course," Brad said.

After everything was set up, the team took a few minutes to change their wet clothes before seeing patients. Brad saw several pregnant women and then Rosa hurried into the tent, rubbing her stomach. Her husband, Jose, was following close behind. Brad asked him to hold his wife's hand while he completed the examination. As Brad moved his hand across her belly, a hard contraction hit. From all indications, the baby would probably arrive that same day, at least by that evening.

Rosa was young and Brad could see the fear in her eyes as another contraction caught her breath. He assured the expectant mother and her husband that everything would be fine and promised to check on her throughout the day.

By midday, the wind was howling and wreaking havoc as gusts blew much of the medical equipment around the tent. Brad heard a commotion coming from the center of the village and wasn't quite sure what was happening until Mario flew through the tent entrance.

Mario screamed at the surprised faces in the makeshift clinic, "A big storm is coming! By the time the buses get up the mountain, it will already be hitting the coast." He turned to Brad and said, "Dr. Brad, they're packing everyone up to leave. This storm is moving fast. The wind gusts are at ninety miles per hour in Guatemala City and coming our way."

Brad asked, "When is it supposed to hit us?"

"We don't know. We need to get off the mountain," Mario explained.

Brad looked around the tented clinic. There was nothing that could withstand a storm of that magnitude. He listened as the wind continued to send flying debris in various directions. But, by this time, Rosa's labor was intense and her cries could be heard even above the wind. Brad hurried over to the area where Rosa and Jose were waiting and saw the panic in Jose's eyes. He quickly examined Rosa; she was fully dilated. Regardless of any storm, this baby was coming.

When the first bus arrived to take people to safety, the villagers packed all they could in large bags and began to board. Brad's team was now packing up supplies. Two of the doctors took several large boxes of equipment to the bus and then came back to round up mothers and children. By then this first vehicle was packed full and it left to start down the mountain.

The driver of the second bus was just driving up and the winds made it nearly impossible for him to park on the narrow mountain road. The bus rocked back and forth and the driver panicked. He simply screamed for all who could fit to get on board and hold on to each other. He wasn't waiting too much longer.

Brad checked Rosa again; the baby was already in the birth canal. She couldn't get on a bus now and he couldn't leave her.

"Dr. Brad, we've got to go!" Mario yelled as he tried to pick up his sister. She screamed out in pain and he stopped. Looking at Brad, he asked, "What can we do? We can't die up here!"

The baby crowned and Jose frantically grabbed his wife's hand with one of his own and used his other to rub her forehead. He made no attempt to leave, but the fearful pressure in that tent was palpable. Just then the wind caught a flap on the tent and within seconds, tore it off. By this time, the second bus was loaded. Medical team members were yelling for Brad to bring the girl and get on the bus. Brad, Mario, and Jose tried to get their arms under Rosa, only to hear her terrifying scream of pain.

Brad knew her pain was too severe for any travel and now he was concerned for the baby's position in the birth canal. The delivery had reached a critical stage. He yelled, "Give me ten more minutes! Ten more minutes!"

Several of the other doctors tried to convince the bus driver to wait, but to no avail. Brad watched the faces of his teammates looking out the back window. He could see their looks of panic mixed with defeat as the vehicle started to rock more severely from the fierce gusts. The driver hit the accelerator, yelled for all to be quiet and to hold on, and rapidly started down the mountain.

Brad looked back at Rosa and saw the mixture of pain and fear etched in her face. Taking her hand, he told her it would be okay, but that now, she needed to push as hard as she could. Within minutes, a baby was in Brad's hands. Looking up at the baby's father, Brad saw sheer horror on his face. Jose dropped

Rosa's hand and ran out of the tent screaming in Spanish, words Brad couldn't understand.

Cutting the cord, Brad handed the baby to Mario as he cared for Rosa. Mario silently looked at his nephew, who had been born with a cleft palate. Mario laid the baby in his sister's arms and began to cry. Rosa, having seen her little boy, just stared off into the distance.

Brad spoke up, "We can fix this!" But at that moment, his first priority was to safely and quickly remove the placenta before the storm worsened. He focused on his immediate task.

As Brad cared for his patient, Mario began to explain that a baby born with a cleft palate was believed to be cursed. Before Brad could argue, the sides of the tent were completely blown away. Knowing survival was unlikely if this was just the beginning of the storm, he began to pray. The screaming of the wind picked up and after looking out at the deserted village, Brad yelled, "Mario! Is there any kind of shelter anywhere?"

Mario thought. "There's a cave in the mountain where I used to play as a boy. But it's not close."

Brad picked up parts of the tent and put them over Rosa and the baby. He ran to what was left of a supply cabinet and grabbed a pillowcase, filling it with formula, straws that purified water, cans of food, first aid supplies, and any medicine he could find. Then he stuffed the filled case into a large bucket and passed it, along with the baby, to Mario. Brad then spread the bloody blanket over his arms, picked Rosa up, and said, "Lead the way to the cave!"

Mario pointed and together they began to trudge through streams of water that had begun rushing down from the top of the mountain. As the water-saturated the ground, the men had to weave in different directions as they dodged falling trees and large fronds. With each step, the wind was pushing steadily against their strides. After what seemed hours of struggling, Mario pointed to a large opening. They rushed into what Brad prayed would be a safe harbor.

Brad cleared a large area, spread the blanket out, and laid Rosa and the baby on one end and wrapped the other end over the two. He and Mario then placed rocks across the cave entrance to keep the water from breaching the opening. Exhausted, the men collapsed down beside Rosa and the baby.

After a few hours, Brad regained some of his strength and walked to the cave's entrance. The might of the mixture of wind and water had cleared all vegetation from the entire area that they had just traveled. There wasn't a single tree standing as water rushed downhill like a raging river. Brad thought he had lived through storms in Atlanta and on the coast of Georgia, but nothing had prepared him for the brutal force of this catastrophic furry.

The storm continued to rage throughout the night and the cave was engulfed in utter darkness. The only other sound was the scream of a hungry baby. Brad felt around the baby's deformed little mouth and knew there was no way for the infant to nurse. The liquid poured out of the sides of his small face whenever Rosa tried to hold him to her breasts. As hard as they all tried to help feed him, with the darkness, nothing could be done until the morning's light. Wanting Rosa to get some rest, Brad carefully crept over and reached for her little son. He rocked the baby until he finally quieted down. Mario held Rosa's hand and sang a sweet Spanish song until brother and sister were sleeping as well. Brad grabbed the pillowcase from the bucket, emptied it, and tore it into strips. He then secured the baby up against his bare chest with the torn fabric pieces. Using the remainder of the pillowcase as a blanket for the child and leaning against the wall of the cave, he and the baby closed their eyes. The worn-out doctor pictured Anne and his children back at home, safe and warm. He couldn't even think of how his wife would deal with the children when she heard the news of the storm. He knew Anne would imagine the worst. Tears rolled down his cheeks as the gravity of his situation became all too clear.

The next two days brought no relief from the roar of rushing water. However, the rocks at the entry held the water at bay and at least they were now dry. The winds were subsiding, but the flooding grew worse. Brad had taught Rosa how to take the cap from the formula bottle and, little by little, feed her baby. They had put the bucket out to catch some of the rainwater and, thankfully, the straws were invaluable for purifying. But by now, the already meager food supply was running low. Brad closed his eyes and prayed for a quick rescue, though he doubted anyone would believe they had survived. And with the flooding, was a rescue even possible? Would any routes have remained intact and passable?

CHAPTER THIRTY-FOUR

HE'S MISSING

L ITTLE B RAD WALKED INTO THE GREAT ROOM WHILE A NNE WAS flipping through a magazine article on Atlanta activities for the month. "Mama, we need to cut the TV on. I was just looking at my iPad. Something bad is going on in Guatemala."

Anne grabbed the remote and clicked on the first national news channel she came to as her heart raced. The lead story was about an unprecedented and rare hurricane that had formed off the coast of Guatemala and was expected to increase to a possible category three by the time it hit Guatemala City. The pictures of the wind destruction of several harbors seemed unimaginable. She held her breath as she listened to the worsening reports.

Anne rushed over, grabbed a card, and called the emergency number that Brad had left; there was no dial tone. She called the hospital's administration office and asked if anyone had an update on the teams in Guatemala. No one had heard a word. Anne felt her arms and legs began to shake; she tried to breathe as deeply as she could. Deciding not to call any of the other spouses in case they hadn't seen the news, she sat down. The frightening feeling that she had felt on the plane had returned. That awful feeling that led her to ask the children to pray for sunny skies. *Where are you, my love? Call me. Let me know you're okay. You've got to come home to me, Brad. I need to see your face.*

Just then her cell rang. She grabbed it. "Hello."

It was Pete Williams, the surgeon who had traveled with the Guatemala medical teams. Anne could hear the hesitance in his voice. "Anne, I don't know how to tell you this . . . but Brad's missing. He was right at the end of a delivery when the buses came to take us to safety. He wouldn't leave his patient and the last bus wouldn't wait."

Anne fell to her knees. "Is there a search team looking for him?"

"Anne, I'm afraid there's nothing to rescue. Everything was practically gone when we pulled out. The clinic . . . our supplies . . . everything. There's no way to get to where he was with all of the flooding. The people in Antigua are afraid that no one on the mountain could have survived this storm."

Fury filled every cell in Anne's body. "You can't tell me that, Pete! I won't listen. If Brad was dead, my heart would be dead too. And it's not. I don't care who you have to hire or what you have to do . . . You have to send a rescue team! Get somebody to where my husband is."

"I don't think you understand—" Pete interrupted.

"No, Pete! You don't understand!" Anne said in her panic. "Brad is alive. You need to get everyone you can find to go look for him."

"Anne, the minute we can get up the mountain, I promise you we will."

"Don't call me back until you've found him," Anne ordered as she slammed the phone down. Then she thought of Margie and her family. She called their church. The pastor answered.

"This is Anne Young. I'm calling about the storm in Guatemala."

He reported good news. "The orphanages and our staff are fine. They were in a protected area and have no significate damage and only minimal flooding in their area, but none near any of their buildings."

"That's wonderful, thank you." Anne put the phone down.

There was a knock at the door. Little Brad ran to open it, hoping it was his daddy. Having overheard his mama's call, he knew Margie and her family were safe. He was sure his daddy was safe too.

As the door opened, Charles Billings asked if he could come inside. Weeping, Anne ran up to Charles. He took her in his arms and said, "I know, Anne. I just heard. What can I do?"

"You can make them, make them find him. I can't live without him. You can help, help make them find him, Charles!" Anne could hardly breathe as she sobbed.

He looked at Anne; her suffering was unbearable for him. He grasped her shoulders and said, "I promise. I will do every-thing in my power to help find Brad. Is there anything I can do for you or your family?"

"Just find him for me, please, Charles," she pleaded.

Charles turned and rushed out. He drove straight to

Peachtree DeKalb Airport. Finding Chuck washing the wheels on his plane, Charles asked, "How good are you at landing on a washed-out runway?"

Chuck looked confused. "What are you talking about?"

"Brad Young is missing in Guatemala. The storm has washed away about everything near Antigua."

"I've been on rescue missions before. Don't see why I can't help now. But we need a plan," Chuck said. "Things have to be well planned for this kind of mission."

Both men went into the hanger, sat down at an old metal table, and started putting their plan in place.

Chuck began, "The way I see it, we have several major problems. The first thing is we don't know where Brad is," he sighed, "or if he is . . . The second is that it's hard to land a plane in a city where everyone is suddenly starving and in a panic. They'll storm the plane looking for food and water. The third thing is how do we get Brad to the airport if we find him? The plane will be destroyed in this situation unless he's right there ready to board. Is there any kind of runway that's intact, not flooded?" Chuck asked.

"I don't know but I'll find out. Now, if I understand you, you're saying the teams have to find him first and get him to the airport," Charles questioned, then said, "You take care of getting supplies on the plane that we can dump off to the people when we first land. Give me twenty-four hours to find a rescue team able and willing to search. Pete Williams is still in Antigua and he knows where Brad was last seen. He and the others can be responsible for getting a search team to Brad's last location." The two men shook hands on their plan and parted ways to start the process.

. . .

Chandler drove up with the twins; she had brought them home from their grandparent's house. She took one look at Anne and asked, "What on earth is wrong?"

Anne grabbed Chandler's hand and pulled her into the laundry room. "I just got a call. Brad's missing . . . and they think he's dead. But I know he's not."

Chandler couldn't respond. She wondered if she could even think.

Anne continued, "What am I going to do? What do I tell the girls? How do I possibly help my son? How do I face his parents?"

CHAPTER THIRTY-FIVE

TRAGIC CIRCUMSTANCES

BY NOW BRAD, MARIO, ROSA, AND THE BABY HAD BEEN IN THE cave for more than fifty-four damp hours. The wetness of the dirt was seeping into the back floor of the cave. They could feel the damp air filling every crack and crevice like cold roaming breaths. Their skin was beginning to sting from being so chapped. Even their hands and feet, all the way to their fingers and toes, were red and painful. But today, there was an even direr situation – Rosa had developed a fever and was experiencing pain throughout her body. Conditions in the cave were hardly conducive for a young mother following a difficult birth. An infection of some sort had set in, which Brad suspected was life-threatening sepsis. The most devastating part was that there was not one single thing he could do. There were no antibiotics in any of the supplies he had grabbed and he knew there was no possibility of outside help. They were desperate and alone.

· · ·

By the next day, it was evident that with her fever, pain, and bleeding, Rosa was in sepsis shock and would not survive. All Brad could think of now was what he could offer her in the way of comfort. He put her baby in her arms, sat down beside her, and reached over to touch her shoulder. He asked Mario to interpret.

"Rosa, try to tell me about your family. I'd love to hear about your mother and daddy. Your home."

The young mother looked back at the doctor and smiled while she caressed the baby. Though she didn't really speak, Brad could see the glimmer of a far-away look in her eyes and her changing expressions seemed to tell her story. He felt sure that good memories were filling her thoughts when Rosa sighed sweetly and took her last breath.

Brad took the baby from her arms and pulled the side of the blanket up to cover her body. Mario leaned down and whispered a prayer over his sister. Carefully picking her up, he carried her to the mouth of the cave and gently laid her in the rushing water. The two men stood there, gratefully watching as the water seemed to slow down, maybe out of respect. Then the river slowly carried Rosa away while each said his private goodbye.

As the men walked back to sit down, a hopeless sadness filled the cave. Its raw gloom closed in like a thick, grasping fog. Only the urgency of the hungry screams of Rosa's baby broke the quiet and morbid atmosphere. Brad glanced at the two bottles of formula that remained; with the cleft palate, so much milk spilled out of his small mouth. Two bottles, even stretched with water, wouldn't last more than two days. With the exception of that small amount of formula and several containers of soup, their supplies were gone.

As the following day progressed, an occasional blue patch of sky appeared and the weather began to normalize. But the flooding only intensified. There was no chance of leaving the cave with any safety, especially with a weak newborn in his arms. Brad walked over to a small pocket of rocks in the cave and lowered his head. As he mourned the death of Rosa, he prayed for all the others who he imagined had lost their lives during the cruel devastation of the storm. He prayed for the baby, one whose parents had not even given him a name. He prayed for his young companion, who had been amazingly stoic throughout the whole ordeal for his tender age of sixteen. And he prayed for himself as he thought of Anne, his son, and the twins. He had to find a way to get back to his family, to his parents, and to all the love he had so taken for granted.

While Brad prayed, the remembrance of the many miracles he had experienced in his medical career began to paint a more positive picture in his thoughts. A peace and strength arose both in his body and his heart. He remembered Anne's words, "Nothing is impossible with God."

Brad felt a new kind of hope surge from deep within. It was as if he could hear the voice of God whispering, almost audibly, "Trust Me." At that moment, he knew he would make it home somehow. He would make it back to Anne.

Walking over to Mario, who was trying to feed the crying infant, Brad put his hand on the young man's shoulder and said, "Mario, what would you like to name your nephew?"

Without hesitation, Mario answered, "Jose."

Brad looked into his deep, brown eyes and said, "Mario, you, Jose, and I will make it out of here. You can trust what I'm telling you."

CHAPTER THIRTY-SIX

DIFFICULT WORDS

ANNE WALKED INTO THE DINING ROOM. SHE JUST STOOD THERE, looking out of the window. Her world had taken on a very different and sullen color. A sad film was skewing any positive perspective. Suddenly, she saw a bright-red cardinal land on the railing along the front steps. Her thoughts began to question. Watching that small creature reminded her of the powerful source of all that is. Nothing was really left up to a hopeless chance. She was now even more convinced that Brad was alive. At that moment, it was like she could feel the actual beating of his heart. It was as if that familiar beating was speaking to the depths of her own heart. She called to Chandler and the children and asked them to take a seat in the great room.

"Your daddy needs our help," Anne began, she repeated, "He needs our help now."

Gretchen frowned and looked up at her mother as she questioned, "Why does Daddy need our help?"

Patsy ran over to wrap her arms around her mother. "We'll help. How do we help?"

Little Brad had been sitting quietly on the floor with his dog. He looked up at Anne and said, "I'll help too, Mom."

"What can we do?" Chandler asked as she wiped her eyes.

Anne told the children about the storm and how several people were missing. She tried to choose her words carefully. "Evidently there was a great deal of flooding and there are lots of people who were hurt very badly." Then their mother smiled and said, "But we are blessed, we have a promise from God. He will never leave or forsake your daddy and he will be with him in times of trouble. We can start praying . . . for the country of Guatemala, for the people of Guatemala . . . and for your daddy's safe return."

Little Brad was eager to begin. "I have a prayer, Mom." He bowed his head and prayed for all the people who were trying to find those that were lost. He prayed that each and every one would be found. When he finished, Gretchen began to pray and asked God to keep her daddy safe and to make sure he wasn't sad. Patsy asked God to give him a friend to be with him until he was found. Chandler joined in as if she had supernatural sight and prayed that God would bring Brad food and water.

Anne closed by praying, "Please, God, bring Brad back to us. More importantly, help him feel our love and prayers, and your strength."

Then all five got into Anne's car and drove over to the Youngs' to tell Brad's parents all they had learned. Anne knew her words would break their hearts. How could she share such tragic news with those whom she loved so dearly?

When they arrived, the children rushed in but had been told

in advance not to say anything until Anne could tell them about their daddy. By the time Anne and Chandler made their way to the kitchen, the twins were already in their grandmother's lap. She looked up, so confused, and asked, "What's going on? Is something wrong with Brad?"

Brad Sr. was trimming shrubbery in the backyard and had seen them drive up. He walked through the back door into the kitchen and saw Little Brad standing by himself, crying. When he saw his granddaddy, he buried his face in his BB's shirt. Anne walked into the kitchen and took Brad Sr.'s hand. With tears, she said, "We need to talk."

Brad Sr.'s cell phone interrupted. He answered, "No, I haven't spoken with her yet. She and the children just came in."

Anne hurried over, grabbed his phone, and laid it on the table. "Dad, I need to tell you before you hear from anyone else."

Little Brad looked at his grandfather and said, "They can't find Daddy, BB."

Brad Sr. turned his head toward Anne. "What does he mean?"

Anne sat down and explained everything she knew. Her father in-law walked over to take his wife's hand and asked, "Who's looking for him and how do they know he's missing?"

"I have told you as much as I know. Charles Billings is getting some people together to go to Guatemala to find out exactly what happened with Brad's team. He promised he will keep me informed with anything he learns."

Tears ran down Anne's cheeks. Patsy sat back, then held her granddaughters tighter. They all realized there was so much to say, but no words to say it.

Brad Sr. walked over to Anne and took her in his arms. "They'll find him, honey. Brad has always been very resourceful. They'll find him."

Patsy took her grandmother's face in her hands as she said, "Gaga, we can help Daddy! We can say prayers for him and ask God to give him friends to help."

Gretchen added, "We can pray he has some food to eat, too."

Patsy looked at all three of her grandchildren and realized they needed to be her priority for now. The thought of them without their daddy was more than she could bear. She gave each of the three a kiss and said, "And we can pray that God will look after him and bring him back to all of us safely!"

Brad Sr. picked his phone up and called Charles Billings. "Anne's here. Tell me what's going on. What can I do to help?"

CHAPTER THIRTY-SEVEN

TRUST ME

THAT NIGHT IN THE CAVE WAS BEYOND BRUTAL. THE temperature dropped significantly as the flooding volume continued to increase, allowing it to creep through the rock barrier and into the cave. Even crouching as far back as possible, the dampness of the pooling water was a serious concern. Besides, there was less than half of a single bottle of formula remaining; the other food supplies were totally exhausted. Brad didn't sleep that night as he and Mario took turns keeping little Jose nestled against their bodies to keep him dry and warm. The men were still awake as the morning light began to appear through the opening of the cave. While Brad sat there, he remembered the words that had been so clear after his prayer.

He whispered, "I do trust you, Lord."

At that moment, a miracle occurred. The sound of the rushing water seemed to subside and even though water continued to flow, the volume was less and the current had slowed. Brad walked to the cave entrance and saw that the puddle inside the cave was now draining out.

Mario tapped Brad on the shoulder. "Dr. Brad, in a couple of hours, we should be able to leave the cave."

Brad nodded in agreement, but wondered what would be waiting for them outside. Would there be any possibility of making it down the mountain on foot? By now he had also realized that he was getting sick. A cough that had only been a nuisance for the last couple of days had deepened and he could read his new chills. He had a fever. Looking down at the floor of the cave, he saw how damp and muddy last night had been. That had not helped his worsening condition.

Calling to Mario, who was trying his best to feed the baby the last of the formula, Brad said, "Mario, grab anything you can find that is dry to wrap the baby inside. We're not going to take a chance on any more rain. We're leaving now." He knew that if his own health was further compromised, the situation would be untenable for Mario. Brad was determined to somehow get this young man and the baby to safety. As they stepped out of the cave into the slippery mud, Brad wondered if the terrain ahead was even passable. But there was no other option. With only one remaining straw for clean water, no food, and no formula, they had to take the risk.

Concern for losing their footing became all too real when Mario slipped several times. Brad was forced to formulate a safer plan. He took off his shirt and tore it into strips. Tying the strips together, he put one end around Mario's waist and around the baby, and the other end around his own waist to secure their connection. He explained to Mario that they were going to find anything that was rooted, would grab ahold of it until they were ready to take another forward step, and then repeat the process. This would be a homemade safety line as they carefully made the descent.

Hours later, when they finally reached the area that had once been Mario's village, they found it was totally obliterated. Not even the foundation of the supply building was intact. Brad thought back over how far they had driven to get to that first village. *How in the world can we make that same distance on foot—with my health and the baby?* It all seemed hopeless. But Brad kept hearing the words, "Trust Me." He was feeling worse, they were so tired, and the baby was screaming from hunger. Trust was hard.

Just then Brad stopped and listened. Mario started screaming, "Dr. Brad! Dr. Brad!"

Both had heard the sound of some sort of engine in the distance.

CHAPTER THIRTY-EIGHT

A SHARED SACRIFICE

BRAD SR. WALKED OVER TO HIS WIFE AND BEGAN TO REPEAT EVERY word that Charles Billings had shared earlier. But by this time, Patsy was inconsolable. Anne walked over and put her arms around her as Dr. Young explained Charles's plan. Patsy looked at her husband and pleaded, "You've got to find him!" Brad Sr. tenderly reiterated that the plan was already in process and that they simply needed to trust the men involved. His wife looked at his face and said, "You're not going to help, are you? It's because of me."

Leaning down, he gave her a kiss. "That's not true, darling. This is a job for younger men . . . I'd only be in the way." Looking at Anne, he continued, "We're going to pray for these men's success. I have no doubt that our son is coming home." Certainty filled his every word.

Charles was checking his phone every two minutes, making sure he hadn't missed a call. Evidently, there was still no word about Brad's plight as he drove back to Peachtree DeKalb Airport. He pulled up alongside Chuck's plane as the pilot was just exiting the cockpit.

"Charles, we've got a problem," Chuck began. "We've got about fifty physicians from Doctor's Hospital that want to go with us. We don't need fifty, but we could sure use ten. But even with ten, my plane won't hold all of the supplies we need and ten passengers. I've called Dobbins Airforce Base and they're willing to lend us a cargo plane, but it won't be equipped and ready for another twenty-four hours."

"Hold on. Let me make a call," Charles said as he pulled out his cell. One of his classmates from medical school was the flight surgeon at Dobbins. He was hoping his colleague's pull could speed things up.

Calling Butch Powell, Charles explained their situation and the need to get the plane airborne as quickly as possible. He asked for medical supplies, even those required for any possible surgery, to be loaded along with the food and water that was sure to be needed.

Butch called back within twenty minutes. "We have the plane, all the supplies you requested, and a copilot . . . and, Charles, I'm coming too." He paused as he remembered and added, "Brad and I became very good friends when he was dating my sister at LSU years ago. We still talk regularly during football season. We'll have this big bird ready to take off in about six hours."

Charles put his phone down as he high-fived Chuck. Their plan had commenced. The two sat down and reviewed a list of volunteer doctors. With no idea what they would actually be facing, they agreed to pick ten physicians in ten different specialties. The two men divided the list and called each one, telling them to pack one bag with anything they felt was medically necessary for their particular needs. All were to meet at Dobbins by six o'clock.

As the two men sat at that old rusty table in the hangar, making a checklist of supplies, Brad Sr. walked in and quietly said, "I'm thankful for what you gentlemen are planning. I just spoke with Butch Powell. Just know that any of your financial needs are covered. As much as I would like to join you, I'm not one of the men you need on this trip. The last thing I'd want to do is take the place of someone that's important to your success. But at least I can make sure the financial side is not a concern." He looked at the two men as his eyes filled. "This way I can assure that anything that needs to be done, will be done." He patted both men on the shoulders and turned to walk out. Over his shoulder he called, "God be with you . . . and with my son."

By six o'clock the plane was loaded and the doctors were filing in with bags full of supplies for any medical need they could imagine. The back of the plane had already been loaded with food, water, diapers, and other sanitary needs. As the last two physicians were boarding, Anne's car pulled up. She parked and hurried over to the plane's stairs. Taking them quickly, she stood at the entrance, looking down the cabin. All eyes turned toward her.

"On behalf of the entire Young family, including my children, I want to thank you for the sacrifice you are making for my husband." Tears rolled down her cheeks as she moved to hug each of the doctors. Finishing, she bowed her head and prayed, "Father, I ask success for this mission and blessings on each and every person on this plane. Please get them there safely, bless them for wanting to help the many who are suffering so badly. And, Father . . . please let them bring my husband home. In Jesus' name, Amen." She turned and walked down the stairs as the plane's door closed and the engines roared to life.

Inside, Chuck came rushing out of the cockpit and shouted to the volunteers who were strapped in around the sides of the plane, "We just received a message! A road crew has found an American."

CHAPTER THIRTY-NINE

ARE YOU DR. BRAD?

IN THE DISTANCE THERE WAS A SPUTTER OF SOME KIND OF ENGINE that was running rough. Brad and Mario began to yell in unison, "Over here! Over here!" Brad realized the rumble of the engine would more than likely drown out any cries for help. There had to be another way to get the attention of whoever might be near, but the two men had nothing that would make a noise above the volume of their shouts. With everything being so wet, even a former boy scout couldn't possibly start a fire.

As Brad continued racking his brain for ideas, the engine sputtered out. Both men yelled with every fiber of their being. They heard the engine come to life once again and its sound magnified as if it were coming closer. The men continued to yell until Brad's voice was gone. However, his silence only encouraged Mario to shout even louder.

The engine stalled once again and, by now, the baby was crying, and Mario was still yelling. Brad could hardly whisper, but was trying to bring any possible sound out of his lungs to add volume. Firing up again, the source of the engine was visible within minutes. A Jeep was nearing as Brad untied the tether and both men ran toward help.

When the three reached the Jeep, the driver took the baby as the two men climbed in the back. Then he handed the baby back to Mario and looked at Brad. "Are you Dr. Brad?"

Brad nodded and whispered, "Yes."

"We have to get you to the hospital as soon as possible. There's a plane on the way."

Brad rested his head back against the seat as he looked at Mario and the screaming little boy. The knowledge that their lives had been saved was overwhelming; his eyes overflowed. He thought back to the culture that would cause a young father to desert his wife and baby, fearing a curse; to a young mother who lovingly cradled her baby as her own life was slipping away. He immediately thought of a young woman named Betsy, who had traded her life for the life of a son as well. He recalled his prayer and the trust that God had reinforced with the sound of a distant engine. Closing his eyes, Brad could feel peace. He was now confident that he would hold Anne and his children once again.

When they pulled up to the hospital, the other physicians from their teams rushed out to greet Brad, a friend they imagined they had seen for the last time days ago. With one look, the doctors immediately knew he was ill. After checking him out, it became evident just how sick Brad and the baby really were. Brad was diagnosed with pneumonia and started on antibiotics and fluids. Mario was basically fine, except for bruises, scrapes, and general exhaustion. A nurse tried to feed the baby as a pediatrician prepared a device that would make sucking easier.

Helping the child receive and retain nourishment was critical. Surgery could be scheduled later that would change everything about his little life, but not until he was at least three months old. As for now, he was safe, dry, and warm. His tummy was full and a kind nurse was rocking Little Jose to sleep.

Two hours later the cargo plane landed on a bumpy, flooded airstrip outside of Antigua. The strip had been constructed years ago to export coffee and was nearly unrecognizable after the storm. It wasn't a pretty landing as the plane rose from each bump, but the fuselage eventually came to a safe stop. The U.S. teams that were already helping at the hospital sent old canvas-covered trucks for the supplies and the new doctors. Each truck was staffed by two guards carrying automatic rifles to safe-guard against desperate crowds storming the trucks for food and water. They needed to get all of the supplies to the hospital where they could be fairly distributed to the many who were in need.

As the physicians, along with Charles, Butch, and Chuck, arrived in Antigua, the sighting of an American had been confirmed. That American was a very sick Brad.

Brad's fever raged for two full days and nights as all of the Atlanta medical teams and local staff worked on him, the sick, and injured. The hospital was packed with hurting people of all ages with every condition imaginable. Without the skills of the medical teams from Georgia and New York, the number of fatalities would have tripled.

Mario watched his nephew get stronger day by day. Little Jose got better at taking his bottle with the new device and every feeding was more successful. His uncle loved watching him keep the milk in this mouth while he sucked and was absolutely sure he could see the baby's weight gain.

On the fourth day, Brad's fever broke and by that night he was able to take some nourishment. Soon he was actually feeling almost human again. On day eight, twenty-seven exhausted, but inspired physicians, including Brad, Charles Billings, Butch Powell, Chuck, the copilot, Mario, and his nephew, Jose, boarded the plane that had been serviced as thoroughly as possible and was now ready to take off for Atlanta.

CHAPTER FORTY

THE CALL

A WEEK EARLIER, ANNE HAD WATCHED AS HER GIRLS CLUTCHED and snuggled with their grandmother, even while they were facing their own fearful thoughts about their daddy. Little Brad sat down on the sofa next to Chandler and was holding her hand as he passed clean tissues that were needed for the constant flow of his grandmother's tears. Anne couldn't help but notice that he took a tissue for himself every now and then. With her medical history, Brad Sr. had decided to give Patsy a light sedative, then he tucked her into bed. The girls had gone in to snuggle in the bed with her and all three were now sleeping soundly.

Anne walked into the living room. She could smell the sweet fragrance of roses in a large vase. Brad Sr. continued to supply yellow roses for his wife year-round. She began to calculate how long her in-laws had been married. Anne has strong hopes for the chance at the same number of years with her Brad.

Brad Sr. was in his study, waiting by the phone. It seemed

the bricks and mortar of the house itself were holding their breath . . . waiting. She walked over to the window and focused on the beautiful day. The sun was going down and the evolving oranges, pinks, and purples were stunning. Bad news could not possibly come on such a day as this. Just then the phone rang.

Brad Sr. grabbed the receiver before it could ring a second time. "It's an American? Do they know anything else? Do they have a description? Anything?" He paced as he listened. "How long will it take them to get to the hospital? . . . If they regain the radio signal, make sure they try to get his name. I'll sit right here . . . Contact me as soon as you hear anything. Thank you for this call."

Hearing the word "American," Anne ran into the study. She stood there with her hands over her mouth, her eyes searching his face. When the call ended, Brad Sr. stood, walked over, and took her in his arms. "They found an American, a young male, and a baby. It has to be Brad."

Anne had a new sense of hope as she joined her father-in-law's confidence.

"He stayed to deliver a baby. It has to be Brad," he repeated.

Little Brad and Chandler came rushing into the room. Brad Sr. rubbed his grandson's head as Anne laid her head on Chandler's shoulder. "We should know something for sure within the next hour," Brad Sr. said.

Just then the phone rang again. He grabbed the receiver to hear Charles Billings say, "We've got him! He's really sick, but we've got fifteen doctors working on him and we can handle what appears to be pneumonia. We've got him!"

Brad Sr. collapsed into his chair and tears streamed down his cheeks. Looking at his family, he said, "They've got him.

He's alive and he's under their medical care. My son will be coming home."

Little Brad went running back to wake up his sisters and grandmother with the good news. Chandler grabbed Anne and shouted praises. Anne looked out the window once again at the ever-changing sunset and echoed Chandler's sentiments. "Yes, praise the Lord!"

Hours later, Anne's cell rang. The weakest voice she had ever heard said, "I love you, sweetheart."

She couldn't get the words out fast enough. "I love you too! I miss you so much. We're so thankful!"

Charles Billings took his phone from Brad's hand and described his condition to Anne. He was quick to add that he was receiving the best care any one person could have and was already showing the beginning signs of improvement.

Anne said, "I'll be on the next plane."

"You can't come, Anne. As much as I know you want to, it's too dangerous. There are no planes landing and this country is in total turmoil." Her countenance changed and he continued, "You have to trust us to take care of Brad and get him back to you. The hospital is full of people in need of every kind of help. I know this will be hard for you to hear, but it will probably be at least a week before we head home. In good conscience, we can't leave this situation without helping."

Somewhere in the feelings of compassion, Anne understood as he explained the magnitude of the need.

Charles could feel her disappointment and added, "Phone service is sketchy, but he'll try to call you every day. Anne, there are some things you can do to help us."

Anne perked up. "Name it.," she replied as she grabbed a pen and pad.

"When they found Brad, he was with a young man and a newborn in need of surgery. There is no home for them to go back to here, but Mario has an older brother in the United States. We've finally been able to reach him but it will be several weeks before the man can make arrangements to come get the two. Mario and the baby will be coming back to Atlanta with us. There is no way Brad will leave them here.

"You'll need newborn clothes for the little boy. Formula, diapers, everything a new baby will need. Mario and the baby will be staying with you and Brad until his brother comes to take them back to Maine to live with him and his wife."

Anne responded immediately, "Tell Brad not to worry. Everything will be ready when he gets home. And, Charles . . . thank you for bringing him back to me."

Charles thought for a moment, and with heartfelt sincerity he said, "Anne, you should know by now that there is nothing that I wouldn't do for you . . . and your family." With that, he said good-bye. Charles had no doubt that Anne understood.

CHAPTER FORTY-ONE

COMING HOME

A WEEK LATER, AS THE PLANE CONTINUED TOWARD ATLANTA, A blanket of peace seemed to cover everyone on board. Most of the doctors were reflecting on the blessing of practicing in the United States. Working with what they had access to, rather than the frustration of needing what they didn't have, had presented so many unique challenges in Guatemala. Other thoughts went to their families and then back to the families in Guatemala facing the overwhelming task of rebuilding. The common theme was the realization that most take far too much for granted; life was more than comfortable for the majority on board. Then there was Mario. He felt a deep sadness for the loss of his village, his sister Rosa, her husband Jose, and the fact that he was leaving the only life he had ever known. And now, his nephew Jose would never even know of Guatemala—the mountains, the coffee plantations, the beauty, the struggle. Little Jose would never experience or even partially understand so much of his Mayan heritage. Chuck's thoughts were thankfulness that he had a copilot. The cargo plane certainly didn't behave like any he had ever flown previously. Butch's thoughts were consumed with countless pending, unopened medical inquires back home. Then there was the possible dishonorable discharge of a fine young man that had made a stupid mistake. And all Brad could think about was pulling his family into his arms.

It wasn't long before the plane began its descent onto the Dobbins airfield and the expectation of a smooth landing this time. Soon the door of the plane opened and the medical teams exited to a hero's welcome. Most of the staff at Doctor's Hospital were waving American flags and greeting everyone as their families ran to meet them. Mario, the baby, and Brad were the last to disembark. Anne and the children were anxiously standing at the bottom of the steps. Finally, Brad slowly walked down and embraced them with the thought that nothing had ever felt that good. He couldn't let go, but knew he shouldn't hold on forever as others were waiting in line. But somehow, he didn't have it within his power to turn them loose.

Patsy and Chandler were sobbing as they hugged Brad. Patsy had just opened her arms; Brad filled them with the assurance that he was okay and home safely. Finally, father and son embraced with an intensity that took them both back to Brad's childhood.

Anne experienced every emotion possible as she now had her husband back. She hurt so deeply when she imagined what he had likely endured. It was obvious that he had lost a lot of weight and his pale complexion made her doubt the reports of improving health as she reached for his hand and slowly led him to the car.

Brad Sr. came over to the car window as Brad lowered it. "Son, I'll be taking your place at the office for the next two weeks to give you time to recoup. We'll talk later."

Sitting around the dinner table with his family later that evening, Brad tried to explain all that had happened in Guatemala. There was so much he left out, not just because he didn't want his children to hear, but if he was honest, he feared reliving it. And he couldn't imagine how Anne would react. How could he tell his family about a new father running away into certain death because of a supposed curse? How could he share watching a new mother take her last breath because there was insufficient medical care available and how her face was such a haunting memory as he thought of her body floating away? As more memories surfaced, Brad excused himself to go upstairs. He took a hot shower in hopes that he could wash away the constant memories and remaining pain.

When the children heard the shower, all three asked their mother if she thought their daddy was all well yet. Anne tried to explain that it would take time for him to put some very sad memories behind him. Their job now was to love him through the next few weeks as he recuperated.

Just then the doorbell rang. It was Charles with Mario and the baby. Because of the disaster and streamlined protocol, all of the immigration paperwork had been completed and he had the documentation to pass along to Mario's brother when he came to take the two to their new home. Anne invited Charles to come inside and have some dinner. As a bachelor, he more than graciously accepted. She fixed plates for both men as

Mario taught the twins how to use the special device for the baby's bottle.

Then Charles handed the bottle to Anne; she began to feed the little boy as she kissed his cheeks and his little hands. Focusing on that sweet face and his brown eyes, she thought of his mother and the love that this little one would never experience. It was all such a reminder of Betsy and her baby boy. Tears filled her eyes and she looked up at Charles. "It's so sad to see a baby who will never know the complete love of his mother."

Charles smiled at Anne. "That baby can never know a more wonderful love than he's getting from you right now."

Anne stood, walked over to Charles, and gave him a kiss on his cheek as she patted to burp the baby. "We're having tea cakes and coffee ice cream for dessert. The children and Mario will have some with you. If you'll excuse me, I'm going to put this tired little boy to bed."

Mario stood and Anne quickly asked, "Excuse me, Mario. Is it okay if I put Jose to bed?" He walked over and gave his little nephew a kiss, then nodded to Anne.

After things settled down and Charles had left, Anne prepared several bottles for later and in the morning. The girls were already in bed, Mario was sleeping in the extra twin bed in Little Brad's room, and the baby was asleep in one of the twin's crib in the guestroom. Brad had been asleep for hours. Sobbing as she stood in the shower, Anne asked herself, "How am I going to approach this man? How am I going to bring him back to where we were before?" She had missed him so badly. She missed the Brad she had left in Guatemala two weeks ago. She missed their unspoken words and their familiar intimacy.

Anne slipped into her prettiest silk and lace nightgown. She tried to be quiet so that she wouldn't disturb her husband. She slowly got into the bed and carefully pulled the comforter up to her shoulders. She leaned over, lightly kissing his check, then turned away. Brad stirred slightly. Moving closer, he softly moved his arm to her waist. Anne felt a tender kiss on her neck and turned toward him. He gave her a brief kiss, then a long, intense kiss. He ran his fingers along her cheek and whispered, "I didn't think I'd ever have you in my arms again."

Anne could feel his tears mingle with hers. "I was afraid too, my love. You see, in your arms is the only place I feel at peace, safe."

He kissed her again and again.

A sense of newness was evident the next morning. The intimacy of their night had reignited the fullness of their relationship. Yet, the next week was still not easy for Brad. Anne would watch as he sat in the study deep in thought, his mind seeming a million miles away. She kept busy and seemed to fall more in love with little Jose each day. Mario was trying his best to adjust to this new life, while the children were back to the routine of all their activities. All of this added normalcy and the feeling that their household was slowly healing.

All too soon for Anne, Mario's brother and his wife arrived to take their two new family members from Guatemala back to their home. Telling Mario and the baby goodbye was difficult for everyone, but excruciating for Anne.

~

As he watched her say goodbye, Brad had seen Anne's love develop more each day for the baby. He could tell how hard parting with little Jose was for her as he caught a glimpse of her tears. Walking upstairs, he shook his head and murmured, "I shouldn't have brought the baby here. I've only caused more sadness for Anne."

As two weeks passed, the thought of returning to his practice, the laughter of his children, and his warm relationship with his wife gave Brad a fragile expectation of regaining his life. But during each day, the weight of the sad memories would surface at the most unexpected moments. At times, he could still feel the damp cold of the cave as he would get caught up in the persistent sounds of Rosa's last breaths, the death rattle that was unmistakable. Then there was that moment that had impacted his life in a way he would only come to understand with the passing of time — "Trust Me." Yet, even with those comforting words, no matter how Brad looked at his future, he saw no clear path back.

CHAPTER FORTY-TWO

FATHERLY ADVICE

BRAD WAS TO BEGIN SEEING PATIENTS THE NEXT MONDAY. THAT was what he and his father had planned. When that morning arrived, he put his hand over his ears when he heard the alarm. He reached over for Anne, but she was already downstairs making breakfast. Picking up his cell, he called his father. "Dad, can you take another week for me? I can't go back today . . . not yet."

"I'll go to the office today, son, but I'll come over tonight and we'll talk. I need to know what's going on with you."

"I don't know how to explain anything, Dad. Walking into that hospital is just not possible. I can't do it yet."

"We don't need to talk about this right this minute," his father offered. "Just get some rest today and I'll see you tonight. I love you, son."

"Thanks, Dad. I love you too."

Sitting up on the edge of the bed, Brad wondered about his

continuing restlessness. He walked into the bathroom and turned on the shower.

Anne was in the kitchen with his coffee ready. She was expecting him to come down the stairs at any moment. By now, Brad must have been awakened by the alarm, along with the familiar smell of his favorite coffee. Just then, she heard her son blowing for his sisters. Calling the girls, she loaded backpacks with their lunch, and ushered them out the door with a kiss. Now, with the house empty, she had time to go upstairs and check on her husband. She walked in the bedroom and saw that the bathroom door was closed. He evidently wasn't getting ready to go to the office; her concerns rushed to the surface.

Feverishly knocking, she asked, "Are you okay?"

Brad opened the door. "I'm getting better, sweetheart, but I'm staying home today."

"You've explained what you went through to a certain extent, my love," Anne began. She reached for his hand and added, "But I need to know it all. I need to know how to help you."

"I just need more time, Anne." He walked past her toward the dresser. "I just need more time."

"Would you like to come downstairs? We can have a cup of coffee right by ourselves."

"Sure," Brad said as he dressed in jeans and a blue sweatshirt.

After they walked downstairs, he sat down to drink his coffee but talked very little. He wasn't interested in talking about Guatemala, instead he asked questions about the Center. He seemed concerned as to whether things were getting done there. But as he talked, she could tell his mind wasn't on the Center at all. He just didn't want to talk about Guatemala.

After assuring him that all programs for the children and women couldn't be better, he walked back into the great room, sat down in his chair, and picked up a medical journal. Anne put their cups in the dishwasher as she sighed; he still seemed so distant. She walked over and stood beside him. He just ignored her and continued reading. With tears, she walked upstairs to dress for the day. Brad looked up; his eyes followed her faint shadow as she disappeared.

That afternoon when the children came home from school, they were surprised to see their daddy at home again. He was sitting in his chair staring at the television that hadn't even been clicked on. Little Brad asked if he would like to go with him to baseball practice.

"Maybe tomorrow," Brad answered before getting up and walking back up to their bedroom.

Little Brad left after shaking his head at his mother. Anne called the girls into the kitchen. "Let's get you two a snack. Then you need to take Bo Jr. across the street to the park." When the twins left, Anne realized Brad's actions were much more complicated than she had understood. She watched out of the dining room window as Gretchen and Patsy walked out the back door with the dog. She asked, "How can I hide my concerns and protect our children? Each day seemed to just get harder."

Chandler came over later that afternoon with another basket of tea cakes that Patsy had made for Brad from Estelle's recipe. But as she walked in the kitchen, he saw the tray she had brought over earlier that week. It hadn't even been touched.

She looked at Anne and asked, "What's going on? What's wrong?"

"I don't know . . . he's just sad," Anne answered. "He's not himself. He seems preoccupied all the time. I can see that's it beginning to affect the children. This whole household is sad." Her eyes welled up. "I caught the twins huddled in their room last week; they were sobbing. They had tried to take their favorite position of sitting in their daddy's lap. He had said, 'Maybe later,' then he got up and walked out to the patio."

Anne's tears spilled.

"It's like he doesn't want to be bothered. Or he doesn't want his thoughts interrupted," she explained. "It's the saddest thing."

Chandler thought back; she remembered hearing how Brad had been as a young boy when his mother's sickness took her away for so many years. She was afraid that same sort of despondency might have returned. It was so hard to watch him turn inward beyond the reach of his family's love. That long-ago depression was said to have lasted for over a year before Brad gradually returned to the young man he'd been before his mother left.

Setting the tea cakes down, Chandler said, "Call me if there's anything Patsy or I can do to help." She took a handkerchief out of her pocket and wiped her eyes as she slowly walked out and back to her car. She felt she needed to talk with Brad Sr., but she also knew that what she had heard would be hard for him to take in.

When Patsy's nurse pulled into the Youngs' driveway, Dr. Young was just getting home from the office. She asked if they could speak together out in the garden; it would be better if

Patsy didn't hear what she needed to say. The two walked over to a table and chairs that sat on the patio.

"Dr. Young, it's happening again."

He asked, "You're talking about Brad?"

"He's gone into a shell. Just like when his mother left."

"How do you know for sure?" Brad Sr. asked.

"I just know."

"That settles it," Brad Sr. said as he stood. "After dinner I'm going over to talk with him. I've been worried for a while now. He seems cordial enough, but he's not Brad. And when he's like this, I know he's hurting somewhere deep, a place that's next to impossible to reach. I need to find out what really happened in Guatemala."

As they walked to the house, Chandler told him about the episode with the twins and how everyone in the family was now feeling the strain. "Dr. Young, they've been the happiest family. How are we going to fix that boy and help him turn the corner?"

"We're going to pray and we're going to find out the details. We have to understand why there is this complete reversal in the life he was leading."

At seven o'clock, Brad Sr. walked into his son's home. Anne was in the kitchen cleaning up from dinner. The twins ran up to their granddaddy to ask if they could sit in his lap while they read him their history lesson. Anne heard the question from the other room and started to cry.

Little Brad came into the room and asked, "BB, can we throw a baseball afterwards?"

Brad Sr. sat down with the girls as they read, then he went outside and threw the baseball with his grandson until the street lights came on. When he came back inside, he walked over and took Anne in his arms. She tried to control her tears, but failed miserably. It was the first time she had felt warmly hugged since Brad's hugs at the airport. "Where's my son?" he asked.

"He's sitting in the chair up in the bedroom," Anne replied.

Brad Sr. walked upstairs and into the bedroom. He quietly closed the door. "Son, what's going on?"

"I don't really want to talk about it, Dad," Brad answered.

"I understand, but we're going to talk. This has to be dealt with right now. You're hurting your wife, your children, and everyone who loves you . . . including me. I can't watch you go through this again. The last time I saw this behavior was after your mother left, when you felt totally deserted."

Brad looked down at the floor. His father took a seat in the chair beside his son.

"Now your wife and your children feel deserted . . . because of something I don't understand; you've left your life."

"Dad, you don't know how it feels . . . to feel like such a failure."

"Oh yes I do, son. I watched your mother suffer for years and there was nothing I could do to help her. I've lost mothers in childbirth, babies that were stillborn or had horrible physical issues . . . I watched my parents die. There was not one thing I could do to stop the diseases that ravaged their bodies. Brad, you are not God. And neither am I. We can only do what we can do." He paused and added, "We have to understand that we're dealing with His plan and not ours. I don't always agree with it and, in fact, sometimes I despise it. But . . . I have to trust Him."

For the first time, Brad looked directly into his father's eyes. "How did you learn to trust Him, Dad?"

"I saw what happened with your mother when she came back to us. I had felt the need to trust God for years, even from the time she first got sick and through the years of failed medical treatments, during those years that we thought things were getting better . . . only to see they weren't. You see, I was only halfway trusting. But since the miracle of the day she came back home to be with us, my trust is unshakable."

Brad thought back to that day and how instrumental Anne had been in getting their house ready to bring his mother home. It had seemed as if she had been placed in his life at just the perfect time.

His father continued, "Trust grew more the day my wonderful daughter-in-law miraculously lived through giving us the twins . . . and as I witnessed miracle after miracle with so many of our patients. That's how I learned to trust Him."

"Dad, I could have helped her! I could have helped that baby's mother if I had had even one bottle of antibiotics. I'm the one who grabbed supplies to take with us to the cave. How could I have forgotten to look for antibiotics in that germ-infested situation?" He shook his head as he wiped his eyes. "I knew to do that, but I cared more about protecting my own life than taking care of hers."

"Son, you were acting quickly, trying to save four lives and get everyone to safety. How do you know there were even any antibiotics left in the village? How were you supposed to know that you'd be in that cave for days? Brad, you've lost patients here when you knew you'd done all you could."

"I didn't forget antibiotics here. I had everything I needed at my fingertips. I understood in those circumstances that it wasn't my fault." Brad paused and sighed. "But I still hated it every time."

"Of course, you did. There's not a physician worth his salt that doesn't hate the losses ... every time."

"But, Dad, she was only fifteen years old. She had her whole life ahead of her," Brad cried.

"Let's look at this more closely, son. You're feeling totally defeated because she was young and pregnant probably long before she should have been. I watched a young woman named Anne talk to a group at the Center about a girl named Donna. Your wife told about the horrors Donna had been through with multiple rapes, being forced out of her home and then having a sick baby with breathing issues. But Anne didn't give up. She figured out how to get busy and help a situation that broke her heart. Today women all over the city of Atlanta are benefitting from Anne's broken heart."

Brad looked up at his father with the initial seeds of understanding.

Brad Sr. continued, "If you're so upset over the living conditions, birth control restrictions, lack of preparations, and even more in the disadvantaged areas of the world ... let your wife be an example. Instead of sitting around feeling like a failure, turn it around and help. Ask yourself, 'If I feel this is so tragic and unfair, what can I do to make a difference in the lives of those who have touched my very soul?' From what I understand from fourteen other doctors who made that trip with you, they'll be willing to help. Your mother and I will certainly help financially out of our gratitude for your safe return."

Dr. Young reached over and put his hand on Brad's shoulder. "Let's take this tragedy and turn it into an opportunity. You probably don't realize this, but the airplane that picked you up was first filled to the brim with food, water, and medical supplies. Getting a medical plane into Guatemala to try and save your life, saved more lives than you'll ever know."

Brad put his head in his hand and said, "I'll need your help, Dad? Can we do this together?"

Brad Sr. smiled. "Have I ever let you down, son? Why don't we form a group with those physicians who went with you and those who came to help afterwards? They've seen the devastation. You all could brainstorm together on workable ideas. Lives, not only in Guatemala, but in places you've never dreamed of can possibly be improved."

A slight glimmer began to appear in Brad's eyes. He wasn't sure how, but there was no doubt in his mind that what had happened to him and Rosa might have a positive outcome after all. He could take that painful experience and change lives, make it into something that would honor Rosa. The two men stood and embraced.

"Dad, thank you. You know me, and all of my shortcomings."

"That's my responsibility as your father. Just like the responsibility you have to three children who are hungry for their father's love. And the duty you have to a wife who needs the companionship of her husband. Now, Brad, I will not be at the office tomorrow. If you're not there, you'll let a lot of people down."

"I'll be there, Dad."

The two men walked downstairs; Brad hugged his father goodbye. The twins ran over to hug their granddaddy, then looked up at their daddy. He sat down in his chair and opened his arms.

Anne watched the beautiful scene unfold and this time wiped away happy tears. She glanced at his eyes, that tender look was back as he embraced his children. That night, Brad listened to his girls read and promised to pitch baseballs with his son when he got home tomorrow. After prayers and goodnight kisses, Brad walked over to their childhood toy box and took out their old Pooh Bears. After their father had handed the bears to all three children as a sign that all was well, they smiled and placed their special stuffed friends, along with so many warm memories, beside them in their beds. Soon the three were fast asleep.

When the couple walked into their bedroom, Brad began, "Anne, I've got so much to tell you."

She gave him a kiss and said, "I've got all night to listen."

In bed that night, Brad shared every gruesome detail of the trip to Guatemala with his wife. More importantly, he shared some ideas for helping with the devastation he had witnessed. He pulled Anne close as he said, "Forgive me, Anne."

She smiled. "Remember an old movie we watched not long ago. 'Love means never having to say you're sorry.'"

He gave her a long, slow kiss as they experienced the intimacy that had always been such a healing part of their marriage. Anne fell asleep in his arms as more ideas entered Brad's mind, or maybe they actually entered his heart. He could still see the face of that young, fifteen-year-old mother. Finally, he closed his eyes and whispered, "Rosa, your life was not in vain. You and I are going to help a lot of people."

CHAPTER FORTY-THREE

A PROMISE KEPT

THE NEXT TWO YEARS OF BRAD'S LIFE WERE FULLY INVESTED IN keeping his promise to Rosa. He first called a meeting of all of the physicians who traveled with him to Guatemala or came to help in the aftermath of the storm. He discussed his ideas of working to establish a network of clinics and training facilities for the local residents. He felt their initial priority should be hygiene, eyesight conditions, and basic first aid. His peers were in agreement, but all understood the plan needed to be taken even further as this initiative became a reality. Doctor's Hospital had just hired a new administrator who was young and enthusiastic. Brad scheduled a meeting with him. Walking into Sid Hudgins' office the afternoon of their appointment, Brad was loaded for bear. As the two men talked, Brad offered Sid a prospectus that explained the plan he and the other physicians were hatching to help Guatemala and other countries.

Sid shook his head. "That's quite an undertaking, Dr. Young. But I had a meeting this week with an individual who may just be able to give you the help you need. A representative from Wellness Pharmaceuticals really wants to get their products into this hospital. As they were describing their services, they offered to supply mobile clinics. He showed me pictures and, Brad . . . these rolling clinics are first-class. I remember the clinic held at least three exam rooms, x-ray and ultrasound areas, a toilet, and I can't remember what else. But I'm telling you they were very nice. Much nicer than the ones we use now for mammograms."

Sid fumbled in his top drawer and then said, "Here's his card." He pulled it out and passed it to Brad. "There's also a group of young doctors at my previous hospital who really have a heart for Cuba. Hold on a minute." He looked through his rolodex, wrote a name and phone number on a piece of paper, and handed it to Brad. "When you talk to this pharmaceutical rep, keep me in the loop. The foundation has some money, in fact, quite a bit. They may be willing to help. I like what you're trying to do and with the current situations in developing countries, they can certainly use some help."

Brad stood and shook Sid's hand, thanking him for his help and his encouragement.

Anne didn't see much of Brad over the next two weeks. He was on a quest. He quickly learned there were groups of doctors all over the United States that had taken on projects for one country after another, besides the numerous charities that were helping. The uniting purpose was to take medical services into areas that had never even seen a doctor. Brad's challenge was networking to share information on the best ways to deliver medical services and supplies, along with solving the myriad of problems that arose with each new project. And then there were the conversations with the pharmaceutical reps. It seemed their mobile clinics met nearly every need the various medical groups had described, but the cost was more than prohibitive. With all of his notes, cost estimates, and input from the other physicians, Brad went to see his daddy.

Brad Sr. couldn't believe how much his son had accomplished in just a few weeks. As he read through all of the materials, he could see where Brad was going. "It's the cost, isn't it, son?"

"Yup. But, Dad, there's got to be a way." Brad was resolved more than ever.

"Have you taken all your notes to Sid?"

"Not yet, but I plan to."

"Have the pharmaceutical companies offered to help in any way?"

"I haven't really known the right questions to ask them," Brad admitted.

Brad Sr. paced as he thought. "Well, let's think this through. You're going to get some flack about medical services being needed in our country first. People are going to question the expense of going to other countries when so many people need affordable medical help in our own back yard.

"And pharmaceuticals are in business to make money . . . not to act as charities. But hospitals, on the other hand, are doing very well. Doctors have a lot of pull and pharmaceutical companies need support from both hospitals and physicians. If you can get Sid working with you . . . that might be good. The two of you could make more progress together. Plus, with the group of physicians you've recruited, your talks ought to go well. They bring in lots of hospital profits.

"Son, why don't you make a deal? Every time a hospital buys three of the rolling clinics, the pharmaceutical companies should donate one clinic to an impoverished area in a country of the hospital's choosing. There are doctors in those countries who would be thrilled to have these clinics for areas in need of immediate help. That way, areas in the United States will be serviced with the hospital's new mobile clinics, as well as needy areas overseas with the donated clinics."

Six months later, the first mobile clinic arrived in Antigua. Within the next year and a half, more than fifty mobile clinics were serving areas across the U.S., as well as in four developing countries. Brad and his teams had made several trips to train and educate. He had kept his promise to Rosa. Her memory and his persistence were helping sick and injured people, allowing thousands of lives to be saved.

Later, as Brad reflected on these last two years, he realized what an incredible help Charles Billings had been. The doctor, who was once his nemesis, had been instrumental in Brad's rescue by organizing the plane to bring him home. He had stood beside Brad at every meeting to secure the mobile clinics, and had even thrown a fit one night when two team members spoke negatively about raising the level of funds necessary to ship the very first clinic. Brad laughed to himself. After Charles' connip-tion, no one had the nerve to utter anything but positive support at any future meetings. He wondered deep down if Charles' support was for him or for Anne. Somehow, now it didn't matter and Brad was grateful.

When Brad came home that night, he walked over to his wife and put his arms around her, kissing her neck and face. He then started to walk into the great room. He turned and nonchalantly ask, "What are we doing this weekend?"

"I thought maybe you and I could go to dinner . . . just the two of us. I made reservations for Pano's on Saturday night," she answered.

"Sounds nice," he said as he picked up the television remote. "I think I'll invite Charles and whomever he's dating these days . . . if that's okay with you."

Anne stood still in amazement. Brad had never wanted to include Charles socially before. She cocked her head and asked, "Are you sure?"

Brad laughed and then gave Anne a peculiarly stern look. "What's your problem? You don't like Charles? I've always thought he was a really nice guy."

CHAPTER FORTY-FOUR

UNEXPECTED GRIEF

ANNE HAD JUST LEFT THE CENTER ON A WARM TUESDAY afternoon. Summer had arrived and with her brood at home, she stopped at the grocery store for some milk, frozen waffles, and lots of coffee. The thought of Brad without his perfect cup of caffeine in the morning was far from pleasant. Reaching for the box of breakfast blend pods, she heard her cell ringing from inside her purse. Placing the box in the cart, she searched and finally pulled out her phone.

"Hello?"

"Anne, it's Chandler. The rescue squad has just taken Dr. Young to the hospital. Patsy's all to pieces . . . I'm pretty certain he's had a stroke."

Anne asked, "Has anybody called Brad?"

"His mother is talking to him right now," Chandler said in an addled tone. "You need to get to the hospital, then let me know where to bring Patsy."

Anne put her cell away, left her cart in the middle of the

aisle, and rushed out.

When she walked in the emergency room it was as if the entire ER had come to a stop. All the staff was crying. Running up to the desk, she asked, "Where is Dr. Young?"

The nurse asked Anne to follow her. She led her to a quiet room. When Anne entered, Brad was already there with his head on his father's chest, sobbing. She knelt down beside her husband. Her father-in-law was gone.

The next few days were excruciatingly painful as they made the necessary arrangements. The children wanted to stay with their grandmother most of the time. Their sadness was heart-breaking for all in the family to watch. Patsy and Chandler were like zombies; it seemed all actions and words were on autopilot. The tragedy had moved each of them to a faraway place and to a whole new realm of grief for his wife. If not for being brave for the children, Anne didn't know what the family would have done. Or how they could carry out the task of planning a funeral.

Watching her husband grieve, Anne felt so sorry for him as he tried to deal with not only his pain, but he was also working hard to take over the family responsibilities his daddy had always shouldered. Anne could see the hurt and stress in his eyes and knew that Brad was mourning in ways he hid well.

The afternoon of the funeral she heard the back door close. She walked to the dining room and looked out the window. Her husband was driving away, not having said a word. But she understood. The night before when they got into their bed, Brad had turned to her with tears in his eyes and shared that he felt overwhelmed. He said he felt that his missing days in Guatemala were somehow partly responsible for his father's death.

Now, standing by the window, Anne thought back to their conversation; she could still hear Brad's words. "Everything that happened to me in Guatemala took more of a toll on Dad than I had realized. You know . . . for so many years, I was all he had."

She choked up as her memories of that conversation continued. "I think about my patients. The ones who have lost children. I've seen so many of them come down with one disease or another . . . That trauma is just too much for their bodies. I can name too many that died before their time simply due to grief. I think that's what happened to Dad when he thought there was no hope that I could still be alive . . . That unspeakable grief began to take its toll that very day."

Anne had wanted to tell him that he was wrong, that Brad Sr.'s death had nothing to do with his son. But in the unspoken recesses of her mind, she knew Brad was right. It took so long for everyone in the family to recover from that horrible time in Guatemala. But her father-in-law never seemed to make that leap. It was as if a part of him had been damaged by the fear of losing his only child. Even though Brad Sr. had learned to laugh again, it was like he had never quit crying on the inside. His movements, his actions, his words were never quite the same. Losing Brad had become an overshadowing possibility that he just couldn't live with.

She thought back to how he even hugged Brad differently after Guatemala. She could almost feel his uncertainty each time they separated. It was evident that he didn't want to be the first one to let go when the two hugged. And the way he looked at Brad; she could tell that he hated to have his son out of his sight. Anne would catch Brad Sr. wiping a tear sometimes when Brad walked away. Throughout his life, that kind man had learned a difficult truth—no matter how hard one tries, protecting the ones we love isn't always possible.

The night of that wrenching conversation, Anne cuddled up to Brad and tried to console him without words. He really hadn't needed words, only to know she was there.

Anne had learned early on in their marriage that there were times when her husband just needed some time by himself. He needed more time with his thoughts. She felt sure that was the case with his disappearance today. The twins came downstairs in their nightgowns and walked over to the window where their mother was still standing. They put their arms around her as though to love her sad thoughts away.

Gretchen looked at Anne and said, "Mama, this is just awful. We're going to miss Granddaddy so much. I don't want him to be dead!" She started to cry.

Patsy burst into tears as she said, "It hurts my heart to see everybody cry."

Just then, Little Brad walked downstairs already dressed for the funeral. He had recently turned eighteen. He walked into the kitchen, grabbed his car keys, and a piece of toast. Walking into the dining room, he said, "Mom, I think I know where Dad went. I'll be back in a little while."

She just nodded and watched her son pull out of the driveway. He was so like his daddy. He just wanted to be with him and see if there was anything he could do to help with any arrangements.

In a couple of hours, father and son walked through the side door with arms around each other's shoulders. Brad broke the bond to walk over to give Anne a kiss as he said, "Dad would be so proud of his grandson." He looked back over at Little Brad and then again at his wife. "We both said our goodbyes. My words paled in comparison to our boy's. I knew those two were close, but I never realized how much my father had shared with his grandson. Things that were so important to Dad . . . things he wanted to be important to Little Brad as well. So many of the same things he shared with me as a boy."

Little Brad smiled shyly as he climbed the stairs to his room.

"When our son said his goodbye, he assured Dad that he would remember and would always try to make him proud. He said all the things I was thinking. I realized what an impact Dad had on so many lives . . . including, most importantly, his grandson's."

With that explanation, Brad broke down and pressed his face beside Anne's, holding her waist tightly. Her thoughts raced as they stood there. *These two men had shared moments that neither will forget. Moments that only fathers and their sons can appreciate.*

As they walked upstairs to dress for the funeral, Anne knew that Little Brad had brought both comfort and strength to his dad. She watched Brad walk into the bathroom to take a shower. Sitting on the bed, she sobbed.

Offering a prayer, she whispered, "Thank you, Father, for a young boy that today took his place as a young man, standing beside his father."

CHAPTER FORTY-FIVE

COMFORTING TIMES

Anne and the girls walked into the chapel. Tears fell as they watched Brad walking through the side door, slowly pushing his mother's wheelchair. She looked weak and so frail, sad and lost, as though all of her emotions had crowded into one, despair. Little Brad escorted Chandler down the side aisle to sit beside his grandmother.

After she was seated, Patsy looked around at the familiar faces of lifelong friends. She had insisted that the funeral be private, as she held her own grief privately and wanted to be surrounded only by the people she and her husband truly cared for. She had planned every minute of the service and it was a beautiful tribute to a man well loved. After the burial, there was a reception at the church and somehow being with all these special friends made the afternoon more bearable for Patsy.

Brad was careful to walk up to each one present and thank them for coming, holding Anne's hand the entire time. He clearly needed her support while there was sharing of favorite stories about his father. The stories brought to life the fact that Brad Sr. had been an exceptional man, along with the sobering reality that he was gone.

After several hours of conversation with Brad, Patsy, and the family, the room was empty. As the family was preparing to leave, Margie and Tommy walked through the door. The minute they had heard the news in Guatemala, they booked a flight to get home to be with the family.

Anne was so glad to see her friend. The two hugged and cried as Brad and Tommy talked openly about the sadness that continued to permeate in the room. Tommy suggested that he and Brad get together for coffee several mornings for a while. He knew the value of talking through grief and was in the best position to listen well as a friend who knew the family. As the two men talked, Brad agreed that Tommy's offer would be helpful and they scheduled the first appointment for the following week.

By now, the family had surrounded Margie and asked if she was coming back to the house with them.

Anne looked at the twins and said, "They are absolutely coming back to the house with us!"

Since Margie and Tommy had sold their home in Atlanta, Anne had fixed the garage apartment to serve as their Atlanta home whenever the two would travel back for mission reports and visits to family and friends. Her first question to Margie was, "How long can you stay?"

Margie gave Anne another hug and said, "As long as you need us."

Anne looked at her friend through tear-filled eyes and confessed, "That will be the rest of my life."

Margie kissed her cheek. "When we have a time to sit down and talk over a cup of coffee, Tommy and I have something to tell you."

"What is it?" Anne asked in a voice that Margie recognized as her friend's concerned tone.

She smiled. "We'll talk in the morning . . . over a cup of coffee. Right now, your family needs you," Margie said as she turned to walk over to check on Patsy. Anne watched as the two embraced. They hugged for the longest time.

Their pastor walked over to speak with Brad. "There's something I've wanted to tell you. About three weeks before your father died, he came by the church. He walked in my office and handed me a check for the new building fund. He was always such a generous man."

Brad had so many thoughts clouding his mind as the pastor spoke. However, one took precedence. He realized from the hand-delivered check that his father must had known how sick he was. There must have been signs that something in his body was failing.

After Brad thanked the pastor, he and his family left for home. Following the familiar route, he was thinking that even as consoling as the day had been with friends and family, he found more consolation in the thought that time with his father had not come to an end. Brad would see his father again one day and, with that thought, he smiled.

Pulling into the driveway, she and Brad spotted Margie and Tommy's rental car. Anne thought back to her conversation with Margie at the church. She knew the couple was tired from their flight and the rush to get to the chapel, so she didn't bother them that night. However, she couldn't wait for their time together over that cup of coffee the next morning. She was curious to hear whatever it was that her friend had to say.

CHAPTER FORTY-SIX

HEARTS ADJUSTING

W<small>ALKING INTO THE HOUSE THAT EVENING,</small> A<small>NNE SIGHED AS SHE</small> thought back. Brad's parents had been an integral part of their lives. She remembered their excitement the night Brad proposed, their wedding, the joy as they watched the ultrasound of Little Brad, and the surprise on Brad Sr.'s face when he realized he would be having twin granddaughters. She recalled watching Little Brad and his grandfather hitting golf balls out in the backyard. The memories were hard even though she knew the exercise of remembering was important to replace her sadness with those happy times. Besides, sweet memories brought happy tears. They felt good.

The next morning, Anne walked downstairs to start the coffee and to slip a coffee cake from a neighbor into the oven. She had promised herself that there would be no more reflecting on the past today. She needed to focus on her family and their guests.

The unanswered ache she was feeling would have to wait until later. Hearing the side door open, she took two cups out of the cabinet. Margie walked in.

The two women embraced without saying a word. Anne walked over to the counter and poured the coffee. She asked, "Margie, what do you have to tell me?"

Margie smiled. "If you don't mind, I'd rather show you." She walked over to the side door and opened it. Tommy walked in with a little girl and a little boy holding his hands. "Anne, I'd like for you to meet my family." She looked first at the little girl and said, "This is Little Estelle, who just turned three," and then she looked at her baby boy, "And this is Tommy Jr., who is twenty-two months old. They stayed with Tommy's aunt while we were at the funeral."

Anne walked over, knelt down, and gave both a hug. Looking at the happy smiles on Estelle's and Tommy's little faces, Anne burst into tears. "Oh, Margie! They're beautiful. Tell me all about everything." She stood up and crossed over to the pantry, taking out a box of graham crackers. After pouring Tommy a cup of coffee, she removed the coffee cake, sliced it, and placed large pieces on plates. Then she ushered everyone to the breakfast room table. "Do not skip a single detail. I mean it, I want to hear everything!" She handed each child a graham cracker and looked expectantly at Margie.

Margie began to explain, "About three months ago, a young woman came to the orphanage in Guatemala. She had been offered a job as a seamstress in California at her sister's work place. She had just received her green card and needed to put her children in our orphanage. We asked how long she felt they would be with us and she said she couldn't answer that question for sure, but imagined three to four years. Anne, everyone at the orphanage immediately fell in love with both of these children. They were so cute and precocious. They fit right in with all of the other toddlers."

By now the children had finished the first graham crackers and as their little hands reached out for more, Anne immediately filled them.

"Three weeks ago, we received a letter from their mother. Inside were legal papers where she released the children for adoption. She was not coming back. Two days later, Tommy and I started adoption procedures to make them our own. Although it will be several months before it will be finalized, our attorney assured us that he saw no problems. We were concerned about the father and whether he might be a stumbling block, but we noted that there was no father's name listed on their birth certificates. That left everything clean for adopting."

"Oh, Margie, I couldn't be happier for anyone. You and Tommy are going to such great parents. Just knowing the way you are with our children makes me so happy for these little ones. The love they will receive from you two will start their life on a wonderful journey. I can't wait for the children to meet their new buddies!"

Margie raised her brows and asked, "And where are those precious children of yours?"

"We were up with them until late last night trying to soothe their broken hearts. You know how they adored their grand-daddy and they miss him already. They must still be sleeping . . . or at least I haven't heard them yet this morning." She thought quickly and suggested with a smile, "Let's go wake them up. They'll be so excited about your news!"

Leaving Tommy with the children and more graham crackers, the two walked upstairs. As they approached the twins' door, they could hear the girls talking. Anne knocked and then opened the door. Gretchen and Patsy were sitting on the floor in their nightgowns, tearfully looking through a scrapbook that their grandmother had made them for Christmas last year. The minute they saw Margie, they jumped up to run and give her hugs.

"Margie, are you coming back?" Patsy asked. "We miss you so much!"

Gretchen chimed in and whined, "We haven't had a banana pudding since you left."

Anne watched as the girls couldn't seem to get enough of Margie's attention. But she soon decided to make the big announcement, "Margie has a surprise to show you. Let's see what your brother is doing and then we'll all go downstairs together."

The four walked out to the hallway. Anne knocked on Little Brad's door. As she opened it and looked inside, he was nowhere to be found. She hadn't checked to see if his Jeep was in the driveway, but she hadn't heard him leave. Watching as the girls and Margie hurried past his room, Anne stepped back into the hall. She smiled when she heard the girls screaming as they saw the children with Tommy. By the time Anne reached the kitchen, the twins had pulled out a basket of books and were reading Winnie the Pooh to four bright eyes.

"Mama, you have to talk Margie and Tommy into staying! We have to help raise their children!" Patsy said.

Gretchen looked at her mother and added to the plea. "We'll know exactly how to do it! We'll raise them like you and Margie raised us!" She then looked over at Margie and added, "And, Margie, we're dying for a banana pudding!"

Their former housekeeper just laughed and said, "We're going to be here for three weeks and I promise to make lots of banana puddings!"

While the girls and Margie were playing with the children, Anne walked to the back door to look out into the driveway. Little Brad's car wasn't there. Brad had spent the night with his mother, and she wondered if Little Brad had joined them after she had fallen asleep. Excusing herself, Anne walked into the dining room to call her husband.

Brad's cell rang as he was talking with Chandler about his mother's medication. "Good morning, sweetheart."

"Good morning. How's your mother?"

"She's still asleep and you won't believe who I just found sleeping under a blanket at the foot of her bed."

"I imagine it's our son," Anne answered with a sigh of relief.

"I have no idea what time he got here, but it had to have been in the wee hours of the morning. When I woke up and went in to check on Mama, they were both fast asleep. I was just getting ready to call you. Chandler and I are about to have some coffee. After Mother wakes up and I'm sure she's okay, I'll be home."

"Brad, the girls and I have had such a nice time with Margie and Tommy this morning. They have a surprise when you get here," Anne said.

Brad laughed. "I sure hope it's some banana pudding."

"It's way better than that!" Anne said with a frown evident in her voice. Then with a more serious tone, she asked, "How are you holding up, my love?"

"It was difficult when I woke up this morning . . . When I came downstairs, I walked into Dad's study. I wanted to call his name like I've done so many times. I feel like there's just a serious void in this house." He choked and continued, "Such an important part of our life is missing. But then I think about Mother . . . and what this must be like for her. I think it would probably be good for the girls to spend the night over here tonight. We can take turns for a few weeks. Seeing her grandson this morning will be the best medicine we could give her."

"I think that's a good plan," Anne said in agreement. "I need to get back to Margie, but call me if you need me."

"I love you, Anne."

"I love you, too, darling."

The next few weeks were easier that Anne had expected simply because Margie and her family were with them. If the girls weren't at Patsy's, they were babysitting for Margie and Tommy. The weather was warm enough to go over to the pool at the club. Anne had alerted the lifeguard to keep an eye on them, but the girls had promised to only let the youngsters swim in the kiddie pool.

It tickled Anne and Margie to watch them get packed up and ready to go out after putting on their little one's new swim-suits. Little Estelle and Tommy Jr. left with "swimmies" on each arm. Sometimes Anne and Margie would go along just to watch them splash in this new experience of a pool. Tommy would tag along to get a peek at the fun before he and Brad headed to the golf course on the weekends.

Margie stepped back into her old life and felt right at home in the Youngs' kitchen. Over the duration of her visit, she fixed all of their favorite foods, including lots of banana puddings. She'd always fill extra plates for Chandler and Patsy. Anne would deliver them on her regular afternoon visits. Margie also prepared several dishes to store in the freezer so the family wouldn't have to go cold turkey when she and her family returned to Guatemala.

By the end of the first week of their visit, Margie and Tommy were asked to please move from the garage apartment to the guest room in the Youngs' downstairs. The girls wanted the children to sleep in their room every night. Their parents needed to be closer in case of homesickness or bad dreams. Everyone was settled and happy.

Anne thought it was such a treat to have toddlers in the house again. Their cute personalities clearly helped the grieving process for the Young children. Anne's grief benefitted from her friend's presence as well. In the mornings, she would sneak downstairs to meet Margie for coffee, as well as to enjoy soothing conversations all by themselves. But late at night, when Anne and Brad climbed into bed, she'd turn toward him and snuggle up. Yet, there were still times that she'd feel his tears. Brad was finding that he missed his father in ways that he hadn't expected, ways that tended to be professionally crippling.

· · ·

At the hospital or office in the past, whenever there would be a high-risk situation with one of their patients, Brad would normally discuss his intended treatment protocol with his father. Once the two had talk it through, he would know exactly what to do. It was different now. Now this confident man found himself second-guessing decisions as days crept by.

Finally, after some personal and encouraging conversations with Tommy, along with Anne's prayers and his mother's pep talks, Brad adjusted and became comfortable in assuming his responsibilities as head of the practice, a role his dad had right-fully held even in retirement. In time, his confidence and acquired knowledge rose to the surface.

Margie and Tommy stayed a few extra weeks due to several decisions that were brewing at their church, financial decisions about funds for the two orphanages they supported. As the church's leadership looked at the benefits provided, generous hearts prevailed. It was then time for Margie's family to head back to their now-funded responsibilities in Guatemala. Anne and the children took them to the airport early one Monday morning. Margie and Anne hugged and hugged. Little Estelle and Tommy Jr. ran around behind the girls and had a hard time letting go of the twins' hands.

Patsy cried out enthusiastically, "We'll keep them! We'll take good care of them!"

"I promise we'll be back soon. We'll come again for Christmas," Margie promised as the hugs continued.

That promise seemed to make things easier for the girls. As they all waved goodbye, Margie and her family disappeared into the terminal. Anne put her arms around the girls and followed Little Brad to the car. Driving away, Anne listened to her girls planning tea at the Ritz with Santa for Little Estelle and a ride on the Pink Pig for Tommy Jr. Christmas couldn't come soon enough.

CHAPTER FORTY-SEVEN

A FAITHFUL FRIEND

SEVERAL MONTHS AFTER BRAD SR.'S FUNERAL, TODD JAMES, THE now-retired CEO of C&C, came by to visit with Brad and Anne. The two were so glad to see him. This man had always been so generous to the Center and Anne and Brad were grateful for his faithful friendship. Mr. James and his wife had been in Europe when Brad Sr. passed way and they had just recently returned to the States. As Brad and Todd moved to the study, Anne left for the kitchen to fix glasses of iced tea. Placing the slice of lemon on the side of the glass, she thought of her first meeting with the infamous CEO and how nervous she had been. She laughed remembering that she had been assigned to recover a sofa and ended up as the senior designer on the C&C account. Taking the tea into her guest, Anne handed him both the cold glass and a napkin.

"I'm so sorry I wasn't here, but I understand your father's funeral was well attended with family and close friends," Mr. James said. "I just came by today because I wanted to express my condolences and tell you what a fine man and friend Brad Sr. was to all who knew him."

Brad and Anne glanced at each other with a shared smile.

"Every time I look at my children, I am reminded of your father's kind nature. Whenever he delivered a baby, it seemed he was just as proud as the parents."

As the visit continued, Anne and Brad enjoyed new stories about Brad's father. The tale of a golf game gone bad more than thirty years ago brought laughter. It seemed Brad Sr. had hit one bad shot after another and took a double bogey on the eighteenth hole just to finish his lousy game. Walking over to his caddy, Brad Sr. had asked, "Buster, do you like these clubs?" The gentleman had agreed that they were fine clubs. The doctor followed up by saying, "Well, they're now yours. May they bring you better luck than they ever brought me." He handed the clubs over to the caddy and walked off of the course.

Mr. James laughed as he shared the story. "But, Brad, two weeks later, your dad was back out on the course with all-new clubs."

Brad remembered going shopping with his father for those new clubs. It was a memory etched deeply, as it was the same day he had gotten his own first set of clubs. After several more stories, Mr. James stood, saying it was time to head home for supper. Before he could say goodbye, Little Brad walked in the house and into the study. Mr. James was surprised at how tall the younger Brad stood as they shook hands.

"Have you started thinking about college yet, son?"

"Yes, sir, I want to become an architect."

"We've got one of the best schools in the country for that

career right here in Atlanta—Georgia Institute of Technology. I believe in keeping our best and brightest right here in Georgia," Mr. James proudly declared.

Little Brad nodded as he smiled politely.

"Son, your granddaddy and I were friends for over forty years. You've got a good name, boy. Your granddaddy was one of the finest men I ever knew. You make him proud."

Little Brad looked at his daddy, then back at Mr. James before asking, "Does that mean I have to be a doctor?"

They all laughed as Mr. James calmly said, "No, son. That means you just try your hardest at whatever you do."

Little Brad answered, "Yes, sir."

Anne walked Mr. James to the front door and gave him a hug. "Your visit has meant so much. We really appreciate you coming by." She watched him walk to his car and noticed that age was beginning to take its toll. His generation, including her father-in-law, had done so much to build Atlanta into the southern metropolis it was today. She slowly waved goodbye as he drove away. Thinking back, she could still remember the night at Miss Carla's, the night he and the other board members of C&C had donated the Center's residence building. Then she recalled how that wonderful man had helped the Center in so many financial endeavors.

She smiled and whispered, "What a good friend."

CHAPTER FORTY-EIGHT

BACK TO THE DIET SECTION

GRABBING A CART, ANNE WALKED INTO THE GROCERY STORE. SHE took out her list. Quickly moving down each row, she selected several boxes of cereal and placed them in the cart. When she glanced up, a picture on the magazine rack caught her eye. Hilda's face was on the cover of Vogue with a caption that read, "Emmy Winning Makeup Artist Shares Her Secrets for Looking Young." Anne picked up a copy and laid it on top of the cereal. She missed Hilda; that woman was always a bright spot in her day. She vowed to give her a call the following week after the hustle and bustle of Thanksgiving had passed.

"Thanksgiving," she sighed. This holiday brought such vivid memories of her daddy and how she had always shared this special time with him. Tomorrow's Thanksgiving would be even more difficult. Brad's mother and Chandler would be joining her family at the club. How she missed Estelle, Brad Sr., and her daddy; then she thought about Margie and all the turkeys she had cooked through the years. Anne couldn't wait for that family to come back for Christmas. She understood that traditions had to change, but what she'd give for one more Thanksgiving with everyone around her table.

Anne had to laugh as her memory drifted back three years ago, when she tried cooking Thanksgiving all by herself. It was a complete disaster; what wasn't burned was undercooked. She could still see the look on Brad's face when he came in the kitchen and caught her staring at the bottom of a scorched pot full of burnt butter beans, with tears streaming down her face. That had been her first Thanksgiving without Margie and her last; they had been eating at the club ever since. And they didn't burn a thing.

Picking up several low-calorie dinners, Anne thought, *I'll start my diet on Monday.* Her cell rang; it was Brad. "I've got an idea," he began. "Why don't we take everybody and go to the Lakeshore Inn on Friday. We can spend the weekend?"

"I love your idea, my love," Anne moaned. "But it won't work. The girls have a ballgame Saturday night and Brad has a date with Molly to go out to dinner with her family."

She could feel Brad's disappointment by his silence. Finally, he said, "Anne, we don't get to do anything anymore . . . except children's activities. We're tied up every weekend with Brad's golf or the girls' stuff. Seems like we never have any time to ourselves or as a whole family. We just rush here and there, trying not to miss anything they have going on."

"I know . . . but do you realize we only have two more years with all three of them at home?" she asked.

"Is it just two more?"

"Little Brad's a junior and the girls are freshmen. It's going by really fast."

"He's still thinking Georgia Tech. Studying architecture," Brad said.

"I think he's sold on both," Anne answered. "Have you seen your daddy's study lately?"

"Not really," Brad said in a curious tone.

"Your son, and your mother, have turned that room into our boy's very own studio. He's got a Computer-Aided Design program on a computer and he's even got an old drafting desk set up to copy antique architectural drawings. I think your mother has bought him every architectural book and gadget that's ever been printed or invented. He's even figured out how to add a bedroom and bath on the first floor for Chandler so she doesn't have to climb those steps forever. By the way, has your mother talked to you about her house?" Anne asked.

"No, what's going on with the house?" Brad shook his head.

"She wants to leave it to Little Brad. She had it appraised so she could leave equal amounts of money to the girls."

"Good grief!" Brad said. "She doesn't need to be thinking about stuff like that already. Sounds like she thinks she's going to die at any minute. I don't like that one bit."

"I know you don't, sweetheart. But apparently, it's important to her. After you've had time to think about things, maybe you two should talk," Anne suggested.

"I called to talk about the Lakeshore Inn . . . and damn, if we're not discussing my mother's death. I wish I hadn't called."

Anne could tell by his tone that he'd had a bad day. "Have you had a difficult morning, my love?" she asked softly.

He was silent for a minute. "I had a baby born this morning with some serious birth defects. If she lives, it will be a miracle. I swear, Anne . . . it's so hard. This is their first child. They'll have to go through lots of genetic testing and be prepared for a high-risk birth should they decide on a second baby. Then the Phillips' younger daughter had her seventh miscarriage. So much bad news to deliver at one time . . . I just need to get away for a few days."

"I agree. I'll work it out if we can leave on Sunday? After the girls' ballgame, they can stay with your mother and Chandler for a few days. You and I will go to the Lakeshore Inn. I'd love to have my man all to myself for a couple of days."

He agreed that Sunday would be great and he'd get Miss Davis working on his schedule and the reservations. Anne hung up with a mixture of a smile and a frown. She turned around to return to the diet dinner section, thinking, *wonder how can I lose at least five pounds by Sunday . . . with Thanksgiving lunch and dessert leftovers in the mix?*

CHAPTER FORTY-NINE

ROMANCE AND ROSES

THANKSGIVING WAS NOW A SWEET MEMORY. PATSY AND Gretchen had cheered their hearts out on Saturday night to no avail; their team had lost 21-14. But by Sunday morning, the tears had dried and they were excited to be going to their grandmother's. Little Brad had packed his and the girls' bags in his Jeep before leaving for church, where they were to meet their grandmother and Chandler. Anne and Brad were packed and followed them out of the neighborhood, before turning left to drive to the mountains and Lake Toxaway. Anne laid her head back against the car's headrest as they listened to Barry Manilow along the way. She had shopped a little on Saturday afternoon and was thinking of the new silk nightgown she had found. It was black and thankfully hid a few of her extra pounds.

Peering out the window as they drove along, Anne was enjoying the colorful drive to the Inn. Georgia hadn't had much rain this fall and the leaves were plentiful and vibrant. Fall colors of orange, gold, reds, and olive greens covered the mountains and made it impossible for the two not to stop for some tart apples at a roadside stand. Finally pulling into the Inn's parking lot, Anne looked at the homey old building. They'd never come here by themselves before, only for medical meetings with a larger, professional group. But, even with a big group crowding the common areas, Anne had always taken the time to enjoy the unique features of the resort.

The construction of the famous old Inn was almost western in style; there were heavy pillars of large, multicolored rocks separating the massive wooden porch and entry. Long expanses of tall windows with thin brown shutters sparkled in the afternoon sunlight and looked so inviting. As she looked toward the second floor, there were endless banks of windows encasing a sleeping porch that had been turned into the Inn's premier room. That room, as well as many others, overlooked Lake Toxaway, a gorgeous body of water, despite its name.

As the valet unloaded their car, a bellman ushered the two to the front desk. "Dr. and Mrs. Bradford Young," Brad said as he pulled out his American Express card.

"Dr. Young, we were able to reserve the specific room you requested and we have you down for three nights. Dinner is served at seven with cocktails beforehand, and we scheduled you both for the activities you asked about. High tea is at four every afternoon and you have a dinner cruise tomorrow night," the receptionist explained as she handed Brad a real bronze key to their room.

Every room in the Inn was decorated in a totally different style, each with its own personality. It made each stay feel like one was visiting the Inn for the very first time. As Anne and

Brad walked by the large, formal parlor, she noticed it had been redecorated since their last trip. Neutral fabrics against the dark paneled walls gave it a stately look. Brad took his wife's hands and pulled her away from the door.

"Come with me, Mrs. Young. You're going to love our room," he promised. Walking up the stairs to the second floor, he leaned over and kissed her cheek.

Passing through a narrow hallway and several open doors, Anne just had to stop and peek in each one. She loved the red room; the walls looked like damask that had been quilted and applied directly to the walls. It was a bright crimson.

Brad followed his wife's gaze. "Looks like a bordello!"

The next room they passed looked English, with green walls trimmed with white lattice work. Several fashionable prints gave the room a feel of a restful gazebo.

Approaching the next door, Brad said, "This is us!"

It was Room Seven; Anne wanted to remember that. Walking in, she smiled. It was the sleeping porch that had been converted into the Inn's largest and most well-appointed room. The bed was luscious – a heavily carved, four-poster king with fluffy linens that were a bright, crisp white. The walls were a soft teal and the rug was more than plush. Furniture in the side sitting area appeared to be comfortable and Brad was thrilled to see the large television with a mahogany coffee bar sitting underneath. It held a huge bouquet of red roses, a bottle of champagne, two bottles of wine, and a silver tray filled with an assortment of hors d'oeuvres.

Anne walked over and breathed deeply as she took the blooms of several roses between her fingers, smiled at her husband, then, opening the shutters, she peered out of the bank of long, clear windows. She called Brad over to see the beautiful view of the lake.

He had just tipped the bellman and closed their door. Walking over to his wife, he pulled her close. After a long kiss, he commented that the lake wasn't the only beautiful view in the room.

Anne closed the shutters. "Would you like a glass of wine?" she asked, but she could tell by the look of love in his eyes that wine was not what he had on his mind. She put her arms around his neck and gave him another kiss. "Maybe wine a little later?" she asked.

He smiled with the same twinkle he had shared with her for so many years. "I told you at the Ritz nearly twenty years ago that I'd never be able to get enough of everything about you, darling. That's as true today as it was then. You, Mrs. Young, are my addiction." He kissed her again and whispered, "Please."

When Anne opened her eyes the following morning, she smiled and thought, *this is as close to Paris as you can get.* Four days and three delightful nights flew by as the couple enjoyed each activity and event provided by the Inn. Meals were formal and everyone dressed for the occasions, the scenery was stunning on the river cruise, and reminiscent of a 5-star travel brochure. Anne had loved high tea with the other interesting guests as Brad played golf.

On the third afternoon, when she walked into the library for tea, Anne was thrilled to see Caroline Green, a client and friend from her life before Brad. The two moved to a small table at the back of the room and sipped tea as they caught up on two decades of family history. That evening, the two ladies along with their husbands shared dinner. As conversation peaked, it was evident that Gerald hadn't given up on hiring Anne as his company's interior designer. Despite his forthright request, Brad laughed and assured him that his company's needs weren't even remotely as critical as their household's needs. He good-naturedly explained that life with all the children's activities and the Center kept her plate more than full. However, enjoying some time with this special couple had been a nice addition to the trip.

After the Youngs said goodbye to everyone at the Inn, who now felt like family, the valet pulled up with their car and the refreshed couple started back to Atlanta. Anne could tell by Brad's crooning Manilow on the way home that he was feeling a lot more relaxed and the time away was much needed by both. The intimacy shared over those few days was like a secret spark that ignited memories of all the love they continued to enjoy.

CHAPTER FIFTY

SWEET CONFIRMATION

SEVERAL MONTHS LATER, ANNE AND BRAD WALKED INTO THEIR house from yet another funeral. Faye Davenport, a friend of Patsy's, had been in a tragic automobile accident. Patsy sadly commented that Faye's eyesight was terrible and she shouldn't have ever been driving in the first place. Her poor sight issues were even more of a problem when the city changed a lot of the stop signs in Atlanta to four-way stops, which only added more confusion for her friend. Shaking her head as she spoke of Faye's age-related issues, Patsy added that Faye was a habitual dieter as well. It seemed she lived between a sugar splurge and fasting most of her life.

"A piece of cake for breakfast was a common temptation," Patsy recalled. "Whenever a group of us would go out for brunch, Faye would order dessert first and say, 'Why not; the rest of the day is uncertain.'" As she was talking about her friend, tears ran down Patsy's cheeks. "I hope she had a huge piece of chocolate cake that morning before her accident."

. . .

After supper later that evening, the couple walked into the kitchen to clean up. When all was loaded in the dishwasher, Brad asked, "Anne, can we sit down for a few minutes? I need to tell you about something."

Anne nodded as she sat down on one of the sofas in the great room. Brad joined her.

"About two weeks ago, I had a dream about Dad. At least, I think it was a dream . . . It seemed so real. I heard someone call my name, I looked up. Dad was standing there, beside our bed. He looked great and he had the biggest smile on his face. He only spoke a few words, but the comfort I felt was indescribable."

Anne looked at her husband with a knowing smile, but didn't say a word.

"He told me that he had come to let me know he was fine and that I was to take good care of Mother until she left to be with him. That was all he said." Brad wiped his eyes and added, "Then I woke up. But, Anne, when I woke up, I could actually smell my dad . . . that Aramis cologne he always wore. Does that sound crazy?" he asked. "Can memories contain smells?"

Anne stood and walked over to the drawer where she kept the tattered floral notebook of her mother's. She pulled it out and said, "Yes and it doesn't sound crazy at all. Let me read you something." Sitting down, she opened the notebook and read Brad the entry about her time with her mother during her daddy's death. About the wrought-ironed bench in the garden, the smell of gardenias, and the uncanny knowledge that her parents were finally back together.

As she closed the notebook, Brad took her hand and said, "Either there really is something to these unexplainable visits, or you and I need some serious help."

Although Brad had been teasing with his last comment, it stirred Anne's curiosity. Later that week, she met with her pastor. Explaining about the two visits, she asked if anything like that was possible and, if so, had he heard other similar stories.

Taking Anne's hand, her pastor said, "I'm going to share something with you . . . but . . . I'd prefer that you keep it confidential. At my first church, right after becoming a minister, a distraught mother came to my office one afternoon. She had lost a child due to a boating accident several months prior to my arrival. I began counseling her during additional appointments for almost a year, but we made little progress. She couldn't let go of the fact that her child, at a mere sixteen years of age, had been snatched from her life. She and her son were Christians and she couldn't understand why God would let this happen. Close to a year later, when she walked in for her appointment, she was a different person."

He shook his head, then continued, "Her son was a star football player for his high school and the night before that appointment, she had a vision, a dream, whatever. She shared that she had walked into the stadium at his school and was just looking around when she heard a voice calling, 'Mama.' She looked up in the bleachers and saw her son sitting on one of the benches. He smiled and said, 'Mama, I just came to let you know that I'm fine and I'll see you again.' The morning of her appointment, everything about her countenance had changed. I knew without a doubt, after she shared her story of the visit, that she had seen her son.

"After that encounter, I started researching the topic and I came across a book that I have since given to many after their losses. I came to the conclusion that these visits or dreams or whatever you want to call them are real in a way that we will never fully understand."

He walked over to his bookcase and pulled out a paperback and handed it to Anne. She looked at the cover; it was a light-blue book entitled, *Hello from Heaven*. "Please consider this a gift for you and Brad. I think it will prove that you do not need serious help."

Anne spent the rest of the day reading the beautiful stories of supernatural visits. The experiences were incredibly clear and she felt both relieved and hopeful. When Brad walked in from the office that evening, she told him about talking with their pastor, then handed him the book.

"Brad, so many people have experienced visits just like we have. Wait until you read the many different ways they saw their loved ones. The stories are beautiful and lives were changed because of the peace brought about by these times together."

He thumbed through the first story. For the first time Anne could remember, Brad didn't turn on the television to watch the news. He was engrossed in the book that gave them both a sense of shared community. After a couple of hours of reading, he laid the book down to rest his eyes. Just then he heard Anne walk to the bottom of the stairs and call the children to supper.

Walking over to Brad's chair, she put her hands on his shoulders and kissed the top of his head. "Now, don't you feel better? We're not crazy after all. Let's eat."

CHAPTER FIFTY-ONE

A WELCOME SURPRISE

"WHAT IN THE WORLD COULD THAT BE?" ANNE ASKED AS SHE looked at the front door. She had gone for a brisk walk and the white object wasn't there when she left. Walking up to the porch, her legs were burning from the three-mile hike. She grabbed the railing for support as she climbed the six steps to the porch. Out loud, she questioned, "What is that large white envelope doing taped to our door?"

Trying to open the door as she removed the envelope, she realized the door was locked. Needing an excuse to rest, she sat on the top step and opened the seal. An unusual note met her eyes as she removed the large white card from the sleeve. It read, "Call this number for a big surprise." Anne figured it was some sort of advertisement and walked around to the garage to toss the letter in the trash can.

Entering the kitchen, she noticed the blinking light on the landline answering machine. *Nobody ever calls that line. I don't even know why we still have it,* she thought. But, being curious, she walked over and hit the message button. "For a big surprise, call this number." The voice then rattled off a non-local exchange.

Anne pulled out her cell. *Why not? There's a chance it could be important.* She laughed as the next thought popped in her mind. *Maybe I've won the Publisher's Clearinghouse Sweepstakes!* She dialed the number; no answer.

Five minutes later, the doorbell was ringing. Opening the door, Sally stepped into view and yelled, "Surprise!"

Anne couldn't remember when she had been happier to see anyone; the two hugged and hugged. Sally had been the children's nanny starting right after Little Brad was born. Anne remembered how disappointed that boy had been when Sally had agreed to a new job outside of Boston. It had been more than ten years since Sally's overstuffed Jeep pulled out of their driveway leading her on a new adventure.

Anne took her hand and pulled her inside, saying, "Come in and tell me everything that's been happening in your life these past ten years." Anne fixed each of them a pimento cheese sandwich, some potato chips, and a Coke before they sat down to reminisce and catch up.

Life had basically gone well for Sally; she had loved the new job, but admitted she missed the Youngs' children so much. Anne remembered how Sally continued to mark every birthday and holiday with a card over the years. The children had grown to love and actually expected to hear from her every year. But the cards never revealed any news on her personal life and never included a return address. Several years after Boston the cards started coming with a postage mark from California. Even later, they noticed the cards came from Portland, Oregon.

Apparently, Sally had traveled from one university to another as her career moved her forward, but she always worked with the children's hospitals wherever she landed.

While in Boston, she had met a young professor and they married quickly. In hindsight, that had not been her best move and she shared with Anne that he was rarely home. Sally had attributed his absence to work and tutoring on the side to bring in more money, but later learned the tutoring was exclusively with young college women. Those late hours included fringe benefits. Sally summed up that leg of her journey by saying, "He was just very good-looking and a cad."

After Sally received a phone call from one of his jilted admirers, she packed her bags and headed for new opportunities in California. There she met a brilliant intern, whom she dated for several years. She felt sure he'd pop the question eventually; instead he broke off the relationship and began dating her best friend. Strike two.

Wanting to rid her memory of both him and her supposed best friend, she packed once again and headed for Portland, having secured a job at one of the hospitals near the downtown area. Sally was still enjoying the same job today and had no male attachments. When it came time for her to decide on a vacation destination, what better than friends in Atlanta? The minute she hit town, her first thoughts went to Anne, Brad, and the children.

"Now, I've told you all about me. I want to hear everything about you and the family." She looked around and asked, "And where's Margie?"

Anne began, "Margie is married to a pastor. She and Tommy live in Guatemala with their two adopted children, Tommy Jr.

and Little Estelle. Our Brad is a senior this year and has been accepted at Georgia Tech to study architecture. The twins will be turning sixteen soon and can't wait to start driving. But, Sally, you want to know the funniest thing?"

She nodded.

"They only want one car. Patsy and Gretchen still go everywhere together . . . do everything together. All three babes are involved in so many activities. Brad and I meet each other coming and going, trying to make sure one of us can watch each event. Brad is doing fine, still delivering babies and managing a huge practice now." Anne sighed. "And I'm the chief cook and bottle washer . . . and enjoying every minute of it!"

Sally raised her eyebrows. Anne admitted, "Well, I guess we eat out a lot. My cooking skills haven't improved much over the years."

"Oh, no. Eating out is understandable," Sally said as she laughed and shook her head. "What about Estelle and the senior Youngs?"

"We lost Estelle several years ago and Brad Sr. more recently. But Patsy is doing great and her nurse Chandler is back with her. You'll have to go by and say hello. She'd love that."

"Do you remember Little Brad's birthday party when he had his first taste of ice cream?" Sally asked.

Anne laughed. "I certainly do. We found out that day that he was a thief. Sneaky little rascal, swiping everyone's ice cream."

After several hours of sharing memories and laughs, Anne heard Little Brad's car pull in the driveway. He was bringing the twins home before going to his baseball banquet. She winked at

Sally and said, "Sit right here." Anne walked to open the back door.

Gretchen was arguing with Patsy as she exited the car. She was fussing about having the wrong backpack. Little Brad walked in the door first. Anne reached out to kiss his cheek. "I have a big surprise for you sitting out in the breakfast room."

He frowned. "Mom, it's not another mother with some daughter you want me to meet, is it? I'm getting pretty fed up with these so-called chance encounters."

Anne laughed. "Quit fussing and come inside."

The minute he saw Sally, his eyes lit up. He rushed over to give her a hug and looked toward his mother as he announced, "This is the woman I'm going to marry!"

Anne remembered that even at three and four years of age, Little Brad always said he was going to marry Sally. He was the saddest she had ever seen him the day Miss Sally left for Boston.

By now, the girls were walking through the door, still arguing over their backpacks. Anne clapped her hands and said, "Ladies, we've got company!"

Both Patsy and Gretchen looked up and screamed in unison, "It's Sally!" Dropping their backpacks, they ran into her wide-open arms.

Anne brought out some cookies and chips as the three sat down with Sally, munching and asking at least a thousand questions.

"Sally, where are you staying while you're in Atlanta?" Anne asked.

"I stayed with a friend last night, but she's going out of town later today."

"Your old apartment is vacant if you'd like to stay with us."

"That would be wonderful!" Sally looked around at the grown children. "It would bring back so many good memories."

Anne explained, "Our cleaning service cleaned it last week, so it should be nice and fresh. We'll expect you to join us for any meals when you're free, either here or if we go out."

Gretchen added, "We want to see a lot of you while you're here visiting."

"But feel free to come and go as you please," Anne said.

After more conversation, Little Brad excused himself to change and leave for his banquet and the twins helped Sally unload her Jeep and carry her bags up the stairs by the garage apartment. Of course, they jabbered the entire time helping her get settled.

When Brad came home, he and "all" of his girls went to Pano's for dinner. He was glad to see Sally and remembered that restaurant as one of her favorites. After dinner, the girls went up to their room to finish their homework and get ready for bed. Little Brad had come home early just to visit with his nanny.

Brad helped Anne take several baskets of laundry upstairs and, once in the room, he asked, 'Have you talked to Mother lately?"

"About what?" She said.

"She and our son are cooking up a plan."

Anne stuffed the last pile of underwear into one of Brad's drawer. Then turned to face her husband as she huffed, "What kind of plan?"

CHAPTER FIFTY-TWO

NOT A BAD IDEA

HER HUSBAND'S WORDS REMAINING A MYSTERY, ANNE NEVER DID get to hear about Little Brad and Patsy's plan that night. The minute her words, "What kind of plan?" left her mouth, Brad's pager went off. He was out the door for an emergency at the hospital. He wasn't able to call until nearly seven the next morning, then only to report that he had suffered through a long night with two difficult deliveries. He planned to shower and see morning patients, then another associate was to take his afternoon appointments. He would finally be able to come home for some sleep around one o'clock that afternoon.

That night was to be Brad's last night on call. After a quick late-morning meeting with the other associates in the practice, they agreed Brad had taken call as many years as needed. The younger associates would alternate call from that point forward unless there was some sort of unforeseen emergency. Brad felt it was good call by the practice, but with that decision, his girls becoming juniors, and his son's plan to move out for college, Brad left for home feeling really old and tired. When he walked in the side door, Anne gave her weary man a kiss and gently reminded him that he needed to fill her in on their son's so-called plan before he was to get a wink of sleep. She followed him upstairs to the bedroom.

Brad sat down in one of the comfortable lounge chairs, propped his elbow on the arm of the chair, and placed his hand on his forehead. He began to explain, "Our son wants the full college experience, so therefore he doesn't want to live at home but he doesn't want to live in a dorm either. Apparently, as he was sharing that thought with Mother, she suggested they remodel the upstairs of her house, construct stairs along the exterior side of the house, and cut an entry door to those outside stairs from his sitting room. That way there would be a private outside entrance . . . for our son's convenience. He would have his very own apartment and, of course, everything his little heart desires with Mother and Chandler meeting his every need: food, laundry, and most anything else, I suppose."

He continued, "Mother is thrilled over the prospect, and our boy has pretty much said it's what he'd like to do, if we agree. He's already drawn up the plans. He'll have a studio, a bath . . . a very fine bath, I might add. My old room and the other guest room will be his bedroom, sitting area, and studio. Mother is getting bids on the remodel as we speak."

Anne sighed. "You know, Brad, it really doesn't sound like a bad idea. Northeast Atlanta neighborhoods are not as safe as they used to be. I'm sure your mother and Chandler would like knowing he's there. Honestly, it sounds like a win-win for everybody to me."

Brad's eyes widened. "I'm sure by the time you get through decorating his new pad, it'll be a win-win for him. I just don't understand why he can't live in one of the dorms. I certainly did fine in a dorm at Baylor prep and LSU."

"Things are different now, my love. Dorms are coed and I'd just as soon he'd have his own apartment." She could see Brad's exhaustion by the look in his eyes. In her sweetest tone, she assured him that after he slept and felt refreshed, he'd see things in a different light. Pulling the spread back on the bed, she cooed, "You've always been a reasonable man and I'm sure you'll be reasonable about this."

"Anne, do you have any idea how inexpensive it is to live in the dorm, compared to a remodel? I can't even imagine what 'this plan' will cost by the time you and Mother are finished. And another thing, I don't like the thought of our children leaving home. I'm not ready for this. I'm serious, sweetheart, I'm not one bit ready."

She walked over to close the draperies as she said, "I know, my love." As she headed toward the door to cut the lights off, she turned and blew him a kiss. "I'll see you after your nap. You're just tired and sleepy. Everything will look better when you wake up." She smiled. "I promise!"

The following morning, Brad was feeling a little better after a good night's sleep and some much-needed special time with his wife. In fact, as he left for the office, he wasn't feeling old at all as he leaned in for a long, goodbye kiss. After waving to her husband, Anne couldn't wait to talk to Patsy.

Stopping by Henri's Bakery, she picked up a dozen glazed donuts and drove straight to the Youngs'. After coffee and their sugary treats, Anne smiled and said, "Tell me about the plan for your new renovation."

Patsy giggled. "I have the most wonderful, handsome young architect and I've gotten all the bids. They're starting next week. Anne, I've never been so excited! Now, I know Brad has had some concerns, but he called me last night. He said he had talked with you and he did not have the strength to take on both of us." She grinned even more. "Plus, he said the more he thought about it . . . he had decided it was a good idea."

Anne smiled. She and Brad really did balance each other out quite well.

Patsy looked around. "The upstairs is going to be much more contemporary than the first floor, but that's just fine with me. Chandler agreed that I need some new things around here. We're also remodeling Brad Sr.'s study and bath for Chandler. I'm not taking a chance on her falling on any stairs as she gets older." She looked toward the banister and said, "Those stairs are wicked!"

Anne nodded in agreement, thinking back to Estelle. They all continued to miss her so much.

"There will still be an entrance to the main level of the house from the upstairs, but our boy will have an outside entrance so he can come and go on his own. Anne, I'm thinking about having the sunroom redone as well. It's where I spend all of my time and I'd like to freshen it up. Maybe just new paint and pretty new wallpaper . . . maybe new cabinets. Not too much. You will help with all the decorating won't you, honey"

"Of course, I think it all sounds great," Anne said. "The apartment will be wonderful to have even into the future. After Brad graduates from Georgia Tech, he might have met some other nice boy who needs a home. Renting out that space makes good sense to me. This house is so big, plus now that we have his daddy on board, we can get to work with no concerns."

That night after supper, Anne sat down with her son. As they talked, she could see his excitement in those big brown eyes of his. "Mom, I'll have everything I need to be able to study in peace and quiet. I'll have my computer system, a drafting board . . . I'd never get all that into a dorm room. I'll have my own bathroom. Coed sharing is not going to happen . . . at least for me."

Anne smiled. With his sisters and their friends, her son worked hard to ensure his privacy by locking doors. That luxury may not be available in a dorm situation.

"So many of the guys are getting apartments. Plus, I want a garage for my Jeep. Gaga said she's giving Granddaddy's car to the girls, so that'll free up a place for my car."

Anne laughed. "Well, I'll tell you a little secret, but you can't tell your Gaga. The girls don't want his sedan, so your daddy has agreed to take your granddaddy's car and give them his new SUV."

Little Brad grinned. "I knew that car thing wasn't going to work, but I wasn't about to tell Gaga. Mom, she has the best time figuring out how she can give us grandchildren anything we need. We're so lucky." His face suddenly changed and he asked seriously, "Mom, can she really afford this renovation and all?"

Anne grinned. "She most certainly can. Don't you worry."

Curious now, Little Brad asked, "Mom, where did Granddaddy get all of his money?"

"Well, he worked very hard and doctors get paid well."

"Gaga said something about Granddaddy's trust fund."

"Your Great-Great Granddaddy was a very wise man. He invested in Coca-Cola from its inception. When he died, he left money in a very generous but sexist way . . . Each male born into the Young family was to inherit money from that trust fund. It's still the rule today."

Little Brad sat up straighter. "Will I get any money, Mama?"

"Yes, you will. But your sisters will not. When your Great-Great Granddaddy put this plan into action, most women didn't work and their husbands took care of their financial needs. Today, all of that has changed. Your daddy felt badly about this, so when he received his money, he shared some with Emma. She was his only girl cousin with no brothers. It was the right thing to do so that she was financially able to look after her children when her husband left her."

"Does that mean I have to split mine with the twins?" He laughed, but she could see that he already knew the answer.

"That will be your decision, but I know you'll do the right thing, just like your daddy did. You won't receive any funds until you're thirty, so you'll have plenty of time to think it through."

"How much will I get?" This was sounding too good to be true.

"With interest, it changes from year to year. You and your daddy can talk about it later. But I don't think you're allowed to know much of anything until your thirtieth birthday."

"So how did Gaga get her money?"

"She married your granddaddy. When he died, she inherited everything that belonged to him."

Little Brad shook his head. "Complicated, huh?"

"It is. But, son, there's something else you need to remember. The men in this family have always tithed off of any money they made or any money they inherited. They felt giving was important to life's success. In His word, God states that He will be no man's debtor. So, when you give to help His people, He will help you."

"We've always tithed on our allowance. You made us. Is that why?"

"Yes, sir, that was to get your heart ready for bigger opportunities."

He gave his mother a kiss on her cheek. "I won't let you down, Mama."

Anne walked out of his room, thinking only of how much she would miss having that sweet boy in their house.

September would come all too quickly and the years even more so. The senior Young house now had an apartment and a young Georgia Tech student settled in his new accommodations. What seemed like in no time at all, her boy was finishing his freshman year, and was more dedicated to the study of architecture than ever. Patsy and Gretchen were already receiving college mailings and sending in their applications. The two had decided to attend Virginia Commonwealth University, if accepted. There, they could both study their chosen majors. Gretchen wanted to follow in her mother's footsteps and become an interior designer; Patsy wanted to go into medicine like her daddy. She was planning to be a nurse and wanted to work in children's hospitals like Sally. Anne asked herself, "How did all of this happen so quickly?"

As she passed a family portrait in the upstairs hallway, tears filled her eyes. The children were so little when that canvas was created; the twins were five and Little Brad was merely seven. How did time go by so fast? Just yesterday, they were baking cookies in the kitchen with Margie. She walked down to the bottom of the steps where Bo Jr. was laying across the floor like a speed bump. She leaned over to pat his head as he slowly rose to allow her to pass.

"You're getting old too, aren't you boy?" Bo Jr. laid his head against her hip, hoping for more pats. "Come on, Bo. Let's go get you a treat."

She felt so melancholy thinking of the night Brad had brought her to look at this house, what he called a very good investment. She remembered thinking that it would be the perfect house for raising a family. It didn't seem that long ago, but this house really had been ideal for her family, which meant that it truly had been a good investment. She grabbed a napkin from the kitchen counter and wiped her eyes. Then she handed Bo Jr. two treats as he wagged his tail in delight.

· · ·

A year later, Little Brad was still loving Georgia Tech and his apartment, although he was always excited over his mother's picnic suppers and a chance to have a man-to-man talk with his dad. With their son keeping an eye on his grandmother and Chandler, Brad and Anne decided it was a good time to take the girls to tour VCU. A week later, parents and the twins boarded Chuck's plane to fly to Richmond. After they arrived, they got settled into their hotel, then the four took a walk around the campus. Walking down streets that Anne had traveled decades earlier, her mind began to wander.

She thought back to one specific afternoon when Doris and Sissy had accompanied her to a furniture store, where she was to sketch several reproductions for one of the store's customers. The most challenging item was a king-sized, Craftique, pencil-post bed. They had all laughed as they wondered why anyone on earth would need a bed that big. They were sure they would just want to cuddle closely in a much smaller space with whomever they chose to share their bed. With the discussion of that decision, the three settled on the number of children they each would have. Sissy adamantly said no more than two, Doris said she'd try one and see how it went, but Anne had wanted a minimum of three and a maximum of six. She could still see Doris' expression as she yelled, "Six! Are you crazy? Can you imagine what that would do to your body?" By the time Doris got through describing droopy breasts and mile-wide hips, Anne wasn't sure she wanted any children at all.

But here she was, walking with her two beautiful and talented young daughters. Walking down the same streets, looking at the same buildings, even that same metal fire escape that held so many late-night memories of her days at VCU. But, listening to Brad's comments and the girls' chatter, she could see that their daddy wasn't so sure about this school. It was right in the middle of the city of Richmond, good and bad sections, and now the university's growth seemed to sprawl in every direction. So many new buildings dotted the campus, and the new streets and paths required an awful lot of walking. However, traveling on foot certainly didn't seem to bother the girls. They were young, excited, and were feeling so grown up. Anne remembered back to her trip with her daddy. Laughing, she murmured, "Fathers often had a different point of view when it came to their daughters. Brad is no exception."

Gretchen and Patsy met several other students and were even invited to spend the night in a dorm, after which, the twins were sold and couldn't wait to enroll.

Arriving back in Atlanta, Brad was still uneasy with the size of their college choice. He thought VCU was huge and he was almost pitiful when he said, "I'm just afraid they'll get lost."

Anne walked over to her husband and wrapped her arms around his neck. "If they get lost, they'll be together. Two are much easier to find, my love."

Brad laughed. "At least Gretchen anyway. If anybody takes her, they'll bring her back so fast it will make your head swim."

CHAPTER FIFTY-THREE

CHANGES...CHANGES...EVERYWHERE

AFTER THE SUMMER, GRETCHEN AND PATSY WERE PACKING FOR college and dorm life. Little Brad would be starting his junior year at Georgia Tech, still loving his apartment and the special attention from his grandmother. Anne was checking to make sure the girls had packed everything she believed would be necessary for the different seasons in Virginia. She opened their suitcases to add a few warmer items and was touched to see that the notebooks she had made for them were laying in the top of each case.

The night before the twins were to leave, their brother came to join the family for supper and to help pack the cars. Anne watched her girls laughing with excitement as her son teased them about how difficult college would be for two scatter-brains. She laughed, but inside, she had never felt so strange. She knew this would be quite an adjustment; the idea that so much fighting, laughter, and activity would be coming to an end made her eyes glisten. She worked hard to hold back the tears; she would not put a damper on their last evening together—at least for a while. Anne looked at Brad and could see they were sharing the same thoughts. He was joining in the conversation, but his heart wasn't in it.

After dinner, the family went over to see Chandler and Patsy; the girls wanted to say goodbye. Anne sat down in the sunroom and watched her mother-in-law. Something didn't seem quite right; her hands were trembling when she gave the girls hugs. Anne dismissed her concerns, thinking their grandmother was just having a hard time letting go. The grandchildren had been her life for so long and now the twins would be far away and only home for semester breaks and holidays. Anne looked over at Chandler and noticed that she was also looking at Patsy with concern. Maybe there was more going on with Patsy's health than she knew.

As the girls gave their last hugs, Anne motioned to Chandler to follow her into the kitchen. Taking her hand, Anne asked, "Is everything okay with Mother?"

"Everything is just fine," Chandler assured. "She's just tired."

The Youngs' caravan headed for Richmond the next morning. Anne and Brad drove her station wagon loaded to the gills with electronics, toiletries, bedding, and decorations for the dorm room. The girls were leading the way with their car filled with clothes, purses, jewelry, makeup—everything a girl believed was necessary to attract the opposite sex.

They arrived in Richmond by mid-afternoon and, as luck

would have it, the twins were assigned to a room on the second level and the elevator wasn't working. But by nine that evening the Youngs had everything placed and hung. The closets were already too full, which made Brad frown, but Anne saw the notebooks placed on each of the two desks and pointed them out to Brad with a smile.

The twins were excited and still had energy to burn, while Brad and Anne were exhausted. Carrying laptops, a television, bean bag chairs, bedding, clothing, and more up the flights of stairs, many times, had been quite a challenge. Brad was in shock at what two cars could hold. Finally, as it was getting late, Anne and Brad embraced the girls for one last time and all four began to cry. Even as excited as Gretchen and Patsy were to explore the campus, the idea of their parents leaving in a few minutes made this transition all too real.

Brad took Anne to a hotel in downtown Richmond, where they enjoyed a late dinner and several glasses of wine. Falling into bed, Anne couldn't wait to close her eyes. But Brad wasn't sleepy. Instead he embarked on constant chatter. "Do they keep those stairwells locked at night . . . in that dorm? And I don't remember seeing any sprinkler heads? Is that building even up to code?" He looked at Anne intently and added, "It really looked sort of old. Did their room doors have locks? I certainly saw more than enough young men milling around those halls. Do you think fellas still have to yell, 'man on the hall' when they enter?"

Anne put her pillow over her head and muttered, "Go to sleep, my love. We'll run by and check that all out tomorrow."

But before she could drift off, Brad aired even more grievances. "What are we doing in Virginia? How did we let this happen? Look at all the fine schools there are in Georgia . . . All of our friend's children are staying closer to home. But no . . . not the twins! They've never made anything easy!" He pulled Anne's pillow to the side so that he could see her expression. "I hope they get homesick. We'll come get them that minute and bring them back to God's country!"

In spite of Brad's delayed hopes, neither Gretchen nor Patsy had any trace of homesickness. It was much easier for them to adjust to this new phase of life than it was for Anne and Brad to adjust to life without them.

Coming home to an empty house was way too quiet and even painful as the couple walked by the girls' clean room. Even Bo Jr. was living with Little Brad at his grandmother's.

After their first semester, Gretchen was doing well academically and dating a pre-med student. Patsy's grades mirrored Gretchen's and she was dating a young man at the University of Virginia. From what Anne and Brad could gather, he was studying law and wanted to go into politics. To Brad, that only meant he was a smooth talker, which did not sit well.

The girls loved their classes and were committed to studying. Gretchen was already working on her first rendering and Patsy could give a perfect injection to an orange. She loved her nursing clinicals and the overwhelming details of medical terminology.

Brad and Anne worked through the quiet stage and had settled into a rather enjoyable routine. The house stayed cleaner and the piles of laundry nearly disappeared. The two were even acting like newlyweds with no regard for time of day or location when inspiration hit.

One night, as they were coming home from enjoying a dinner out, Brad's cell rang. After saying hello, he just listened. Anne whispered, "Is everything okay?" Brad took a turn away from the direction of their home as she repeated the question.

He could only shake his head. "It's Mother."

After pulling in her driveway, Brad was the first to run into the house with Anne close behind. Chandler met them inside the back door. "Your mother had a seizure. She's resting comfortably now, but I know how this works. I've seen her like this before, many years ago . . . The symptoms are returning and we need to get her back to her doctor in New Orleans."

Brad thought back to how hard it was for him to know his mother was so sick when he was a young boy. He was thankful that his son had gone to see the twins for the weekend. He had no plans to tell the children anything until he knew exactly what they were facing.

The next morning, Chuck's plane was fueled and ready. Patsy had endured a rough night and slept during the entire flight to New Orleans. Later that afternoon, Brad and Anne had a conference with his mother's physicians. The news was not good. His mother was lapsing back into the old symptoms and there was nothing they could medically do at this point. Her primary doctor told Brad that it was a miracle this final stage hadn't come much earlier. After so many years, the body is simply tired and the defenses relax. What was happening to her wasn't unusual and he warned that the seizures would increase in number and intensity. With Patsy's resistance to the anti-seizure drugs, at her age, her overall health would decline quickly.

But the doctor added a hopeful scenario. "Chandler has been through all of this before with your mother. You couldn't have a better companion by her side. She'll know how to keep Patsy as comfortable as possible."

Brad thanked him for his candor as they stood to leave. Then he remembered and asked, "Should we take her home?"

He physician smiled and said, "After listening to Patsy talk about her family and her wonderful grandchildren, home is where she needs to be."

All four boarded the plane to return to Atlanta the following morning. Brad sat with his mother and held her hand.

Looking at her son, she asked, "Haven't we had so many good years?"

Leaning over to kiss her cheek, he could only answer, "Not enough."

With Chandler's help, Patsy enjoyed another wonderful year of life. Anne worked hard to make Christmas, with all of the children home, the most festive one ever. Six months later, Patsy peacefully passed away in her sleep. The seizures had indeed become more prevalent and all who knew and loved the gentle, yet strong, woman were relieved to know that her pain had finally ended.

Little Brad continued to live in the apartment of his grandparent's home for several months after Chandler moved back to South Carolina to help her sister with their family's bed and breakfast. Ultimately, Little Brad decided it was time to come home, until he had time to think everything through. Simply put, he missed his Gaga terribly.

After a long, hot, busy summer, with all three children back at the house, the fresh feel of fall returned. The girls went back to VCU and Little Brad started his senior year. Late one Saturday afternoon, their son called Anne to ask if she and Brad had any dinner plans. He had been to the Georgia Tech vs Clemson game. His team had lost miserably. Yet, Anne still heard excitement in her son's voice, despite the loss.

She asked, "What would you like to do for dinner?"

"Let's go to Pano's," he suggested.

Anne was stumped. Her boy hated going to fancy restaurants; he claimed they were a waste of his time and money. "Pano's?" she asked.

"Yes, ma'am. Will you make reservations for four? I'm bringing a friend. We'll meet you there at seven."

Anne quickly made the reservation and then looked at the time. She and Brad were enjoying a lazy day and hadn't even gotten around to taking showers. It was after five thirty when she walked into the great room. Brad was supposedly watching another football game on television, but he was snoring in his favorite chair. She gave him a gentle kiss and said, "Wake up. We need to get ready for dinner."

Brad groaned, "I'll eat later."

"We're going out to dinner." She nudged him again. "Get up, we need to hurry."

"Why are we going out?" He grumbled, "We've got plenty of food here. I'm not in the mood to get cleaned up and besides the LSU game comes on at seven."

"We're meeting our son at seven . . . and he's bringing a friend." She smiled. "From the sound of his voice, I'd bet it's a girl."

Brad got up and headed toward the stairs with a loud sigh. "She'd better be really special if I'm going to miss the LSU game on her behalf."

At seven, the two walked into Pano's and saw Little Brad standing by the reservation desk with his former high school sweetheart. Molly was now a student at Clemson and was spending the weekend in town with some of her Atlanta friends. She had run into Brad at the football game. Though they had texted some early on, they had lost touch over the last couple of years. With the look on their faces, Anne could see their hearts hadn't lost touch for a minute.

Molly explained that with her father's transfer to London, she had finished high school there, but was determined to get back to the United States for college. She smiled and took Brad's hand. "And I missed this fella! It's so good to see him again."

Little Brad had never seriously dated anyone after Molly

moved overseas. Looking back, Anne could count on one hand the number of dates he had told her about. Both she and his father were glad to see him looking excited and somewhat embarrassed over Molly's comment.

Molly spent that night at the Youngs' house and Anne clearly picked up her dread of leaving to start back to Clemson. Their son moped around for the entire week and headed out for Clemson after his Friday classes. That became a pattern for the entire academic year. Either Molly was in Atlanta, or Brad was at Clemson on the weekends.

Meanwhile, the twins had decided that they weren't interested in dating any one person seriously. With Grandmother Boyd's plan in the notebooks, dating one special person just got too complicated. And they rationalized their decision by stating that increased study time was needed as their courses increased in difficulty. Brad could not have been happier and he loved their choice to follow in Anne's footsteps—career first.

CHAPTER FIFTY-FOUR

ANOTHER DAUGHTER

ANNE WAS GLAD TO SEE SUMMER RETURN; IT MEANT HER GIRLS would be home for Little Brad's graduation. Molly had basically become a member of the family. Her parents were still in London, so they had invited her to spend the summer with them as well. Anne enjoyed watching the young couple. Little Brad reminded her so much of the younger version of her husband. Molly's long, dark hair was similar to her own and when she'd sneak glances at the two sharing a kiss or holding hands, she could only think of herself and Brad, twenty-five short years ago.

The night before the graduation ceremony, Little Brad and Molly walked in after leaving his rehearsal. Molly climbed the steps toward the guest room and their son asked his parents if they had a few minutes to talk. The three of them sat down as he began to explain his intention to marry Molly.

"Mom, Molly's the only girl I've ever loved. I'm not interested in anyone else and I just want to marry her. Her parents will be here in mid-August for a few weeks, and I think that will be a good time."

Brad looked at Anne, and then back at his son. "You've just turned twenty-three, son. That's mighty young."

"Dad, if you had met Mom when you were my age, what would you have done?"

Brad thought back and he knew there had never been anyone like Anne in his life. "I'd have married her on the spot."

Anne walked over and sat on the arm of Brad's chair and gave him a kiss. She turned toward their son. "We love Molly. She'll make a delightful daughter-in-law." She paused and then asked, "Have you already asked her to marry you?"

"No, ma'am. I wanted to talk to you first." He sighed. "I guess I need to buy a ring."

"Your Grandmother Boyd's ring is in the safety deposit box," Anne said. "You and I can go see it tomorrow if you want. Even if you don't like the setting, you might like the diamond."

Brad butted in, "And, son, you need to make this a romantic proposal. Women like that . . . flowers, down on one knee . . . the whole deal. And you need to call her daddy to get his permission first. If I were you, I wouldn't mention a word of this to your sisters. They are absolutely incapable of keeping a secret."

"I was thinking about taking her to dinner. Then we could go over to Grandmother's place. Molly's never seen the apartment there. And, Dad, I just want something happy to happen in that house now . . . to bring back the good memories. Besides, that's where we'll be living if she says yes."

"Well, after graduation tomorrow, you and I can run by the

bank," Anne said with a smile. "I like your plan, honey, and I think Molly will too."

Following the pomp and circumstance of graduation, the twins went to an engagement luncheon for one of their friends. Anne and her boy headed for the bank. When they opened the safety deposit box, she took out a small, white silk box and handed it to her son.

Opening it, he smiled. "It's perfect, Mom. Molly will love the old-fashioned look. That's her style."

"Mother would be thrilled to know you're giving it to your bride-to-be. So would your Granddaddy Boyd." She gave him a hug and asked, "When do you plan to talk with Molly's father?"

"I thought I'd give him a call in the morning. And I've made reservations at the Club for Friday night." He laughed and added, "That way I can charge it to Dad. I'm going to order champagne and the works. With grad school and a wife, I'm sure going to have to watch my pennies."

Anne smiled.

"But the way I figure it . . . with the money that Gaga left . . . the house should be free. I'll use that money for utilities and stuff until I'm making money as an architect. And Molly has already been offered three teaching jobs locally, so we ought to be okay."

"It sounds like you've thought this through. Remember, you have some money from your Granddaddy Boyd if things get tight."

"Mom, I'm not going to spend any of that. It's for starting my career. I don't want to work for anybody else; better to have my own firm, and that will take capital. I want to be free to take on construction that interests me, not just run-of-the mill assignments. I think Granddaddy Boyd would like knowing that's where his money is going."

Anne patted his hand. "I think you're absolutely right. He would love that."

Brad and Anne were on pins and needles Friday night. Molly's father had been receptive to Little Brad's intended proposal and they couldn't wait to see Molly's face when the couple returned home. About ten-thirty, the side door opened and the two strolled in. Molly had her left hand up by her face, wiggling her ring finger.

Anne rushed over and took her hand in her own. "Oh, it is perfect!"

Brad gave her a kiss and hugged his son.

Molly looked at Anne and asked, "Will you help me plan our wedding? Mother won't be here until August and besides, that's not her strong suit, and I don't even know where to begin."

Brad laughed as he looked at his wife. "You've just made her night, Molly. By the time she's had a week to think about this, you two will be well on your way."

"My daddy has already given me a budget," Molly said as she looked at her husband-to-be. "But Brad thinks it's way too much money and we need to put some of it in the bank." She rolled her eyes. "He says wives are expensive and that he learned that fact from overhearing your conversations. Even my daddy jokingly told him, 'a good woman costs a lot of money.'"

Frowning, Anne looked at her husband and said, "My spending has been nothing compared to this man's collection of cars."

The side door opened again, this time it was the girls. After hugs and screams, the normal excitement following a marriage proposal, both grabbed one of Molly's hands and led her upstairs.

"We have so much to talk about! Are we going to be bridesmaids?" Patsy asked.

Gretchen echoed, "What colors are we wearing?" She then turned around quickly on the steps and looked straight at her father as she grinned. "And Daddy will have to get you birth control pills."

Little Brad's shook his head. "Dad, can you believe she just said that? Good grief! Look at Molly's red face."

"That's your sisters for you. The way they talk is like a gumball machine. When a thought comes into their mind, it rolls down and comes off their tongue," Brad said with a sigh. "We might as well all go to bed. Those three will be up there talking all night."

"How did Molly like your grandmother's house?" Anne asked.

"She loves it, but we'll be living in the apartment at first. I need to finish grad school and the heat and air-conditioning will be too much for the whole house. Besides, we don't need all that room right now." He laughed. "I'm going to go get a kiss and then I'm going to bed. See y'all in the morning."

Anne, the twins, and Molly spent the entire summer planning a wedding and reception for late August. Their time was well spent as it was a beautiful ceremony, so much like Anne and Brad's. Molly's dress was perfectly designed just for her, all lace. She was lovely. Both sets of parents enjoyed their time getting to know one another and as the newlyweds drove to the airport for a honeymoon in Hawaii, the four parents wiped tears and waved goodbye.

It was already time for the twins to head back to the campus for their junior year. The two planned to spend the first semester in Richmond, but would be studying abroad in their spring semester. They were starting out in London and were actually spending their first week with Molly's parents sightseeing and adjusting to the time change. From there, they would go to Scotland and Ireland before they flew into Italy, where they would be studying in Florence and Rome. Following that, they would spend a week in Paris on their own before returning to the states.

One night as Anne was talking to the girls in Scotland, she had an idea. "Why don't Daddy and I meet you in Paris? We could spend a week together enjoying all the places we love. For almost thirty years, he has promised me another trip to Paris. I think it's time we make that trip a reality."

When Brad walked through the door that night, Anne called him into the dining room. The table was set with her finest china, meringues were on a dessert plate, champagne was chilling, and a passport and a flight itinerary were lying atop each dinner plate. "What's all of this, Mrs. Young?"

She walked over and put her arms around his neck, giving him a long kiss. "I'm taking you to Paris."

"And when are we going there? I have a lot on my schedule at work," Brad said.

"Your schedule has been cleared for two weeks in late April. Therefore, we are going to have April in Paris . . . just like you've promised for well over twenty-five years ago. The first week we'll be with the twins. We have a driver and we're spending a day at the Louvre, a day at Versailles . . . the girls and I will do a little shopping and we'll let them enjoy seeing the countryside and sampling all of the good foods. On Saturday, we'll put them on a plane headed back to school and we'll have another whole week by ourselves."

The second part of her pitch brought a wide grin to Brad's face.

"We're staying at the Victor Hugo," Anne continued. "And I promise you'll have a wonderful week."

Brad began to kiss her neck as he said, "Do we have to wait until April? All this talk has me in a Paris state of mind."

CHAPTER FIFTY-FIVE

THE PARIS STATE OF MIND

Brad and Anne exited Terminal A at the Charles De Gaulle airport and saw two happy faces as the twins rushed up to greet their parents. They had arrived the day before and were already enjoying the Parisian cuisine.

"Mom, we want to do everything you and Daddy did on your honeymoon," Patsy began. Then both girls giggled and she quickly added, "Well, almost everything."

That's exactly what the four did, following the same itinerary that Brad had planned so long ago. Museums, great restaurants, even dinner in the Eifel Tower. They visited the little town of Chantilly and enjoyed waffles with the special Chantilly cream. After talking with several tour guides, they found a quaint little antique shop that carried bolts of the Chantilly lace that used to be manufactured in the town. Anne explained that this was where the lace for her wedding dress had come from, which gave the girls inspired ideas. Each bought bolts of their favorite lace to ship home for future wedding gowns. They wanted their dresses made a lot like their mother's, except they wanted long trains; there was no concern that there weren't any grooms on the horizon at this point in time.

With Gretchen's keen interest in art, she and Anne didn't pass a single museum, while Brad and Patsy visited a few Parisian hospitals. All too soon, it was time for the girls to go back for one more month of classes before their summer break.

Brad and Anne were left all to themselves. This trip proved to be different from their first, but not too different; mornings were still the same, and the remainders of each day were spent in all sorts of relaxing ways. They had lunch at several outdoor cafes, bought art at the Left Bank, and meandered through tiny streets they had missed on the first visit. By the time they finished a gourmet dinner with wine and after-dinner coffee, the two were admittedly sleepy and would cuddle in bed, simply listening to the various sounds that echoed through the windows.

As their last night in the City of Lights arrived, Anne and Brad dressed up and went to a little bistro with quite a famous reputation. Apparently, it was best known for baked chicken breast smothered in a special sauce that Brad recalled as "French gravy." They toasted, while smiling over the multitude of memories that defined their history as man and wife. Afterwards they held hands as they leisurely walked through the many glowing street lights along the Champs-Elysées. She snuggled into his arm as they reached their hotel.

∾

Their life had come full circle, starting out with just the two of them and returning once again. That night as they slid into bed, Brad pulled Anne close, remembering back to their first night together in marriage. He had never wanted anyone as much as he desired every inch of her that night. The night he learned what making love truly meant. Everything about Anne had been new and different in amazing ways and the intimacy they experienced that night was like none other. He could still see the movement of the soft lace on her wedding dress as she walked down the aisle with her father. Not believing she could look any prettier, he realized the morning of their wedding day that she surpassed all of his expectations.

Then he thought about how close he came to losing her with the birth of the twins. What a good mother she had been to their three children. What a good wife she had been to him. He remembered the night of their engagement and even as he placed the ring on her finger, he had no inkling of the joy she would bring to his life. His thoughts sped forward to the cave in Guatemala when he worried that he would never be able to hold her again. It was as if everything wonderful in his life was wrapped around Anne.

He looked over at the curves of her body and thought back to the first time, about her softness. A passion rose up in Brad that he hadn't taken the time to experience in years. Their lives had been so busy. It seemed like everything else took precedence over any leisurely time for making love. But tonight, they were by themselves and time was not an issue. He was with the love of his life in Paris and she was all his.

～

Cuddling together the next morning, Anne felt that she had experienced Paris in the truest sense of the word. They had been carried back in time and the lovemaking they had shared was such a gift. It was as though they'd never left the Victor Hugo hotel or the room that held their innermost longings and childlike playfulness.

Brad disappeared into the bathroom and when he returned, he took Anne's hand and led her to the shower. Candles were lit and the pleasant fragrance of roses filled the room as they stepped into the warm water. It was the perfect ending to this second honeymoon. A little later, Brad ordered breakfast to be brought up to the room. He voiced a blessing while tears fell from Anne's cheeks.

She looked in his deep brown eyes and said, "There's nothing like being with you in Paris, my love."

CHAPTER FIFTY-SIX

DANCE WITH ME

TEN YEARS LATER, THE YOUNG FAMILY RETURNED TO PARIS, BUT this visit was with a much larger family. Brad and Molly had been blessed with two young sons, who had immediately stolen Anne's heart and their grandfather's afternoons when they started playing T-ball. It was great fun to have another set of twins in the Young family. Patsy had finished undergrad studies and had received her Master of Science degree, while Gretchen had completed a two-year internship in design at Emory University. Both women were fully committed to their careers until love entered the picture.

Patsy had literally run into a young cardiologist when she turned to sit a tray of instruments on a surgical cart. As all the items scattered on the floor from the unexpected jolt, the two rushed to pick up the mess and bumped heads. Strange as it sounds, that was the beginning of a beautiful love affair. Six months later, Patsy and Will Creech were married in a ceremony reminiscent of Anne and Brad's, just much larger. Within two years, they welcomed a daughter, naming her Anne.

Gretchen, on the other hand, became a sought-after designer in Atlanta. Calling her brother one afternoon, she had begged for his help on a necessary addition to one of her projects. Declining his sister, he laughingly vowed he would never work with her nit-picking personality, under any circumstance. With more thought, Brad remembered Austin, an associate and newcomer to his architectural firm. Brad had learned that Austin had three sisters and was used to being bossed around. He was the perfect architect to work with Gretchen. Two years later, Gretchen and Austin were married in a ceremony exactly like her sister's.

Within a year, the twins and their husbands had built houses side by side. Even since college, the girls never missed a day talking with each other for at least an hour, or better yet, a personal visit. Little Anne never seemed to be confused with the two of them; she simply called them both "Mama." She was perfectly content in either home and in either set of arms. Now, Patsy was pregnant again and Gretchen was expecting her first. Almost as if carefully planned, their due dates were exactly the same and the new grandchildren were expected in four months. Anne and Brad couldn't have been more pleased, especially when they learned that both babies were girls. It would be like having the twins all over again.

One night when Brad and Anne had the whole family over for supper, Brad was sifting through the mail before they sat down at the table. He came across a travel brochure to Paris and handed it to Anne with a big grin.

Anne took the flyer and held it up for Patsy and Gretchen to see. "Remember this, ladies?"

Patsy took the brochure and passed it to Molly, while both of the twins quickly recounted how much fun the trip had been. By the time Gretchen finished describing the restaurant at the Eifel Tower, the small town of Chantilly, and the incredible meringues, Molly turned to her husband with imploring eyes.

"I want to go to Paris, Brad!"

From that first request, the conversation took on a life of its own as their father watched the girls' twinkling eyes and listened to the mounting excitement in the voices. By lunch the next day, Brad had a ten-day trip planned as a surprise for the whole family. Molly's parents had moved back from London to Atlanta following retirement and were always willing babysitters for the twin boys. And Will's parents were thrilled to come visit at a moment's notice. Little Anne had stolen their hearts as well.

After talking with the other grandparents and discussing schedules, Brad zeroed in on the best dates for the big trip; they would leave on the fifteenth of April. With the girls' pregnant conditions, he booked the flights and decided business class would be necessary for any chance of comfort with the growing bellies.

Brad called a family meeting the following night to share his good news. All four of his girls were ecstatic and the husbands knew to mimic the same excitement. Handing out the itineraries, Brad explained about the already secured childcare arrangements.

. . .

A month later, the family boarded their flight and in what seemed like a very short time, they landed in Paris. Brad had arranged a van rental and over the ten glorious days, the Youngs didn't miss a thing. From Versailles to the wine country of the Loire Valley, the younger couples scurried around while Anne and Brad would find a comfortable chair or bench . . . and two glasses of wine.

One afternoon, Anne took her husband's hand as they sat down for an afternoon break on a bench along one of the bustling streets that led to the Louvre. The girls and their husbands were checking out the various shops for final souvenir purchases.

"How were we so blessed?" Anne asked. "We've had such a good life together. Suppose I had never moved from Richmond to Atlanta. Suppose I hadn't been an interior designer and suppose you never had a new office to decorate." She smiled. "But I did move and I met you. My life has been exceptional ever since I looked into those big, brown eyes of yours. Such a good life, my love."

Brad leaned over as he softly touched her lips with his own. "I know, sweetheart. Now, at the ripe old age of sixty-eight, as I enjoy the grandchildren and think back over the years, it's easy to see that we've experienced more than I could have ever imagined."

That night, after taking the rest of the family to the airport for their flights home, Anne and Brad returned to the Victor Hugo, to their special suite, for another few days in Paris. Brad walked over to the bar and poured two glasses of Beaujolais, bringing one to Anne. They talked about the excitement of the past week and a half, how fulfilling it was to see their children and spouses together enjoying each other as they explored the many sites of this historical city.

Sipping his wine, Brad watched Anne's eyes begin to glisten. He could still read those eyes like no one else. Talking of the family and the beauty of what their love had created always brought tears. He set his glass on the side table and walked over to the stereo in the room. Having learned years ago how to order up Manilow in Paris, he cut on his selection, *Somewhere in the Night*, then walked over to his wife.

Taking the glass out of her hand, he set it on the coffee table and looked into her soft brown eyes as he said, "Dance with me, please."

CHAPTER FIFTY-SEVEN

PLEASE, MY LOVE, PLEASE

ANNE AND BRAD NEVER MADE ANOTHER TRIP TO THEIR BELOVED Paris. But they did get to celebrate their fortieth wedding anniversary with their three children, spouses, and nine fabulous grandchildren. Gretchen, Patsy, and Molly worked hard to make sure the party was up to Anne's standards. So many friends and so many memories filled the evening.

Three years later, Anne was sleeping soundly when she felt a tug on the sleeve of her nightgown. Opening her eyes, she looked over at her husband and smiled. Then she heard his voice say her name. The word was strained as he gasped for air. She raised up. Looking at her, Brad moaned, "911."

Anne scanned his face; she could see that he was in intense pain. She grabbed her cell off the nightstand and made the call. With tears streaming down her face, all she could say was, "What can I do? Tell me what to do!"

Brad patted the bed for her to lie down by his side. Anne curled up and wrapped her arm around his waist. "They'll be here any minute. Please don't try to talk. Don't you dare leave me, Brad Young. Stay with me, my love."

Then she heard his whispered words, "I love you, sweetheart. I always have and I always will."

They were the last words Brad would ever speak. Anne held him as tightly as she could, trying not to let him go, but she knew he wasn't breathing. She couldn't feel his chest move at all and his gasping had stopped. Within minutes, the doorbell rang. She quickly ran downstairs. Opening the door, she motioned for the paramedics to go upstairs.

In just a few minutes, an EMT walked back downstairs and asked, "Mrs. Young, who do we need to call to come be with you?"

She didn't answer; she ran back upstairs.

The emergency team appeared in the doorway to their bedroom. Her husband's body was on a gurney; it was covered. Anne told them to stop as she stood on the landing. She moved the sheet and took Brad's hand; it was still so warm. She fell across his chest and sobbed, "No, please no. Don't leave me." She began to kiss his hand, then his face.

The EMT took her hand and softly whispered, "Mrs. Young, Dr. Young is no longer with us."

Anne backed up, trying to think, but she couldn't. She slowly leaned over and gave her husband one last kiss as her lips met his. Replacing the sheet, she nodded. The team slowly carried her husband away. He was gone and she wanted to scream, "Bring him back!" Anne wanted all of this to be a terrible mistake, a horrible nightmare, but it wasn't. A woman with the team offered to stay with her until a family member arrived. Anne just shook her head and walked into her bedroom. Closing the door, she walked over to the window.

Watching the ambulance drive away, she couldn't imagine how she would face the children. For that matter, how would she take her next breath? Life as she knew it was no more. How could she even wake up tomorrow morning without Brad cuddled by her side? She walked back downstairs and into the kitchen, sat down at the table, tried to compose herself, and called her son.

The next week was just a blur. Anne remembered trying to soothe the feelings of her children and grandchildren, knowing they were equally devastated. Her son tried to be so stoic for his mother and his sisters, but Anne knew her sweet boy and how difficult this loss was for him. He and his dad were such pals. All he could say was, "Mom, Dad never had any heart problems. How did this happen?"

Anne had no answers, but she learned over the course of that week what a treasure Molly truly was to the Young family. She stepped in and made good decisions when Anne and the children couldn't quite function enough to take the reins. Molly cared for all the little details with calm confidence.

After a while, as always happens when there's a death, everyone has to get back to their lives. To their routines and responsibilities. The children were careful to coordinate schedules so that at least one of them stopped by daily to check on their mother.

Anne tried to be pleasant, yet, without Brad, her life was broken and there was nothing that she truly wanted to get back to. Heartache had taken control of her thoughts and her days.

Two weeks later, as Anne was pouring a cup of tea, she heard the doorbell. Walking to the door, she looked out of the glass panel. Charles Billings was standing on the front porch. She opened the door and failed to hold back the freefall of emotions that she had stifled for days.

Watching tears as they slid down her cheeks, her friend simply stepped up and put his arms around her. "I'm so sorry, Anne. I was on a medical mission in the mountains of Peru. When they finally got the message about Brad to me, all I could think about was getting home to check on you."

She and Charles talked for hours that day, reminiscing about Guatemala, the Bellamy House, and the many times he and Brad played golf together. As the sun began to set, he asked if she would like to go get some dinner. Anne could only shake her head no. Thanking him for the visit, she walked him to the door. He promised that he would be checking on her regularly.

Charles kept his promise. Not many days passed for the next two years that he didn't call, come by, or send flowers to try to comfort her. But then one week, Anne realized that several days had passed without hearing from her friend. She had to admit how dependent she had become on his attention. It certainly wasn't more than friendship, but she had gotten used to his company. It helped in ways she hadn't really seen until his companionship wasn't there anymore. Even the children had been thankful for Charles' kindness to their mother as they watched her resume her life.

More days continued without any word from Charles. Finally, Anne felt the need to call. When he answered, the tables were turned—she asked how he was doing and if he was okay. She could hear a definite hoarseness to his voice.

"I'm fine, Anne. Thank you for calling. I've had the flu, but today's a little better."

Anne hesitated, then said, "I would have brought you soup or something if you had let me know."

"Well, I'm letting you know now . . . and I'd love some soup."

From that point forward, their friendship and kindnesses toward each other were mutual. Charles never pressured Anne for anything more than a comfortable relationship. He knew her heart would always belong to Brad. But he also knew his heart would always belong to Anne. They would go out for dinner once a week, sometimes to a movie or a play at The Fox. Anne spent the rest of her time attending various activities with her children and grandchildren or lunches with friends. Plus, there were always needs at the Center.

Late one afternoon, Anne walked in the side door of her house after spending close to seven hours on her feet selecting new paint colors for the Bellamy House. She smiled as she thought of Sarah. Memories of how that generous woman had never moved to an assisted living home. Instead, she had lived out her days, spry and happy, surrounded by the love and gratitude of all her adopted daughters, young women who had passed through the welcoming atmosphere at Sarah's donated building. Anne couldn't help but shed a few tears that day when she selected the last two colors that she felt sure Sarah Bellamy would have approved.

After the tiring day, Anne was undressing to get ready for bed when she suddenly felt weak, nearly to the point of feeling faint. She attributed her light-headedness to her long and emotional afternoon. However, by the next morning, she felt no better. Calling Charles, Anne explained her symptoms, especially the dizziness she would experience when she tried to stand. He told her not to move and promised to be there within fifteen minutes. Running in the side door, Charles took one look at Anne and could tell by her unusually pale coloring that he needed to get her to the hospital for tests. He was afraid it was her heart.

Waiting for her test results, Charles paced. He knew how much she missed Brad and wondered if these strange health issues were related to her grief. Soon her test data was in his hands. As he reviewed the results, the paperwork showed nothing of any great concern. A tear formed in his eyes; he remembered seeing her exact symptoms many times before in other widowed patients. He had been convinced by those unexplained conditions that people could literally will their hearts to stop beating. He now believed that was happening with Anne. He thought of all their conversations about eternity and her hope in that promise. Charles took a deep breath as he recalled that this hope seemed to be the one thing she was hanging on to.

. . .

Charles admitted Anne to the hospital for several days to monitor her and run more tests, but day after day he could see no change. Gretchen, Patsy, and Molly took turns staying with Anne day and night. When she showed no improvement, they even agreed that their mother seemed to have lost her will to live. One afternoon when the three girls were in the room at the same time, Anne asked them to sit down. She said she had something important to ask.

"I want to go home . . . so your daddy will know where I am. He will not be happy if he has to go all over Atlanta looking for me." She managed a smile, then repeated, "I just want to go home."

After hearing their mother's plea, Gretchen called Charles. He agreed, as there was nothing else he could do for her that he hadn't already tried; it was time for Anne to go home. Nurses were arranged to be with her and their mother's request was honored.

Days passed, but Anne's strength never returned. In fact, her breathing became even shallower. Yet, every night the nurses could hear her talking; sometimes they'd even check to make sure she was alone in her bedroom. One of the nurses decided to call Gretchen and discuss what she thought must be Anne's hallucinations.

Gretchen asked, "Can you tell what she is saying?"

"I could hear her saying 'please' and then what sounded like an endearment."

Gretchen knew exactly what those words meant. Her mother was asking for her daddy. Patsy and Gretchen decided to stay the following night to listen to their mother's words themselves. Charles was there when they walked in the room.

He looked at them and shook his head as he quickly wiped his eyes. Then he kissed their mother's forehead and said, "Her heart is so weak, it's even hard to find a pulse. I'm glad you two will be with her tonight. I've got to make rounds, but I'll be back. Call me if there is any change, or if you need me."

After fluffing her pillow and straightening her comforter, the twins gave their mother kisses and sat down on the small sofa in the room as they whispered to one another. In just a little while, both daughters heard Anne softly speak several words, "Please, my love, please."

Looking over at her bed, Gretchen and Patsy could see that a smile was appearing on their mother's face as she briefly opened her eyes. Both girls recognized that smile. It was the one their mother had always reserved just for their daddy. Gretchen's mouth silently formed the words, "She's calling Daddy." Reaching over, she took her sister's hand. Walking over to their mother's bed, the two watched Anne slowly close her eyes. The girls stood motionless. Just then the room was filled with the delicate fragrance of red roses, their mother's favorite.

Patsy squeezed her sister's hand as her tears began to fall. Hugging Patsy, Gretchen smiled and said, "It's okay, sissie. Don't cry. She's with Daddy now."

ETERNITY...

Anne and Brad Young had the assurance of eternity. They had made a decision, early on in their marriage, to enjoy a relationship with Jesus. As their life together experienced the normal ups and downs, even some difficult trials and tribulations, the two learned to trust His promise below and so can we.

John 3:16, "For God loved the world so much that he gave His only Son, so that anyone who believes in Him shall not perish but have eternal life." TLB

After the birth of their son, and with gratitude for this precious child, Anne and Brad prayed the simple prayer below as the two committed themselves to the Lord and His plans for their future.

"Jesus, come into my heart, forgive my sins, and give me eternal life. I confess you as my Lord and Savior."

After this prayer, life as the couple had known it would never be the same. In the end, as with Anne's mother, the two left a legacy that would stand in their stead . . . a life of substance, a life well lived. You and I have that same choice. The choice to leave a legacy of a well lived life, as we rest in the assurance of eternity.

Ecclesiastes 3:11, "... God has planted eternity in the hearts of men." TLB

May God abundantly bless His glorious design for your beautiful life,

J Boykin Baker

DISCUSSION QUESTIONS

1. As 'By Design III' began, could you identify with Anne's chaotic attempt to handle a morning when everything goes haywire?
2. When Anne and Brad deal with the first attack from Mark Ivy, do you feel they should have been more concerned? Would you have taken security issues more seriously?
3. Did Estelle's death bring back any personal memories of the loss of a dearly loved individual? How did you cope with that loss?
4. Were Brad and Anne naïve about dangers of Guatemala? When Anne and the children returned to Atlanta, were her concerned feelings justified?
5. Could you understand Brad's grief when he returned from Guatemala? Anne's sadness? The children's confusion?

6. What were your thoughts about Dr. Charles Billings' infatuation with Anne? Brad's jealousy?

7. When Brad Sr. died, could you understand Brad's feelings that he may have contributed to his father's death?

8. As the children grew into young adults, how would you rate Brad and Anne's parenting skills and why?

9. Do you believe the manner in which Brad and Anne handled their discussion with the children about Gretchen's Plan was on target? How could you tell?

10. Have you ever experienced a "hello from heaven"? What are your thoughts on this subject?

11. When Anne and Brad met their girls in Paris, were you surprised at the rekindled passion that they experienced as the two seemed to travel back in time?

12. As the Young family matured do you feel that Anne and Brad could claim a life well lived? Why?

RECIPES

A FESTIVE SOUTHERN HOLIDAY FEAST WITH FAMILY, FRIENDS, AND THEIR SIGNATURE DISHES

JANAREE'S EGGNOG

(Yields 2 quarts)

Ingredients

1 can Eagle Brand milk
1 teaspoon vanilla
¼ teaspoon salt
1 quart whole milk
1 cup heavy whipping cream

Directions

1. Mix first four ingredients.
2. Whip cream in a separate bowl.

3. Fold whipped cream into the milk mixture.
4. Serve cold and sprinkle with nutmeg.

Tastes like liquid ice cream ya'll!

SISSY'S CRAB BISQUE

(Serves 4)

Ingredients

6 tablespoons butter, divided
4 tablespoons green pepper, minced
4 tablespoons onion, minced
1 green onion with top, minced
2 tablespoons parsley, minced
1 ½ cups sliced fresh mushrooms
2 tablespoons flour
1 cup milk
1 teaspoon salt
¼ teaspoon pepper
1 drop Tabasco sauce
1 ½ cup half-n-half
1 ½ cup crabmeat

1 tablespoon dry sherry

Directions

1. In a skillet, heat 4 tablespoons of the butter and then add peppers, onions, parsley and mushrooms. Sauté until soft, about 5 minutes.
2. In a saucepan, melt remaining 2 tablespoons of butter and stir in flour until smooth. Gradually add milk, stirring over medium heat, until thickened and smooth.
3. Stir in salt, pepper, Tabasco sauce and half-n-half and bring to a boil.
4. Reduce heat to simmer and add crabmeat. Simmer uncovered for 5 minutes.
5. When ready to serve, add sherry.

ESTELLE'S TURKEY AND GRAVY

Ingredients

1 whole turkey (your choice of size)

Gravy:
½ cup melted butter
½ cup plain flour
4 cups chicken or turkey broth

_____

Directions

Turkey:

1. Salt well and rub with melted butter. Stick a few celery sticks in the cavity.

2. Enclose in a large Reynolds oven bag and follow the instructions on the bag (for the weight of the turkey and temperature).

Gravy:

1. Simmer the turkey neck and giblets in salted water for about an hour. This makes good broth to use.
2. In a saucepan, combine butter and flour and cook over low heat for 5 minutes, stir occasionally.
3. Slowly stir the mixture into the boiling broth and stir until thickened.
4. Simmer 30 minutes on low heat.

ANNE'S HONEY-BAKED HAM

Get directions to your nearest Honey Baked Ham store, rush in and purchase appropriate size ham needed, carefully bring it home so that no sweet juices spill out of packaging. Attractively place spiral slices on a silver meat tray. Add fruit and parsley garnishes. Smile and enjoy the compliments while you dodge any cooking questions. Mums the word!

MARISA'S SAUSAGE DRESSING

Ingredients

1 pound mild Italian sausage in bulk
1 bag cubed stuffing (I use Pepperidge Farm, Herb Seasoned Stuffing)
½ stick butter
1 medium onion, diced
1 large stalk celery, diced
1 large carrot, diced
32 ounce chicken stock (I use Swanson's low sodium)

_____

Directions

1. Preheat oven to 350 degrees. Grease a large (15 x 10 in.) baking dish or foil roasting pan.

2. Brown sausage in a large non-stick skillet until no pink remains. Break sausage, as it cooks, into crumbles or small pieces. Using a slotted spoon, remove cooked sausage to a paper-towel lined plate to drain.

3. Sauté onion, celery and carrot in pan drippings, adding butter (to taste) as needed. When vegetables are soft and onion is translucent, transfer to a large bowl.

4. Add cooked sausage and stuffing to vegetable mixture. Add stock, a cup at a time, until the mixture is combined well. Transfer stuffing mixture to baking dish.

5. Bake for 30-40 minutes, basting occasionally with remaining stock (I like dressing a bit on the dry side and use turkey gravy at the table, to moisten if needed).

SARAH'S SWEET POTATO CASSEROLE

Ingredients

3 cups fresh sweet potatoes
½ cup sugar
½ cup firmly packed brown sugar
Juice of one orange
½ stick butter
1 teaspoon vanilla
Cinnamon and ginger to taste
Miniature marshmallows (optional)

_____

Directions

1. Bring sweet potatoes to a boil covered in water in a

large pot. Reduce and simmer until potatoes easily prick with a fork.

2. Cool and peel potatoes and then put in a mixing bowl. Beat until smooth.
3. Add remaining ingredients (except marshmallows) and mix well.
4. Place in a casserole dish and cover top with marshmallows.
5. Bake at 350 degrees until warmed through and marshmallows are lightly browned.

K. DURHAM'S SQUASH CASSEROLE

Ingredients

4 cups sliced yellow squash
½ cup chopped Vidalia onion
35 buttery Ritz crackers, crushed
1 cup shredded cheddar cheese
2 eggs, beaten
¾ cup cream
¼ cup butter, melted
1 teaspoon salt
Ground black pepper to taste
2 tablespoons butter

_____

Directions

1. Preheat oven to 400 degrees.
2. Place squash and onion in a large skillet over medium heat. Pour in a small amount of water.
3. Cover and cook until squash is tender, about 5 minutes. Drain well and place in a large bowl.
4. In a medium bowl, mix together cracker crumbs and cheese. Stir half of the cracker mixture into the cooked squash and onions. In a small bowl, mix together eggs and milk, then add to squash mixture. Stir in 1/4 cup melted butter, and season with salt and pepper. Spread into a 9" x 13" inch baking dish. Sprinkle with remaining cracker mixture, and dot with 2 tablespoons butter.
5. Bake in preheated oven for 25 minutes, or until lightly browned.

DEBBIE'S BROCCOLI CORN BREAD CASSEROLE

Ingredients

1 package Jiffy Corn Muffin Mix (8 ½ ounces)
¾ cup cottage cheese
3 whole eggs + 1 egg white
1 10 ounce frozen chopped broccoli or fresh, chopped very small
1 can corn or 2 ears of fresh corn (good way to use leftover corn on the cob)
½ cup melted butter or margarine
Onion powder or fresh finely chopped onion
Dash salt

_____

Directions

1. 1Thaw frozen broccoli & drain.
2. Combine melted butter, onion, salt, cottage cheese and eggs, beat until smooth. Stir in broccoli and corn.
3. Stir in muffin mix, mixing lightly.
4. Pour into a greased 9" x 13" pan. Bake at 400 degrees for 20 to 25 minutes. Broil slightly at the end to brown top.

DORIS' STRING BEAN CASSEROLE

(Yields 10-12 servings)

Ingredients

2 cans of French-style green beans, drained
1 can cream of mushroom soup
1 can cream of chicken soup
½ cup milk
1 cup shredded sharp cheddar cheese
1 can bean sprouts, drained (optional)
1 can sliced water chestnuts, drained (optional)
1 1/3 cups French's Crispy Fried Onions
Dash of pepper

_____

Directions

1. Mix soups, milk, cheese, sprouts, chestnuts and pepper in a large bowl.
2. Stir in beans and 2/3 cup fried onions.
3. Pour into a 2-quart baking dish.
4. Bake at 350 degrees for 30 minutes. Stir.
5. Top with remaining 2/3 cup fried onions and bake 5 minutes longer or until fried onions are golden.

JEAN'S EASY PEASY MAKE AHEAD MASHED POTATOES

Ingredients

5 pounds of Yukon Gold potatoes
6 ounces of cream cheese
8 ounces of sour cream
½ cup milk
2 teaspoons onion salt
White pepper to taste

_____

Directions

1. Cube potatoes and place in boiling salted water. Cook until tender, but still a bit firm, usually 15 minutes
2. Drain and mash.

3. Combine potatoes with all other ingredients & mix extremely well with mixer.

4. Place in a greased casserole pan. I use a 9" x 13", and I use a nice one as I will put completed dish right on the table.

5. Bake at 325 degrees for 50 minutes. This can be put in the fridge and used 2 or 3 days later, just take it out of the fridge 30 minutes prior to baking in the oven. It can also be heated up in a well-buttered crock pot.

6. If you need to save calories, change all the ingredients to the light version.

7. Garnish with some parsley around edges for a fancier look.

MISS CARLA'S WILD RICE

(Yields 2 ¼ cups)

Ingredients

¼ cup wild rice
3 cups boiling water
1 teaspoon salt
Butter

_____

Directions

1. Wash the rice in 4 changes of cold water to clean.
2. In a saucepan of 3 cups boiling water, add salt and gradually stir in rice to keep the water boiling.

3. Cover and reduce heat to simmer. Stir occasionally with a fork. Cook 30 to 45 minutes or until rice is tender and water is absorbed.
4. Add butter and stir before serving.

HELEN'S TIPS FOR COOKING VEGETABLES

Some of our favorites

Butter Beans
Sweet White Corn
Black Eyed Peas
Fresh String Beans

_____

Directions

1. I always use PicSweet frozen vegetables if fresh are not available. I cook them in a can of Swanson's chicken broth instead of water and add a little salt and a pat of butter.
2. For baby butter beans, I bring to a boil and cook for about 10 minutes uncovered. Then I remove them

from the stove, cover and let them stand for about an hour. Reheat if necessary to serve.

3. I cook sweet white corn the same except for only 5 minutes.

4. Black-eyed peas usually need to cook longer until they are tender. Allowing the vegetables to sit in the broth gives a much better flavor.

5. For fresh string beans, I like to find a very lean piece of pork seasoning meat for more flavor. I boil the meat for an hour and then add the beans. Cook until tender and allow to sit for another hour.

AUNT FRANCES' CURRIED FRUIT

Ingredients

1 can pear halves
1 can peaches
1 can pineapple chunks
1 can apricot halves
Maraschino cherries
¾ cup light brown sugar
2 teaspoons curry powder
1/3 cup melted butter

_____

Directions

1. Drain all fruit except cherries.

2. You can either layer the fruit into a baking dish or cut it into bite-sized pieces.
3. Mix brown sugar and curry with the melted butter. Pour this mixture over the fruit. Top with Maraschino cherries.
4. 1. Bake covered at 325 degrees for 30 minutes, and then uncovered for another 30 minutes.

KATHERINE'S CRANBERRY ORANGE RELISH

Ingredients

1 orange - peeled, seeded and cut into wedges
¾ cup chopped pecans (toasted if you like)
½ cup of sugar
½ cup orange juice
1 tablespoon Grand Marnier liqueur

_____

Directions

1. Pulse cranberries and oranges wedges in a blender or food processor until coarsely chopped.
2. Transfer to large bowl. Stir in pecans, sugar, orange juice and Grand Marnier (or other orangeliqueur).

3. Serve cold.

WENDY LOU'S NEVER FAIL YEAST ROLLS

Ingredients

2 cups milk
2 cups Crisco/lard
½ cup sugar
1 package yeast
4 cups flour
1 teaspoon salt
½ teaspoon baking soda
½ heaping teaspoon baking powder

_____

Directions

1. Bring milk, Crisco and sugar to a boil. Cool.

2. Sprinkle yeast on top of mixture to let it begin to work.
3. Stir in dry ingredients and let rise in a warm place until double in size.
4. Add enough flour for soft dough and knead if you are going to make the rolls right away. Roll out, use biscuit cutter and put on parchment covered cookie sheet.
5. If you aren't going to roll them out, refrigerate dough until you are going to make the rolls. When ready to use refrigerated dough, drop by tablespoons on parchment covered cookie sheet.
6. Either way you make them, bake at 425 degrees until brown, about 8-10 minutes.

DEBRA'S PECAN-PUMPKIN PIE PERFECTION

(Yields 28 2" x 2" pieces)

Ingredients

Crust:
1 stick of butter, melted
1 package Pecan Sandies style cookies

Filling:
15 ounce can pumpkin
8 ounce package cream cheese at room temperature
1 stick butter, softened
2 large eggs
2 teaspoons vanilla extract
1 teaspoon pumpkin pie spice
1 teaspoon cinnamon
1 teaspoon nutmeg

1 ½ cups powdered sugar

—————————

Directions

1. Preheat the oven to 350 degrees (325 if using a convection oven).
2. Line a 9"x 13" baking dish with parchment paper and spray with cooking oil.
3. Place the cookies in a food processor and grind them completely. Option: can place them in a gallon-size Ziploc bag and pound them until completely crushed.
4. Add the melted butter to the cookie crumbs and mix well.
5. Press the cookie-crumb crust into the baking dish evenly and bake for 10 minutes.
6. Mix the pumpkin, cream cheese, eggs, vanilla, pumpkin pie spice, cinnamon and nutmeg until mixed well. Gradually add the powdered sugar until the filling mixture is completely smooth. Place the filling mixture into the pre-baked crust and spread evenly.
7. Bake at 350 degrees for 55 to 60 minutes (until toothpick comes out clean). Let cool, cut 2x2 inch squares, top with whip cream and enjoy!

HILDA'S CHOCOLATE CHESS PIE

(Yields 6 – 8 pieces)

Ingredients

1 unbaked pie crust
1 stick butter
2 ounces Bakers Semi-Sweet Chocolate
1 cup sugar
2 eggs, beaten
1 teaspoon vanilla
Dash salt

_____

Directions

1. Melt butter and chocolate over low heat.

2. Blend other ingredients and then mix in with the warm mixture.
3. Pour in the unbaked pie crust. Bake at 350 degrees for 35 minutes.
4. Top with whipped cream or ice cream to serve.

WENDY M.'S PEACH COBBLER PIE

(Yields 6 – 8 pieces)

Ingredients

1 crust for a deep dish pie
1 ½ cups sliced peaches
1 cup sugar
1 cup self-rising flour
1 stick butter
1 teaspoon in another
1 ¼ vanilla extract (optional)
Optional, but great for variety, add 1 ½ cups blueberries

_____

Directions

1. Layer peaches in bottom of pie crust. If desired, add the blueberries now.
2. In a bowl, mix sugar, flour, butter and cinnamon (vanilla flavoring too if desired) with a fork.
3. Pour and gently press mixture over top of fruit.
4. Bake at 350 degrees for 45 minutes until center is bubbling.

GRANNY'S CHOCOLATE CARMEL BROWNIES

(Yields 24 servings)

Ingredients

1 chocolate cake mix (18.25 ounce size)
1 cup chopped nuts
½ cup butter (1 stick) melted
1 cup evaporated milk, divided in directions
35 caramels (10 ounce package)
2 cups semi-sweet dark chocolate morsels

_____

Directions

1. Preheat oven to 350 degrees.
2. Combine cake mix and nuts in a large bowl.

3. Stir in butter and 2/3 cup evaporated milk (batter will be thick). Spread half of batter into ungreased 9"x 13" baking pan.
4. Bake for 15 minutes.
5. Heat caramels and remaining evaporated milk in small saucepan over low heat, stirring constantly, until caramels are melted. Sprinkle morsels over brownie, drizzle with caramel mixture.
6. Bake for 25 to 30 minutes or until center is set. Cool pan on wire rack. Melt butter and chocolate over low heat.
7. Blend other ingredients and then mix in with the warm mixture.
8. Pour in the unbaked pie crust. Bake at 350 degrees for 35 minutes.
9. Top with whipped cream or ice cream to serve.

KIM'S CHERRY PINEAPPLE ICE CREAM

(Yields 1 quart)

Ingredients

1 egg, beat until frothy
¾ cup sugar
1 can carnation milk
1 can sweetened condensed milk
Pinch of Himalayan sea salt
1 cup cherries cut into quarters
1 20 ounce crushed pineapple with juice

_____

Directions

KIM'S CHERRY PINEAPPLE ICE CREAM

1. Beat egg, sugar and carnation milk. Add sweetened condensed milk and salt.
2. Add pineapple and cherries.
3. Pour into freezer container and freeze for 3 hours.

ABOUT THE AUTHOR

J Boykin Baker grew up in the small town of Wilson, North Carolina. She knew from the age of seven, after seeing the old movie "Pillow Talk," that the only career for her was interior design. After college, marriage, and babies, her dream of being an interior designer came true with the start of her own design firm in Atlanta, Georgia. As luck would have it, she just happened to be in the right place—at the right time—with the right look and ended up designing hospitals, corporate offices, and high-end residential projects across the nation.

During her years as President of Baker Interiors, Inc. she had the privilege of working with countless women. Due to a caring nature, she was led to mentor young women through familiar struggles of a reoccurring nature. Eventually, she carried her love for women and children even further when she founded a non-profit, Widow's Mite Experience, Inc. to provide emergency water relief for families in the United States and around the world. With the help of hundreds of women volunteers, the ministry is now active in 32 countries.

The author's writing career began with a series of children's books illustrating the unusual travels of a doll named Mary Margaret. She has written two pilots that explore the lives of Southern women and has had various interiors and commentaries published in slick-cover magazines from coast to coast. Under duress, she has even written two professional manuals. Currently, she is continuing to write about her passion—the joys, challenges, and struggles of the life of a modern woman. Her first novel of this trilogy, *By Design: A Love Story with a Twist*, was first published in 2018. Holding cross-over appeal to women of all ages, *By Design* touches the hearts of women who are experiencing, or remembering, the intensity of a new love. The second book of the trilogy, *By Design II: Matters of the Heart*, published in 2019 connects with busy women who are trying to establish fulfilling lives in the ever-changing complexities of our modern culture. This third novel, *By Design III: A Life Well Lived* speaks to the hearts of those who understand the brevity of life and desire to pass the torch to future generations.

With humor, tears, and professional insight, this author enjoys sharing her wide-ranging experiences in her writings, on national television, radio interviews, and speaking to international audiences. She was recently named one of North Carolina's Women of Achievement. In a nutshell, J Boykin Baker continues to thoroughly enjoy a full and adventurous life!

Thank you for purchasing *By Design III*. By doing so, you are helping to send clean water to flood-ravaged areas in the United States and disparate water-deprived countries abroad. Thirty percent of all author profits from this book will be donated to Operation Blessing, a 501(c)(3) non-profit ministry.

https://www.ob.org

THE BY DESIGN TRILOGY

Books, Kindle and Audiobook available on Amazon.

Books available in all of your favorite bookstores.

Made in the USA
Columbia, SC
16 February 2020